# *A Duchess by Midnight*

"She's here," Miss Trelayne whispered softly, so softly he barely heard. "Do. Not. Move."

Moving had not occurred to Ian.

"She's where?" he asked in a rasp.

"*Shhh*," she warned gently.

The bird called again, a sound, Ian thought, not unlike most birds. But then he saw a flutter; he heard a swooshy sort of pumping of air—and there it was. A small bird, lighting on the balcony railing mere feet from where they stood. In the dimness, her feathers registered as only dark and light, her shape decidedly . . . birdlike.

She hopped twice and opened her beak and trilled.

Miss Trelayne sucked in a delighted breath. A gasp. It was the sound that accompanied newly opened jewelry boxes, or grand anniversary cakes wheeled out on a trolley. Ian had also heard that sound in bed.

He shifted, just a little. He could feel the outline of her body up and down, from her thin shoulders to her long legs. Lithe, thin, like a corded rope, but with the softness of a woman. She tensed when the bird sang, something like ecstasy seizing her muscles. He could feel her warmth through his coat.

"I can't believe she's so close," she whispered.

"Yes," he agreed. "Close."

**By Charis Michaels**

*Awakened by a Kiss*
A DUCHESS A DAY
WHEN YOU WISH UPON A DUKE
A DUCHESS BY MIDNIGHT

*The Brides of Belgravia*
ANY GROOM WILL DO
ALL DRESSED IN WHITE
YOU MAY KISS THE DUKE

*The Bachelor Lords of London*
THE EARL NEXT DOOR
THE VIRGIN AND THE VISCOUNT
ONE FOR THE ROGUE

# CHARIS MICHAELS

# A DUCHESS BY MIDNIGHT

## AWAKENED BY A KISS

AVONBOOKS

*An Imprint of HarperCollinsPublishers*

A DUCHESS BY MIDNIGHT. Copyright © 2022 by Charis Michaels. All rights reserved. Printed in the United States of America. No part of this book may be used or reproduced in any manner whatsoever without written permission except in the case of brief quotations embodied in critical articles and reviews. For information, address HarperCollins Publishers, 195 Broadway, New York, NY 10007.

First Avon Books mass market printing: July 2022

Print Edition ISBN: 978-0-06-298499-9
Digital Edition ISBN: 978-0-06-298500-2

*Cover design by Nadine Badalaty*
*Cover art by Alan Ayers*
*Cover image © totally out/Shutterstock*

Avon, Avon & logo, and Avon Books & logo are registered trademarks of HarperCollins Publishers in the United States of America and other countries.

HarperCollins is a registered trademark of HarperCollins Publishers in the United States of America and other countries.

FIRST EDITION

22 23 24 25 26  BVGM  10 9 8 7 6 5 4 3 2 1

*For Elle Keck*
*Genius editor for seven books,*
*serendipitous friend for always.*
*Godspeed (!)*

# Chapter One

*Kew Palace*
*Richmond Upon Thames*
*October 1818*

The antechamber to the Throne Room at Kew Palace was crowded that day, and Drewsmina Trelayne took stock.

To her right, a stern-faced woman in starched wool and a black cape. She stood close to the door and clutched a bulging satchel. A charity crusader, Drew guessed.

To her left, a military man in dress uniform and his fidgety aide-de-camp.

Near the window stood three nuns with a huddle of boys, likely orphans, or a choir, or an orphan choir.

Milling somewhere in the middle were two men of

academic bent; one bearing a spinning piece of scientific equipment and the other a taxidermized specimen of a mouse.

There was also the elderly couple with the birdcage; and a rouged woman (opera singer or similar?), her maid, and two small dogs.

Finally, in the shadowy corner slouched a lone man. Tall, face averted, motionless, possibly asleep.

And then there was Drew herself, front and center, an enterprising young Woman of Business, on the cusp of both Enterprise and Business.

Inventorying the other callers had taken up all of five minutes. Drew was bored but also anxious. It was not her first time to the palace.

Drew's stepsister, Cynde, was married to Prince Adolphus, son of King George III. Although Adolphus was the king's seventh son and tenth in line for the throne, he was a prince nonetheless. As such, he and Cynde made their home in Kew Palace. Typically, when Drew called on her stepsister, she was received in Cynde's opulent private chambers.

The Throne Room, in contrast, was where the royal couple granted audiences to supplicants, charities, and petitioners, and Drew was here because today was not a social call. Today was business, the day Drew would be introduced to the new client who would change her life.

If said client turned up.

And if he could be persuaded.

If everything went exactly, perfectly according to the plan.

This plan, which until today existed only in theory, had been thrust into reality when Drew received a hasty note from Cynde last night.

> *Throne Room tomorrow, Drew. Can you please come? Arrive early and bide your time in the antechamber with the other callers (apologies—but the wait will be worth it, I hope!).*

*An old friend of Adolphus's is meant to call. He's
in desperate need of help with twin girls in advance
of their first Season. He's called the Duke of Lachlan, very rich, but rather bumpkin-y or reclusive or
socially inept or some such . . . cannot say for certain. He's Cornish? Almost Cornish? Something to
do with Cornwall?*

*But did I mention: twins! That's two girls on
whom you may work your magic, so come prepared
to charm and convince, etc., etc. Follow my lead, alright?*

*Hoping this is the opportunity for which we've
waited.*

The note had made Drew a little breathless, and she was
generally in full control of her breathing. Drew had been
biding her time, waiting for exactly this sort of introduction for the better part of a year. The note had made her so
hopeful, she sought out her brother-in-law, the tedious Lord
Madewood, to ask him what he might know of a "nearly
Cornish Duke of Lachlan."

Madewood had welcomed her inquiry with his usual
creepy aplomb; inviting her to his dark library, sprawling
on a settee to pontificate for a half hour. In the end, the
theatrics had been worth it. She'd learned that there was,
indeed, a Duke of Lachlan. The dukedom was in Dorches-
ter, very near to the Dorset coast. Three years ago, the
duke had been at the center of a scandal that consumed the
country. He'd shown promise in the House of Lords before
the scandal but had since retreated to the ducal estate and
hadn't been heard from since.

"But what of twin daughters?" Drew had probed. "Girls
he might wish to bring to London and launch into society?"

"Daughters?" Madewood had repeated speculatively. "I
cannot say. His family was not discussed in the papers. Marrying off daughters would be very ambitious, indeed. No
young woman, and especially no debutante, would benefit

from association with such a recent controversy. I don't care if her father is a duke."

"Did the scandal involve some . . . indecency?" Drew ventured.

"Indecency? No," assured Madewood, "it's nothing like that. He was involved in a Luddite riot. Got a man killed and injured several others—a youth, I believe? That is, his *mismanagement* of unruly tenants . . . *led* to a riot . . . that killed a man . . . and injured the youth. Lachlan rabble-roused alongside his tenants, going so far as to join their ranks as if he was one of them. After whipping them into a fevered pitch, he played the turncoat and gave them up to the guard in Portsmouth."

Drew considered this, weighing the risk of attaching herself to a family with a direct link to Luddite rioters. The so-called Luddites were skilled craftsmen—weavers or stockingers or lace makers and the like—angry that new textile mills were putting them out of work. Lives were lost, men were hanged.

Still, rabble-rousing and "mismanagement" didn't sound so very bad, did it? Hardly ideal but it wasn't as if the duke was a marauder, or a letch, or a highwayman. This was a situation with which Drew could do some real good—for the daughters, if nothing else. She had to begin somewhere.

"But perhaps enough time has passed," suggested Drew hopefully, "and gossip about the riot will have died down? It was three years ago, did you say?"

"Yes, '15. But, it was fuel to the fire for so many subsequent uprisings. It has not been forgotten, I assure you. Ask anyone about the Honiton Uprising and you'll get an earful. There was outrage on every side. The villagers were furious that their landlord warned the garrison; and the regiment in Portsmouth was angry that a duke had aligned himself with peasants. Poor leadership, that's what it was. He pitted the two sides against each other out of sport. Or he was out of his depth. Either way, he was too inexperienced and too arrogant."

"Yes," said Drew absently. She was thinking again of his daughters. What challenges would they face if their father was considered a rabble-rouser, turncoat, and instigator of civil unrest?

*I can help them*, she thought.

*I can be of very great help to the lot of them.*

Drewsmina Trelayne was in the business of—or rather, she *would embark upon* the business of—coaching young debutantes through their coming-out Season in London society. Her specialty was—or rather, *would be*—outsiders. Outcasts. So-called ugly ducklings. Girls who hovered on the margins of society life.

In short, exactly the type of girl that Drew herself had one time been.

She would specialize in snipe-prone, screechy girls; silly, giggling girls; or silent girls forgotten in the back of the room.

She would coach slouchy girls to stand up and quiet girls to speak up and chatty girls to pause and silly girls to listen. She would polish brashness and embolden shyness.

She would take on girls with scandal-shamed fathers who needed to rise above gossip and enjoy an untarnished debut.

She would do for her clients exactly what heartbreak and resilience had forced Drew to do for herself.

And she would charge a fee for the service, which would finally allow her to leave her miserable situation as a spinster sister in the home of Anastasia and the tedious Lord Madewood.

But first she required this client.

"Not very quick-like with the visitors, are they?" asked the old woman who stood beside Drew in the airless antechamber outside the Throne Room. She and her companion held a birdcage between them. The weight of the cage, not to mention the twelve or so Dartford warblers flapping about inside it, was heavy and unwieldy.

Drew had avoided the couple (in as much as anyone

could be avoided in the tiny room) because it pained her to see any animal caged, especially birds, especially Dartford warblers. She'd developed a fondness for bird-watching these last five years, and she was familiar with the beautiful, reclusive warblers. They were partial to the dense, scrubby heathland in Surrey and not at all given to captivity.

Doubtless, the couple meant well. If Drew had to guess, they'd brought the birds as a gift. Later, when Drew and Cynde were alone, she could urge her stepsister to release them.

"We've been waiting an hour at least," said the man holding the other side of the cage. His wife nodded indignantly.

"Well, that cannot be," remarked the stern-looking charity woman. "Subjects are meant to call to the palace gate no sooner than a quarter to eleven. And it is currently a quarter *past* eleven. So you could not have been waiting an hour. If you'll recall, I arrived to the palace gates *before* you lot. So. When Their Royal Highnesses Prince Adolphus and Princess Cynde admit the next caller, that caller is certain to be *me*."

"If we're splitting hairs on the matter," declared one of the scientists, "I arrived before all of you." He stroked his stuffed mouse.

"Surely you are mistaken, sir," said the charity woman. "I was undeniably the first to arrive, not to mention my appointment has been scheduled with the prince's secretary for weeks."

"I am *not* mistaken," the scientist replied, digging in his satchel for some proof.

Drew sighed and cast a glance around the small, dim room. Had the duke arrived? She saw no young women who might be the twins, so she assumed the girls would not be present. But the duke himself was meant to be a caller, just like her. Presumably he would be in the company of a wife. But surely a duke and duchess would not be subjected to the antechamber with orphans and birds in a cage?

She looked again. Perhaps he would be the officer? Although the military man looked very old, indeed. The twins in question would have to be granddaughters, if not great-granddaughters.

Or could Lachlan be one of the scientists? Also likely no.

Her gaze fell on the still, silent man slouching in the shadows. Theoretically, he *could* be a duke and theoretically he *could* be the correct age; but he could also be an undertaker who was ninety. Everything about him invited Drew to redirect her gaze . . . but curiosity caused her to glance back.

He stood so far from the lamps, she could make out little more than a voluminous overcoat, a face obscured by the brim of his hat, and tall boots. He shouldered against the wall, arms crossed, the posture of someone who was present in body but whose consciousness was far away.

Not that any of these details mattered, because he appeared too informal to be a friend of the prince's. And again: dukes did not convene in antechambers with the masses. Lachlan would arrive by another door; he would not cue, nor would he slouch. The slouching, in particular, unnerved her, and Drew had enough reasons in her life to be unnerved. She had no wish to invite more.

"May I look at your birds?"

One of the boys had broken ranks from the nuns and stood peering inside the birdcage at the terrorized Dartford warblers.

"Not now, yeah?" whispered the owner of the birdcage.

In the same instant, her companion enthused, "Of course you can."

"Are they sparrows?" asked the boy, suddenly accompanied by a second boy, then a third. Soon a semicircle of boys had formed around the birdcage.

"Keep back, if you please," said the woman, trying to

wrench the birdcage away. "These Dartford warblers are a gift to Prince Adolphus and Princess Cynde. They make a terrible mess when agitated, and I cleaned the cage this morning."

"We won't agitate them, madam," assured the first boy, stepping closer. The others followed.

"There's no harm in letting them look," the man scolded gently. To the boys he said, "Admirers of birds, are you, boys?"

Behind them, the charity woman had continued to grumble. "You'll see. When the footman admits us, *you will see*. Guests are not shown in willy-nilly. This is a palace, after all."

"And who asked you? That's what I'd like to know," said the old woman, distracted now from the birds.

"But would one of the birds sit on my finger?" asked the first boy. "If I stick it in?"

"He would bite it off," assured the next boy.

The first boy ignored him and raised a pudgy finger to the cage, working it carefully between the bars. Above them, the owner of the birds quarreled with the charity crusader.

"Let me have a go," demanded the second boy, and then a third. More fingers wiggled between the bars of the cage.

Looking back, Drew could identify *this* as the moment when everything went terribly, irrevocably wrong.

The cage wobbled. Thrashing, hysterical warblers flapped about, landing beaks and miniscule talons against the invading of fingers. The boys startled and yelped, jerking back their hands.

The collective jostling caused the door of the cage to unhinge and swing open. Within seconds, a dozen Dartford warblers, flying hell-bent for Surrey, launched from the cage and swarmed the antechamber.

Pandemonium filled the tiny room in a literal swarm. Birds, boys, yelping dogs; feathers rained down.

The owners of the birdcage leapt into action, trying to recover the birds with windmilling hands and flapping apron.

Nuns crouched beneath their coifs and reached blindly for orphans. The boys scattered, leaping and swiping for the birds, hooting in delight. The opera singer embarked on a rolling scale of breathy screams. The other waiting callers ducked, shrank away, or swatted at the birds.

"Everyone, please," Drew heard herself call, "*keep calm.* If we are still and quiet, the birds will settle."

Calmness, it was clear, was as far away as Surrey. As Drew watched in horror, the terrified birds careened to the ceiling, swooped low, and collided with walls. The impact of each collision stunned them into disoriented flapping. One boy managed to capture a bird, and it lay gasping for air in his palm. The military officer swatted at a low-flying warbler with his newspaper, sending the little bird spiraling through the air like a leaf.

Drew's eyes swam with angry tears. The birds hadn't asked to be caged, nor carted to a palace antechamber, nor terrorized. The room was too small for them to flee and too spare for them to hide.

"Stop," Drew tried again. "If we simply remain calm, the birds will not be so panicked. They can be—"

No one listened. Drew gaped about the room, helpless and angry. Now even the slouching man was joining the fray. He shoved from the wall and stalked through the chaos to the double doors that led to the corridor.

"Why not," he was asking under his breath, "just open the bloody door . . ." he reached for the knob, ". . . and release the bloody beasts—"

"No, wait!" Drew gasped, lunging.

Drew caught his large, gloved hand just as it pulled the doorknob.

He looked up, and suddenly she could see his eyes. A chilling, piercing blue, the focal point of an exceedingly handsome face.

He was not, she now saw, ninety years old.

Nor was he an undertaker. Unless he was the most perfectly formed undertaker in the history of dead people.

He stared at her from beneath the brim of his hat in direct challenge. *Yes?* his expression asked.

Drew recovered and squeezed his hand to stay him. "No, please," she said in a rush. Their faces were close, as close as two people sharing the same doorknob.

In that moment a Dartford warbler made a disoriented dive perilously close to her face. Drew yelped and jumped closer still.

"I'll *open the door*," the man explained slowly, plainly, as if speaking to a mad woman, "and the birds will fly through it."

"No." Drew shook her head violently.

An orphan boy bumped into her hip and she was shoved almost into his chest.

"No," she repeated, righting herself. "If you please. If the warblers escape into the palace, they'll become separated, they'll fly mindlessly into far corners and never find their way out. They'll die of starvation or be killed by staff. We'll never recover them."

"These . . ." he speculated, "are your birds?"

"No," she said desperately, trying to make him understand. "Dartford warblers are not prone to domestication. The compassionate thing to do is to release them—but into the wild. Not into a palace."

"And what do you propose?" Now an orphan crashed into him and clung. He used his free hand to lift the boy by his collar and set him back on course for the chaos in the room.

"If we can stop the panic and simply keep calm, the birds will settle. Then we might collect them one by one into the cage and release them properly. But we must all . . ." she looked with frustration at the room of revolving birds, shouting people, rampaging boys, and barking dogs, ". . . settle."

"Right," he said, following her gaze at the room. "Only mildly ambitious."

Drew let out a distressed laugh. She couldn't help herself. He was handsome, and he was funny. And she was holding his hand.

Drew's heart beat very hard and heavy in her chest. It felt like an egg that contained something very new and wild trying to hatch out.

"Please, sir," she said, swallowing, "I should like to try."

Drew stared at him, shocked that he didn't argue. He looked back with wintery eyes, and the egg of Drew's heart thumped again. Finally, he gestured to the room with a go-on-then nod.

Drew blinked, snatched her hand away, and turned back to the room. It was a din of wild birds and shouting people and braying dogs.

"Stop!" Drew called, pitching her voice at a shout. "Please! Everyone, if we could keep calm, and allow the birds to find somewhere to light. Please!"

There was no response. Not a single glance. She opened her mouth to try again.

"What about . . ." the man shouted to her, "the window?"

He pointed to a small, high window that looked out onto a stone wall.

He continued, still shouting, "Would you permit me to release them through the window?"

"Yes, that would be perfect," Drew shouted back. "If you can manage it."

The man wound his way through scrambling people and careening birds. The window was high but he reached it with little effort.

"It's painted shut!" he called to Drew.

"There's no help for it!" she called back, halfway to him.

A boy darted in front of her and she caught him up by the wrist. "You must stop *running*," she pleaded. Another boy followed and she caught him with the other hand. The boys pulled and squirmed against her hold, trying to rejoin the fray.

He pushed at the window again but it wouldn't budge. Meanwhile, a diving warbler swooped low and almost collided with his head. He swore and ducked. He was re-adjusting his hat when a second bird hit him, this time in the ear.

"Are you hurt?" Drew called, releasing the boys. He ignored her as he scanned the room. His gaze lit on the smokey fire, and he reached for the metal poker propped on the hearth. Before she fully comprehended his intent, he took up the poker, thrust it through the window, and thrashed it around, shattering glass and breaking panes.

The commotion cut through the din in the room, and for a long second, all the shouts, arm waving, and barking fell silent.

The man continued his task, tracing the poker along the outline of the sill, knocking it clean. Shards of glass and splintered wood rained down. When he retracted the poker, only the open square remained. They immediately felt the morning chill and smelled the murky River Thames.

Silence took up gradual residence in the room, all sound filtered out the window. Everyone gaped from the absent panes, to the man, to the shattered glass at his boots.

In less than a minute, the first warbler seized freedom. A dozen flock-mates immediately followed, launching them-selves from the terror of the small room into the free world. Feathers wafted to the ground. A dog whimpered. A breeze swung the door on the birdcage with a creak.

They recovered their voices all at once.

"By what right do you have, sir? I ask you—"

"How dare you, them birds belonged to—"

"Oy! Did you *see* it?"

The callers were angry and confused. Every comment was punctuated by glass crunching underfoot. The dog chorus resumed.

The man ignored them all, removed his hat, and pulled a gray feather from his ear. He wound his way through angry people to the doors to the Throne Room. He glared at the thick oak as if he could open it with his mind. He replaced his hat.

Drew watched him in disbelief. She'd encountered many people in her life. Well-meaning people, compassionate people, hardworking and capable people, but she could never remember anyone doing anything quite so demonstrative or dashing as this.

Without realizing she'd moved, she came to stand beside him.

"Thank you," she said.

"I did it for the birds," he said.

She chuckled. Another joke.

One of the boys skidded to a stop beside him, brandishing the fireplace poker like a sword. He ignored him.

"Any notion of how long they usually make us wait?" the man asked Drew.

"No." She shook her head. She forced herself to stare at the door and not at him. "Shattering windows cannot hurt. If we mean to move things along."

Another boy appeared, and the first boy began to jab at him with the poker. Two nuns descended and hauled them away. Behind them, the argument about order of admission had resumed.

"What are you in for?" the man asked Drew.

"I beg your pardon?"

"Why are you calling on the prince?"

"Oh," said Drew, and she paused, trying to think of the best way to explain.

Later she would realize that the true damage of the day hadn't happened when the birds were released or the window was broken.

Later she could see that the real damage of the day would happen *now*.

*Now* was when things went horribly, irrevocably wrong.

She said, "I've come to make the acquaintance of a potential client. Princess Cynde is my stepsister, and she is to make the introduction."

And here, she should have stopped. He'd not asked for more details. She knew only that he was handsome and clever and together they had saved the warblers.

Unfortunately this was all she required to continue talking. Drew was a spinster and rather good at it, but she wasn't dead. She'd excelled at style, and cleverness, and even confidence, but when it came to speaking to men, she was out of her depth. So very far out.

"I am in the business of turning out debutantes," she said. "Not in the manner of a finishing school, not yet, but I provide a similar service. For private clients."

The man beside her said nothing, but he slowly turned his head in her direction.

Now that she had his full attention, she felt compelled to add, "The potential client is a duke, actually. Lachlan, he's called. A friend of the prince's. He has twin girls that he wishes to bring out—that is, to launch into society for the next Season."

The man narrowed his eyes. Was he intrigued? Fascinated? Her stomach flipped. She continued, "He is in need of help with the girls, and it is *his* business I've come to solicit. The duke's. For his girls."

Still, the man said nothing, but he was staring at her with intense interest. Drew was made a little dizzy by the attention.

She kept talking. "The duke in question was the cause of some scandal several years ago. His reputation was so damaged, he was forced to leave London."

And now, Drew could actually *hear* herself saying too much, but she couldn't seem to stop.

"It was a pity, really," she went on, saying it all, saying things she didn't even know to be true. "He'd shown great potential in the House of Lords. But he was responsible for an early Luddite riot. He incited the march and then betrayed his own tenants to the authorities. It was widely reported in the broadsheets. It ruined him really, which will make the debut of his girls very challenging, indeed.

They'll need to tread very carefully. But never fear, I specialize in these scenarios. It is my favorite sort of project."

She had just said it, the words barely out of her mouth, when the doors to the Throne Room were thrust open. A liveried footman appeared.

"His Grace, the Duke of Lachlan," the footman intoned, half question, half proclamation. A summons.

"Aye," answered the man beside Drew. "Lachlan."

To Drew's great horror, the man beside her—*the Duke of Lachlan*—stepped around the footman, strode through the door, and disappeared into the Throne Room.

He did not look back. The doors slammed shut.

Drew stared in horror at the thick gray wood while her words revolved in her head like a swarm of Dartford warblers.

# *Chapter Two*

"Mystery solved," muttered Ian Clayblack, the Duke of Lachlan, coming to a stop before Prince Adolphus. He affected a stiff bow.

"What was that, Lachlan?" called Prince Adolphus, sitting on a throne that looked very much like an upholstered wingback chair. Beside him on a matching wingback-like throne was a young woman in streaming pink ribbons and bouncing yellow curls.

"Good morning, Your Highness," Ian corrected in a clipped voice.

To the woman he said, "How do you do, Princess. Felicitations on your nuptials." The words were pleasant but his tone was not.

"What mystery?" demanded the prince.

"The mystery of why you summoned me." He looked around. *"Here."*

"I summoned you because you amuse me, Lachlan."

"Yes, but typically I amuse you over a pint of lager at the Ferryman Public House in Cumberland Road. I wasn't aware that Kew Palace *had* a Throne Room. Nor that you held court."

The prince made a dismissive gesture. "It's no small thing to share the royal family with fifteen siblings, Lachlan. I must fight for my stake in this family. This is Mama's embroidery room, if you must know. She allows my wife and me to use it the second Monday of every month to entertain causes that interest us."

"So I'm a cause?" asked Ian, frowning.

Ian and Adolphus had served together in the army. They'd slept in a field and eaten gruel and roots and spit-fired salamanders. Ian considered Dolph an ally and a friend, but it was possible to cause real offense here; he was a bloody prince. He should force himself to tread lightly.

"Of course you're not a *cause*," the prince was assuring him. "And we shall drink together at the Ferryman soon enough. But now that I'm properly married . . ." he reached for his princess's small hand, ". . . I am endeavoring to take my royal duties more seriously. We've a friendly history, it's true, but let us not forget our larger roles. *My* father is Sovereign; *you* are a duke. You have goals in parliament, and I want to help you achieve them."

"*Right*," said Ian, not believing it for a second. This meeting was not about Ian's goals, it was about—

"Pray tell me," ventured the prince, "how are Evelyn and Ava?"

And there it was. Ian swore in his head. "Who?" he asked, knowing the answer—*hating* the answer.

"Your *nieces*, Lachlan."

"Oh," said Ian. *"Imogene and Ivy."*

"Right, forgive me," corrected the prince. "How are the dear girls?"

"My nieces are well," bit out Ian, not entirely a lie.

"You're cross," said the prince.

"I'm confused, Highness. You've a waiting room filled with loyal subjects who are about five minutes from coming to blows. Someone has broken a window. I would not wish to waylay your allotted Monday with your many adoring supplicants."

"Ever a selfless man of the people," mused the prince sarcastically.

"Indeed," said Ian, still trying to gauge his motives. When the prince said nothing, Ian took a deep breath and dove right in.

"Fine," Ian said. "Since you've asked, I've urgent need of a recall to the export duties in Bournemouth. The livelihood of my tenants—of so many craftsman in Dorset—will cease if they cannot ship their goods beyond England without being taxed to the teeth."

"Oh yes, yes, tenants and taxes," mused the prince. "I will see what might be done. But let us return, for the moment, to the diverting topic of *your nieces*." He gave his wife a wink.

Ian suppressed a growl. He reminded himself that he'd expected this. His old friend had summoned him, but Adolphus had almost no power. The export levy was an issue for parliament or the king.

As to Ian's nieces . . . Ian marveled that Adolphus had remembered the girls. If Ian had ever mentioned them, he had no idea why. Furthermore—

"Pray keep your dagger glares and ground teeth in check, Lachlan," snapped the prince. "We're not in a barracks and you're distressing my wife. She is endeavoring to do the lot of you a very great favor."

"Pardon, ma'am," Ian bit out, bowing stiffly. "*What* favor?"

"Your two nieces have accompanied you to London, have they not?" asked the prince.

"They have," Ian said, but in his head, he thought, *No, no, no, you must be joking—No.*

But of course the die had been cast.

The flame-haired woman in the antechamber had made this abundantly clear. What a terrible, seemingly unavoidable surprise. And Ian *hated* surprises.

"And you intend to host them in a Season and launch them into society?" said the prince.

"Something of the sort. If I can manage it."

"You're a duke of some means, Lachlan. Of course you

can manage it. If you're worried about that scandal with the rioters, surely that's nearly forgotten."

*Or,* thought Ian, *it's been remembered vividly—as evidenced by the woman who recited a distorted version of it to me just five minutes ago.*

He said, "Yes, Highness."

"Tell me what challenges you face with the girls?"

*Nothing that has anything to do with you,* thought Ian, but it was clear by the look on the prince's face that he would have an answer.

"Ah, my sister—their mother—is a bit . . . distractable," ventured Ian. "And the girls are very . . . raw."

"Quite," soothed the prince, his voice sympathetic. "This is what we'd heard."

"Heard from *whom*?" Ian ground out. Beyond sending staff ahead to open the London townhouse, he'd told no one he was returning to London. Even less had been said about the girls.

"Oh, we have our sources, don't we, Minnow?" the prince was saying, grinning at his wife. The princess scooted as close to him as their separate chairs would allow. She leaned over to whisper something in his princely ear. She was a pretty little thing, if your taste ran to sugary and young and petite, which Adolphus's always had. And good for him. It was difficult enough to be a duke. Ian was certain that seventh son to a king came with a great many more challenges. Dolph should have his doll-like wife, but he should have her without treading on Ian's already complicated life.

"If you can conjure the appropriate amount of respect and courtesy for my wife," said the prince, "she would like to extend an offer—to you, for your nieces. Regarding their advancement."

Why couldn't people, Ian wondered, leave well enough alone? His only wish for himself and his family was to live their lives without comment or interference except to eradicate the bloody export duties on the livelihood of his tenants.

"My wife is offering to *sponsor* the girls," said the prince. "Next spring. In their presentation at court. To Mama."

Ian blinked. Surely he'd misheard.

"*Presentation to the Queen*," Dolph clarified. "Of England."

Ian forgot to be rude or respectful or even angry. "She's what?" He gaped at Princess Cynde.

"You've heard me," sighed the prince, leaning back.

Ian looked from his old friend, fat and self-important; to his petite wife, yellow hair framing her sweet face like curtains around a brightly lit stage.

"Thank you?" Ian ventured.

"You're welcome," chirped the princess, her first words. She had a twee voice that matched her ribbons.

Ian ignored her and waded through this wholly improbable offer in his mind.

Truth: he'd brought Ivy and Imogene from Dorset to host them in a London Season.

Truth: he'd intended to see the thing done properly, in the manner befitting a duke and his family.

Truth: returning to London was the absolute last thing he'd wanted to do, and he wasn't certain, even now, if it was best for the girls.

*Un*true: he'd expected Imogene or Ivy to be presented at court to the Queen of England.

It was a gross understatement to describe the girls as "raw." They'd returned to Avenelle three months ago, and he'd yet to determine exactly what his sister had done to cultivate their strange combination of sheltered and wild. What was worse, he had no idea how to correct it. He'd brought them to London at significant personal toll; honestly, he'd been at his wit's end. Wasn't this what young women did when they turned sixteen? They embarked upon a proper London Season?

Ian's vision for their Season had involved their making

the acquaintance of other girls, fittings for new wardrobes, a handful of carefully chosen parties, and a modest debut ball. And nothing more.

The Lachlan title amounted to an inconsequential dukedom in Dorset. His own scandal had put a stain on the family name. The girls would not run into lofty circles or pursue life at court. If they were very lucky, they'd pick up one or two refinements in London and return to Dorset by summer.

The thought of Imogene or Ivy, God bless them, surviving a royal presentation without incident seemed impossible—as likely as him returning to parliament without inviting public scorn. At best, wildly aspirational; at worst, a disaster.

"I knew you would be ungrateful and difficult," sighed the prince, selecting a sticky date from a bowl.

"Forgive me, Highness, I'm—"

"And that is why I intend to sweeten the deal," continued the prince.

"The deal?"

"As part of the girls' introduction to Mama, I will further facilitate a meeting between you and my brother George."

"The prince regent?" Ian rasped. Surely he'd misheard.

"Of course the prince regent. That is your larger goal, is it not? To persuade George to release the export duties on your tenants' lace? My brother, in turn, will pressure the Lords. George owes me a favor, and now *you* owe me one."

"Highness," said Ian, the only word he could manage.

If the regent could be convinced to support the eradication of export duties on textiles and lace, Ian wouldn't have to return to the House of Lords. He wouldn't have to navigate the gossip or endure public scorn and relive the riots in every paper in London. He could slink back to Dorset and never be heard from again.

But at what personal cost? Imogene and Ivy presented at court? God help them all.

Ian cleared his throat. "If I might venture an amendment. With regard to my nieces . . ."

"You may not," cut in Dolph. "The offer remains exactly as I've said. Your nieces are important to my wife and therefore, they are important to me. I cannot guarantee an audience with my brother if we don't combine it with your family's introduction to the queen. I'm a prince, but I'm not a bloody miracle worker."

"No," conceded Ian. "I don't suppose you are." If nothing else, Dolph was honest.

"But why is Princess Cynde so very invested in my nieces?" Ian was honest, too, and this arrangement made no sense.

"Don't trouble yourself with the details," Dolph drawled. "Take the bargain, Lachlan. Trust me that you won't regret it."

Ian stared at him, trying to comprehend the choice he was being forced to make.

His relationship with the Avenelle tenants hinged on the eradication of this export duty and the prince regent could be instrumental in making that happen. Regardless, one did not turn down an audience with the future king. It simply wasn't done.

Perhaps he could also use the audience to explain himself. Salvage some part of his reputation at the highest level—God only knew what the prince regent thought of him or the riots.

He'd called on the prince with the dim hope of making some progress on the export duties. An audience with his brother, the prince regent, was so far and away better than his wildest dreams. If his nieces were also somehow tied to the deal—so be it. In Ian's experience, very few things in life came easily.

"The next appropriate response, Lachlan," lectured the prince, "is to ask the princess how you might repay this great generosity. What you and the girls must do to make her so very proud—both throughout their Season and on the day they meet the queen."

"Right," rasped Lachlan, snapping to. Of course he already knew. His nieces were only one half of the arrangement. There was also the young woman in the ante-chamber, her cheeks likely as red as her hair.

"Ian, for God's sake!" shouted the prince, clearly annoyed.

"Ah, sorry, Dolph—ah, Your Highness."

Ian looked at the princess. "But what can I do to best facilitate this great generosity, Highness?"

"Well, actually . . ." began the princess in her high-pitched voice. She raised her tiny hand and snapped at the footman standing sentry by the double doors. "I should like to introduce you to my dear sister . . ."

*Chapter Three*

With only one look, Drew would know. Cynde's face would reveal what words need not.

Either the Duke of Lachlan had exposed her incredible rudeness or, by some miracle, he hadn't.

The opportunity to train his girls was out, obviously; but the Throne Room could not be avoided. Drew braced for the worst and began to walk forward. Footmen swung the doors open with a whoosh. In the fuzzy distance, Cynde and Prince Adolphus sat side by side in overstuffed chairs.

The duke—*oh God, he'd remained*—stood before them, his posture radiating impatience.

Drew sought Cynde's face. Her blond curls and pastel silk were easy to spot. And there she was, beaming . . .

. . . hope.

She appeared hopeful.

By some miracle, Cynde did *not* know.

Slowly, with measured steps, Drew advanced through

the long, narrow room. She'd heard the notion of walking on air, but now she wondered if the opposite could also be true. She was tunneling into the ground.

*What* had she been thinking? After all of these years, all the progress. She'd *transformed* had she not? She'd transformed so thoroughly, she was *endeavoring to coach other young women to do the same.*

And to charge money for it.

Except now—

"There you are, Miss Trelayne," called Cynde, shooting her a look that said, *What's happened?*

"I am here, Highness," Drew heard herself reply.

Drew stopped before the dais and curtsied gracefully. If nothing else, she knew how to curtsy.

She glanced at Prince Adolphus. He nibbled dates from a bowl, watching his wife with lazy approval. Drew glanced at the Duke of Lachlan. He crossed his arms over his chest and stared stonily ahead, projecting displeasure.

"Your Grace," began Princess Cynde, speaking to Lachlan, "may I present to you Miss Drewsmina Trelayne. My sister and dear friend. She is the answer to the debut of your nieces."

*Nieces?* Drew swung her gaze to the duke.

"So you're saying," asked Lachlan, his voice sardonic and disbelieving, "this will actually *happen*? This surprise . . . woman with whom I'm being—"

He sighed. "We're all meant to simply go along?"

Prince Adolphus choked on a date and then cleared his throat, coughing into his fist. "*Lachlan!*" he barked.

"Right," the duke sighed. He sounded exhausted.

"Do not test me, Lachlan," Prince Adolphus warned, "I am doing you a favor—two favors—and your rudeness knows no bounds."

The duke closed his eyes. He took a deep breath. He looked to Drew.

"How do you do?" the duke droned, his voice dripping with sarcasm.

Drew glanced miserably at Cynde. She nodded encouragingly. *Go on . . .*

"I—" Drew cleared her throat. "Very well, thank you, Your Grace. You have twins you hope to launch in society?" Drew's voice was as pretty as it was false. The two of them were unwilling actors in a play, forced to say their lines.

"Indeed," confirmed Lachlan. He glared at the prince and then returned his icy stare to Drew. "I'd say the word *launch* overstates my goals for them. *Society?* Also a stretch. They are sixteen years old and I've brought them from Dorset to London to prepare for a modest Season."

"Modest?" asked Drew.

"The girls are very green," Lachlan went on. "And all of us—the girls, their mother, who is my sister, and myself—intend to return to Frampton, in Dorset, by summer. Until then, I should like to make some effort toward a Season, allow them to enjoy Town, kit them out. Make an appearance, if you will. I believe that's how it's done."

"I see," said Drew, although she did not see. Hosting a debutante Season—and not just one debutante, but two—was expensive and time-consuming and would have far-reaching impact for the rest of any girl's life. If money was no object, it was not something to be embarked upon by halves.

"You are trying my nerves, Lachlan," warned the prince. "We've summoned Miss Trelayne to *help* you. She is in the business of styling and training girls for their Season. She can aid Eunice and Opal—"

"*Imogene and Ivy,*" gritted out the duke.

". . . in a most gratifying debut. For all of you. She can be the difference between smashing success or lackluster tedium. But of course you've not mentioned the most important bit."

"*I've* not mentioned it?" asked Lachlan. "*Me?* I'm not the engineer of this coercion."

"You're fortunate that I'm so very fond of you," said the prince. "It's no surprise that you're disliked in most circles."

Drew nearly gasped at the insult. The prince popped another date into his mouth. Lachlan was slowly shaking his head.

"As we've said, Drewsmina," continued the prince, "the task at hand is to train up the nieces of my old friend Lachlan here; prepare them for their debut. You know this bit. What has not been said is that the girls will be presented *at* court to Queen Charlotte in the spring. It's no piddling thing, being presented to the queen, and you'll have your work cut out for you. However, it's an arrangement that should benefit both you and the duke. And the girls, of course."

To the duke he said, "Miss Trelayne is a future style maker and will soon be the most sought-after finisher of debutantes in all of London. You are lucky to have her before she is impossible to book, even by me."

"Yes," mumbled the duke on an exhale. "How lucky."

"I beg your pardon?" asked the prince.

"Thank you, Highness," said Lachlan.

"Drewsmina," continued the prince, "Lachlan has plenty of money and no wife to siphon it away. Spare no expense in outfitting the girls nor billing him for your time."

"Wait," cut in the duke, "I'm to *pay* her?"

The prince continued to Drew, ignoring him, "You will work with the duke, his sister Lady Tribble, and the girls to prepare them for their presentation at court and whatever else is necessary for a proper Season. I apologize in advance for his obstinacy. What can I say? He is not *well-liked* by most people."

"The feeling is mutual," Lachlan grumbled.

"Any problems you may encounter, please apply directly to me," finished the prince. He took a deep breath and beamed at Princess Cynde. "That's sufficient, wouldn't you say, Minnow?"

"Lovely," said Cynde sweetly, clapping her hands together once. "It's all settled. You can manage, can't you, Miss Trelayne?"

"Ah," began Drew. Words escaped her overwhelmed brain.

The duke was unmarried.

The twins were his nieces.

Lachlan hadn't been interested in hiring a stylist for the girls. She'd been *assigned* to him.

And this was *after* Drew had insulted him in the antechamber.

Now the prince gazed lazily at his young wife, chewing a fresh date.

Cynde beamed hopefully at Drew with a look of accomplishment.

The duke stared straight on, his eyes stony.

Drew looked at her hands for longer than necessary, trying to summon the correct words. Finally, she said, "Thank you so very much, Highnesses, Your Grace. And yes—I can manage."

The truth was, Drew knew very little about court presentation, although she could easily learn. The real challenge here would be an employer who had no wish to hire her. And whom she'd insulted.

Cynde chimed in, "You will not regret this collaboration, Your Grace. There is no match for my sister's talents. Your nieces will have guidance on wardrobe, styling, manners, proficiency with hobbies and diversions, introductions, modesty—there are so many things Miss Trelayne can teach them. They will learn to navigate London, how to manage city servants, to write tactful correspondence, to make sparkling conversation. Best of all—and this is the bit that only Miss Trelayne can offer—she will teach the girls to believe in themselves. To be confident. To make informed choices based on their own best interest and to choose wisely."

"Oh, *good*," drawled Lachlan, his tone steeped in sarcasm.

Drew stole a glance at him. He looked trapped. He looked as if he'd been forced to endure a very long, very tedious meal, and now he wished only to go, but someone had suggested songs around the pianoforte.

"Brilliant," said Prince Adolphus. "Off with you then. We've other subjects. You may mete out logistical details however you like. But please take note, we'll be keeping watch. Cynde speaks routinely with Miss Trelayne. I'll also wish to learn of the girls' progress. Perhaps monthly visits to the Throne Room would be a useful tool in their training."

"Oh lovely!" said Cynde, clapping her hands again.

"Very good, Highness," said the duke, and he bowed formally. "Thank you for this . . . introduction."

"You're welcome, Lachlan. Now, there's a good fellow. My steward will send word about that drink at the Ferryman. I'm glad you're back in London, whatever the reason. It's long overdue."

Drew hesitated, allowing the duke to reply, but he said nothing.

"May God save you both," Drew put in and curtsied again. "I am ever so grateful for this opportunity. I . . . I will not disappoint you, or the duke, or his family. As you know, this is my life's purpose."

"Of course it is," Cynde enthused, her voice almost a squeal. "How very welcome you are. I am positively brimming with anticipation."

Lachlan mumbled a curse beneath his breath and bowed again.

Drew hovered, not entirely certain if they'd been dismissed or if a footman would lead them out.

She glanced at the duke.

He stared at her with cold, impatient eyes.

Drew took a small step in the direction of the door, a test.

He made an exaggerated nod, *Yes, that's it*.

Drew blinked, swallowed, and made for the door.

But now would they *leave* together? she wondered. Must this terrible conversation be prolonged?

"Miss Trelayne?" the duke said, following close behind.

Drew did not stop.

Footmen held open the doors, and she stepped out. Inside the antechamber, bickering persisted. The commotion of little boys filled every corner. Drew sailed through, ignoring it all. The next doors led to the landing that would take her to the grand staircase. She hit them at a near sprint.

"*Miss Trelayne*," the duke repeated, his voice curt and impatient. He kept pace behind her.

Outside the antechamber, Drew stopped. She closed her eyes. A railing lined the balcony, and she reached out to steady herself. She turned.

The duke came up short behind her.

"Forgive me," she breathed, throwing out the words like a protective hand over her face.

"Look at you," he said dryly, "quick as the birds."

"I beg your pardon?"

"Never mind," he said. "Look, congratulations. Apparently this will happen."

"Your Grace . . ." she began.

"Forgive me, I loathe surprises. The truth is, you'll do as good as any."

"I beg your pardon?"

"Look—Miss Trelayne. *Royal edict* would never be my first choice for making decisions about staff, but honestly, I don't care who manages the twins. They must have someone. Dolph and his wife have every faith in you clearly."

"I—" began Drew, but she paused.

Cynde had faith in her because Cynde held her in great affection.

The prince had faith in her because he loved Cynde.

Their loyalty was sweet, but this job had been earned through nepotism, there was no way around it.

"I am very devoted to the craft of styling debutantes," Drew finally said. The truth.

"Devoted, are you?" said the duke. "Diplomatic, too, I take it."

"I beg your pardon?"

"I may be a pariah Miss Trelayne, but I'm not an idiot. Can we both agree that you have no experience, no credentials, and we are likely your first clients?"

"Ahh," hedged Drew.

"If not, you'd have a full roster and no need of the influence of the royal family. Your 'devotion,' however, is not in question. You seem very devoted indeed."

He looked her up and down then, his gaze nothing like that of an employer. He looked at her . . . *person*. Not at her styling. Not her posture. Not even her face. He was looking at her . . . well—at *all* of her.

Drew fought the urge to duck her head. She was not accustomed to being assessed by men. For one thing, her very tallness meant that most men had to look up to see her. Although not *this* man. *This* man had a good three inches on her.

When men had taken the time to study her, it was to marvel. They showed the same kind of sneering appreciation they might show a dog who'd eaten a living turtle, shell and all.

The Duke of Lachlan looked at her like he'd been stopped by something unexpected that had caught his attention. A treasure in a shop window. A peacock. A shooting star.

Drew was uncertain how to go on.

"I really don't care about your credentials," the duke finally said. "The twins are, in a word, *disasters*. My sister is a widow and entirely out of her depth as a parent. Correction: she is out of her depth in most things. They have only just returned to Avenelle, my estate in Dorset. Oh, but wait—perhaps you already know all of this?"

Drew shook her head.

"So your misinformation is limited to my sins alone? Fine. Rest assured, ours is a complicated family. If you are prone to gossip—which you've proven yourself to be—you'll get an eyeful. But, with regard to what you said earlier to me, I should like to make myself perfectly clear—"

"No apology is sufficient for my indiscretion," Drew rushed to say. "And my regret could not be more complete. Please know this. It's no excuse, but: the birds. I was overcome with—I wasn't thinking."

"Whatever the reason, I cannot tolerate gossip about the riots, not inside my household or out. If I were to hire you—and it seems I've been given little choice but to do so—your colorful description of me would be entirely unacceptable. *Any* discussion of me would be entirely unacceptable."

"Yes, of course," Drew assured, her voice choked. "I understand."

"I extend this same discretion to the twins," he went on. "The less they learn about their disgraced uncle, the better. But also, the less you say about the girls, the better. To anybody. I cannot say what they've been through, but I'm doubtful any of it is fit for public consumption. Their lives hold challenge enough without—well, without a swirl of gossip chasing them through London. I must insist upon complete silence when it comes to my family."

Drew wanted to ask what challenges the girls faced. She wanted to ask why his nieces were a mystery to him. She wanted to ask why he so readily accepted the title of "disgraced."

Instead she nodded and said, "Absolutely, Your Grace. I understand completely. It won't be a problem."

"None of this may matter. When you meet the girls and my sister, you may run screaming for the hills, despite your royal patrons."

"Never you fear," Drew said. "I should be delighted to work with your nieces. That is, if you truly wish it. But please—there has been no royal edict. I can speak to the princess about removing the obligation from—"

"I cannot decline the arrangement. The twins' presentation in court is tied to an audience for myself with the prince regent. It's an opportunity I cannot refuse. We'll have to make the best of it—all of us."

"*Right*," Drew said thoughtfully, nodding along as if

she understood his many vague references to disasters and complications.

"If nothing else, your very newness may make you the perfect candidate for the twins. I prefer to keep out of the public eye. For reasons you've already explained."

"If nothing else, I am . . . *new*," she agreed. Another truth.

"Right," he said distractedly, looking around. "Very well then. It's settled. Can you begin tomorrow?"

"I can," she said, her chest filling with buoyant hope.

He gave a nod and stepped around her. "The house is number 14 Pollen Street. Say, ten o'clock?"

And then he strode away, not waiting for an answer. She lifted a hand to wave at his retreating form.

When he was gone, Drew spun back, staring at the closed doors of the antechamber. She released the railing. Tears began to sting her eyes, and she blinked them back.

She'd done it.

By some miracle.

Despite all her mistakes.

She had an actual client—*two actual* clients.

She'd managed the first leap toward the rest of her life.

# Chapter Four

Ian was pacing the entryway when Miss Trelayne called the next day.

Pacing? More like lying in wait. Ian was impatient, but he was not delusional. He'd lain awake last night, wondering if the *royal assignment* of a strange woman could possibly, miraculously, be the answer to the question of Imogene and Ivy.

*Oh, Imogene and Ivy.*

He'd only brought his twin nieces to London because he'd run out of options in Dorset. Now here they were, but he'd made no immediate plans for what to do next. He'd intended to settle in for a bit. To allow the girls to grow accustomed to city life. To *wait and see*.

Now Prince Adolphus had thrust this . . . this . . . woman upon them, and she could easily make a bad situation worse. She could be wholly indifferent, or—

Well, he was too much of a realist to believe she could do any good. Her presence in their lives had been too much of a surprise.

Still, *something* had propelled him to the entry hall to wait for her.

Fear, likely. Fear that she'd turn up to say all the wrong things. Fear that she'd turn tail and run the moment she met Imogene and Ivy. The girls were fragile, for all that. The person he ultimately hired to train them would require a very particular brand of patience and compassion.

Or perhaps he was afraid that she might not come at all?

Oh no, he thought. She must come. Surprise royal assignment or not.

If she didn't come, he'd be alone with the girls.

For the fourth time, Ian paused to squint through a rain-streaked window into the street. He checked his pocket watch. Ten o'clock. He looked again and—

*And there she was.*

Right on time.

The raindrops on the windowpane distorted her to a smear of orange and burgundy. She'd come on foot. Apparently, she was not deterred by rain.

Ian stepped back, and let out a breath.

"Greenly!" he bellowed, summoning the butler.

"Aye, Your Grace," the old man called, shuffling to the door with glacial slowness.

"You're sacked, Greenly," Ian said.

"Pray do not tease, Your Grace," said the old man.

"All staff. The lot. I'm replacing you with a wagon of circus performers. They couldn't do worse."

Miss Trelayne's knock was firm and professional, and Ian froze for half a beat. It was a confident knock. Prepared. Intentional. No wonder it startled him; didn't she know everyone in this house flew about by the seat of their pants?

"Her, too," Ian grumbled, leaning against the wall, crossing his arms over his chest. "Sacked."

"Very good, Your Grace," appeased Greenly, pulling open the heavy door.

Ian would sack no one, of course. His problem was too few people in his life to help him, not too many.

Or, he *supposed* that was the problem.

*If I knew the bloody problem*, he thought, *I would solve it.*

"Yes?" Greenly called to the stoop.

"Hello," said the voice of Miss Trelayne.

The sound conjured up the image of flame-orange hair, lithe tallness, a jarring splash of freckles on pale white skin.

Ian frowned again. He was not fond of red hair. Or freckles. He didn't like remembering the distinctive details of people he barely knew. Given the choice, he preferred to forget most people.

If only he'd not devoted quite so much time in Kew Palace to studying her distinctive orange hair, and freckles, and litheness. But there had been nothing else to do.

"How do you do?" Miss Trelayne continued to the butler, "I am Miss Drewsmina Trelayne. I've an appointment with Lady Tribble and her daughters, Miss Imogene and Miss Ivy. It was arranged by His Grace, the duke."

Of course she would not ask for him. Naturally, *rightly*, she would ask for Timothea and the girls. It was for the girls that she'd been hired. In a normal household, inhabited by a normal family, the girls would be under the purview of their mother. She'd said exactly the correct thing.

And maybe that was why he'd been lying in wait; he'd wanted someone, anyone, to come here and say and do the correct bloody thing.

"Very good, miss," said Greenly. "The family are expecting you. Follow me, if you please."

Greenly, damn him, had ushered her inside before Ian had had a chance to slip away.

"Thank you," said Miss Trelayne, stepping briskly inside. The entryway filled with the smell of rain, and morning chill, and something else, a smell he could not identify. Another memory unfolded. The two of them, lunging for the door in the same moment. The birds. He'd been struck by the same smell; a musky, personal, vanilla-y scent. Very feminine, intimate.

Ian frowned.

"Shall I take your wet things, miss?" the butler requested, unburdening Miss Trelayne of a burgundy coat. Ian wouldn't have noticed the color, except the dress beneath was shockingly pale—a light blush color; too pink to be ivory, too white to be pink. The skin of a pomegranate pulled back to reveal the creamy sheath that protected the wet, succulent fruit.

Ian frowned more deeply. She should not put him in the mind of a pomegranate. Or of layers being pulled back. Or wet succulence. She should not remind him of anything except solutions.

Ian glowered at Greenly as he disappeared around a corner.

"Oh, hello, Your Grace," said Miss Trelayne.

"Hello," he muttered. Of all the benefits of being a duke, perhaps his favorite was that he could say as little as he pleased.

"I'm looking so forward to meeting Lady Tribble and the girls."

"Yes," he said.

Now there was even less to say. His sister was ridiculous; for as long as he could remember, he'd dreaded introducing her to people.

Awkward silence rose like water in a tub. Ian studied her. She looked less abashed than yesterday, more hopeful. Her hair was the same, as orange as the cylinder of a Dutch lily. Her eyes were an odd mix of blue-green, and she stared at him with the direct and alert look of someone who expected you to say something important. She was as straight and as tall as a candlestick.

"How *tall* are you?" he asked suddenly. Ian stood six foot, two inches, and she was almost as tall as him.

"I beg your pardon?"

"I am well over six feet. Rarely do I meet a woman anywhere approaching my height."

"I cannot say," she finally said. "Not quite so tall as . . . six feet."

He frowned at this. He was going to tell her that she should know her own height, that it was a remarkable thing, that it might be useful for dressmakers or bed builders, but Greenly was back.

"Shall I, Your Grace?" asked the butler.

"Carry on," Ian said.

Their progress down the grand hall was as slow and foreboding as a funeral procession. He felt he should say something, duke or not. He should explain about Timothea and the girls, go over some expectations, remind her about gossip.

"Will you remain for the introduction, Your Grace?" Miss Trelayne asked, turning halfway back to him.

"I had not considered. I hope not, honestly. What do you advise?"

He'd not intended to reveal the breadth of his ineptitude, not right away, but Drewsmina Trelayne emanated a sort of . . . proficiency. A knowing. She had a reliable air that made him want to—

Well, to get his money's worth while there was still time. She would not remain. No sane person would. He should've made a list of questions to ask her before she fled from the house.

"Let us make no plan," she suggested lightly. "If the girls are as untried as you've said, nimbleness and versatility may be our most useful tool."

"That sounds like a trick," he mumbled.

"Call it what you like. The idea is to embrace the unexpected rather than recoil from it."

"You mean embrace surprises," he said. "I hate surprises. Unfortunately, no preface could be better suited to meeting my family."

"Whatever do you me—?"

She was cut off by Greenly, who stood in the open doorway. "Miss Drewsmina Trelayne, here to see you, Lady Tribble, Miss Ivy," the butler announced.

*Chapter Five*

"How do you?" Drew said, speaking to the large yellow room.

Her voice was bright and brisk; a disguise for her nerves.

The greeting was met with silence and she scanned the room, seeking out the only other adult face.

Lady Tribble, the duke's sister—it could be no other—was sprawled upon a sofa in a posture of half repose. In her lap, she held a small stringed instrument. She stared out, unsmiling, and picked out three, sharp notes—*ping, pang, pluck.*

Drewsmina, determined not to say the wrong thing, waited.

"Hello," the woman said, her voice was testing, cautious.

*Oh, but she is nervous*, thought Drew. She affected a warm, pleasant smile. She dipped into a small, head-bobbed bow.

"It's a pleasure to meet you, my lady," said Drew.

Lady Tribble played three more notes. The baroness wasn't dressed in a gown so much as nestled deep within a swath of green fabric. She reminded Drew of a plump bird in a grassy nest. Was this garment a . . . shroud? A night rail? The dress managed to look, at once, like too much and not enough. She was covered from neck to hem, but unexpected body parts—a shoulder here, a knee there, two bare feet—protruded in a way that was oddly provocative. Her hair had been bandaged in an uneven turban.

"Oh for God's sake, Timothea," said Lachlan, stepping up. "Cease with the mandolin."

"It is a lute," informed Lady Tribble. "Modified, of course."

"And this is no concert. Where is Imogene?" he asked.

Lady Tribble looked slowly around the room, her eyes narrowed as if she peered through a veil of smoke. "She was here a moment ago. Ivy, darling, where is Genie?"

Drew looked to the other side of the room. A young woman sat in a far-flung chair in the corner. She wore a beige morning dress in a very poor fit—Drew saw this immediately—and she had long, dull hair, possibly in need of a thorough washing, pulled tightly back from her face. Drew smiled at her, but the girl ducked her head and clasped the seat of her chair, the gesture of someone on a harrowing ride in a runaway wagon.

"I cannot say," the girl murmured to the floor.

Drew took a step closer. Balanced on the girl's lap was a large book, on the book, a small wire cage. The cage appeared to contain leaves and twigs and stones. Drew's excitement, already at a fever pitch, climbed higher still. Oh, but this was going to be so very fun, indeed.

"You cannot say, or you do not know?" Lachlan was saying, beginning to pace. "Did no one hear me say that the new . . . new—"

He glanced at Drew. "How do you fancy yourself? Are you a governess?"

"No, no," assured Drew, eyeing Ivy, "these girls are too grown-up for a governess. I am a stylist."

Across the room, the girl introduced as Miss Ivy tipped her head ever so slightly to study Drew.

"Right," said Lachlan. "*Stylist.*" He emphasized the word as if he were naming an exotic and gratuitous profession such as "sword swallower," or "food taster."

"Did I not say," Lachlan went on, "that the new *stylist* was due at ten o'clock?"

"Oh, you did say it," assured Lady Tribble, strumming her lute, "obviously. As it is ten o'clock, and I am here."

"Yes, but where is your *daughter*?" Lachlan grumbled, dropping into a chair and rubbing his eyes with one hand.

Drew looked around, checking cracks in doorways and gaps beneath floor-length curtains. The girl could be absent, but she could also be hiding. She was just about to ask Ivy about her book and wire cage when a giant cat, as fat as a spaniel, slunk into the room.

"And who is this?" Drew asked. "Not Miss Imogene, I presume."

"That is a cat," declared Lady Tribble with no trace of irony.

"Miss Trelayne can identify a cat," said Lachlan tiredly, his hand still over his eyes.

"Well, some people," refuted Lady Tribble, "are of the belief that human spirits can be embodied within the physicality of animals."

"No one believes this, Timothea," said Lachlan.

"Well, not of Mephistopheles, of course," replied Lady Tribble—here again, no irony. "He is merely a cat. As I've just said." She strummed a soothing chord on her lute. "As far as we know."

The duke scraped his hand downward, palming his face.

Drew cleared her throat. "Your cat is called Mephis-topheles?" she asked brightly. "Now, that is a mouthful, although . . ." She examined the cat. He had flamboyantly thick fur, horn-like pointy ears, and an expression of haughty disdain. ". . . rather fitting, I believe."

"He's called Meph, for short," whispered Ivy Starry from her chair in the corner.

"How clever," enthused Drew. "'Meph.' And who is the proud owner of this beast?"

"Meph belongs to no one," proclaimed Lady Tribble, her voice taking on a reverent tone. She replayed the same chord, the beginning, perhaps, of the creature's signature march.

"The cat was a stray found at Avenelle," said a new voice from behind them. Lachlan dropped his hand and sat up. Drew turned. Lady Tribble plucked a different progression of chords.

In the doorway leaned a girl. Imogene Starry.

"Imogene," observed Lachlan tiredly, "how lovely of you to turn up. Miss Trelayne, I give you my second niece, Imo-gene Starry."

"There you are, darling," said Lady Tribble. "I knew you'd been here a moment ago."

Drew smiled cautiously at the young woman. While Lady Tribble had a lazy sort of eccentricity, and Ivy was timid and mousy, this girl? This girl . . . ?

And now Drew's heart beat very fast indeed.

Imogene Starry was, at once, unkempt and beautiful. Hair unbound. Dress a faded crimson. Had she . . . ? Yes, she had. She'd altered the décolletage into the neckline of a saucy widow. Eyes: cornflower blue. Hair: sunlight blond. Figure: lush but not thick.

In two words, the girl was dangerously alluring.

She assessed Drew with a boldness that bordered on challenge. At the same time, she gave off a lazy, half-lidded detachment that said, *You don't see me.*

Like her sister, her dress was ill-fitting and the color did nothing for the tone of her skin.

And yet, she all but glowed, even in the rainy-day light of the mustard-painted room. In some other girl, her drooped posture might suggest a back injury; but Imogene projected lazy defiance. Everything about her said, *Make me care, I dare you.*

Despite Drew's own manners and poise, her first instinct was shock. She couldn't say what she expected, but it was not this.

On the heels of shock came wariness. Drew had transformed herself, but she'd never been a beauty, not now or ever. If she was being honest, Drew was a little intimidated by beauty. She felt the urge to step back.

But her *third* impulse, which was rooted in survival (and had been with her far longer) was to remain where she stood, meet the girl's challenging gaze, and show absolutely no reaction at all. Not to the rudeness, nor to the beauty.

"Avenelle is your home in Dorset?" Drew asked the girl, taking up the conversation about the cat.

"Well, it's the *duke's* home, isn't it?" said Imogene.

"Avenelle is your home, too," reminded the duke on a sigh.

Imogene did not agree or contradict. Instead, she studied Drew with cool detachment. Drew allowed the girl to stare. She'd taken care with her styling today, like every day. Her wardrobe was one of her greatest vanities. Fine clothes were a necessity for a stylist; also a necessity for someone so very tall and thin, with carrot-colored hair. The correct clothes helped to make Drew . . . if not pretty, then at least attractive.

"Won't you join us?" Drew asked. "I'm eager to become acquainted."

Imogene shrugged, the gesture of someone who consented because there was nothing else to do.

No one had invited Drew to sit, refreshment had not been offered, and the duke's introduction had been very spotty, indeed. Normally she would defer to the girls' mother for these salutations, but Lady Tribble was playing her lute in earnest now, humming softly to match the notes. Lachlan stared at the floor as if a hole might open up and he could jump through it.

Drew cleared her throat. Someone needed to establish authority, but no one else seemed inclined. Surely Lachlan or Lady Tribble would contradict her if she overstepped.

"Let us *all* sit, shall we?" Drew took a chair adjacent to Lady Tribble. The baroness did not look up.

"Ivy?" Drew called. "Won't you come closer? Perhaps share a refreshment. Who can ring for tea?" Drew smiled expectantly, hoping that one of the girls might take the initiative.

Ivy trudged to the opposite end of her mother's sofa. Imogene drifted to the cat. Dropping to the rug beside the animal, she tucked up her legs and rested her chin on her knees. Idly, she twirled her fingers above the cat's head. He flopped on his back, mesmerized.

No one rang for tea.

"Your Grace?" asked Drew. "How might I send for a pot of tea? If you do not mind?"

"Tea. Right," said Lachlan. He rolled from his chair and strode from the room.

"Will one of your duties be to issue orders to Uncle and staff?" Imogene asked with faux innocence.

"Ah," Drew began, trying to formulate an answer.

Imogene cut her off. "Are you not a *servant* yourself?"

Carefully, Drew began to pull off her gloves and place them in her lap. "I am not a servant, in fact," she said. "I am . . . an instructor. Like a music teacher or a tutor, although more comprehensive. How glad I am that you have raised the topic, as now might be a good time to go over some of the duties I will perform while I am here. If the two of you and your mother are amenable."

She glanced at Lady Tribble. The baroness appeared to examine some malfunction on the bridge of her lute.

Drew continued, "I will teach you how young ladies are

expected to dress and behave when in public and in private. We'll look at how you should behave around ladies and gentlemen and, similarly, how you should behave around shopkeepers and dressmakers and servants. Manners convey respect, and respect is owed to everyone we meet.

"Much of this, you may already know. Some of the teaching will be my demonstration of this or that custom or task while you observe. Just as I've done now. Do you see how I've sent for tea? Other times, you'll want to jot down a few notes and memorize, as you've done in the schoolroom. We'll practice it all again and again among ourselves and then we'll call on friends and practice—"

Imogene raised her hand and Drew stopped speaking.

Imogene looked at her with pronounced boredom. She cocked her head as if to say, *I'm waiting.*

"Of course raised hands will not be required for questions," said Drew. "The three of us will be more like . . . collaborators. Although, it is very polite of you not to interrupt. You may speak freely, Imogene."

Imogene did not lower her hand, nor did she speak.

Drew swallowed. "Yes, Imogene?"

Imogene's hand fell. "We were never in school. In case you didn't know."

"Imogene," whispered Ivy, her cheeks reddening.

"Nor do we have any friends on whom to call," Imogene continued. "Again. In case you didn't know."

"Oh," said Drew. "In fact I did not know. We have . . . so much to learn about one another."

Drew heard footsteps behind her. She glanced back, using the moment to collect herself. Lachlan stood in the doorway, his face was tight and shrewdly interested, the expression of a man trying to decipher a coded passage.

Drew turned back. "So . . . you've not had *formal* schooling," she said, reframing the comment. Imogene would not have raised it if she did not wish to discuss it. "No tutors, perhaps, but you would have had nannies and a governess."

"Well, there was Matron," remembered Imogene, her tone suspiciously forthcoming. "And Proctor."

Drew studied her beautiful face. *Matron and Proctor?* Had they been figures of some authority in their lives? She named them with equal parts foreboding and relish. Did she embellish to make a point?

"And we learned to read scripture," Imogene went on. "And the Temple tracts. But most books were banned, of course."

Drew ceased hiding her shock. "I'm afraid I don't understand," she said.

She looked from Imogene to her sister. Ivy had dropped her face into her hands. Lady Tribble put aside the lute and chewed a fingernail in the nervous manner of someone deep in thought. She refused to meet Drew's eyes.

"Oh, I see," realized Imogene, sounding a little excited. "No one's told you?"

"No one has told her *what*, Imogene?" demanded Lachlan. He shoved from the door. "What does that mean, 'no school and no friends?' And who the devil are 'Matron' and 'Proctor'? I've been hounding you for a month to explain what happened after Tribble died, and you've said nothing. Now you wish to elaborate? *Now?*"

"Perhaps I didn't remember," said Imogene thoughtfully. "Until now."

"Imogene," Lachlan said, his frustration clear, "I want to help you, God knows I do. I want to help all of you. But you must communicate with me when I ask, or when I don't ask, or whenever you can bear to tell me. Please."

"But . . ." concluded Imogene, "not in the company of Miss Trelayne? She's been brought in to—"

"Why not?" Lachlan cut in. "If that's what you wish—to shock and alarm Miss Trelayne, why not? My priority is to learn what has happened."

The girl chewed her bottom lip, saying nothing.

Lachlan continued. "I've no idea what I'm doing, Imogene. I've said this again and again. There is no guidebook for sorting out one's *wayward* nieces, is there? I am a bachelor. I've no experience with nieces or children of any stripe. I'm doing all of this for you: the Season, the city, and *Miss Trelayne*. But you must help me." He began to pace.

Drew looked back to Imogene. She smiled the spiteful, self-satisfied smile of a child who'd pushed an adult beyond the limits of his patience. Meanwhile, Lady Tribble had closed her eyes and balled her hands into fists at her sides. Ivy stared at her lap with wide, worried eyes.

The mood in the room had gone, Drew thought, from expectant . . . to strange . . . to something like a runaway cart. Now they dealt in the realm of wayward nieces, unsaid things, proctors and matrons, and girls with no friends.

Drew was put in the mind of the birds in the antechamber. Yesterday, she'd wanted only to bring calm to the room, to settle the birds. Meanwhile, Lachlan had wanted to shatter glass and chase chaos out the window.

At Kew Palace, they'd done it his way. Here, they would do it hers. They would bring calm to the room. Everyone would be given time to settle.

With truly enlightened timing, a young maid hurried into the room bearing a tray of pastries. Two footmen followed with a rolling cart.

"Out, Meredith," intoned Lachlan, "not now."

The maid froze, stricken by the reprimand.

"Meredith, is it?" Drew cut in. "Is that tea? Lovely. Perhaps the duke would allow you to station it near the window? Close the doors as you leave, if you please. That's it, thank you ever so much."

"Very good, miss," said Meredith, hustling out with the footmen and closing the doors with a whoosh.

"Most things are improved by tea," recited Drew. "Lady Tribble, do you mind if I pour?"

"None for me, please," sighed Lady Tribble, not opening her eyes. She nestled more deeply into her shroud, now fully reclined on the sofa.

"Very good," said Drew. "Ivy? Can I ask you to lay this small table with four cups and saucers? Yes, that's it— lovely. Imogene, perhaps you can locate the strainer? There it is, brilliant. I see the pastries, but does the kitchen typically send up some savory choice—oh wait, here is a tray of sandwiches. Brilliant. But this *is* a proper tea."

The girls did as she bade, laying the tea with ungraceful but dutiful movements. Spoons were dropped. Napkins were unfurled in the manner of a flag waving surrender. Pastries were claimed in an escalating volley of, "Do not *think* you'll have the apple tart. It's *mine*." "I will think of it, and I will eat it."

When the time came to pour, Drew glanced at Lachlan, worried she'd overstepped. The duke stood in the middle of the room, arms folded, face bleak.

Drew flashed a smile that she hoped was both encouraging and professional, the smile of a woman who knew just what she was doing.

"Now," Drew said, distributing cups of steaming tea, "shall I continue going over what can be expected from my time here? I should also like to hear of any special interests or areas of training the girls would like to learn more about. Or to avoid, if we can indulge in a few omissions."

The girls stared at Drew, munching on tarts and sandwiches, and said nothing. Despite their lack of knowledge about laying tea, their table manners seemed in perfect working order. There was no smacking or slurping. The duke drifted to the window, propping his hip on the sill. He drank his tea and stared into the street.

"Perhaps I should go back. Do we all understand what is meant by a *London Season*?"

More silent chewing. Ivy's eyes were large and wary. She looked as if Drew was explaining how to rout a charging bear. Imogene's expression was wholly disinterested, as if Drew recited the taxonomy of moss.

In a perfect world, Drew and the girls' parents would

have reviewed their plans and budget for the scale of their Season. But Lady Tribble seemed willfully detached, and the duke had hardly chosen Drew as a collaborator. He'd been saddled with her. Furthermore, he seemed not to know or not to care about the fine details of their Season. Drew saw no other option but to make it up as she went along.

She continued, "As you may know, young ladies are regarded by the world as children until the very week of their debut. After that, and only after that, they are considered 'out' in society."

Ivy took a quick, hungry bite of sandwich, rapt. Imogene rolled a grape between two fingers and sighed in boredom.

"Perhaps you have experienced this," Drew said, "being regarded as children, despite being very nearly grown. If I might inquire, how old are you girls?"

"We are sixteen and a half," provided Ivy.

"Very good," said Drew. "You are sixteen, and not yet 'out,' and so you are not included in adult social events; you are not engaged in conversation by adults, especially men outside your family."

Drew waited for a resentful chorus of *it's true* or *I hate it* or *we are not children*—but none came. The girls simply drank their tea and waited.

Drew cleared her throat. "However, *after* you are introduced into society, this regard will switch almost overnight. After your debut, you will be permitted, nay, encouraged, to attend parties, dinners, balls, and the theater in the company of adults—men and women. You will be engaged in conversation with men and women, and asked your opinion about topics ranging from the weather, to literature, to exhibits at a museum, art, politics, and society gossip. You will dance, you will drink champagne, you will be courted by men of all ages with romantic intent. As you do all of this, you'll project the most authentic and interesting version of yourself so you

might match up with a potential husband, enter a courtship, become betrothed, marry, and begin a family." Drew
took a sip of tea. "Among fifty other things, at least."

"Oh no," said Ivy, a whisper.

Drew glanced at Lady Tribble, hoping she would either
assure her daughter or contradict this (admittedly) frank
description of a Season. The baroness said nothing.

"Never you fear, Ivy," Drew went on. "We have plenty of
time to prepare. I explain it not to alarm you, but because
neither deceit nor willful ignorance improves our chances
of success. And please keep in mind this is a broad, gener-
alized view and I color it with my own opinion of the enterprise. I am happy to entertain objections or amendments
to this view."

Drew poured herself more tea, waiting again for someone to object or amend.

Lachlan stared into his teacup.

Lady Tribble had not opened her eyes.

Ivy had taken on a faint *purplish* hue, as if she might be
ill; but Imogene's detachment faded, and Drew leaned in,
just a little.

"If I may be even more frank, I do think it's a rather
odd custom, and not entirely fair—rather like a whipsawed
version of growing up. It is meant to protect a system that
keeps a certain set very close-knit and tends to reward
those who marry their first cousins." She made a face. "But
that's the way it's done, whether any of us likes it or not.
Your uncle was correct to bring you to London months in
advance. And I am here—'brought in,' as Imogene has
suggested—to ease the way for you, to make sure you're
smartly dressed and aware of what is expected at any given
event. I'll also help you bolster the bits of your personalities
that will best serve you."

"What if we . . ." ventured Ivy, ". . . cannot be bolstered?
What if we've no wish to be bolstered?"

Before Drew could answer, Imogene cut in. "Your own
debutante Season must have been a smashing success," the

girl remarked. "You made a brilliant match with a husband met during your debut?"

Drew blinked. She opened her mouth and then closed it. *This girl* . . .

"What an excellent question . . ."

She glanced in the direction of the duke. Naturally, he listened with rapt attention.

"In fact, my Season was a great disaster," Drew said brightly. "I was rather a different girl then, and I made many mistakes. Embarrassing mistakes. A pity, really; because for all its challenges, a Season can be jolly good fun. Unfortunately I did not have proper guidance; in fact I received quite the opposite of what one might call 'guidance.' As we go along, I'll share with you the tragic tale of my Season—or should I say, *Seasons*. The details are not important now. What's more important is that I have transformed from that unpopular girl to the woman I am today. I have changed. It's too late to enjoy my own Season done properly, obviously—"

"How old *are* you?" Imogene inquired.

Drew glanced at the duke. He stared at her.

Drew cleared her throat. "I am twenty-eight years old. Old enough to understand what it means to embody the very best version of myself but not so old that I'll insist upon netted veils or chastity belts."

"But do you live with your parents?"

Technically, these were not overtly rude questions; however, the delivery and intent toward rudeness were very apparent. They had such work to do. Luckily, Drew had once been very rude, herself. She could manage.

"My father is deceased," Drew said. "I live with a sister, Ana, and her husband, the Earl of Madewood."

"Oh, but you are a spinster," realized Imogene.

"Imogene," Lachlan warned, "must you be deliberately obtuse?"

"I am a spinster," confirmed Drew, "yes. Unrepentant. Proud, really. I did not marry—this is true. But I am making my own way. Not having a husband or family allows me the freedom to work with girls like you. And it is work that I enjoy very much."

"Why?"

"Well," she began, "several reasons. First, I love fashion and millinery and colors and fabrics; and finding the most advantageous wardrobe for you girls and styling your hair will be among our very first steps.

"Second, I am excited by the notion of making the debutante Season a bit . . . less onerous and, if possible, *fairer* for everyone involved."

"Will the Season be . . ." ventured Ivy in a whisper, ". . . terribly unfair?"

"Not in as many words," began Drew. "How can I explain? Before the Season gets underway a flood of young ladies will arrive in London from all over England. Some girls will come from America as well . . . Scotland . . . there will be so many girls. Some will be well prepared for the great whirl of it and so very eager. Others will be anxious and reticent. Some will be thrust into the parties and outings before they are fully comfortable with the city and the crush and the expectations. Many will be overwhelmed and out of their depth. Every level of preparedness and enthusiasm or awkwardness and disdain will be seen. Even so, a handful girls will, in a way, shine. With little effort, they will take to the enterprise like a fish to water. They'll exude poise, manners and wit, beauty—they will appear *incomparable*.

"Some will have been brought up to triumph in this moment, with perfect manners and natural beauty; others will float along on a river of Mama's jewelry and Papa's money. Others seem inherently confident or somehow naturally popular. And good for them.

"I have no interest in these girls," Drew proclaimed, warming to her favorite topic. "None at all. They are pretty, they are droll—fine. I'm lulled to sleep by the sheer boredom of girls such as this.

"*Instead*," she went on, "the girls that interest me are the ones who have not, perhaps, been brought up to shine; those who may have no dowry or no jewels; who are clever but perhaps not yet so very witty, who are talented but not yet polished. I admire the girls whose beauty is unconventional; whose humor is sharp or subtle or evolving; girls who are, perhaps, more . . . 'interesting' than poised.

"*These* are the girls who fascinate me; and these are the girls who I am excited to groom and guide into confidence."

"Really?" challenged Imogene. "But what care have you for a girl such as this?"

"Well, Imogene," sighed Drew, "if I'm being totally honest, *I* was this girl. And as difficult as it was to transform into the woman I am now, the journey was exciting and rewarding. I merely want to usher along other girls on the same path."

If Imogene had something to say about this admission, she did not articulate it. Instead, she narrowed her eyes and subjected Drew to open scrutiny. She stared at Drew's tidy pink hat, her red hair, secured tightly in the signature braid that ringed the crown of her head. The girl looked at her face, including the generous spray of tapioca-colored freckles, down her long neck to her pale pink dress.

Drew stared back, allowing it. Color rose to her cheeks, her heart pounded, but she did not look away.

Finally, Imogene said, "Uncle fancies us to be this sort of girl, then." She looked thoughtful, as if trying to reckon with this notion.

"Your uncle made no assumptions—that is, he made no such mention to me," Drew hurried to say. "Please do not misunderstand; no one is speculating about the potential for your success. And anyway, the truth is that His Royal Highness, Prince Adolphus, and the Royal Princess Cynde actually . . . er—"

"My old friend Prince Adolphus has arranged for you to be presented at court, Imogene," finished Lachlan, coming away from the window. "A court presentation means you'll be introduced to his mother, the Queen of England. Perhaps you've heard of her? It is a very great honor and, from what I understand, not easily managed without copious practice and instruction. Miss Trelayne's tutelage comes in conjunction with the invitation to meet Queen Charlotte. If you have a problem with her, you may take it up with the prince."

"Hmm," mused Imogene, popping a grape into her mouth. "Here we go again."

Drew wanted to study Lachlan's face, to see the expression that went with his highly edited version of their arrangement, but Imogene's comment took precedence.

What did she mean, *Here we go again*?

Drew waited for her to elaborate, but she said nothing. *No one* said anything. The silence closed in on all sides, squeezing the room.

*Fine*, thought Drew. *If no one else will ask, I will. But not yet.*

"Now that you know what I intend to do with you and why," Drew said, "I'd like to share my philosophy on *how* we shall go about it."

"Beatings, no doubt," said Lachlan idly, drifting to a stack of papers on a desk.

"Very clever," said Drew, "but I'm not paid enough for beatings. And anyway, I'm referring to my regard for the girls, not how I'll bend them to my will."

"I am less cooperative after a beating," offered Imogene. "Just to be perfectly clear."

Drew stared at her. The girl appeared entirely earnest. She glanced at Lachlan. He'd frozen in the act of rifling through the papers.

"Noted," said Drew carefully. She cleared her throat.

Again, she waited. Imogene said no more.

Drew went on, "What I meant to say is, I shall be respectful of your feelings and preferences. I will listen to your points of view. I'll also be honest. You will hear what I truly think in all things, from which fabrics look best with your skin to my honest opinion of the rules and customs of London society. My one request—no, that's not true, one of several requests—is that you show me the same respect, openness, and honesty.

"As such," Drew forged ahead, "I wonder if we might return to the topic of your prior schooling? And your friends."

"What about it?" asked Imogene.

"Well," began Drew, "has your home . . . always been in Dorset?"

"No," sighed Imogene, bored again.

Drew narrowed her eyes. "Where else have you lived?"

"Gloucestershire."

"Oh, lovely. Near the sea, perhaps?"

"Near the pigs."

"So you *prefer* Dorset to Gloucestershire?"

"We prefer anywhere to Gloucestershire."

"Why is that?"

"*Because*," said Imogene, "Gloucestershire is where we lived under the fat, sweaty thumb of Reverend Sagg, isn't it? And the Temple of Order in Eden."

"Ah . . ." Drew said. If there was a reasonable reply to this, Drew could not think of it.

And now the silence was a suffocating, choking sort of noose.

"I beg your pardon?" Drew managed.

"Our last home was on the grounds of the Temple of Order in Eden. It is a church. Or rather . . . a community? It is a community and a church."

Drew stared at Imogene. The girl had finally achieved her goal. Drew was not only shocked, she was shocked into speechlessness.

Behind her, she heard Lachlan drop his paperwork and come closer.

"Do you know it?" asked Imogene. "The Temple of Order in Eden? Or T.O.E., if you prefer it."

Drew shook her head.

Lachlan, now standing behind her said, "You're joking, Imogene. Timothea, sit up and tell me she's joking."

Lady Tribble did not move except to squeeze her eyes more tightly shut.

Drew carefully asked, "How long did you reside at—there?"

"For five years," said Imogene. She worked very hard to sound bored, but her voice had taken on a hardness. The girl wasn't bored, Drew realized, she was furious. "From the year after Father died until summer."

"*Imogene*," whispered Ivy, sounding distressed.

"Five years?" demanded Lachlan, his voice a rasp.

Imogene took her time selecting another grape and rolled it into her mouth. She said nothing.

"And this . . . church did not suit you?" ventured Drew.

And now Imogene laughed, a humorless, bitter sound. "No, T.O.E. and I did not suit. Did we, Mama?"

With no warning, Lady Tribble reanimated. She sat up so abruptly the lute rolled to the floor, twanging off several bad notes.

"I am not feeling well at present," Lady Tribble said. "I should like to retire to my rooms. You'll tell me if I miss anything important, won't you, girls?"

"Timothea, no," implored Lachlan. "Let us—"

The baroness rose and he trailed off. With a faint smile to no one in particular, she collected her instrument and wound her way to the door. The long tail of her green shroud followed her out like a snake.

The girls watched, reactionless, as she exited.

When she was gone, Drew allowed herself to look at the duke. He stared after his sister with a mix of disbelief and disappointment.

When she was gone, his eyes met Drew's. They exchanged a look. It was the sort of shared expression that conveyed one part *did you hear what I heard?* and another part *bloody, bleeding hell*.

The duke cleared his throat.

"Perhaps you might join me in the next room, Miss Trelayne?" he said. "Allow me to elaborate on one or two . . . points?"

"Perhaps that would be best," said Drewsmina, rising.

Ordinarily, she would press for openness and honest speech in front of her young clients.

Ordinarily, secrets were discouraged.

But nothing about this was ordinary.

"Girls," said Lachlan tiredly, "carry on with your tea." He strode from the room.

Drewsmina smiled at them tightly, smoothed her skirt, and followed.

# Chapter Six

*Don't go, Don't go, Don't go.* Ian strode down the corridor with only one thought.

*She must not go.*

He pounced on the third door he came upon, a small cloakroom that serviced the ballroom. Snatching a lit candle from the hall, he ducked inside, motioning for her to follow. When she stepped in, he swung the door shut behind her.

"Please do not go," he said.

She spun around. "Where are—? What is this?"

"Cloakroom," he said dismissively. He was lighting sconces. "The servants. I cannot abide eavesdropping."

He blew out his candle and tossed it on the countertop. "The Order of Temple in Eden? *What* in God's name?"

"I believe your niece said, 'The *Temple of Order in Eden.*' Which allows for the initials—"

"T.O.E.," he finished. "Bloody, bleeding hell. This is so much more dire than I—well, than I had hoped. How foolish of me. Of course it's worse. Have you heard of this . . . this T.O.E.?"

She shook her head. "If nothing else, Imogene has found a way to poke fun."

"Oh yes, how hilarious she is," Ian said. "The Temple of Order in Eden. What has my sister done?"

"The girls and their mother have not shared their recent history with you?" ventured Miss Trelayne. "Nothing at all?"

He turned his head to look at her. "No. They haven't. Most brothers and uncles would have elicited this information. I shouldn't blame Timothea, this is my fault."

"Before we lay blame, Your Grace, will you say if you've been . . . estranged from your sister and nieces?" She did not accuse so much as suggest.

"No, not estranged. That is, my sister and I were never close. Our childhood was unhappy. She's ten years older. Also, she's a—a breed apart."

Standing in one spot suddenly seemed like an exercise he could not endure. He began to pace. "She was married to an odd duck of a baron, but they got on well enough. I wasn't yet duke when the twins were born. We exchanged infrequent letters and saw each other less. I did several years in the army, fought in Spain. After her husband died, I sent for her and the girls, imploring them to return to Avenelle, but she refused. She wrote that they would recover best in their own home. I—God help me, I took her at her word. My life had grown complicated; I didn't have the will to argue—I left it.

"When next I inquired, she wrote that a local clergyman had begun to minister to them. Again she refused to return to Avenelle. Her letters suggested that they were improving.

"'Friends from church are a comfort to the girls and me,' she wrote.

"'Please do not disrupt our grief,' she wrote.

"'I shall send for you if we require more.' Bollocks.

"Problem was, I *needed* so very much for this to be true; I had my own crisis with the riots."

He stopped pacing and turned to her. "I have no idea why I'm telling you this. The end point is, I was neglectful and selfish. I took her at her word because I was ill-equipped to cope with the alternative."

"You cannot force someone to return home if they do not wish it," said Miss Trelayne.

"Beatings?" he asked, ignoring her. "Did Imogene say 'beatings'?"

Miss Trelayne cleared her throat. "But how did they return to your . . . purview? If you've only now learned of their . . . situation, I assume it wasn't you who retrieved them from the, er, temple?"

Ian shook his head. "They turned up on my doorstep in the summer, the three of them. Unannounced, no explanation. Timothea told me nothing except that she 'felt it was best they return home.'

"Ivy has barely spoken," he continued. "I've heard her voice more this morning than ever before.

"Imogene—" He shook his head. "Well, you see how she is. Defensive, cagey, the goal of every conversation is to provoke."

In his mind's eye, Ian saw the cold, wet huddle of Timmie and his two nieces, now so grown he barely recognized them, crowded on Avenelle's stoop. Dressed in dour, sad clothes, their cheeks hollow, their possessions little more than a small basket shared between the three of them.

He swore and spun away, walking to the wall. He leaned his head against it, forehead to the cold plaster.

"I am to blame," he said to the wall. "I should have gone to them after Tribble died. I was too involved with the disaster in my own life. There are no excuses."

"But did the girls appear . . . unwell?" she asked. "When they returned to Avenelle?"

Ian rolled sideways, his back against the wall, facing her. "Who can say? They looked wild and unkempt. Their clothes were god-awful. I know bollocks about female attire, but even I could see this. Timothea has always preferred to burrow in her clothes more than wear them; there's no accounting for the way she dresses. The girls looked underfed but they did not complain. That first night, I had Cook bring out everything in the larder, but they barely ate. There was no crying or carrying on. They simply walked through the halls of Avenelle, gazing at ceilings and stairs as if they'd never before seen the inside of a manor house."

"But how would you categorize their life before Lord Tribble died? Were they . . . comfortable?"

Ian shrugged. "He was a baron of some means. The house was not so grand as Avenelle, perhaps, but perfectly suitable. A country manor."

"Have they no claim to this house?"

"A nephew inherited. The new baron invited my sister and the twins to remain, but she claimed she did not get on with the man."

Slowly, mindlessly, he began a rhythmic tapping with the back of his head against the wall.

Miss Trelayne eyed him, her misty blue-green eyes enigmatic. How calm she seemed, standing there, asking logical questions. She rested a hand on the counter, like someone for whom a solution might be within reach, written on a recipe card, perhaps beneath the countertop. In his mind's eye, he saw himself grabbing up her hand, pulling it to his chest, absorbing some unknown . . . proficiency from her.

Retaining her.

*Do not go, do not go, please do not go.* He couldn't believe he'd doubted her just an hour ago.

"But do you believe that the girls were entirely sheltered when they resided on the grounds of this . . . church? No outside contact?" she asked.

"Your guess is as good as mine, honestly. They have steadfastly refused to discuss it. I've asked a thousand questions since their return. Only today have I learned even the slightest clue of their situation."

"*Right.* Well, they claim to know how to . . . read and write. They are not illiterate."

"God only knows." He shoved from the wall and began prowling the room.

"I only brought them to London," he explained, "because

I was at my wit's end. I knew they required . . . *something*, but I'd been unable to identify what. Timothea was no help, although she consented to the idea of a London Season. I thought perhaps a change of venue might do them good. I thought, what young lady does not relish the idea of new frocks and parties and dancing? I was grasping at straws." He ran a hand through his hair.

"It was not a bad plan," she ventured. "Anything could go wrong I suppose, but they do not seem opposed to the idea of a debut. Ivy is anxious but I shall work with her. Imogene pretends to be indifferent, but she is intrigued."

Ian stopped walking. He turned to her. "You'll stay? This means you'll stay on."

"I—Well, I was under the impression that I served at your discretion. The prince—"

"Yes, yes, but that was before you learned how very complicated this all is. Yesterday amounted to Adolphus meddling to impress his wife; today I'm asking you to join bedlam. They require—I require—so much more than what was discussed at the palace. I would not blame you if you fled and never looked back."

"They will require rather a lot, I'm afraid."

"Should I simply pack up the lot of them and return to Dorset? I am determined to do right by them, first and foremost. It's the least I can do. And God knows I have duties there. But what is right? I've no idea."

"Well, I'm no expert, mind you. I could only venture to—"

"Tell me what you think," he cut in. "You've elicited more knowledge in thirty minutes than I'd managed in three months. You make it seem . . . like an adult has entered the room."

Miss Trelayne cleared her throat. "Ah . . ."

"Tell me honestly," he ordered, coming to stand before her, hands on his hips. She was so tall, he barely needed to dip his head to look her in the eye. He'd always felt beastly, squinting down at smallish women, and he liked having a discussion with a woman of reasonable height.

"Well, honestly?" she replied, "If they were making no progress in Dorset, I think you did the right thing by bringing them to London."

"Right—yes. Good." He let out a breath. "Thank you. No progress was being made in Dorset."

This time, when he thought of taking up her hand, he did it. He snatched it up with both of his own, squeezing it. It was . . . a way to say thank you. With emphasis. A way of imploring her not to go. A way to touch her, something he hadn't realized until now that he'd wanted very much.

DREW STARED AT the duke's hands encasing her own. She was not accustomed to being touched. Her sister, Ana, tolerated her to a degree that precluded touching. Her mother barely spoke to her, let alone touched her. Cynde snatched her into a quick embrace now and then, but her stepsister was so very slight, touching her was like touching an empty column of petticoats and lace.

The duke's hold was the opposite of empty. His large hands formed a cocoon. He squeezed, a physical demonstration of something like, *Here, Now, This.*

*We.*

The words were not said, but she felt some . . . point being made. An urgent cooperation between them. A signal. They'd departed their previous arrangement and stepped, in unison, to something new.

She looked into his eyes. Her expression must have alarmed him, because he dropped her hand.

Drew's hand felt cold and bare and she pulled it back.

*Here, Now, This. We.*

She realized she'd lost the thread of the conversation.

"But should their end result be a bloody . . . debutante come-out?" Lachlan was asking. He ambled away. "Meeting the queen? Does it compound the problem to put the girls through the paces of a Season? What if you worked with the girls but we removed the pressure of a debut?"

"Well," Drew ventured, forcing her brain to think, "we should not rule it out. My rapport with the girls might be easier if we are working toward some goal. In this way, the Season could serve as a distraction. From what little we've learned, I believe the girls have had quite enough unconventional and, er, strange history. Why not offer them this normalcy?"

"Yes, perhaps you're right. Normalcy. If they can be taught to manage it."

She watched him make another jittery circuit of the room. Their situation should have been unsettling; instead, his agitation meant he was affected by his nieces' plight. His questions meant he was paying attention. He cared. And he wanted Drew to make some improvement.

She was captivated by the contradictions of him. Yesterday he'd been stern and reluctant; now the circumstances had changed and he'd managed to change with them. He freely admitted he needed her help. How long had she waited for the opportunity to affect real change?

She had not been entirely honest when she'd said he was right to bring the girls to London. London would be a very dangerous place for girls as unprepared as they seemed to be. But this didn't figure in Drew's influence. She could help these girls. London was possible with Drew here.

And with him. With his . . .

Well, she couldn't say what he might bring, but it was clear that he wanted the best for all of them.

It made her want to . . . to—

She wanted to watch him pace the room and listen to him talk about his family and his life. She wanted him to take up her hand again and beg her to stay.

Suddenly, Lachlan snapped his fingers and spun back. "Whatever we do, Miss Trelayne, you must stay here—that is, stay here *night and day*. In the house. You should be constantly engaging the twins. You must *live* here."

"Ah . . ." Drew stammered. This, she had not considered.

She hadn't even known if he would receive her this morning. And now night and day?

"Their mother either doesn't know or doesn't care how to help them, and I am the clueless, derelict uncle they've only just met. You have a way with them; it was obvious from the first moment."

"But, Your Grace—"

"It's all settled. I'll have one of the family rooms made ready."

*"Your Grace—"*

"I'll double your salary. You'll have copious days off, a pension, letters of reference—whatever you require."

His tone did not ask her so much as inform her. She let out a little laugh.

"What? You are occupied with other demanding clients?" he guessed.

"No, it's not—"

"You are needed at home to care for an aging grandmother? A maidan aunt? A beloved family hound?"

"No."

"But what is it? You've said you are unmarried and you live with a sister. Do you find the house unsuitable?" He glanced around the dim cloakroom. "Please do not take this particular room into consideration when you answer."

She laughed again. "No, it's none of those. It's merely that I'd not thought of . . . living in. For this, you'd want a proper governess, wouldn't you? I fancy myself a stylist, as I've said. A sort of . . . consultant. If you need help beyond this, perhaps a—"

He was shaking his head. "I don't want anyone but you."

Drew paused. She felt a chip fall from the shell around her heart.

She cleared her throat. "I'd hoped to veer away from the designation of governess. It's fine work but not my area of interest. I am in the business of finishing girls, not bringing them up."

"Unfortunately, T.O.E. seems to have done the work of bringing them up." He made a face. "Finishing is exactly what they require. Only, a very great amount of it. If you labored from morning till night—nay, if you put in an *unlimited* amount of labor, it still might not be enough. I wish to hire you an unlimited amount. Surely you can manage this?"

It was a ridiculous question, and his expression said he knew this. He did not look entitled, only desperate.

"Please?" he finished.

Another flake of eggshell popped from her heart. Drew closed her eyes, bolstering herself. She opened them again.

"You speak as if refusal is not an option," she observed. It had to be said.

"But how could you refuse?"

"Well, I could say, *No, thank you*, and see myself out, couldn't I?"

"You cannot go."

She laughed again. Of course she could go and they both knew it.

Lachlan frowned at her laughter, and for whatever reason, this made her laugh even more. His face was no less handsome when he frowned—lucky thing, because he frowned rather a lot. It wasn't a sad frown or an angry frown, but a look of frustrated irritation. He didn't appear irritated at her, but at *himself*, perhaps? At fate?

"Oh yes, go on then. Laugh," he urged. "It's not your nieces who've been abducted by the religious zealots of T.O.E. these last five years. Beaten by 'Proctor' and 'Matron' and God only knows who else."

"Forgive me," she said, covering her mouth with her fingertips. "I was thinking of yesterday. Remember *yesterday*? When I was the amateur instructor with no clients and no prospects, and you only agreed to take me on because the prince commanded it—"

"Just to be perfectly clear," he corrected, "I agreed to you because I wanted you. Adolphus was the indulged party in this, not you. I do as I please. Forgive me for allowing you to think otherwise. I am uncomfortable with surprises, and you were, quite literally, a very great surprise. It was to the *surprise* aspect that I . . . objected—not to you. And you're no surprise now, you're—Well, you seem suddenly essential. If ever there was an indulgence, I'm asking *you* to indulge *me*."

He took a deep breath. "I need help, Miss Trelayne."

"Yes," she heard herself whisper. "Yes, you do."

Their gazes locked. His eyes were so very blue. She had the urgent wish that he would take up her hand again. She closed her fingers into a fist.

She forced herself to ask, "But what of the girls? Or Lady Tribble. They may not wish for my round-the-clock presence."

"I don't care."

"They will not cooperate if they resent me."

"They've shown no objection to any other person I've trotted out, including several doctors, a boy to wrangle their demon cat, and an artist to paint a mural in the music room. Nothing seems to faze them. If they've responded to anyone, it's been you. You made so much progress in thirty minutes."

Drew thought of how the girls intrigued and excited her.

She thought of the money, and the references, and freedom from Ana and Madewood.

Mostly, she thought of the duke and how she liked to watch him and how she wanted him to touch her again.

*Foolish girl*, she scolded in her head. That part of her life, the part where she noticed handsome, interesting men, where she dreamed of a future outside of spinsterhood, had ended long ago—had ended before it had scarcely begun. Her heart, fragile shell that it was, had been completely broken, shattered by a short little courtship that was so insignificant, it felt like a fluke, a once-in-a-lifetime trick of fate. It would not happen again, and certainly not with a duke. Absolutely not with *this* duke, handsome and energetic and all but begging for her help. She'd given up on this long ago, and good riddance.

"Miss Trelayne?" Lachlan prompted.

"Yes," she said, squaring her shoulders; squaring her expectations. "If the girls and Lady Tribble consent. If you send a carriage, I will pack some things and see myself transferred by tonight. I will help you."

*Chapter Seven*

"I should like only *plants* on my plate, if you please, Barton," said Ian's sister, shooing away the footman and his tureen of beef tips. "I've explained this to Cook again and again."

Ian studied Timothea over them rim of his goblet. As ever, she seemed to reside in the Land of the Upside-down. If the house burned, she would complain about the tightness of her shoe. If her daughters were odd and mute and possibly stunted in some way, she would complain about the food.

"The staff cannot keep up, Timothea," Ian told her. "Last week your plate was to be void of any food *white* in color. The week before that, it was no fish." He motioned for the footman to double his own portion of beef.

Ian rarely took a formal dinner in the dining room, although not because of Timothea's ever-shifting dietary restrictions. It wasn't what was *said*, it was all the things that were *not* said—the bloody silence. Since the riots, Ian himself had grown silent and pensive. Seclusion did that to a man. But the resounding quiet of a meal passed with his nieces was worse than silence. It was the sound of secrets.

Tonight, however, he felt he should make some effort. He glanced at Miss Trelayne seated between the twins; her orange hair twisted up and secured with a wide ribbon, her blue dress looking smart and bright and formal next to the girls' cobbled-together drabness and his sister's shroud.

Miss Trelayne had dressed for dinner. He'd noticed immediately. She hadn't overdone or swanned to the table with the intent to show off, but he'd remembered the pinkish dress from before, and now she wore a blue gown of considerably less fabric but more shine. She also wore a lone piece of jewelry—a moth made of some sort of blue stone. Or was it a beetle? He couldn't care less about women's jewelry, but the insect had caught his eye, and he found himself returning to study it again and again. And not just because the pin was interesting. Her gown's swooping décolletage did not afford enough fabric to host the pin on her shoulder or . . . or anywhere else. Instead, she'd attached the shimmery little sparkle just above the hollow between her breasts. He'd hardly describe Miss Trelayne as a voluptuous woman—he wasn't in the business of describing the endowments of any woman in his employ—but he would be lying if he said the beetle didn't draw his eye, and his eye hadn't lingered on the outline of her breasts, small and pert, on either side.

He wondered why she'd made the effort—not about the beetle necessarily, but the dress, the ribbon—all of it. Nothing about his family suggested formality at home, surely this had been perfectly clear to Miss Trelayne. Why bother?

How long had it been since anyone in his company had bothered with anything?

"You *misunderstand*," Timothea was insisting, signaling for another glass of wine. "*No one* understands. I admit that my palate is complicated, but I am happy to remind. The servants must be willing to learn. As for you, you'd do well to embrace more plants in your own diet, Ian. The girls and I swear by it."

Ian looked down the table at his nieces, both tucking in to beef tips in a hearty sauce. If they heard their mother's statement, they gave no sign. He glanced at Miss Trelayne and saw her make the same observation. She glanced back at Ian and they shared a look. Ian felt himself relax, just a little. That look alone was worth the salary he was paying her.

And here was another moment that begged the question: *How long has it been?*

He couldn't say the last time he'd felt the kinship of something like a *shared look*. By definition, the life of a recluse offered limited eye contact. And kinship? Out of the question.

"Girls," began Miss Trelayne, "I should love to know more about your interests and passions. It would make my planning easier for your lessons."

This inquiry was met with silent chewing; a pattern Ian knew well. He'd passed the last three months tossing out general, pleasant inquiries only to be met with the sound of crickets. In truth, the twins' blank stares had begun to drive him a little mad. He'd tried everything from bribery to holding his plate over the open stone floor and dropping it.

He was keenly interested to see how long it would take before Miss Trelayne began shattering crockery.

"Ivy," continued Miss Trelayne, "did I noticed a small cage in your lap when I arrived this morning?"

Ivy's face turned red and she stared at her plate, saying nothing.

"I believe you also had one or two books in your possession. My guess is . . . reference books? Scientific journals or something to do with naturalism?"

Ivy acknowledged this question with a bashful shrug.

Miss Trelayne smiled gently and turned to Imogene. "And what of your interests, Imogene?"

"Oh, I have no interests," said the girl nonchalantly.

"No interests?" marveled Miss Trelayne. "None at all?"

"Indeed," said the girl, now with a trace of pride. "*I have no interests at all.* If you wish to polish or promote an interest of mine, you may start and end with . . ." And now she made a strange fan-like gesture with two hands, slowly arching her palms open like a magician. This was accompanied by a blowing sound—presumably the noise of an abyss.

Ian was just about to scold the girl—a futile effort, he knew, but something should be said—when Timothea suddenly spoke up.

"No, no, *no,*" Timothea said, waving a fork back and forth in front of her face like a metronome. "There is a *butter glaze* on the radishes, Barton, I can taste it. Send them back. I swear, Ian, your cook is trying to kill me."

Ian's brain felt heavy, he wanted nothing more than to drop his head back and blink at the ceiling. He glanced at Miss Trelayne. She showed no reaction as she nibbled a carrot at the end of her fork.

"But how do you spend your days, Imogene?" continued Miss Trelayne, speaking to the carrot. "Perhaps that's what I should have asked."

"My days?" mused the girl. "Oh, I gaze out the window."

"This I cannot believe," said Miss Trelayne. "Far too boring."

Imogene flashed an ingratiating smile and did not answer.

"I see you've altered the neckline of your dress," commented Miss Trelayne. "This tells me that you've put off window gazing long enough to take up a needle and thread."

"I was overwarm," said Imogene, the smile still in place.

"Perhaps you like fashion, then?" asked Miss Trelayne.

"Perhaps it's none of your business what I like or what I don't like. Perhaps you can ask all night, or perhaps you can ask every night for the rest of my life, and perhaps I will not tell you *my interests.*"

"*Genie,*" whispered Ivy, a plea.

"That's it," said Timothea, slamming her cutlery down

with a clatter. "I must speak to the kitchen myself. There is *fish* in the soup."

Ian closed his eyes, the gesture of a coward. He knew this; he embraced it. Closing his eyes was the quickest way to remove the scene before him. He could still hear it, of course—his sister ignoring the extreme rudeness of her daughter, hear footmen scramble out of the way as Timothea huffed her way to the door, hear Ivy's squeak of distress.

*We should have never left Dorset*, he thought.

*There's no hope for it*, he thought.

And finally: *She'll go. Miss Trelayne. Why in God's name would she remain?*

What an ambitious folly it had been to add another player to the farce of their lives. He had enough to worry about in Timmie and the girls; now he must worry about the flight of Miss Drewsmina Trelayne.

He opened one eye to peek at her.

She was eating her carrot with practiced calm; as if she hadn't just been insulted, as if his sister were not as batty as a loon.

He opened the other eye and studied the flashing blue insect pinned to the neckline of her gown.

*Why dress for dinner?* he wondered again, signaling the footman for another drink.

*Who gifted her with the gemstone broach?*

*What other—*

"Perhaps," Miss Trelayne said, forking up another bite, "I *could* ask again and again. Or, perhaps you and I could find some peace between us?"

"We are not friends, you and I," Imogene said. "So let us not pretend."

"No," agreed Miss Trelayne, "we most certainly are not. I would never remain friends with someone whose regard for me is so very low. However, I've not come to be your friend. I've come to help you and your sister realize your own best potential for life in society and life in general."

"Just to be clear," said Imogene. "Uncle Ian is *paying* you to do this. You've come here *for money*. So let us also not pretend that there is some higher calling."

"Yes, the duke is paying my salary. However, it is my pleasure to work with you."

"You must need money very bad indeed," said Imogene.

"And why is that?"

"Because we are terrible," said Imogene, her tone enigmatic. Ian did not know if she was testing, or joking, or proclaiming.

"*Terrible* is a relative term, Imogene," said Miss Trelayne, "and I'm sorry to say that I do not find you terrible."

"*Yet*," provided Imogene.

"The truth is," said Miss Trelayne, "you could be terrible, or I could be terrible, or we could both choose to be perfectly pleasant. And why not? Time spent in London . . . a new wardrobe . . . the Season . . . a debut ball. How very fortunate you are that your uncle will provide all of these for you."

"And how very fortunate that you are being paid to prevent us from embarrassing him."

"*Imogene*," breathed Ian, feeling defeat deep in his bones.

Miss Trelayne forged ahead. "In fact I am fortunate. The money I will earn from this job is very important to me."

"You are destitute?" Imogene guessed, sounding hopeful.

"Oh no," said Miss Trelayne, unruffled, "I live comfortably in the home of my sister and her husband, as I've said. But I have plans for the future which involve relocating into a respectable flat of my own."

"Is your sister your twin?" This came from Ivy, her voice small and whispery.

"In fact she is not, Ivy. Ana is my younger sister by several years. I live with her out of necessity, actually. I am unmarried—but also estranged from our mother."

"And now you aim for estrangement from your sister as

well?" calculated Imogene. "Perhaps it is your goal for everyone to hate you."

"Hate? No. Estrangement? Also no. But if you want the real answer—and something tells me that you appreciate the real answer in all things, Imogene—my sister and I do not get on. Our girlhood was contentious and no one in our life stepped in to force us to make peace. It was horribly unpleasant. However, I've grown up, I've changed in a myriad of ways. Bickering no longer appeals to me, but she cannot see past it. I cannot blame her entirely, she is an unhappy woman. She and her husband, Lord Madewood, quarrel almost every day, miserably—sometimes violently. The situation is uncomfortable for me on the best day and hazardous on the worst. And that is why I require the money from this job, not to mention any jobs that come next. To *move on*."

"You dislike contention?" asked Imogene, sounding inspired.

"That is not a challenge," said Miss Trelayne quickly. Her fork was halfway to her mouth. Her face took on a contemplative look. She set the fork down.

Looking to Ian, she said, "Your Grace, can I impose on you to leave the table for just five minutes, so I might speak to the girls alone?"

"Go?" asked Ian. Coward that he was, he'd wanted to leave the table since the meal began. But now things were just getting interesting. He wanted to know more about her bickering sister and her estranged mother. Perhaps they shared a wretched childhood in common.

"If you don't mind?" asked Miss Trelayne. "It's terribly rude, I know, with your supper growing cold on your plate. But I'd like to say something very private to the girls, and I think perhaps it might be easier to ask you to leave rather than the three of us."

"Yes, of course," said Ian, pushing back. He stood at the head of the table, uncertain.

"Just five minutes?" she pressed. Her expression somehow said *trust me*, and *this is important*, and *I am a professional*.

Again, Ian felt himself relax. He no longer wanted to flee the room, but he did want to be useful, to make things easier.

With a nod and a rap to the table, he quit the room.

# Chapter Eight

What will be done now that Uncle has gone?" whispered Ivy Starry with a quavery note of fear.

Each time the girl spoke, Drew's heart felt like a wet cloth being wrung out.

Imogene spoke next. "Do not worry, Ivy." Her voice held no fear.

"I asked your uncle to go, Ivy," Drew said calmly, "because the very last thing I wish, ever, is to embarrass the two of you or make you feel . . . abashed or chagrined."

"Never you fear," drawled Imogene. "We are not troubled by 'abashment' or 'chagrin.'" She made a scoffing noise and rolled her eyes. It was an unnecessary boast; her hubris was dimming.

"Right," said Drew, "I've no wish to embarrass you. Not ever. *My wish* is to teach you confidence and self-assuredness, to raise your spirits, not to skewer them. Some conversations go better when fewer people listen in, that's all I mean. I believe this is one of them."

"You believe you can *embarrass* us?" asked Imogene.

"No, no," said Drew, refusing to rise to the bait, "I believe your uncle is a great ally to you, and it's not necessary for him to hear our every conversation, especially this one."

"This conversation is to be very bad, is it?" Imogene asked. And then, God love her, she actually braced; her posture square, chin high. She leaned, just a little, to shield her sister.

*What had these girls endured?* Drew wondered. Ivy looked petrified and Imogene appeared ready to hurl herself in the path of a flying object.

Drew looked away for a moment, composing herself. From the corner of her eye, she saw Lachlan hovering in the shadows of the servants' entrance. He'd gone, but not far. Another protector. Or perhaps he was just curious. Either way, he was invested in these girls and what happened next. She tucked away this particular selflessness for later examination. She'd not known her own father, so it was difficult to predict the attitude of male guardians.

Given the choice, she'd prefer for him *not* to hear what she was about to reveal, but this job was not about her or her pride, it was about the girls. And either she conducted herself with honesty and forthrightness, or she was no different than other stylists. So be it. It made no difference if he overheard.

"What I wanted both of you to know," Drew said, turning back, "is that there is nothing you can hurl at me—no rudeness, no insult, no accusation—that is more terrible or damaging than the things *I* have hurled . . . or said . . . or done. To friends, and members of my family, and servants, and even strangers. Nothing.

"You call *yourself* terrible? Drewsmina Trelayne—" she pointed to herself "—was the Originator of Terrible. When I was younger, I was known to be mean-spirited, conniving, hurtful, sour, loud, and deceitful. I've been petty and ungracious. And I made no effort to disguise any of it. I was, in a word, *terrible*—just as you've threatened, Imogene. I existed only for myself, and I was very good at it."

"What do you mean?" challenged Imogene.

"Oh, let's see," sighed Drew, thinking back. "For example, my sister Anastasia and I could have doubled our wardrobes if we'd *shared* dresses and jewels between us, but I was shrewdly proprietary over every stitch of clothing and scrap of ribbon—I shared nothing—meanwhile I would steal from her wardrobe and either swan about in her things when she was out or, on more than one occasion, I pawned her things for money.

"I tattled on Ana constantly, including about things she had *not* done.

"If she received letters from friends or, God forbid, a young man, I would read them and put them in the fire without telling her. I lied about which of her friends called and what they wanted and misrepresented the nature of parties so that Ana would turn up at the wrong time or dressed out of keeping with the event."

Drew took a deep breath and pressed on. "I was the very devil to servants. Shouting, complaining, criticizing. I was demanding beyond all reason.

"I was a malicious gossip to my friends—what few I had—and I falsely accused tutors of sleeping on the job or lying about my poor marks.

"Worst of all," she finished, "I had another sister—a *stepsister*—and I was particularly hateful to her. My mother disliked her and forced her to do chores in our house like a serving girl. Anastasia and I, who were crushingly jealous of her beauty, leapt at the opportunity to march her about, berate her, and invent new chores for her to do. It is, perhaps, my greatest regret, because unlike Anastasia, who was just as terrible as I was, Cynde was a sweet girl, innocent, who'd just lost her father; and she was ill-equipped to combat the petty cruelties that I heaped upon her.

"And that just names a few of my many sins. I've done penance for the terrible treatment of the people in my life, I've asked forgiveness, I've endeavored to find some peace. However, I shall likely never forgive myself for the way I treated Cynde. The great irony is that she has treated me with nothing but forgiveness and grace. She rose above my mother's terrible household and is actually married to a royal prince and lives in Kew Palace. Your invitation to be presented to Queen Charlotte at court came from her."

"But how did you stop?" whispered Ivy.

"Stop?" asked Drew.

"Being so terrible? You are . . . You've not—"

"Never you fear, Ivy," said Drew. "I'll not unleash my Terribleness on the two of you. I've actually *retired* that part of myself, and good riddance. It is a long story, perhaps for another time, but the short of it is, I had my heart broken, terribly, so badly that I lost the energy to lash out and be spiteful. I lolled about, suffering in a miserable sort of . . . well, hopelessness, really. And it was actually my stepsister, Cynde—who by this time had escaped my mother and caught the eye of Prince Adolphus—who reached out to me in a manner so very kind and forgiving. The shock of her compassion, of how little I deserved it yet how willing she was to show it, reordered the way I viewed the world and, ultimately, the way I behaved. There's more to it than that, it's a long, rambling story, and I'd be happy to tell you all about it some time. This night, however, I should like to hear more about you.

"Just keep in mind . . ." Drew paused, trying to find the correct words. "That is, I should like you to be aware: There is nothing you can say or do that I've not already said or done. Call me names if you like, suggest that I am poor, or unsuited, or self-interested. You may say I'm terrible company, or ill-mannered, or too ugly to sit across from you at breakfast. You may ignore me or refuse to cooperate. I will not be bothered and I will not be deterred. I am not afraid of rudeness, and I am not afraid of you."

"You do not know us," declared Imogene, this retort a little hollow. "You do not know *me*."

"How correct you are, Imogene, I do not know you. I feel certain, however, that the . . . unpleasant behavior you've shown me since I arrived does not come from you—not the *authentic* you—but instead from some very burdensome place in your personality that *protects* the most authentic 'you.' You are not *inherently* mean-spirited or ungenerous or unwelcoming or rude. *This*, I know."

Drew paused, taking a sip from her goblet. The girls stared at her with wide eyes.

"Do you know *why* I believe this?" she continued. "It is because my own heart, deep down, was never mean-spirited or ungenerous or unwelcoming or rude—not to Ana or Cynde or anyone else. When I said and did all the terrible things to all the undeserving people, there was . . ." and now she fluttered her hand in the air, ". . . another 'bad-ness' that compelled me to be so very small, petty, and mean. I am not afraid of whatever causes you to challenge me and call me names—and, it can't be said enough, I'm not afraid of you.

"I am committed to working with you, no matter how rude you become; partly because I need the money and partly because I enjoy the work. I have a sentimental place in my heart for girls who do and say terrible things. Lucky you.

"We are stuck together, the three of us. We can make the most of it, we can ignore it, we can fight until the bitter end, or we can do some combination of the three. But I cannot be put off."

The twins sat before her in silence. Either they had taken this under advisement or they were planning their next volley.

And by "they," of course she meant Imogene. Beautiful, defensive, prickly, expertly rude Imogene.

Drew watched them. When no one spoke, she ventured,

"The reason I asked about your various interests is because I'd like to arrange lessons for each of you. Some of this instruction, I'm afraid, will be mandatory. Whether you like it or not, you must learn to dance; if you know a foreign language, you should brush up on it; if you play a musical instrument or have voice training, we will continue with this; if there are gaps in your schooling, we should arrange for a tutor. Horses are not mandatory, but if you've an interest in riding, I believe there is benefit for every female in proficiency on horseback. Beyond these required lessons however, if there are areas of interest near and dear to your own hearts, these may also be included—assuming your uncle agrees. Tutors and instructors can be hired to instruct in countless areas of study."

Imogene remained silent, watching her with suspicious, narrowed eyes. Ivy, however, finally looked up from her plate.

"What areas of study?" Ivy whispered.

"Well, as an example, my very favorite hobby is actually bird-watching. I adore birds and whenever I have free time, I spend it out of doors, usually hidden within a bush, sitting very still and quiet and watching birdlife. I have a sketchbook and pencils and record what I observe with drawings and notes. I have studied migratory patterns and seasonal behaviors. I also have a small reference library of books about birds."

No surprise, Imogene opened her mouth to make some reply. The impulse to ridicule bird-watching was irresistible. It wasn't glamorous or fashionable or exciting. As hobbies went, it was quiet and boring, popular mostly to pensioners.

But Imogene did not tease. She closed her mouth.

*Progress*, thought Drew. *Or, the joke hadn't been worth the effort.*

Drew forged on. "Up until several years ago, my bird-watching prowess was entirely self-taught. But then I discovered a professor at London University who offered guided tours of popular birding trails, including lectures about the British birds and advice on where and how to view various species. I paid the fee and joined the tour and learned so much more. After his tutelage, I enjoyed my hobby a hundredfold."

They looked at Drew as if she, herself, were a bird and they'd convened at the dining table to study her.

Drew joked, "You'll not appreciate this, but I am now something of a *birding expert*."

If their silence was any indication, they did *not* appreciate it.

Drew chuckled and continued, "That is a way of saying, think of your own interests, no matter how obscure, and we'll see if we might locate an expert to help you learn more. Or do it better. Whatever it may be."

"You'll arrange this simply to . . ." Imogene speculated, ". . . indulge us? Or to spend Uncle's money? I don't understand. You do it because your heart is so very touched by our . . . our . . . by whatever appeal you claim we possess?"

"Oh no, I do it because being passionate about something will make you more interesting. Which is part of my job."

More blank stares.

"When the Season begins," she explained, "you'll see that every debutante offers some curated mix of harp playing, French speaking, quadrille dancing, with the possible addition of flower arranging or watercolors tossed in. And good for them. If either of you wish to pursue these, we shall arrange it. However, the most *interesting* girls are the ones whose passions look beyond the expected repertoire of ladylike diversions; the ones who learn a skill or follow a passion because they truly enjoy it, rather than simply because generations of grandmothers deemed it suitable and tidy and serene. Do you understand? You should do what you love—and not only because you love it, but because it makes you more of who you are."

"Do you believe that watching birds makes you more interesting?" asked Imogene, and Drew laughed. Whether the girl meant to insult Drew or birds, she couldn't say. It didn't matter. They were listening.

"To the correct people—that is, the people who *I* wish to know and with whom I spend my time—bird-watching is perfectly interesting. Or at least, *I* am interesting because I have this passion. Also, I should like you to have interests that enrich you, independent of making a splash at your debut or finding a husband. A woman should have something to sustain her—multiple somethings—no matter how the Season falls or what the future holds. And also, the more you know about anything, the better off you are."

And now they'd returned to silently watching her. Drew made a mental note to teach them to *respond* when people addressed them. The blank stares must cease. But for now, perhaps she'd said enough.

"Think on it, both of you," she said. "By tomorrow, I'd like to hear a few ideas on lessons or hobbies that interest you—and window gazing does not warrant. Let us also think on what you may already know. I mentioned languages and instruments and the lot. Gaps in these skills should be filled right away."

"We'll need all of it," said Imogene, turning to look at her square in the face. "Every. Single. Thing you've said."

The direct answer—and an answer lacking in hostility, to boot—caught her off guard. Her goblet was halfway to her mouth. She put it down.

"Oh," she said. "Very good then. Thank you, Imogene. All of it."

She wanted to glance over her shoulder, to see if the duke heard—moreover, if he approved—but she dared not lose the engagement.

"What language?" Drew asked lightly.

"We know only English," said Imogene.

"What instrument?"

"We've been made to sing hymns . . . so many hymns . . . but with no particular skill or finesse."

"Do you *like* singing?"

"No," the girls answered in unison.

"Do you derive any enjoyment from music?"

"Not really," said Imogene at the same moment Ivy whispered, "I am curious about the xylophone."

Both Drew and Imogene turned to stare at Ivy.

"I read about it," she whispered. "In a book."

"Very good," said Drew, smoothly. "Xylophone. So be it. Perhaps Lachlan can have one brought in."

"Horses?" Drew asked, her heartbeat increasing.

"We rode a little before Papa died," said Imogene. "Anything after that, I've sorted out on my own. Ivy has ridden only behind me on a shared mount. We have not used a saddle in years. No tack."

"Oh, well done. Alright. Riding instructor, a mare or two. Proper saddles . . ." Pound notes swam in Drew's head, and she ignored them.

"Imogene," Drew asked, "it occurs to me that sport may interest you. If music does not."

"Sport?"

"Yes. Archery. Lawn bowling. Or tennis, perhaps?"

And now the silence was better than words, because Imogene's face lit up. It was the most genuine look of hopefulness she'd yet seen.

"Right," said Drew. "I'll see what we can do about a little of each."

Drew was just about to make some concluding statement about how well this had gone and how excited she was, but a footman interrupted them, descending on the room with trays of pudding.

"Oh, lovely," Drew said, fighting to keep the excitement from her voice. They'd made progress. Perhaps the three of them could get on. "Who will take pudding?"

On the heels of the footman, Lachlan strode in from the opposite door with Lady Tribble on his arm.

"Timothea has returned for pudding," he announced.

"Which I understand is neither beef, nor fish, nor white in color. Chocolate, I believe?"

"Yes, Your Grace," said a footman, setting a tiered confection at the baroness's place.

Lady Tribble settled into her seat, glancing at her daughters. It was a quick look but Drew saw her search their faces, to *assess* them. She made no comment, asked nothing, and quickly transferred her attention to the chocolate.

The baroness seemed to employ a strange mix of neglect and performative oddness to shield herself from any useful interaction. She wore it like a nun's habit, projecting to the world, *I adhere to a different set of expectations.*

Drew was no stranger to terrible mothers, but Cynde had assured her there were many different ways to be a good one. She would hold out hope for Lady Tribble.

Not that it mattered. Manners and good sense could spring from even the rockiest history; Drew's survival of her own childhood was living proof of this. If Drew could conduct herself like a reasonable human, if she could be useful and fulfilled, anyone could. And honestly, the less Lady Tribble engaged any of them, the more Drew was able to do as she pleased.

The pudding was rich, and cold, and delicious, and the five of them devoured it in near amicable silence. Twice Drew glanced at the duke—she couldn't help it—wondering what he must think of her admission as the Originator of Terrible, praying he would consent to the many expensive enrichments she'd just promised the girls. Most of all, she wondered how a man who seemed as clever and full of energy and as . . . *vital* as the Duke of Lachlan wound up living in near seclusion in Dorset.

As new clients went—well, as *first* clients went—the girls were nothing like she'd expected, but she was very fond of them already.

As employers went—

Well, she dare not scrutinize her fondness for the Duke of Lachlan.

*Put him out of your mind*, she thought, taking the last bite of compote.

*Finish the meal.*

*Review plans for the morning.*

*Excuse yourse—*

Just then, the girls' giant cat ambled into the dining room dragging a fat, squirming mouse between his teeth.

The girls reacted with gleeful horror, their pudding forgotten. They leapt up and darted around the table, rattling china and turning up corners of the rug. The cat, suddenly aware of his error, froze for half a beat and then galloped away in a fluffy blur. The girls let out a yelp and gave chase.

Drew made more mental notes. *They must ask to be excused from the table.*

*Activities such as cat chasing and yelping are allowed, but only in the privacy of family meals at home.*

"Pray, Ian," said Lady Tribble, rising next. "What direction does my bedroom window face? I should like to read the stars while twilight is unclouded."

The duke cocked his head, studying his sister. His expression was disbelieving but also sad; like he'd watched every last passenger disembark from the mail coach only to find that his long-awaited guest had not made the journey.

"Is it . . . north?" Lady Tribble speculated.

"*West*," corrected the duke. "Your bedroom faces west, Timmie."

"Oh, lovely," said Lady Tribble, arching her wineglass in a simulated wave. Following an s-shaped path that only she could see, she quit the room, dragging the tail of her shroud behind her.

And just like that, the dining room was empty except for Drew and the Duke of Lachlan.

Footmen, previously more numerous than family members, had suddenly vanished.

Up and down the table, the remains of chocolate compote congealed in crystal goblets.

Candles jumped and gutted.

From a distant room, she heard a grandfather clock. The slow tick mocked the sudden fast drum of her heart.

All the terrible behavior to which she admitted when talking to the girls came rushing back to her mind. Had he heard?

It didn't matter, she reminded herself. Her place in this house was to guide and advise the twins. Anything else, especially the times she found herself alone with the Duke of Lachlan, was not important.

She felt inclined to look at him—one generally *acknowledged* the only other person in a room—but she couldn't. It was as if her head wouldn't swivel left. She felt suddenly intrusive. She felt as if he'd designated the end of the table for the highly private work of signing secret documents, or scolding a servant, or removing his shirt.

*Well, he's not doing that*, she thought, blinking at the empty doorway.

She heard a creaking noise from his end of the table.

Next, the heavy, *thump, THUMP* of something slamming into the tabletop. She jumped.

"Miss Trelayne?" he questioned.

"Yes." A whisper.

"Are you—?" He stopped.

She waited, her heart pounding like marbles spilling from a crate.

He sang, "*Hello?*"

Another pause. She auditioned various responses—*Oh, I didn't see you there, Look at this, here we are, If you'll excuse me*—but said nothing.

He continued, "Perhaps you failed to see me sitting at the head of the table."

She could not admit to this and said nothing.

He prompted, "I wasn't sure if you were aware."

"Oh yes," she said, "I am aware."

Stupid, silly girl.

This was always going to be part of working with families, she reminded herself. Speaking with fathers and uncles and brothers and guardians. She could not be missish and she could not . . . imagine them without shirts.

"Are you . . ." he tried to guess, ". . . so dumbfounded by my nieces that you cannot bear to look at any of us, myself included?"

"Oh no, Your Grace," she assured. She forced herself to pivot to him.

He was reclining in a balanced sort of lean, his chair propped on two legs. His boots were on the table, crossed at the ankle. This had been the thumping noise.

*Lovely*, she thought, *casual repose.*

Now that she'd looked at him, she found herself unable to look away.

"Should I apologize for Imogene?" he asked, rocking slightly back and forth on his balanced chair. "I feel compelled to apologize, but I wouldn't know where to begin."

"Oh no. I am unaffected by Imogene." *And I am unaffected by you.*

"Hmm," he said, his voice a tumbled sort of growling sound.

*Unaffected*, she repeated slowly in her mind.

Suddenly, three footmen pushed into the room, laughing at a joke. They'd thought the room was unoccupied, clearly. When they saw the duke, they came up short.

"I beg your pardon, Your Grace," said the oldest footman; followed by, "Oof" as his colleagues collided into his back.

"Come in, Barton," the duke said, beckoning them with a tired wave. He slid his boots from the table and righted the chair with a *thwack*.

"Balcony, Miss Trelayne?" he proposed, jabbing a thumb in the direction of glass-paned double doors in the rear of the dining room.

"Balcony?" she repeated dumbly.

"Just here. It was a deathtrap when I inherited, but never you fear. I've unsealed the doors and restored it. It overlooks the garden."

"The garden," she repeated. She sounded like a language student learning English.

"We'll only be in Barton's way if we remain." He shoved from his chair.

"Yes," she answered.

*Yes, yes, yes.*

# Chapter Nine

The balcony presented three mildly troubling yet very exciting challenges for Drewsmina.

First challenge: the manner in which the duke held the door.

He didn't open it and step back. He didn't push through it and proceed her. He turned the knob, cracked the door, and then held it above her head. She was given no choice but to pass beneath the arch of his bicep and chest to step into the night.

She smelled him as she went, a compelling mingle of claret, and soap, and *him.*

The stroke of a feathered wing brushed the pit of her stomach.

She shuffled onto the stone balcony and blinked, trying to adjust her eyes to the night. Two lanterns burned low on either side of the door. Below them, stone walls hemmed in a dark rectangle of a garden. Within those walls, a smattering of mounded shrubs, winding paths, and arched benches took vague shape in the night. Somewhere, a fountain gurgled and plopped.

Second challenge: The night was cold and her gown was bare, and she sucked in a little breath, taken by surprise. She grabbed her arms around her torso without thinking. Lachlan was behind her immediately.

"Sorry," he said and whipped off his coat and settled it on her shoulders.

The simple offer of a warm coat from an obliging gentleman was a gesture she'd never experienced. For a moment, she wasn't certain it was really happening. Had he *dropped* the garment by accident and it landed on her shoulders? Had he grown overwarm and needed some place to hang it?

The offer of garments did not occur to men when it came to Drewsmina Trelayne; she did not appear delicate enough to affected by the cold. And so few men's coats would actually fit her.

The duke's coat hung about her shoulders, perfectly large and perfectly warm. Now she *wore* the smell of him. She was swamped with it. The cold was forgotten. For a long moment, everything she ever knew was forgotten.

Third challenge: the duke sprawled.

He didn't sprawl *to* her or *near* her, but he leaned against the thick stone banister with an elbow, and crossed his boots at the ankle. It was the standing version of the casual repose he'd enjoyed in the dining room.

He was, she'd noticed, no stranger to leaning or sprawling. Or pacing. Or laying his head against walls. Or shattering windows. The Duke of Lachlan did as he pleased in any given space, more comfortable with his large body than anyone she'd ever met.

She should not, she lectured herself, find this charming. In fact, she should make no notice of his posture, or whether he leaned, or whether he stood on his head.

She bit her lip to keep from smiling.

*None of this is done to delight you,* she told herself. *He is who he is, and you happen to reside in his home.*

*Make no assumptions.*

*Do not grin.*

"Tell me, Miss Trelayne," he said, eyeing her, "how did you know how to . . . do and say all the things you've done and said? To the girls?"

"I'm not sure what you mean," she said modestly. "We've simply shared a meal."

He ignored this. "I thought you were inexperienced and untried. Adolphus pawned you off to me, his scandal-ridden friend, as if you have no other work. Meanwhile, you've been brilliant with the girls. A mesmerist."

"There's no magic to it, I assure you. I was simply honest with them. Perhaps honesty is so rarely afforded to young women, it feels like sorcery. Or worse. I endeavored to show some measure of humility, which I've found to enhance most situations, and I refused to show fear."

He barked a laugh and now she did smile.

"Well," he mused, looking out over the misty garden, "you were very forgiving. Most tutor-y, instructor-y sort of women would have scolded. Punished, even. Imogene is unforgivably rude. She's damn near brought a tear to my eye on several occasions."

Drew laughed again. "This, I highly doubt. But I do have a sense that Imogene's been scolded and punished enough these last five years. Besides, it's not . . . my way."

She looked to him and their gazes locked. A snap of energy passed between them, a taut string pulled back and *plucked*. Invisible vibrations rippled the air.

Drew swallowed hard, riding it out. She didn't look away.

"You are generous of spirit," he mused.

"Generosity will now be *your* purview, I'm afraid," she said. "You were listening at the door, were you not?"

"I was."

"Then you heard me promise the moon in terms of private

instruction for the girls? I hope I've not overstepped. It will be rather expensive."

"*Rather expensive*," he repeated slowly. He tipped his head back to stare at the sky.

"Indeed. Especially the horses. However, there is confidence and even power to be gleaned from the proficient handling of a horse. I . . . I should like to expose them to it."

The duke said nothing. While Drew watched, he pushed his elbow off the wall, grabbed the stone banister, and hopped up to sit on it. Next he swung his legs up and actually *reclined* on the railing.

One moment he was leaning, in the next he was laid out before her like a man on a bed. He tucked his hands behind his head and crossed his boots at the ankles.

When Drew looked down, she stared directly at his thighs. Her head snapped up.

"Honestly," he mused, speaking to the sky, "I would pay anything to set them to rights. If I failed them in duty, at least I can open my purse. I'm doubtful it will work—money made no difference in the aftermath of the riots—but I should like to try." The last bit was said on a bitter exhale.

Drew took a small step back. She wasn't certain how to respond. "The first step, perhaps, is wanting what is best for the girls, which clearly you do. For their own reward, not yours."

"Meaning?" His blue eyes cut to her. He cocked an eyebrow. The air between them strummed again.

Her gaze dropped from his blue eyes to his body, laid out like a man-shaped buffet. She licked her lips.

"Miss Trelayne?" he prompted.

"That is to say," she managed, "it was my mother's most fervent wish that I should make a brilliant match when I debuted." There was no more sobering topic than her mother.

She took a deep breath. "It was her only goal. A brilliant match for her daughter would elevate her own status. She gave no thought to my own happiness—not during the Season or in a future marriage."

"Perhaps I should dispatch Imogene to elevate my status as part of her Season," Lachlan mused, teasing. "It would be a fight, actually, to see whose wretched behavior—hers or mine—could more effectively sabotage the other."

Drew chuckled and pressed on. "*In contrast*, you seem to be motived by the girls' best interest. Purity of motive, I'd say. It's an excellent start."

And now he sat up, swinging his legs down. "Purity. You are surely the first person to pin me with that."

Drew blinked, uncertain how to respond. She felt her cheeks go pink.

"We cannot be your first clients," he said. "You're too wise."

Wisdom, she could address. "You are my first *paid* clients," she said. "I have worked with other families in the role of friendly advisor. A volunteer. My consultations have been like a favor to the families. Princess Cynde has friends who've needed help with their daughters, and I was happy to oblige."

"Ah yes, the royal couple. So how did *I* become the lucky friend from whom *payment* was to be extracted?" He rolled back to his reclining position.

"Oh," she said, taking in the very great length of him, his balance on the wide railing, how easily he moved.

*He is magnificent*, she thought, her brain sending up useless observations that made very little sense. Or the only sense.

"Just to be clear," he said, speaking to the sky, "I should pay double to have you, and likely it will come to that. Ultimately your salary will feel like a fat bribe. The money will trap you here with us long after your patience for Imogene has run its course."

"I am not afraid of Imogene. I quite like her."

"Oh yes, the great many similarities the two of you share. What did you call yourself? The Originator of Terrible? I'll admit, I was just as intrigued as the girls, but I fail to see it, these sins of your younger self. Surely you exaggerate."

"Surely I do not. I regret that you were forced to hear that list."

"Should I relay *my* sins, Miss Trelayne?" he asked.

*Yes*, she thought. *Yes.*

"Tell you all the mistakes I made as a younger man?" he continued. He stared into the distance. "You've never gotten anyone killed, I reckon."

His face had gone stormy, his blue eyes closed.

"I . . . I cannot say, Your Grace," she said lowly.

"Nor should you," he said, opening his eyes. His expression was twisted; he was fighting his way back from somewhere dark and desperate.

"Go on then," he said. "Tell me how very much like Imogene you have been."

"Oh no, I am nothing like Imogene. That is—I was difficult as a girl, and *she* is difficult, but there is one crucial difference in that she is very beautiful. I was a bit of a—of an ugly duckling. My appearance was the source of my willfulness—or a very large measure of it. I cannot say what feeds Imogene's, but it's not the way she looks. Her beauty gives her confidence—which I also did not have."

"An ugly duckling?" he questioned, shooting her a look.

Now it was Drew's turn to close her eyes. He was studying her now and she couldn't endure the scrutiny. He looked at her like a man searching for a hidden lock on a very plain box, lined inside with velvet.

*Please leave it*, she thought.

*Please ask again*, she also thought.

"Miss Trelayne?" he asked, sitting up again. "What do you mean 'ugly duckling'?"

THE CHIEF BENEFIT of the new governess—no, the new *stylist*—was that she'd taken his nieces in hand. Ian knew this.

Another was that she hadn't blamed or ridiculed his sister—at least not openly.

She also hadn't openly blamed or ridiculed him. This was less a benefit than a bloody miracle.

Mostly the benefit was that she hadn't fled screaming into the night.

But a fourth, no *fifth*, was that he genuinely enjoyed talking to her.

He rose from the banister, eyeing her. It had been so very long since he'd spoken to anyone at length, least of all a clever, pretty girl.

He was out of practice, but even his long-suffering solitude was no excuse to pry. He would not have pressed her about the alleged "ugly-duckling" years if her blue dress hadn't struck him as quite so . . . so . . . striking. The opposite of ugly, surely.

Nor if her ginger coronet hadn't intrigued him.

If her insect pin hadn't—

He glanced again at the blue stone twinkling in the moonlight. She'd attached the beetle in such a way that it slanted, just a little, every time she moved. Its antennae were constantly pointing the way to another creamy expanse of her freckled skin. Her shoulders had been swallowed by his coat, but she'd not bothered to button it, and it gaped in exactly the correct spot. He could see the pin. He enjoyed looking at the pin.

"Oh yes, well," Miss Trelayne was saying, "no woman escapes a lifetime at this particular height, or with this particular shade of hair, or with these great many freckles, without considerable attention paid."

"Quite. But how is this a *challenge*?"

She stared at him.

He ventured, "The fawning becomes a nuisance, no doubt?"

She frowned, the look of someone who'd been asked to spell her name a fourth time.

"Sorry," he said. "You've mentioned your great humility. I won't force you to boast."

"Boast?" she repeated.

"About your bright hair or intriguing freckles or—"

He stopped himself from saying *body*. Even he knew this crossed some sort of line.

But then he cast his eyes up and down said body—he couldn't help himself. She'd been designed like a marble statue in a garden. Perfectly formed. She wanted only a toga. Although the blue dress, as he'd already noted, was also very nice.

"I, er—" she began.

"Sorry," he cut in. "Ignore me, please. I am . . . out of practice with . . . conversation. I might as well have been consigned to T.O.E. these last five years."

He was just about to ask her about her disagreeable sister or her estranged mother—more inappropriate topics, but why stop now?—when she spun toward the garden below.

"What?" he asked.

Miss Trelayne held up a hand to silence him. Her gaze was fixed on the misty lavender vegetation.

Ian forced his brain to shift, going on high alert. Nighttime interlopers were not uncommon in London, even in a walled Mayfair garden. He narrowed his eyes and squinted into the garden. He cocked his head to listen. Nothing. No informants, no pirates, no sailors.

He looked again to Miss Trelayne. She ignored him, peering into the birch tree. He used the opportunity to study her profile. A trio of heavy blue stones adored her small ear. Her full lips were parted, just a little. Her nose was proud and it suited her. He had a flash vision of how it would feel to nuzzle that nose in a kiss.

She put him in the mind of a tall, thin book that poked above the others on a shelf. The book that said, *Pick me*. The one with colorful illustrations and maps.

She was like a very rare book that was best enjoyed when laid open on a desk and poured over. A book for which you wet the pad of your thumb to turn the page, where you glided your fingertips down the foolscap to fully appreciate the engravings.

"Do you hear that?" she whispered.

"What?" Ian had forgotten to listen.

"It's a song thrush," she whispered. "There she goes again. Do you hear? Her song is distinctive because she repeats different phrases in mixed sequence. It's said to be like poetry. I've only heard it once before. Song thrushes are nocturnal, and I'm rarely out this late."

Ian squinted into his garden. "Song thrush," he repeated.

She was leaning on the banister, arms locked, bottom out. His coat smothered her, but the heavy wool didn't disguise the contour of slight waist swooping to round bottom.

Suddenly, his fingers were restless, twitchy. He put a hand on the stone banister, idly tracing the shape of the curved lip.

"Oh!" she exclaimed, breathless, standing upright. She hopped back from the rail and softly collided with his chest, her back to his front.

Her body felt nothing like a book.

He opened his hands and hovered them on either side of her waist.

"She's here," Miss Trelayne whispered softly, so softly he barely heard. "Do. Not. Move."

Moving had not occurred to Ian.

"She's where?" he asked in a rasp.

"*Shhh*," she warned gently.

The bird called again, a sound, Ian thought, not unlike most birds. But then he saw a flutter; he heard a swooshy sort of pumping of air—and there it was. A small bird, lighting on the balcony railing mere feet from where they stood. In the dimness, her feathers registered as only dark and light, her shape decidedly . . . birdlike.

She hopped twice and opened her beak and trilled.

Miss Trelayne sucked in a delighted breath. A gasp. It was the sound that accompanied newly opened jewelry boxes, or grand anniversary cakes wheeled out on a trolley. Ian had also heard that sound in bed.

He shifted, just a little. He could feel the outline of her body up and down, from her thin shoulders to her long legs. Lithe, thin, like a corded rope, but with the softness of a woman. She tensed when the bird sang, something like ecstasy seizing her muscles. He could feel her warmth through his coat.

"I can't believe she's so close," she whispered.

"Yes," he agreed. "Close."

Her head bumped against his jaw, and he felt springy curls. The braid that ringed her head was softer than he expected; not a tight plat, but loose, pillowy. Curls tucked and woven, secured with the ribbon.

The bird called again; again Miss Trelayne clenched. After another trill, and another, it let out a final song, hopped twice, spread its wings, and flew away.

Miss Trelayne gasped again and tracked her progress into the sky. When she turned her face, her braid brushed his jaw, snagging on his emerging beard. His skin tingled. He breathed in, smelling her vanilla scent.

"*What a sight,*" Miss Trelayne whispered.

"Yes," Ian murmured, tipping his head down to watch her watch the bird.

"Sorry. I'm a bit of a fanatic." Her eyes were trained on the horizon.

"Good for you." He jostled forward, closing the infinitesimal space between them. Now the roundness of her bottom was pressed deliciously against him. His body, already half erect, hardened fully. The urge to nuzzle was overshadowed by the very real need to clasp her hips, hold them in place, and grind into her. He inhaled again, savoring her vanilla scent. He heard her breath catch, but the bird had gone. She was responding to *him.*

He said, "It was true what you said to the girls. About a passion making a woman more interesting."

"You may abandon this hope when Ivy begins the xylophone," she whispered.

He laughed and reached out, a breath from encircling her

with his arms, from pulling her to him. But the sound had somehow broken the spell.

She shivered and stumbled forward, reaching for the railing. She turned her face away, sucking in a breath.

Ian swore to himself; he felt her absence like a hood falling over his eyes. Every sense suddenly dull, crying out. He wanted to reach for her, to pull her back.

He wanted—

"But do you have a passion, Your Grace?" she asked, her voice thin and forced. She addressed her words to the railing.

"Passion?" he rasped, willing his brain to function.

"Forgive me. I didn't mean to pry." She raised up and took another step back. He swore again in his head. *Don't retreat*, he urged. *Come back.*

She glanced at the door.

"My passion," he repeated again, hoping to distract her. Hoping she would not go. "My passion was meant to be Avenelle. The dukedom. My tenants. I was determined to do justice to the land and the families and the title. My father was bollocks at managing it. But I—"

He stopped again. Arousal was still thick in his veins. He struggled to form coherent thought. He felt cagey and agitated. He turned away. The banister at the edge of the balcony was thick and flat, more of a ledge than a railing and without warning, he stepped one booted foot on top of it, like he intended to mount a giant step.

"Your Grace," she said.

He made a grunting noise and matched the move with his second boot, stepping up. He'd never stood on this railing, but the view of the garden was considerably better from this height.

"Your Grace, please take care," she said.

"I bungled the dukedom very early on," he continued. "*Gravely.* As you've heard. No one in my purview has recovered. Is it a passion? Oh yes. Do I enjoy it? No, not for several years now. With no end in sight."

"But will you come down, Your Grace?" she asked.

He glanced at her. She had the worried look of someone trying to recover a shoe from a mad dog.

"Sorry. I am a moving target." He jumped down. "My demons are crack shots."

"If I might suggest, Your Grace," she began gently, "'Lachlan' is a title. And being a duke and managing Avenelle—these are responsibilities, not passions. A *passion* is something you do purely for pleasure. For the delight of it. To stimulate and enrich you. To drive your curiosity."

His brain caught on the words *delight* and *stimulate* and *passion*. He stared at her, wondering if he'd heard the same things.

She couldn't hold his gaze, and he cursed again. What the bloody hell was he doing? He couldn't terrorize the stylist on top of everything else. She was only now bringing the twins in line. And he was many things, but a marauder was not one of them. He mustn't scare her.

He cleared his throat and looked away. "Avenelle is all of those things and more," he said. "Or it was."

"I suppose I understand a little," she said, turning to sit on the banister. "Most everything I know about fashion and styling, I learned from observing birds."

Ian considered this. "Oh, you mean hats? Feathered bonnets?"

"No—not hats. Or. Not only hats. I won't bore you with the particulars, but you asked about the challenges of my appearance. I'll give you *one*. No girl wants hair the color of a boiled carrot."

"You cann—" he cut in.

She held out a hand to silence him. "Despite what the grannies may say about the beauty of redheaded babies, *ginger hair* is an oddity and a nuisance, and I've hated mine for as long as I can remember. It overtakes my head, obscures my face; no lady's maid has ever been able to manage—to *subdue* it. All bonnets and most fabrics only serve to make it . . . orange-er."

"*No*," he denied, intrigued. He came to sit beside her, staring at her head.

"*Yes*," she countered. "For years, whenever I entered any room—be it church, or a shop, or as a guest to a tea—the bright, shining beacon of my hair was the first thing anyone saw. The great, audacious *orange-ness* of it."

He shook his head, frowning. "You imagine this."

"Oh no, it has been said to me again and again. 'But look at your *hair*, Drewsmina.' 'I don't think I've ever seen hair quite that *red*, Drewsmina.' 'But has your hair always been so very red, Drewsmina?' 'Was your father a leprechaun?' 'Perhaps your mother took something during her lying in to cause your hair to be so very—?'"

"Let me guess," said Ian. "Red?"

"Orange," she corrected. "And that says nothing of the assumptions about my temper."

"I would suggest that you exaggerate," he said tiredly, "but I've known the same single-minded fixation. Only with me, it's, 'There he stands, the traitorous duke who led his tenants in seditious riots.' No matter where I go. The pub. The garrison that houses my former regiment. If I walked into the corner butcher's shop, someone would proclaim it, I assure you."

"I said it," she admitted softly. "In Kew Palace."

"Yes, but at least you said it about a poor sod you thought you'd never meet. If you'd known it was me, you would not have said it."

"If I had known," she whispered. "I would not have. I'm so very sorry."

"Thank you," he said.

There was a pause. He looked at the railing beside his hip and saw her hand, pink from the cold, splayed against the stone. He wanted to cover it with his own palm. To warm it. To possess it.

He wanted to feel anything but the loneliness of the last three years; the worry for his nieces; the desperation of his tenants.

He mustn't touch her. It made no sense to touch her. Even so, he stared; he memorized her long fingers and the smooth ovals of her nails.

"One thing I've learned about people," she said, "is that most of them *really* struggle—truly, they rack their brains—to think of anything useful to say."

He laughed and looked into her face. Their eyes met. They were teal, her eyes. The color of the tall reeds at the edge of his pond.

"When I first began observing birds," she said, determination in her voice, "I saw again and again how the orange breast of a common robin actually looked very pretty against the blue feathers of his wing. Are you familiar with robins?"

"Yes," he said, wishing she would look at him again.

"Right. Well, I thought, if this robin can manage to make his orange body look so very nice in contrast to his blue markings, perhaps there is a lesson there."

"Your blue gown," he realized.

"Yes," she confirmed. "Since that realization, I've commissioned so many gowns in blue. Not all of them, but more than any other hue. The correct shade of blue strikes a sort of harmony with my hair and makes it less of an oddity and more of a coordinated effort, I should say."

"But I can barely see your hair," he said, a complaint.

She opened her mouth to say something but then closed it.

"You've hidden it," he continued softly, frowning at the braided coronet ringing head.

"Yes, well," she finally said, "that is another technique. Not learned from birds."

He nodded. What more could he say? He could hardly ask her to elaborate; enough had been said about her hair. And his passions. And likely every other thing. Had three years of seclusion made him . . . *chatty*? This had not occurred to him at Avenelle. At Avenelle, he'd hoped to never speak to anyone ever again.

He took a deep breath.

The sounds of the night—rustling wind, and buzzing insects, and scurrying mice—rose up from the garden below, animating the silence.

Her nose, he noticed, was red from the cold. The light through the dining-room door had been reduced to a dim glow, an ember fire in one grate. The staff had cleared the table. They were alone.

He said, "I'm grateful you are working with my nieces."

"Thank you." A whisper.

"You are wise and compassionate. I do not know you well, but you seem to understand what is truly important in life."

"This I cannot claim. But perhaps I have experience with what is . . . not important. In life."

"I apologize for my sister," he said.

When he'd circled the dining room to return for pudding, he'd encountered Timothea, hovering just outside the door. Her face was wet with tears. She was wringing her hands into a knot. He'd whispered a question, but she'd only shaken her head. He'd reached out to her and she cried for a moment against his shoulder.

"No apologies," Miss Trelayne said.

"Just to be perfectly clear, I'll not survive your tenure without copious apologies. Ask anyone. It's the only way I get by."

"I prefer it. I've learned to avoid people who cannot say I'm sorry."

"One thing I've endeavored to do, despite everything, is take responsibility."

"One thing I've endeavored to do is permit myself to move on." She looked to him and again their eyes locked.

"From what?" he asked, a whisper.

For a long beat, she said nothing—that is, she said nothing with her voice. Her expression was filled with some unnamed intent, and anticipation, and portent.

"From what, Miss Trelayne?" he repeated, still whispering.

"Actually, Your Grace," she said, pushing to her feet, "I'm afraid I must ask you to excuse me. It's rather late, is it not? I believe we may have said—that is, surely we've reviewed all of the—"

"I'll ask you again," he threatened. She couldn't go now.

"Yes," she said, taking two steps back. "Perhaps you will ask again."

Ian rose.

She slipped her arms from his coat and it slid from her shoulders. She held it out. The bulk of it sagged between them. Moonlight refracted off the sheen of her gown, setting her aglow. Her eyes shone turquoise.

He accepted the coat, absorbing the lingering warmth.

"Good night, Your Grace," she said, backing to the door.

"Wait. What do you have planned next? For the girls."

She paused. "The modiste," she said, turning to open the door. "In a day or two. As soon as I can schedule an appointment."

"Should I plan to come?"

"It's up to you, really." She looked back.

*I'll come.* The thought popped into his brain, but he said, "Let me know your plan."

"Very good, Your Grace," she said and slipped through the doorway and was gone.

# Chapter Ten

Mrs. Jericka Tavertine (real name "Jane Tooth") operated a custom dress shop in a cobblestone alley behind Bond Street. Tavertine's Fine Apparel for Ladies and Girls was Drewsmina's favorite type of merchant: little known, talented, trustworthy.

The shop was frequented by opera singers, ballet dancers, diplomats' wives, wealthy bourgeoisie, and (if they were brave enough to leave the hallowed halls of Bond Street) ladies of the ton. Mrs. Tavertine welcomed everyone with only one condition: ability to pay.

The Duke of Lachlan, by all accounts, should meet this condition, but Drew knew the invoice would come as less of a shock if the duke witnessed the commissioning of the girls' wardrobes firsthand.

That is why, when he entered the carriage three days later, her stomach had flipped like a cake in a pan—and not because she was thrilled by the mere sight of him. Or the prospect of spending more time with him. Not because she'd lain awake these last two nights, buzzing and fizzing with the memory of their time on the balcony. Not because her heart had taken flight with every fleeting encounter in the light of day.

She was also gratified because Lady Tribble had declined to come, and the girls should have some family present to sanction this day and share in the fresh start it represented.

"I shouldn't have come." This was Lachlan's first statement a quarter hour later. He said it, rather pointlessly, as they stepped through the deceptively modest door of Tavertine's.

Jericka Tavertine stood proudly in the center of the showroom, scissors and measuring tape in hand, flanked on either side by six seamstresses and tailors, each bearing their own instruments of the trade. Collectively, they had the voracious look of eager surgeons, prepared to save someone's life.

While the duke grumbled, the twins froze in the doorway. Drew ushed them in with cheerful encouragement and gentle pats. She had told them about her own experience of being overlooked and dismissed by established dressmakers who found Drew's height daunting and her red hair impossible. No patron at Tavertine's, she assured them, was ever reduced to second-best. They would not have to jockey for attention or hound the staff to assist them. Jericka gave every client her full attention.

"Good morning, Mrs. Tavertine," called Drew. "Thank you for seeing us on such short notice. May I introduce His Grace, the Duke of Lachlan, and his nieces, Miss Imogene Starry and Miss Ivy Starry. Lachlan, girls, *this* . . . is Mrs. Tavertine and her very talented coterie of artisans. They'll work with us to create your new wardrobes."

Moving as one, Jericka and her staff dropped into a head-ducked bow. Drew, who had devoted an hour after breakfast to proper introductions, cleared her throat and stepped back.

Reluctantly, the girls dipped into a wobbly bow. "How do you do?" they mumbled. The expression on Imogene's face said, *I'm not a dancing bear*, while Ivy's face said, *Do me no harm.*

Drew accepted both. Anything was preferable to the blank staring.

"Lovely," said Drew. "Right. Mrs. Tavertine, if you are amenable, I should like the girls to peruse the showroom, taking in fabrics and patterns. It may help them to ease into the process and set their minds to the task at hand. If you have any commissions that you're willing to share, we would welcome a peek.

"And, oh," she added, "perhaps some tea and a comfortable chair for His Grace?"

"Absolutely," said the dressmaker, dispersing the assembled staff with a silent twitch of her head. "I agree completely. And if I might say, how beautiful your clients are. A dozen fabrics spring to mind that would suit each of them. But do make yourselves at home. Explore, touch, drape, or set aside anything that sparks your fancy."

Drew shot her a grateful smile and turned to the girls. "Now, as I said at breakfast, Mrs. Tavertine procures fabrics from around the world. There is a mind-boggling array, but do not be daunted. Think of favorite colors, think of textures that feel comfortable and easy to wear—warm for winter or cool and light in the spring sun. The Season will extend from February until May.

"Think also of what I told you about the robin, and why I, personally, choose to wear so much blue. Think of what beautiful things you have seen in the countryside or garden, what fabrics you've noticed on pretty ladies in London. Or simply go where the eye draws you."

"But will you help us?" whispered Ivy. She looked like a girl set to walk home in a dark wood.

"I will help you," said Drew, "but I'll want to see your first impressions. If you must, follow Imogene for a time. She's got the hang of it already. It's meant to be enjoyable, Ivy."

Imogene had drifted to the open shelves of fabric like a sleepwalker wading into a pond.

From across the room, the duke called, "But do not feel guilty, Ivy, if you do not enjoy it. Scrutinizing your wardrobe is, surely, an *optional* part of anyone's day, even for females. My valet selects all of my clothes and we're both happier for it."

Drew's heart squeezed at his protectiveness. "Lachlan is correct," she said. "If the task grows tiresome, we'll bid Mrs. Tavertine to select the lot. But I should like you to *try*."

Ivy nodded dutifully and turned in a slow circle, eyes wide at the shelves and shelves of colorful fabrics.

"Is it necessary to force her?" the duke asked lowly, causing Drew to jump. He had materialized beside her like a ghost.

"Force her to select fabric?" she asked. "No. But to manage a new situation? Yes. We cannot release her into the world with a look of anticipatory fear on her face."

"No," he said, "I suppose we cannot."

He crossed his arms over his chest, watching the girls. He sighed, but did not move away.

Drew forced a professional smile and compelled herself to drift. She would settle somewhere. A footman had pushed a chair beneath a sunny window and wheeled in tea. A broadsheet had been folded beside the pot.

Drew came to a stack of fabric on a nearby shelf and stared at it. She sighed. The fabrics, formerly a favorite indulgence, might as well have been a pile of bricks. Instead, her mind's eye conjured up memories of the balcony and the song thrush. And Lachlan—standing on the railing, lying on the railing, telling her about Avenelle.

*You've run mad*, she thought. *Stark, raving.*

"You're not wearing blue," said Lachlan, suddenly beside her again. Not in the chair, not taking tea, not reading the papers. Not . . . settled.

"No," she said.

Today she'd worn one of her favorite of Jericka's creations, a dark yellow day dress with black velvet trim.

Drew had been unconvinced that yellow—really a sort of rich gold color, the yolk of an egg—would suit her, but Jericka had persisted and the resulting frock was sophisticated and different and just a little ironical. Drewsmina loved it. She'd worn it to show Jericka how much she loved it. She'd never expected Lachlan to remember their conversation about blue.

"No insect jewelry, either?" Lachlan asked.

Drew's hand froze in the act of reaching for a fold of silk. He'd noticed. The blue garnet beetle. He'd *seen*.

She looked to him. "Insect jewelry?"

"Yes. The first night, you had a beetle pinned to your—to just . . . *here*."

He raised a gloved hand and hovered his index finger over her chest; then he seemed to think better of it and turned the finger on his own chest, tapping twice just below his cravat.

"I . . . I've worn the caterpillar today, actually," she heard herself say. "A bracelet." She raised her hand between them and shook it so the carved ebony bracelet slid loose and peeked between the lace of her sleeve and the edge of her glove.

"A caterpillar," he repeated, his voice marveling, delighted, as if she'd worn the bracelet as a surprise for his pleasure.

He caught up her hand and flipped it, setting off a swirl of sensation.

Tapping gently, he inched the carved beads around her wrist with his index finger.

"Do you wear an insect bauble every day, Miss Trelayne?"

"Most," she said.

Their eyes locked, and the dress shop, the twins, London—they all fell away. She saw only her hand held within his, her beloved little caterpillar bracelet winking in the sunlight.

No one ever noticed the beetle or the caterpillar, not even Cynde. They were small indulgences, just for her.

"These were gifts?" he guessed.

She shook her head. "Oh no. My own collection. Bought over the years. Not valuable, except to me."

"What do you like about them?"

"Well, they are different, aren't they? Unexpected."

"Like you," he concluded, and something inside her chest hatched to life. A fresh hope. A chance. He *saw* her. And the sight did not cause him to dismiss her or turn away.

If he could *see* her, he could *want* her.

If he could *want* her, he could—

*Stop, stop, stop.*

*Silly, stupid Drewsmina.*

She pulled her hand away and turned. She stalked to an adjacent shelf and squared herself before a stack of fabric, staring at it with all of her might, seeing every color and no color and a great, blank void.

*You must* want *your heart to break*, she thought.

By some miracle, she remembered to check the girls. Imogene was industriously building a stack of bold, shiny silks on a counter. Crimson, ebony, royal blue, purple. Beside her, Ivy watched in baffled nervousness.

*Good. Progress. At least someone was in the correct frame of mind.*

Drew took a deep breath and reached for a bolt of fabric, any bolt. Putrid green wool fell into her hands.

"Imogene appears to be fashioning a flag for King Arthur's court."

The duke was beside her again. He'd acquired a stool, and he plopped it down next to the shelf and sat.

"Imogene wants to look like a grown woman," Drew said, forcing their conversation into the realm of the professional. "To be provocative and assured and formidable."

Drew replaced the green fabric and pulled down another bolt. "She is also daring me to tell her *No*."

"Just to be obstinate," Lachlan guessed.

"Perhaps. She also wishes to make a point. The task of a new wardrobe is impossible; we'll never agree."

"What will you do?"

Drew shrugged. "I'll work with her. We'll find appropriate colors that allow her to feel a bit daring and noticed without being garish or too mature. I'll prove that a new wardrobe is possible. Imogene's coloring actually lends itself to mauves and tans and muted, mossy colors," she went on. "She will hate these until she sees how they enhance her beauty."

"Like your blues," Lachlan observed, and Drew fumbled the fabric in her hand.

"Careful," he said, leaning to catch it.

Drew plucked it from his grasp and returned it to the shelf.

"I'm not accustomed to discussing myself with anyone," she blurted in a whisper. "Least of all a man. Perhaps it's best that we discuss the girls. Primarily."

She pivoted and trudged away.

"I thought we were discussing the girls."

*He did?* Heart pounding, she crossed to a counter stacked with velvet trays of decorative lace. She leaned over the samples and stared as if she'd never before seen lace.

He was beside her in the next moment, dragging his stool. Her insides ricocheted with a pinging current of energy. She was mad, possibly ill. And breathless.

"But surely we're keeping you from some important work, Your Grace?" she said to the lace.

"What work?"

"Whatever it is a duke may do on a daily basis?"

"Oh that. Not really. I deal with correspondence from my steward first thing in the mornings. Harvest is over, so traveling to London for a time has been manageable. Oh look," he finished, tapping the glass with his finger. "Lace. That's ours. Not that one, this one. The delicate, handmade, frothy bit." He frowned down at the glass.

"Yours?"

"Well, my tenants'. Many of them are of Flemish descent, going back generations, and lace making is in their blood."

"Oh, but you mean Honiton lace?" asked Drew.

"I do mean," he said heavily.

She was confused. "But you just mentioned a harvest. Is Avenelle not primarily supported by farming and sheep?"

"Oh, we do it all at Avenelle. Farming, mining, sheep. Lace making. Whatever the tenants prefer, actually. The estate is a collaboration, and I prefer that each family has some choice in their livelihood."

"But you're not in favor of the lace makers?" she surmised.

"Let us just say the lace makers are not in favor of me."

Drew thought of this, waiting for him to explain. He said nothing, turning his back to the display and leaning against the counter.

She tried again, "Honiton lace is considered among the finest in the world. If you see it in this case, it will be the most expensive and most beautiful trimming in Mrs. Tavertine's shop."

"Aye. It's very precious, indeed. I've just as much pride in Honiton lace as the next man. I've risked life, limb, and reputation to find a way for my tenants to carry on with it. But it's becoming a lost art, isn't it? Labor-intensive, expensive, and takes hours and hours to weave. Meanwhile, mechanized textile mills—several of which are *also* on my land—turn out bolts of cheaper lace, far faster. Most importantly, perhaps, the mill owners can afford the export tax that enables them to sell their lace around the world. My old-world weavers cannot keep pace. As duke, I want all of them to succeed, the mills and the craftsman. It's a problem with no obvious solution, and the struggle has dominated my life these last three years. It was the impetus for the bloody riot that nearly sent me to Newgate."

"I didn't know," she said, "the reasons for the riot."

He let out a weary sigh. "It's a miserable tale, honestly.

No one cares enough to learn what really happened, they want only someone to blame."

"*I* should like to know," she said softly.

He glanced over at her with a look that said, *You're the first*. He gave a sad smile, and the hatchling from her heart hopped and tried to fly.

"The lace makers will never be able to compete with the new textile mills, but there is high demand for Honiton lace around the world. We need only a level field of play."

He was shaking his head. With due emphasis he breathed, "Which is why the export duty for small craftsmen *must be removed*."

"Your audience with the prince regent," she remembered. "The girls' presentation at court."

"Yes. The prince doesn't make the laws but his influence in parliament is significant. Meanwhile, mine is . . . a joke at the moment. With one fell swoop he can do what I never could. In the meantime . . ."

"*You* pay the export duty for the lace makers?"

He let out a bitter bark of laughter. "If only it was that easy. The lot of them despise me too much to accept my help."

He looked up to her, gave a sad little wink, and turned back to the lace. "The less you know, Miss Trelayne, the better. Believe me."

Drew stared at him, her heart hopping into her throat. She wanted to tell him that she didn't care for what was best. She was riveted. She loved Honiton lace—she loved all artisan-made, handcrafted textiles—and she loved the notion of progress and tradition coexisting side by side. And she loved—

She stopped herself.

There were things that one loved, and then there were things—well, men—you'd only just met.

*Silly, stupid girl.*

She stared down at the lace, trying to think of something

more to say. Fifty questions tumbled in her head. She was just about to ask him to identify the mill-produced lace, when they heard the *tap*, *tap*, *tap* of demanding footsteps behind them.

"What are you doing?" said a familiarly suspicious voice.

Drew and Lachlan turned.

Imogene Starry stood behind them, hands on her hips, glaring at Drew and her uncle.

## Chapter Eleven

"We are looking at this lace," Ian replied, turning his back to the counter and leaning against it. "What are *you* doing?"

"I've chosen fabric. Choosing fabric was our stated purpose for this outing. And *Ivy*—" she scowled in the direction of the window "—is taking tea. And reading the papers. She has chosen nothing. So . . ."

"Oh lovely," clipped Miss Trelayne, hurrying away. Her cheeks glowed red. "Let's have a look, shall we?"

Imogene followed Miss Trelayne to the counter and flung a hand in the general direction of her heap of fabric choices. Her message was clear: *I've graduated from this process.*

Miss Trelayne smiled an I-don't-think-so smile and beckoned her back.

Unfurling the top bolt with a dramatic whoosh, Miss Trelayne compelled Imogene to explain her choices and her vision for potential dresses.

Imogene complied with a mix of boredom and irritation—a girl forced to show off her watercolors to Auntie's friends—but Miss Trelayne asked so many questions and appeared so very interested, Imogene eventually warmed to the task.

For the next half hour, they mulled over the fabrics, summoning Mrs. Tavertine to join them with her sketchbook.

With nothing to contribute, Ian poured himself a cup of

tea and sat in the windowsill, drinking in companionable silence next to Ivy. She was reading the broadsheets with a small dog who'd wandered in from a back room.

The tea had gone cold, but he drank it anyway, staring at Bond Street in the distance.

"Who do you see outside, Uncle?"

Ian glanced down. Ivy was watching him with a look of— What had Miss Trelayne called it?

*Anticipatory fear.*

"No one is outside, Ivy. I'm merely woolgathering. Staring mindlessly into the street."

"It's not safe?" Ivy guessed. She rose up a little to peek out the window.

"Oh no, it's perfectly safe. Bond Street is just through those buildings and round the corner *there . . .*" he pointed, ". . . and it will be bustling with fine ladies and gentlemen dandies at this hour. Entirely safe, I assure you."

"But you hate it," she guessed.

This suggestion gave him pause; he wondered what his expression must show. "No, Ivy," he admitted, "I don't hate it. I find shopping for luxury trinkets to be tedious, perhaps—"

"But not dresses?"

"Well, I've come along today to support you girls. It's hardly luxury to replace your current wardrobe, if you don't mind me saying. Necessity, more like. If you see me frowning, it's due to the *inhabitants* of Bond Street, not the shopping—the ladies and dandies I mentioned."

"Why?" Ivy asked.

Ian replaced his cup. Miss Trelayne felt the girls were owed honesty, but there was honesty and then there was simply not wanting to talk about it.

Then again, this was the most conversation he'd had from Ivy since the girls had come to Avenelle.

"Well," he began, "three years ago, when you were . . ."

"With T.O.E.," she supplied.

"Right. When you were with T.O.E. I was in the midst

of a fight between my tenants, the town counsel, and the owner of a mill in our village."

"Was the mill so very sinful? Reverend Sagg is very much opposed to mills."

"Actually I was in favor of the mill *and* the tenants. The mill provided a great many jobs for some villagers. Others were dedicated craftsmen who felt the mills were destroying their livelihood. I wanted to find a way for both sides to succeed. I had mediated a sort of truce. But ultimately that truce fell through, and the tenants marched on the town and incited a riot. There was a terrible night of fighting and violence. A man was killed and many others were injured."

"Right here in Bean Street," she surmised.

"*Bond* Street," he corrected. "No. The tragedy happened very near Avenelle, actually, in Dorset. But it was such a terrible disaster that the newspapers reported it here in London, and Londoners, especially the people who frequent places like Bond Street, wanted my head."

"Wanted your head?"

"They wanted to blame me." He made a slicing gesture at his neck.

Ivy's look of anticipatory fear returned. "But why? If you only wanted what was best for everyone?"

"The Londoners were angry because I'd indulged the craftsmen for so many months. I was only trying to understand their point of view, to listen and possibly find a compromise, but many people in government—many other landowners—saw what I was doing as *collusion*. Do you know what that means?"

Ivy shook her head.

"The other dukes and earls and such thought I betrayed all landowners by stirring up violence and sedition among the tenants."

"And they wanted you to go to jail for it?" she guessed.

"Nearly," he said. "A tribunal of judges found me innocent of blame. However, in the court of public opinion—meaning what most people thought and said about me—I was entirely to blame. As a result, there are many places in the city that I'm not welcomed, at least not without accusations and scorn. Name-calling. *Ill will.* Bond Street is likely one of them."

"Oh, so you are *hiding*?" she surmised.

Ian considered this. Did he hide from the people of his own class? Is that what he'd been doing in Dorset these last three years? *Hiding?*

Probably, he thought. But he hadn't discovered any other way. He was hated by his tenants and hated by the establishment. And his culpability in the riot, despite good intent, could not be denied. He'd endeavored to justify his actions, but no one wanted excuses. They wanted only someone to blame.

And so he'd allowed it—what else he could he do? And when he could no longer tolerate the guilt and scorn, he'd disappeared. He was hardly welcomed back in Dorset, but Avenelle was his home, whether his tenants liked it or not. He was determined to restore their trust in him. This was why it was so very important that he eradicate the export duty. His craftsmen must be allowed to legally trade with the rest of the world and earn a living wage.

"Let us just say that I prefer to be invisible," he said.

"*Me, too,*" Ivy enthused. "I prefer to be invisible."

Ian paused, the wrongness of this statement as clear as his face in a mirror.

"No, no, Ivy," he began gently. "You mustn't strive for invisibility." He glanced to Miss Trelayne. He was out of his depth. She would know what to say.

"It is my strong preference," she declared.

"Well, you may value privacy, and you may keep your circle of trusted friends very small, but true invisibility is rather lonely. And it doesn't allow you to do much good for anybody else. It's sort of an . . . indulgence for all of that— invisibility. I never intended to stew in it myself. I'm using the time to make amends with my tenants."

"I intend to remain invisible as long as I can," declared

Ivy, stroking the dog. "But now Miss Trelayne has come, and she's forcing us to *be seen*."

"Yes," said Ian, staring at Miss Trelayne. She must have felt his gaze because she looked up. "I suppose she is rather forceful on that score. It's not a bad thing, in the end. You've nothing from which to hide. That is the difference between me and you."

He was just about to summon Miss Trelayne when movement outside the window caught his eye. He leaned in, squinted, and saw it again. A tall, broad-shouldered man, dressed like a highwayman, was signaling to him with a bob of his hat. He lurked in the shadows near the drainpipe of the adjacent alley.

*Rucker Loring*. Ian blinked twice, shocked to see one of his Avenelle stewards standing in a Mayfair alleyway. Loring bobbed his hat again, the look on his face purposeful and a little urgent.

Ian swore and shoved to his feet, upsetting the dog. He'd hoped his tenants could get on without him for the early weeks of his time in London. He'd spent a fortnight briefing his stewards.

And now this. How long had he been away? Less than a month. Ian had bade the stewards to write if something went wrong—he'd no wish to return to any surprise crises—but he'd never expected one of them to actually leave Dorset to seek him out in London. Things must be very bad, indeed.

The young steward, like his other estate managers, was not a learned man, but one of the few locals Ian could trust. What leadership was required here, now, Ian couldn't imagine.

"I need air, Ivy," Ian said, not looking back at the girl. "I'm going out."

"Oh, but may I come, Uncle?" asked Ivy.

"No, I'm afraid not. I've business with a man from Dorset. Be a good girl and do not leave the shop until I return."

Miss Trelayne must have heard the note of command

in his voice, because she took three steps toward him, her eyes wide.

"I've an errand, Miss Trelayne," he called to her. "I'll be back presently. Can you and the girls wait for me here?"

"Yes, of course, Your Grace," she said.

Ian nodded and shoved out the door, upsetting a trio of customers—a young man and two women—reaching for the door at the same time.

"I beg your pardon," exclaimed the young man, clearly offended by his haste.

"Mind yourself," grumbled Ian and strode out the door.

# Chapter Twelve

"Did the duke say where he was going?" Drew asked Ivy after he'd gone.

"No." She was trying to lure the dog back into her lap.

"But was he upset? He seemed rather agitated when he left."

"Perhaps he was bored of the dressmaker's," said Ivy.

"Yes, perhaps," mused Drew, settling her hip on the arm of Ivy's chair. She peered out the window but the street was empty. The duke had vanished.

She sighed, confused and a little unsettled. There had been very little role for him here, but his sudden absence felt disappointing, like an unexpected letter with bad news.

She looked down to Ivy, determined to keep on task. "There were no fabrics that interested you, Ivy?"

Ivy collected the dog and held him to her chest, hiding her face in his fur.

"Right," Drew said. "But tell me: Would you mind if myself and Mrs. Tavertine made the selections for you? We could show you samples of what we choose, and you could say yea or nay?"

The girl did not answer.

"*Ivy*," she cajoled, "you must have some prefer—"

She was cut off when the shop door opened, admitting a gust of cold wind and another family. The group was comprised of a grandmotherly woman; a young lady, short and thick; and a young man, tall and strapping. The three of them shared the same prominent noses and pale blond hair. A brother and sister out with their grandmother or aunt, Drew thought.

Mrs. Tavertine greeted them and then hurried to Drew and Ivy.

"Forgive me, Drewsmina," Jericka said. "I tried to re-schedule my one o'clock, but they've come despite my note. I miscalculated the number of hours Miss Imogene and Miss Ivy would require. I'll need to step away to compel this other family to return tomorrow."

"No, no," Drew said, "do not turn them out. I am to blame; sorting both girls in one morning was too ambi-tious. If the other clients can share you long enough to make some small progress with Miss Ivy, she'll stand for measurements with a seamstress and then *we'll* return an-other day."

"Very good," gushed the proprietress. "Thank you." And she swept off to placate the new family.

Drew returned her attention to Ivy, but not before she saw the young man from the newly arrived family staring in the direction of Imogene.

*Oh dear*, Drew thought. The man's gaze followed Imo-gene's progress about the shop; his eyes roving voraciously from the tumble of her blond hair, to her long eyelashes, to the effect of her tight corset. He began to drift in Imogene's direction.

Drew swore under her breath and weighed her options. It would be a mistake to underestimate Imogene's po-tential to make a very big fuss. A quarrel with the girl would, ultimately, be more disruptive and damaging than simply allowing some small exchange. Drew would keep a close eye.

Ivy chose this moment to become philosophical. "I can-not see why it matters how I look," she mused.

"Well," said Drew, watching as Imogene took notice of

her admirer, as she *beamed* at him, "it may not matter to you—which is acceptable when you are at home. However, it is a sign of respect to the people outside the house to make some effort, to look clean and pressed and presentable. It says to friends and strangers, 'You matter enough for me to pull myself together.'"

Now the young man leaned on the counter with an elbow, making some joke. Imogene giggled and he followed with a second statement, this one whispered nearly in her ear.

Drew swore again. This could go very badly if Imogene felt curtailed by Drew, but soon she would be given no choice. She glanced at the boy's family. The granny and the young woman had unfurled a bolt of muslin and examined the threading with Mrs. Tavertine.

Keeping an eye on the room, Drew turned back to Ivy. "What if I'd turned up to your drawing room in Pollen Street wearing a sad, bedraggled dress, with my hair unkempt and my fingernails dirty? You might have thought, 'Her view for this job is very low indeed. She regards our introduction in the same way she regards bath day for her dog.'"

"You have a dog?" asked Ivy.

"No, no, Ivy, but I'm trying to make a point. Do you see how sloppiness might be distracting? We want people to hear what you have to say, not be distracted in how ragamuffin-y you may look."

Drew barely heard her answer. Imogene and this strange boy strolled together up and down the shelves of fabric, their heads bent in conversation. Every fourth or fifth word, Imogene laid a lingering hand on the boy's arm.

"I don't care if people hear what I have to say," Ivy admitted.

"This may not always be the case," Drew managed, watching Imogene disappear around the corner of a tall shelf. "The older you become, the more you will wish to be taken seriously. Your appearance needn't take two hours, neither in commissioning the wardrobe or in your daily toilette, but ten minutes would not be remiss, would it? Here's what we'll do. We'll charge Mrs. Tavertine with pulling together a collection of very practical, simple dresses in colors that suit you, and be done with it. A maid will keep them clean and pressed. And that's it."

"Well . . ." began Ivy. "I suppose . . ."

Drew barely heard. To her very great frustration, Imogene and the young man had reached the doorway to a corridor in the rear of the showroom, hovered for half a beat, and then disappeared from view.

"Oh," droned Ivy, bored. "Imogene's made a friend."

"I'll have to go after her," resigned Drew, springing up and walking in quick but restrained pursuit.

Jericka rushed to her side, and Drew called, "Four day dresses and four gowns, if you please Mrs. Tavertine. Simple design. Whatever muted colors you think may suit her. Can someone take her dimensions quickly? I must look in on Imogene."

"Very good," said Mrs. Tavertine, changing course. "Can I trouble you to follow me to a sitting room, Miss Ivy?" She plucked the dog from her lap.

"Do not worry, Miss Trelayne," called Ivy as she tromped away. "Imogene makes friends wherever she goes. No one was more outraged than Reverend Sagg, but even he was powerless to stop her."

## Chapter Thirteen

Drew asked Lachlan to ride outside the carriage for the journey home. Perhaps he could hear and perhaps he could not, but the conversation would be painful enough without Imogene enduring his strangely silent, plainly obvious outrage. He'd returned from his errand agitated and tense, and when he'd learned Drew's very modest retelling of what had happened, his mood (naturally) became stormier still. The situation only wanted his tinderbox match touched off against Imogene's simmering flame.

Drew sat with the girls inside the vehicle—it would not hurt for Ivy to hear, and she could hardly ride on the coachman's box, too—and endeavored to speak with calmness and graciousness.

"Can you tell me, Imogene, about the rules at your *previous* home?" she asked gently. "Were young ladies allowed to slip away, alone, in the company of men?"

The girl said nothing.

"T.O.E.? Did it allow this?"

Not for the first time, Drew wondered if this particular conversation would not be better held between the girls and their mother.

"You must engage with me, Imogene, you must. It's too important to leave unsaid."

No reaction.

"Unless," Drew tried, "you'd prefer to discuss this with Lady Tribble?"

"My mother," Imogene said finally, "does not care."

"She *does* care," insisted Drew, hoping this was true.

"I've done nothing wrong," insisted Imogene. "We walked into the street. We were talking. This diatribe is misplaced."

"Perhaps you simply talked and perhaps you did not. Perhaps this is a diatribe and perhaps I'm telling you something that you already know. Regardless, it cannot be left unsaid: all interactions between young ladies and men of any age must happen within plain view of other adults. You cannot disappear together. You cannot be alone. You cannot go missing together, and you cannot be discovered alone together—by anyone. Even servants."

"It's a stupid rule," said Imogene.

"Call it stupid if you like," said Drew, "but it has endured for centuries. Of all the rules, it is among the most heavily guarded by the matriarchs and patriarchs who control society. And the most *re*garded—by everyone. Your very future depends upon it. Girls discovered alone with men are considered unmarriageable. Their innocence is believed to be lost. Their friends turn away. They struggle, even, to find honest work."

"*Stupid*," repeated Imogene, turning away.

When Drew had burst through the rear door of the shop and stumbled into the street, her priority had been to check for bystanders. It mattered less what Imogene was doing and more who was watching. Thankfully, the little back street was deserted.

Following the sound of Imogene's laughter, Drew rounded the corner to see Imogene flattened up against the bricks, and the boy leaning over her, one hand propped above her head. Her face was tipped up, his mouth was descending. No pose represented more yearnful, breathless, *youthful* longing. Add in Imogene's beauty and the young man's boldness—he'd met her just ten minutes ago—and their pose was almost clichéd.

Thankfully, Imogene had not put up a fight when Drew had called to her. She ignored her—twice she refused to acknowledge Drew calling her name—but when Drew circled close enough to take her by the wrist and tug her away, she'd come. The boy, also thankfully, had fled somewhere between the first request and the extraction.

"How can my *entire life* hinge on kissing a boy behind the dressmaker's shop?"

A loud *thump* rattled the carriage. The sound, Drew thought, of Lachlan's head hitting the back of the coachman's bench. He *did* hear.

"Innocence, as I'm sure you know, is valued most of all in any lady, Imogene," Drew recited.

"More than cleverness?"

"Yes."

"What of spirit? What of courage?"

"If lost innocence comes first, these are not even considered, I'm afraid. Not by society at large."

"What of compassion?" Imogene's voice climbed higher with each incredulous question.

"It's the same for any quality you could name, I'm afraid. Even riches or beauty."

"*Upside-down*," hissed Imogene.

"Perhaps it is. But I did not make the rules; I have, however, been charged with impressing them upon you."

"And what of Harold's innocence? Does his future hinge on it?"

"Who is Harold?"

"The boy! From the shop!"

"Oh. Harold. But did you *know* this boy, Imogene?"

"Of course I didn't know him. I've only just arrived in London. I don't know anyone but you. And I find you rather tedious, I don't mind saying."

"Yes, I'm certain that you do. However, this point cannot be overlooked."

"Would it have made a difference? Kissing Harold, if I'd *known* him?"

"No. It makes no difference. The only thing that matters is that your reputation remains untarnished."

Drew paused and took a deep breath. "Is everyone in this carriage aware of the . . . er, *intimacy* shared between a husband and wife after they are married?"

Imogene glared at her. "Surely you jest."

"Is that a yes?"

"*Yes,*" articulated Imogene, leveling her with an indignant glare.

"Ivy?" asked Drew.

"Ivy knows enough," Imogene cut in.

"Very well," said Drew, appreciating Imogene's protectiveness of her sister, even now.

Drew continued, searching for the correct words, "That intimacy is afforded only to husbands and wives. Only *then* can they be alone together. Only *then* may they enjoy closed doors, and stolen kisses, and private conversations in the back streets."

"You mean afforded to only *wives,*" said Imogene. "Husbands may do as they please. *Men* may do as they please. Harold is probably already kissing some other girl, not a care in the world."

"You are correct. This rule applies only to females. Again, I am not the architect of this rule, however, I would be remiss in my duties if we did not review it."

"And review it, and review it," droned Imogene.

"Excellent point," said Drew, "let's review: In public settings, you may speak with young men, men of any age. But if you are discovered *alone* with a male . . . in a garden, in a library, in a street, *anywhere* . . . the assumption will be made that you have shared some . . . some intimacy with him. Even if you've done nothing more than stand about, gaping at each another, you'll be presumed 'ruined.'"

"It's a terrible thing to presume about a person," whispered Ivy, all traces of the emerging confidence she'd shown at Tavertine's had slipped away.

"It is terrible," agreed Drew. "Unfortunately, it accurately describes the way a girl is regarded if she violates society's rules of chaste, respectable behavior. It means she is no longer innocent, no longer suitable for a gentleman, no longer marriageable."

Ivy looked with concern at her sister, reaching out to take her hand. Imogene was in no mood and flicked her away.

"Do not feel threatened, Ivy," said Drew. "Despite Imogene's complaints, the rule doesn't have to be difficult to follow."

"Perhaps not difficult for you," said Imogene. "I like men and having a laugh and larking about. How much fun can anyone expect to have under the watchful eye of sanctioned observers?"

"But, Imogene," said Drew, "you have your whole life to subvert the watchful eye of sanctioned observers. It's only now, at age sixteen, without the protection of marriage, that you must be mindful. There is still fun to be had in the company of chaperones. You have so many balls and garden parties and races ahead of you."

"But what is everyone afraid of?" asked Imogene. "This is what I'd like to know. So what if I cannot properly 'guard my innocence'? What if I find it a great, bloody burden and I'm ready to be rid of it? Where's the harm in this? How can my lack of innocence result in such . . . doom? *Total ruination?* Spare me, please."

"Honestly?" sighed Drew, "I cannot say. I believe the suggestion is that ultimately, men have very little control over their . . . desire, and if females cannot be relied upon to keep away from them, then—?"

"Then what?"

"They will run amok and society will collapse?" ventured Drew weakly. She'd never really given it a great deal of thought. No man had ever wished to steal away with her, and her lack of desirability was not her favorite topic on which to dwell.

Imogene was laughing bitterly now. "Society will collapse?" She tipped over sideways, laughing. Ivy looked on with bewilderment.

"Consider this," said Drew, patting Ivy's knee. "Independent of societal collapse—which I agree, does sound ridiculous—the threat of pregnancy is very real, if you are *actually*, er, intimate with a man. The rules against unchaperoned time with men are intended to stave this off. It's one thing to be ruined, it's quite another to be unwed with a baby on the way. This makes not just one life very challenging, but two.

"However, before we get carried away with talk of unwanted babies," said Drew, "let me raise the topic of unwanted husbands. Do you fancy yourself married right away, Imogene? This month? To a stranger?"

"What do you mean?"

"I've mentioned that the London Season is a way to match up with a future husband. So, looking forward, let us say for the sake of argument that you happen to be very popular this Season. It's a real possibility, I assure you. And if, during the Season, a man takes a fancy to you, and you to him, *and you follow all of the rules*—after that, the two of you will enter into a proper courtship. If you continue to suit, he will ask your uncle for your hand in marriage. When Lachlan agrees, you will be betrothed. After that, possibly even a *year* into the future, you will be married.

"*However*, if you are discovered alone with a man—any man, even this *Harold*—and if he possesses even a modicum of honor, the two of you will be forced to marry. Immediately. Whether you're suited or not. There'll be no courtship. No planning of a lovely wedding. Your reputation will be saved only if you hie away to a conveniently discreet vicar and become immediate husband and wife. The only alternative to saving your honor would be pistols at dawn with your uncle."

To this, Imogene said nothing. She shook her head and glared out the window. Ivy made a small sound of distress and wrung her hands.

"Would you be amenable to marrying Harold, Imogene?" Drew pressed. "Are you aware, even, of his family name? Because if I'd not kept your uncle at bay, if I'd not extracted you from the street myself—and if we'd not been exceedingly lucky that the street was empty—Harold Family-Name-Unknown would be well on his way to becoming your husband."

"You cannot force me," she said.

"Yes. Perhaps we could not. But we would beg you. Because if word got out, you would have no other options and it would be necessary to shield Ivy. Because her reputation would be tainted by association."

"Well, that makes even less sense!" said Imogene, whirling from the window. "Who would ever suspect *Ivy* of kissing anyone?"

"I've not said it makes sense, Imogene," said Drew quietly, "only that it is."

They rode on in strained silence for two blocks, Drew allowing her words to take root.

"I'm only trying to protect you, Imogene," Drew finally said, her voice soft. "Can you tell me that you understand? Can you tell me that you will be mindful of your reputation and what it means?"

"You think I'm a strumpet," Imogene shot back. "You've pretended to be an ally when really you're no better than the cruel overlords at T.O.E."

Drew paused a beat before she responded, taking a moment to comprehend all this accusation inferred.

"I do not think you're a strumpet," Drew finally said. "I'll make no judgment on your innocence, and, in fact, my only stake here is that we maintain it. *If you wish to live the life into which you've been born.* That life means eventual marriage to a gentleman. Acceptance into polite society. Etcetera, etcetera. We can argue the merits of this rule until kingdom come, but in the meantime, we'll need to be realistic about how the world works."

It was a bold statement indeed. The widely held view was that innocence was eternally linked to purity, good judgment, and restraint, *not* realism. However, Drew was realistic above all else. No spinster-y woman with orange hair and six inches on most other girls could survive without practicality, first and foremost.

As to the Temple of Order in Eden, she would be remiss in not acknowledging the accusation.

"Furthermore," Drew said, "I should be happy to listen if ever you girls are ready to discuss your life in the . . . er, T.O.E. community, but please do not align me with your 'cruel overlords' unless you can cite specific examples."

"You want specifics," spat Imogene. "How about this? Now, we all know why you're not married, don't we? You were ruined by *some man*, and no other man would have you."

"Wrong again, Imogene," said Drew tiredly. "If my reputation had been jeopardized, I would not be allowed to work with young ladies. Women who are considered 'ruined' cannot find honest work even as a clerk in a shop, let alone with impressionable debutantes."

Imogene made a scoffing noise. "You've probably never even fancied a boy. You've not had the opportunity to be 'ruined.' You're setting out this rule, and you don't even know what it means."

"Also untrue," Drew said. "I did fancy a young man, once upon a time. I fancied him very much, indeed. He was a sergeant in the Royal Marines, a very fine man, a perfect gentleman. Never once did he impose any impropriety on me."

"Well, then I feel sorry for you," said Imogene. "*And* for the good sergeant. Because kissing is lovely. I rate it very highly, indeed. It is one my favorite things to do. And perhaps if you'd allowed him to steal a kiss, then we would not be speaking of him in the past tense. Perhaps you would still be sweethearts."

"We are not sweethearts," corrected Drew, her throat suddenly thick, "because my mother spoke to an acquaintance at the War Office and arranged for his immediate posting to India."

Silence. The carriage hit a rut and they were all tossed to the left.

"Why?" Ivy whispered.

"Because," said Drew, "she did not approve of the match. James was a gentleman in spirit but a commoner by birth. We were powerless to stop her, and he was sent away.

"So," she finished, looking to Imogene, "perhaps I've not been subjected to the great unfairness of freely kissing men whenever the mood strikes, but other arbitrary laws of society have been imposed on my happiness."

She'd barely survived the heartbreak of her mother's interference. To this day, she invoked the simple tactic of putting it out of her mind and never speaking of it, just to get by. Even this abbreviated version of the story reopened old wounds.

"*We* are not the same, you and I," gritted out Imogene. She turned her face back to the window. "I don't care what you say."

"*Genie*," whispered Ivy, a scold.

Imogene ignored her.

"It's *alright*, Ivy," assured Drew. She took a deep breath, allowing the defensiveness and hurt to drain away.

"We've had a long morning," she continued gently. "We're hungry, and out of sorts, and it's freezing in this carriage. We'll have a lovely luncheon, perhaps take a nap, and then the French tutor will arrive after teatime."

Imogene dropped her head against the window, the gesture of someone whose endurance had run out.

"An hour only to begin, Imogene," said Drew. "Perhaps you'll like French. It's the international *language of love*."

## Chapter Fourteen

Drewsmina Trelayne's Rule of Style and Comportment #6:
A young woman may never steal away alone, out of sight
and unaccounted for, with a man. Not once. Not even for
a moment. The ramifications of being discovered are not
worth risking the strict inflexibility of this rule.
[Repeated as #6 for emphasis.]

"Miss Trelayne?" Lachlan asked at the close of dinner. "Might I have a word with you in private?"

"Very good, Your Grace," Drew said, agreeing without
really hearing the question. She'd been laughing over Imogene's joke about Jericka Tavertine and her slavishly vigi-
lant staff.

Dinner, she was happy to note, had been peppered with
intermittent laughter; the mood around the table being . . .
if not loving and jovial, at least civil and far less strange.
They were making progress. In five days, they'd made actual
progress.

"And what was your impression of the dressmaker's,
Vee?" Lady Tribble, more engaged than ever before,
asked Ivy.

"They have a dog there," volunteered Ivy, pushing back
from the table.

"Ivy?" Drew prompted carefully. "We spoke this morning about something pertaining to the end of mealtimes. Do you recall?"

"May I be excused?" recited Ivy softly.

"Oh lovely," praised Drew. To Lady Tribble she said, "Baroness, I believe Ivy has directed this request to you."

"A dog in a dress shop, how clever," said Lady Tribble.

"Not the dog, my lady," said Drew gently, "the request to be excused."

But Ivy was already to the door, her nose in a book.

"Everyone is excused," declared Lachlan. "I need to speak to Miss Trelayne. Get out."

"But, I've not finished my pudding," complained Imogene.

For the second night in a row, Drew had watched Imogene use a series of nudges and scoots to reposition one of her mother's *two* wine goblets close enough to be absorbed into her own place setting. Now she casually sipped claret in between bites of soufflé.

"Fine," said the duke, "we'll go. What is your progress on the pudding, Miss Trelayne?"

"Oh," said Drew, unprepared for his urgency. "Quite finished, Your Grace."

"Excellent. No more wine, Imogene, if you please," said the duke, stalking to the door.

Drew was given no choice but to follow him. He'd said very little throughout the meal. At the time, she'd allowed herself to believe he'd been stunned into silence, overwhelmed by how quickly the girls had progressed from disagreeableness to lively chatter. Now he strode down the corridor at a pace that could mean anything from *what an outrage* to *the house has caught fire*. Drew hurried to keep up.

Perhaps, she thought, he had reconsidered her handling of Imogene's entanglement with the boy in the shop. When the carriage had returned to Pollen Street, Imogene had stomped into the house with self-righteous indignation. Lachlan had climbed from the coachman's box, determined to go after her, but Drew had stayed with him, suggesting that enough had been said. It had been a quick exchange—he'd actually seemed a little relieved at her advice—and she'd not seen the duke since.

Now he paused in the corridor, looked right and left, and then poked his head into an open door as if he'd never seen it before. After a moment, he stepped inside.

"Leave us, Meredith," she heard him call from within. The beleaguered maid fled the room in the next instant, her ash pail swinging wildly.

Drew paused outside the door, took a deep breath, smoothed her skirts, and stepped inside.

"I cannot believe it," Lachlan declared from behind her.

She turned to the sound of his voice, and he swung the door shut with a *thwack*.

Drew jumped. "I beg your pardon?"

"The girls. The talking. Even Timothea. There was *laughter*. I simply cannot believe it." He began to pace.

Drew blinked at him. He wasn't angry, he was in disbelief—*happy* disbelief. She let out a breath and glanced around.

They were in a large airy room that encompassed two floors. Expansive paintings lined the walls like murals. There was little furniture, save scattered benches, presumably for gazing at the art. Fluted pedestals with marble busts stood in a grid in the center of the room, interspersed with life-sized sculptures of muscled people in togas, Romans in repose, and frightened horses.

"Where are we?" she ventured.

"Gallery," he said with a dismissive wave of his hand.

"Your home is a showplace, Your Grace. Tomorrow the girls and I shall embark on a tour."

Lachlan stopped pacing and looked around. "My great-grandfather was an art enthusiast."

He squinted at a sweeping landscape as if it were an advertisement for lye soap. "I haven't gotten around to redoing it."

"You don't share the previous duke's passion for art?"

she asked, slowly pivoting. She was no connoisseur, but the value of such a robust collection would be significant.

"I don't care about the London house," he said. "My devotion lies almost entirely in Dorset."

He crossed to the newly laid fire and stoked it with a poker, launching a swirl of sparks.

"And to the girls. It cannot be overstated. Today seemed . . . remarkable. They're typical, ordinary girls. After all of their oddness. I'm overcome. Honestly. They are behaving normally after just *a handful of days*."

"They were always typical girls," she said, drifting in his direction. "I believe they have not been afforded the opportunity to do normal things. Most girls will have something to say about shopping or French tutors, even if it is to complain."

"It is such a relief, you've no idea," he said, jabbing the poker into its cage. He spun away, stalking the length of the gallery, hands in his pockets.

"It's better, perhaps, not to boast of a victory too soon," Drew cautioned. "Imogene is more forthcoming, but she is not happy. It may be normal behavior to step out with a young man, but her recklessness is very risky. And I worry that Ivy may not be ready for a Season this year. I hope this does not upset your agreement with the prince. But it would be a mistake to force her if she doesn't want it."

"I don't care about the Season. The prince would be useful but not at the cost of the girls." He came to a bench and hurled himself on it, an exhausted boxer after a fight. "I want to get this bit correct. Or at the very least, I want *not to fail*."

"If I might suggest: Your desire to do right by the girls is the opposite of failing them. I am somewhat of an expert on adults who have failed children, and you are a good uncle to the girls, Your Grace."

Drew came to a stop near his bench. Their proximity had begun to feel too natural. Wherever he was, she went to him. If she could not go to him, she looked at him. Had the girls noticed how frequently she glanced at him? Admiring the way he joked with the footmen? And the shared looks. This had rapidly become second nature. If they occupied the same room, they punctuated any meaningful comment by locking gazes, by communicating without saying a word.

And that said nothing of what they were doing now.

She should not be here, alone with him. She should not stand beside him as he sprawled on the bench.

A proper lady would be put off by his casualness, by his poor posture, his deflated neck cloth, his boots akimbo; but Drew wanted only to stare, to admire, to laugh. He was so naturally uninhibited. It delighted her. She wanted to remember it for later, when she could recall the image and study it in detail. When she could imagine herself getting close enough for him to reach out a hand, take her by the wrist, and—

"I was lucky enough to have the figure of an uncle," he volunteered suddenly. "A decent, engaged uncle in my life. He cared where my parents did not. It made all the difference."

"A brother of your mother, was it?"

"God no. My mother has so many brothers I'm not sure I've made the acquaintance of all of them."

"Your mother is still alive?" Drew asked, surprised.

He waved the notion away. "I'd not look to her as a resource, if I were you. She lives in the Scottish Highlands, and she is loath to leave it. Ever. She had almost no part in raising Timothea, the legacy of which is still felt today, I think you'd agree. She had even less to do with me."

"Oh," said Drew. "I . . . I'm sorry." She took a few more steps, now almost even with him.

He shrugged. "If you take into consideration my mother and the twins' mother, it's an *advantage* that you can manage the girls without their interfering. The girls listen to you; they respond to you."

"They listen, I'll give them that. Respond? I'm not so sure."

"Your handling of Imogene after the . . . incident with the boy was brilliant." He slid his boot from the bench and tapped it against her foot.

Drew stared at the hem of her skirt where his foot had arced beneath.

"Oh. Well," she said.

Was he touching her? Or kicking her?

No, not a kick. It was the brotherly gesture of kinship, the boot-to-slipper equivalent of clinking glasses after a toast.

"You could have shamed her," he went on, "which you didn't, but you made your point just the same."

"I wasn't certain what could be heard from outside the carriage." Had he listened as she detailed her broken heart? Had he heard Imogene's accusation that she'd never been kissed?

"It occurs to me I should ask you to sit," he said, dropping his head to the side and considering her. This made no sense, because his body currently occupied all of the bench. To join him, they would have to . . . crowd.

"I am admiring the art," she said.

"You'll force me to stand," he threatened. "Gentlemanly custom and all that."

"It's not necessary to play the gentleman on my behalf, Your Grace. I'm merely . . ." She paused. Drew's father had actually been a baronet of some means. Her sister was married to an earl, and her stepsister was a royal princess. Humility had been part of Drew's transformation, but she found herself suddenly unable to assert that she was not a lady.

She turned away, stepping around his leg. A marble bust loomed nearby and she came to stop before it.

"Never tempt a man *not* to act like a gentleman," he said from behind her.

Drew's heart sprouted wings and began to flap inside her chest.

She stared at the bust. He was an olive branch–crowned ancient, with flat, white eyes. He saw nothing, and Drew saw nothing. Her every sense was trained on the booted footsteps coming up behind her.

"I could hear your conversation from the coachman's box," he said over her shoulder. "Tom showed me how to listen in. The servants know everything, in case there was any doubt. I've no idea why I endeavor to meet with you behind closed doors."

"Why, indeed?"

"The point is, Miss Trelayne, this afternoon could have ended in a very great disaster for Imogene, but it did not. You reached her in time. You lent exactly the correct amount of muscle to the situation without inflicting lasting damage, I hope. Well done. I cannot believe our luck, honestly."

Drew turned round. "Luck?"

He propped a hand on the pillar beside her head and looked down at her. "Yes, luck. Prince Adolphus could have attached anyone to us, couldn't he? We're very fortunate to have you. You've not made out so lucky, I'm afraid."

She smiled at the praise, looking up into his eyes. Surely she could permit herself to bask in statements like this. Compliments to her professional proficiency?

"Did you hear the bit about T.O.E.?" she ventured, trying desperately to speak only of her work.

"Yes. She's said nothing more about it?"

"Nothing."

"God only knows what she meant. Then again, it sounds as if T.O.E.'s rules about fraternization are not so different than society's."

"I had the same thought," she said. "Imogene has a world of frustration ahead of her if she intends to challenge what it means for a girl to be 'ruined.' I cannot think of a more unyielding law of social order."

"Unyielding," he repeated lowly. He was staring at her lips.

Drew's mouth watered. She held her breath. She dropped her own gaze to his mouth.

"You're very pretty, Miss Trelayne," he said. This came out slowly, as if he realized each word as he said it.

"Your Grace," she whispered. Her heartbeat was a peck in her throat; a fast, sharp, relentless peck. Her cheeks were on fire. She couldn't breathe, and yet she no longer seemed to require breath. She subsisted on whatever he would say next.

"Clever *and* pretty," he said. "What insect jewelry have you worn tonight?"

Her gown was aquamarine; a favorite of her evening frocks. She'd hoped to show off another of Mrs. Tavertine's creations to the girls. She'd also hoped, foolishly, that he would notice that it matched the color of her eyes.

"I wear butterflies," she rasped, "with this gown."

"Where?" he wanted to know, leaning back to study her throat, ears, and wrists. She felt a burning sort of buzz everywhere his gaze fell.

"They are pins," she said. "In my hair."

He leaned in, searching the top of her head.

She laughed. Only the Duke of Lachlan was tall enough to study the top of her head.

"At the nape," she whispered, gently touching the spot where she coiled her coronet braids into a bun behind her head.

The duke stooped and leaned in, following her hand.

He was close, so very close. She felt his breath on her neck. The smell of him was all she knew, soap, and wine, and the musky scent of him. It blotted out the acrid smell of the cavernous room. The thick barrier of his body was warm against the draft.

"Miss Trelayne?" he whispered; his words slid across her skin like a foot sliding into a slipper. The perfect fit.

"Your Grace," she whispered back.

"I . . . want." It was all he said.

She waited. His eyes left her mouth, darted to her eyes—a question—and then looked back to her mouth.

Drew tried very hard to assign some reasonable excuse for him to look at her this way.

His hearing had gone off and he needed to read her lips?

Some piece of her meal was stuck in her teeth?

He'd suffered a dizzy spell and needed to keep his eyes on a fixed point in the room?

He was . . .

She'd run out of possibilities.

"'*You want . . .*'" she repeated, a breathless prompt.

There was no air to be had in the world. She existed in that underwater moment when your lungs needed air, but the surface of the water seemed leagues away. She was consumed by a little bit of panic and a great amount of need.

"Would you be open to a kiss, Miss Trelayne?" he asked.

"A kiss?" she asked, barely speaking.

"*Mmm-hmm,*" he rumbled, as he dipped his head. His nose was just inches from her jaw.

"To test the unyielding societal rule?" she guessed.

"No."

"To celebrate today's progress?"

"No."

"But . . . why?"

"If I must think of a reason . . ." he said, but then he trailed off.

They stood so very close, they shared the same air. Warm, whisker-rough angles of his face brushed against her nose, her chin, her ear. With every tantalizing scrape, sparks rose in her chest, and she raised her chin, seeking, wanting.

Desire unspooled inside her, a tight, corded rope stretching to the limit.

Again, she repeated his words, prompting him, "'*If I must think of a reason . . .*'"

"Right," he breathed, and he nudged closer. Her shoulders leaned into the arm he'd propped on the pillar. The wool of his coat and the silk of his waistcoat rasped against the ruffle of her bodice. His thigh pressed into the layers of her skirt.

"The reason is," he began lowly, speaking against her neck, "you told the girls you'd never had a kiss, and

I couldn't believe it. I haven't been able to stop thinking about it. I've been driven to distraction, Miss Trelayne, thinking about your unkissed . . . state. *You* are a distraction to me. *You* and your unkissed mouth."

"Oh," she said.

"*And* because I want to."

*I want*, she thought, agreeing. The two words sang through her; there was a chorus of want.

She didn't trust her voice. She nodded instead.

God help her, she ducked her face to seek out his lips.

*LIKELY, THIS IS a very bad idea*, Ian thought, his last truly coherent thought before he kissed her.

But then she was there, *really* there. Not nearby. Not jostled against him. In his arms, against his chest. Her lips were parted, seeking him—and he descended. The kiss was harder than he'd intended. Actually, he'd had no intention, like so many pinnacle moments in his life, he'd not seen it until he lived it.

One minute they'd been talking about the girls, and then they *hadn't* been talking about the girls, and then his brain lost track of the conversation, and he could only think how very close she was, and how very curious he'd been about how she would feel and taste.

He'd had the forethought to ask permission only because he'd been a gentleman once upon a time. This was a new role: Portrait Gallery Stalker. Also new: Kisser of Staff. After acknowledging these, all forethought and afterthought and good sense evaded him entirely, because kissing her was (this, he *had* predicted) so thoroughly incinerating, his consciousness caught flame like a very dry log, every hollow and nook suddenly engulfed, licking hot.

She didn't know how to kiss; she hadn't lied about this. If curiosity had led him to this moment, his reward was the incredibly arousing act of slowing down, of sliding his hands to her shoulders and squaring her in front of him, of widening his stance, of starting from the beginning. Teaching. Coaxing. A soft, slow peck. Once. Twice. The third time, he lingered, fitting his bottom lip below hers. She responded to each soft peck with a little jolt, leaning in to follow him. He smiled at her eagerness and then nibbled, ever so softly, just at the corner of her mouth. When her lips parted, he hovered there, his mouth bussing against hers, waiting for her. Immediately, gratifyingly, she sought more, and he deepened the kiss, swiping his tongue across her bottom lip.

She let out a delicious little gasp and he inhaled it, allowing her to seek more still, to take the lead. It was exhilarating and mind erasing and thuddingly erotic.

Ian couldn't remember ever teaching a girl to kiss—his dalliances generally involved eager tavern girls or merry widows, women who'd been in the correct place at the correct time. When their ingenuity and eagerness managed to distract him from a card game, or overtake his departure from the theater, who was he to stop them?

But this? This was something else entirely.

She offered plenty of eagerness but there was no ingenuity, and he loved it.

His hands slid down her arms and swept her back, and he stopped trying to define any of it. What use were definitions when he held her—finally held her. She was so gracefully tall, and lithe, and thin—yet not so thin that her waist didn't dip; that the slope of her hips didn't swoop. Wherever his hands roamed, she trembled and melded closer. The swirl of lust and sensation sucked him under, and he allowed it. He happily drowned in it.

When a working thought did flash into his brain, it was a simple, animalistic demand. *Let me show you. Let me taste you. We'll want more of this. We'll want everything.*

He cupped his right hand against her hip, anchoring her to him, and traced her arm with his left. When he came to her hand, he tugged it up, wrapping it around his neck. She took hold immediately, threading her fingers into the hair and holding on. Now she wasn't simply being held, she was holding; now she wasn't simply seeking his mouth, she was slanting her head, deepening the kiss.

*Yes*, he thought. *That's it.* He staggered back a step; she was kissing him nearly off his feet. He caught her around the ribs, squeezed the delicate smallness of her waist and pressed her to him, balling handfuls of her skirt. He wanted to pick her up, to wrap her legs around him, to carry her.

He broke the kiss for a moment to scan the room. Where could he—? His grandfather's useless room with useless statues and nowhere to—

The bench. There was no other option. Literally, it was the bench or the floor because this kiss was sapping him of his ability to stand.

"Miss Trelayne," he whispered, scraping his emerging beard across her mouth, pressing her lips to his ear, feeling her breath.

"Mmm-hmm?" she whispered, a moan, seeking his mouth again.

"Up you go," he said, and he slid his hands from her waist to palm her bottom and lift her, sliding her up his body. She didn't know enough, God love her, to straddle him, her body remained straight, although languid and loose, her neck bent and face downturned to maintain the kiss.

On a gasp, she broke away. "You can't," she panted. "I'm too—You haven't the strength."

"Never say it," he breathed, backing to the bench. "I could carry you anywhere. Don't tempt me to carry you anywhere."

She giggled against his mouth, a magical, delighted sound, the laugh of a much younger woman, a debutante.

When he made contact with the bench, he fell back with little grace. His only care was to brace her, to bring her down with him. He hit the velvet with a thud and guided her, hands just above her hips, gently on top of him. When she was stable, he used his knees and thighs to align her *just right.* He had the idle thought that no woman had ever felt like such a perfect fit. When her face was close, he allowed her to fall the last six inches, dropping her against his chest until they were nose-to-nose.

"Oh!" she said, and he devoured the sound, recapturing her kiss-swollen mouth, smoothing his hands down her back to grab up large handfuls of her skirts. He stretched one leg down the bench and bent the other at the knee, supporting them with a boot on the ground.

She'd grasped him by the shoulders when he'd lifted her, and she still hadn't let go.

He broke away to whisper, "Touch me?" A plea.

She answered immediately; diligent, seeking hands sank into his hair, roved his neck, cupped his face. She explored down his chest and found the edge of his coat. Moving quickly, she slid a tentative hand beneath the wool of his lapel. Ian hissed in pleasure, encouraging her, and she delved deeper. The coat suddenly became a burden he could not bear, a barrier to her touch, and he lifted them slightly to strip out of it, hurling it to the side. The waistcoat came next and he ripped the thing, sending buttons flying.

She sat in his lap, her legs now straddling him properly, watching with an intoxicating expression of lust and excitement. In his shirtsleeves now, he fell back, but not before he took up her hands and planted them on his chest.

"Touch me," he implored again; and again she complied, sliding her hands up over the bare skin of his throat, down his shoulders, and along his ribs. She didn't just touch him, she *felt* him, as if she was memorizing his anatomy, as if she was searching his body for a deeply hidden area in urgent need of immediate attention.

*Search southward*, he thought, painfully aware of the most urgent, attention-seeking area, but he said nothing, kissing her again, reveling in her enthusiasm and her innocent exploration.

Without thinking he rocked to the left, making it easier for her to slide her hands inside his shirt. He caught her about the waist with one hand and cradled the back of her head with the other, sliding his fingers into her soft, springy braid. The butterfly pins pricked his palm. He toyed with them, loosening their hold and plucking them free—first one, then another, then another. He dropped them to the floor and returned to the braid, digging his fingers in, loosening, massaging. Soft strands of seemingly endless curls fell loose, his palm full of them, and he tugged gently, eliciting a moan.

"Miss Trelayne," he mumbled against her lips. "You're— This—Please—"

His hands left her hair, roving over slim shoulders, swiping fingers beneath the sagging rim of her bodice. One hand slid down her body and hitched her skirts. Her legs were encased in silk stockings.

"*Yes*," she gasped, shimmying against him. Her hand clutched the shoulder of his shirt.

"You are perfectly formed," he marveled. "Exactly, perfectly correct. Every delicious bit."

"I'm—" She didn't finish. He kissed away whatever she would say.

She made a sound that was part sigh, part coo, and his fingertips delved deeper inside her bodice, tracing the shape of one perfect breast. The hand on her leg climbed higher, finding the spot on her thigh where the stockings dropped off and warm skin emerged.

He was just about to flip her flat on her back, to do—well, he'd not thought of precisely what he would do—when voices, excitable, high-pitched voices, a chorus—no, *a mob* of voices—and a very bright light forced their way into his lust-slogged brain.

Ian paused, listening.

He snapped his head up, squinting into the light.

He frow—

"Uncle? Uncle? *Uncle*?! Whatever are you doing to Miss Trelayne?"

His niece Imogene stood in the center of the gallery, one

theatrical hand on her throat, another clutching what was surely the largest lamp in the house.

Beside her, Timothea stood in her dressing gown, studying Ian's position with Miss Trelayne like an artist preparing to sketch life models.

Beside *her*, stood Ivy, looking on with concerned interest, her arms filled with their demon cat.

Behind this trio stood a scrum of servants, from Greenly the butler, to Mrs. Hearst the housekeeper, to seemingly every last maid and footman and, unless he was mistaken, the boy who delivered the milk and eggs at dawn.

Ian looked down at Miss Trelayne. She stared up at him, teal eyes wide with disbelief and horror. She slid her hand from his shoulder and dropped it over her eyes. She turned her face away.

When she moved, one long curly strand of hair slid from the bench and swung back and forth, nearly sweeping the floor.

Ian swore, looked back to the assembled witnesses, swore again. He sat up, maneuvering his body in front of Miss Trelayne to shield her as best he could.

He acted on instinct, as he always did in his many wrong-minded, ill-advised, disastrous moments of life reckoning.

"Everybody out but Lady Tribble," he said, whipping his wilted cravat from the bench and draping it across Miss Trelayne's chest.

"Uncle?" Imogene tried again, but Ian cut her off.

"Miss Trelayne and I have found ourselves . . ." he cocked his head and considered the best word to describe how they had found themselves, ". . . overcome. We'll require five minutes of solitude and twenty fewer people in this room. Everybody but Lady Tribble—*out*!" This he bellowed, and servants began to back away. The cat leapt from Ivy's arms and galloped toward the door. Ivy spun and gave chase.

Imogene studied them a moment more, a look of—unless Ian was mistaken—spiteful satisfaction on her face. Then she turned and followed her sister and the cat.

Only Timothea remained.

Ian waited until the room had cleared and then he looked up at his sister.

She was running her fingers through her hair, idly combing it. "You'll have to marry her now, Ian," she said tiredly. "Even I know that."

"No, we don't have t—" he began, but then he stopped. What could he possibly say?

Miss Trelayne had just explained the precise guidelines governing this precise situation.

She'd explained that it wouldn't matter if they didn't know each other. And that no one would care about their personal preferences.

Ian stood up. Miss Trelayne made a noise of distress, and he was reminded, stupidly, numbly, that she lay prone on the bench.

"Can you stay with her while I see to my clothes?" he asked his sister.

"Ian, you must speak to her," said his sister.

Ian craned around to look at Miss Trelayne. Of course he should speak to her. She looked like the victim of a shipwreck washed onto rocks. One unfurled braid hung to the floor. Her skirts were a tangle, and she'd drawn up her knees to conceal her legs. Her bodice was askew. She'd not removed the slim hand from her eyes.

"Miss Trelayne?" he began, uncertain of what else he would say. He hated not having time to prepare what he might say. "Miss Trelay—"

"Not speak to her *now*, Ian, for God's sake," cut in Timothea, "give her a moment."

"Right," he said, uncertain. Slowly, he turned back. He stood. He stooped to pick up his discarded garments. "I will leave you. Can you accompany her to the library in ten minutes?"

"I was already in bed, actually," observed his sister.

"*Timothea*," he growled.

"I'll not stand for your beratement," Timothea declared, "and neither should Miss Trelayne."

"No one is berating anyone else," Ian said tiredly. "Forgive me. I . . . I—"

Ian had no words for what he had or hadn't done. His mind was a riot of shock and regret. He didn't regret what they'd done so much as that they'd been caught. And wasn't that a grievance as old as time?

It wasn't self-interest; he simple hated being caught by surprise. Kissing Miss Trelayne had been the opposite of a surprise. He'd been fixated on it for days; he'd imagined it fifty times. The dreadful surprise had been—well, it had been that they'd been forced to stop. Of course he would bungle whatever came next.

He glanced at his sister. Timothea had not agreed to ferry her to the library, and for once he prayed she would simply do as he asked. If he was a failure at surprises, she was the enemy of reasonable requests.

"Timothea?" he prompted. "The library. Will you assist Miss Trelayne?"

"Yes, Ian," she sighed, "of course, I can hardly leave her here, in the gallery, with Grandpapa's soulless statues, can I?"

"Thank you," he said and stalked to the door on hollow legs, his leaden footsteps the only sound in the room.

*Chapter Fifteen*

Drewsmina was overcome with panic.

It was the sort of stomach-pitching, mind-blanking surge that precipitated the hurling of crockery. Or maddened sprinting into the night.

But Drew could neither shatter plates nor sprint away. She could only trudge, eyes forward, face aflame, as Lady Tribble endeavored to find the library.

"It was on the second floor, I am certain of it," mumbled Lady Tribble. "He wouldn't have *moved* it, surely. There are a great many books. It would take *days* to *move a library*."

Finally, a statement ridiculous enough to pierce her stunned state. Drew was tempted to steal a look, but she kept her gaze straight ahead. She was terrified of catching the eye of a passing servant, or the girls, or even of Lady Tribble herself. The baroness might be lost in her own home, but she was still a gentlewoman, and the mother of her clients, and she could sack Drew in a heartbeat.

Instead, she led Drew through a warren of corridors that

would end, presumably, at the Duke of Lachlan, who would sack her.

*What in God's name*, she thought, *had I been thinking? Truly?*

Kissing her employer, however natural it felt, however a two-person crime (when they came down to it), would be considered worse than stealing the silver or fisticuffs with a servant.

Kissing her employer invited banishment—and not just from this job—from all future jobs, from all decent society.

Her sister, Ana, (who, let's be honest, had done her fair share of illicit kissing), would have every right to terminate Drew's privileges as the Spinster Sister Who Lived Upstairs, and she was just spiteful enough to do it. This meant Drew could add "homeless" to the reordered version of her future. That said nothing of the heartbreak it would cause Cynde.

Drew squeezed her eyes shut, staving off the sting of tears. Her throat felt painfully thick, as if she choked on smoke. How fitting, as the life she'd been carefully building for herself rapidly burned to the ground.

"Ah, here 'tis," said Lady Tribble, opening a door to reveal . . . a tiny room with one bricked-over window.

"Oh, perhaps not," the baroness sighed, crestfallen. "Perhaps—"

"*Timothea*," said Lachlan, calling from an adjacent door. His voice sounded curt and irritated. "Here."

Drew's gaze had been fixed on a point in the middle distance, but she turned at the sound of his voice like a weed following the sun.

*Silly, silly, stupid girl.*

She caught a glimpse of him before he disappeared through the door. He'd restored his clothing. His movements were brisk and efficient. He looked like he had before he'd shattered the window in Kew Palace. It would be no effort to dismiss her.

"Oh right," said Lady Tribble tiredly. "I knew we'd nearly found it." She drifted inside.

Drew paused, hovering on the precipice.

If she felt outrage in this moment, if it felt unfair that they'd both been discovered but only *she* would stand for shameful judgment, Drew tamped it down. What could she possibly expect? Glorified governesses were not entitled to outrage. They were entitled only to survive this moment without more indignity, then to leave this house, possibly to leave London. To transform again, assuming there were any incarnations left of Drewsmina Trelayne.

She took a deep breath and squeezed her eyes shut, trying to wring out unshed tears. Her heart, which had felt like a cold, dead stone these last ten minutes, now sprang to life, thumping like the wings of a large bird.

"Where is she?" clipped Lachlan, his voice carrying from inside.

"She is in the corridor, Ian," said Lady Tribble defensively. "Keep calm, for God's sake."

"Where?" demanded Lachlan.

"I am here, Your Grace," said Drew, stepping inside.

"Oh," said the duke. "Right. Very good. Come in."

He was seated behind a massive desk in the center of the room. He picked up a folio of papers and tossed them aside. He slid a piece of parchment in front of him and took up a pen, dipping it in the ink pot.

*He cannot look at me*, she realized, the flapping bird of her heart sank into a dive.

"Miss Trelayne," he began. "I—"

"I'm so incredibly sorry," Drew said in a gush. The words fell from her mouth like stolen silver from a pillowcase.

"It's not—" he began.

"Ian?" interrupted Lady Tribble absently.

Drew and Lachlan turned to Lady Tribble.

"Where are Grandpapa's books on Roman mythology?"

While they watched, Lady Tribble drifted from the desk to wander between two bookshelves. She disappeared down the aisle.

There was a moment of silence. Drew glanced at Lachlan. Remarkably, he met her gaze. The bird in her heart swooped upward again. Lachlan's expression was not angry or cold or bitter. He cocked his chin toward the bookshelves and then looked back to Drew. His face said, *Surely she's joking?*

Drew blinked, a flash of delight momentarily blotting out their terrible reckoning.

"Why am I not surprised?" he mumbled. He cast another quick glance at Drew and then back to his paperwork.

He started again, "What is your view, Miss Trelayne, on what comes next? What would you tell us to do, if you, yourself, were not part of . . . of the 'us' in question?"

Drew stared at him. "You're asking me, Your Grace?"

"Yes, of course. It's an odd request, I know. Honestly, I wasn't aware how desperate I was for useful counsel—"

"You were clearly desperate for something," came the voice of Lady Tribble from behind a shelf, "but 'useful counsel,' it was not. If I'm being honest."

The duke froze, flicked his eyes to Drew, and then looked away.

"I was going to say," he continued, "how much I required useful counsel until you came along." He cleared his throat. "This runs contrary, I know, to my need to, er, draw you into a kiss."

"Oh, that was far more than a kiss," came the voice of Lady Tribble again.

The duke pivoted in his chair to stare down the aisle.

"I stand corrected," he said, turning back. "*Far more than a kiss*. I should like to point out that I do not make a habit of kissing and . . . 'and far more' . . . members of my staff. Not on a regular basis. Not ever, actually. Just to be clear. In fact, this would be my first ever time to commit such an infraction, so—"

"Not true," sang Lady Tribble from the back of the room. "What of the milkmaid from Frampton?"

Lachlan swore. "The milkmaid was not a member of staff. And I was all of fourteen years old. If you cannot join the conversation here, at the desk, Timothea, pray do not interject."

Drew watched him struggle with irritation, with chagrin, with something else she couldn't name.

*He is human*, she thought. In her mortification, she'd allow herself to forget this.

He began again. "What are your thoughts, Miss Trelayne?"

"Ah," she began.

"Ignore my sister," he said.

"Well," ventured Drew, "if I'd witnessed the . . . the incident, I suppose I would ask you how well you could contain the gossip among your staff. Do you trust them? If they can be asked not to discuss what they've seen, then perhaps we could all . . . walk away without anyone being the wiser. The girls are another story, but if I took them into confidence, if I explained . . . explained . . ."

Here Drew faltered, because she had no idea how she could explain. What could she possibly say? That she'd felt a deep, unshakable attraction to the duke from the moment she'd seen him lurking in the antechamber of Kew Palace? That the attraction had mounted, like a thirst she could not quench? And when he offered—nay, when he'd pulled her to him—she'd seen the chance, at last, to drink? The sheer bliss of that moment had drowned all reason, and good sense, and her future. She swam about in the sensation of it and, at the time, considered it so very worth the cost. Until . . . it wasn't. Until this moment, standing before him, helping determine some way to be dismissed while pretending to be grateful that he wasn't tossing her out on her ear?

She could hardly tell him *that*.

"No, no, that would never work," Lachlan was saying. He rolled from the chair and began to pace. "We traveled from Avenelle with a very small staff. Few servants were willing to remain in my employ after the riot—not near enough to keep pace with a London household. I hired ten city servants, at least, when we arrived. They'll have no loyalty to me, not when it comes to a morsel as delicious as this. The Duke of Lachlan kissing a governess? God help me."

"Not just kissing," interjected Lady Tribble from the back of the room.

"Bloody hell, Timothea—can you not attend us and make some useful suggestion? What in God's name are you doing in the shadows?"

"I've been searching for this library all week," said Lady Tribble, emerging from the shelves with a small stack of books. "Books were frowned upon at the Temple."

"Right," gritted out the duke, "but your search for leisure reading is not the goal of this conversation. We're making some decision. About . . . about Miss Trelayne."

"I would like to return to my rooms," declared Lady Tribble.

"Do not leave us alone together," Lachlan countered.

"Do not leave me, asleep on my feet, in this library," shot back Lady Tribble. "I'm tired and I wish to go to bed."

"And tell your daughters what?" Lachlan asked. "Timothea? Second to your great fatigue and search for a bedtime story, we've convened here to work out some answer for the girls."

Lady Tribble flipped open the topmost book and stared at the page. She did not answer.

"Are you aware that, just this morning," began Lachlan, "Miss Trelayne explained the consequences for assignations between unmarried men and women to the girls? In no uncertain terms, she explained it. It was beautifully put. And not untrue. So *now what*?"

"So *now*," said Lady Tribble, speaking to the book, "Miss Trelayne, whom you've hired for this very purpose, may interpret the scene in the gallery *to* them and *for* them. 'Tis her job."

"Interpret it for them *how*, Timothea?" bit out Lachlan. "She is involved—chiefly, *primarily*—she is involved. She can hardly make a lesson of it when she was one of the . . . er, players."

Humiliation, hot and sticky, melted down Drew's body like wax down a candle.

"It'll be ever so easy to explain if you *marry her*, Ian," said Lady Tribble.

The melting sensation stopped cold.

Lady Tribble clunked down the books on the desk. "There, I've said it. Now may I be excused from this conversation?"

"Timothea—" he began.

"No!" refused the baroness. "Do not 'Timothea' me. I've said it. *Twice*, I've said it. What other choice do you have, Ian? This effort to cast around for any other option confuses me. Do you intend to turn her out? Claim something like 'indecency' or some such? Nonsense—please think again. I've witnessed enough piety and sanctimonious scorekeeping to last a lifetime. It's exhausting. And unsporting. And boring, really. I'd recommend anything but."

"Of course I would not turn her out for indecency," Lachlan said. He glanced at Drew and then away. The conversation had begun to feel like a tennis match, with Drew's future as the ball.

"So you believe you can pass it all off as a trick of the light? Or a misunderstanding?" Lady Tribble went on. "Please. Imogene and Ivy may have been sheltered these last five years, but they are not stupid. And certainly the servants know what they've seen. The only choice is to marry her, Ian. If she will have you. Now—" she took a deep breath and gathered her books "—I've a headache. And I've said all I can on the matter."

"You're going?" Lachlan stated.

"Yes, I'm going. I was already abed when Imogene roused me."

"Roused you, did she?" he asked. "And what reason, pray, did she give for summoning you to a room of the house into which no one ever goes in the middle of the night?"

"She heard a terrible ruckus. Fighting, she thought. Or a fire. She is very astute."

"Oh yes, she's devilishly astute. At least now we know how she convened the vast audience."

Lady Tribble was headed to the door. "If you intend to implicate Genie in your dalliance, I urge you to think again. This is your problem, Ian, not Imogene's."

"Oh the irony," he shot back. "Just this morning, Miss Trelayne was given to chase one of Imogene's would-be paramours down an alley. She recovered her before Imogene was forced to consider anything like . . . like *marriage to a stranger*. Imogene was spared, but we are not."

*He is a duke and I am a stranger, and they keep repeating the word* marriage *as if it is a real consideration.* Drew wanted to crawl out the window.

"Oh yes, so ironic," scolded Lady Tribble. "Except Imogene is sixteen and you are thirty-three. Perhaps you should adhere to your own counsel on the matter. Good night, Ian. You've evicted me from my bed, marched me about the house, implicated my innocent daughters, and now you've *trapped* me here to hound me for the opinion I've already stated."

"I'm not trying to inconvenience you, Timothea, I'm—"

She spun back. "Who else do you intend to marry, Ian, I ask you? Your evasion of the obvious is so very great, you've made me curious. And it takes quite a lot to pique my curiosity, believe me. So, congratulations—now for the reckoning."

"What the devil does it matter who I marry?" he shouted back, glancing at Drew.

"Who? Say it," pressed Lady Tribble.

Lachlan went silent.

Drew closed her eyes shut.

The only thing worse than being turned out by the duke would be to hear him say what all of them already knew: he would not have her.

TIMOTHEA JOSTLED THE stack of books in her arms, shaking her head back and forth. He'd provoked her to anger, and he'd done it on purpose. She did not overstate the threat of a "reckoning." Ian didn't care. He *needed more time*. He had his own reckoning—with Rucker Loring and the distressing news he'd brought from Avenelle, with his tenants, with Imogene and Ivy—the last thing he needed was to unexpectedly acquire a surprise wife.

"I like Miss Trelayne," Timothea was now declaring. "She reminds me of Diana the Huntress."

An image of Miss Trelayne in a toga, her long legs peeking from the slit, her hair loose down her bare back, flashed in Ian's mind.

"If there is no other girl," Timothea demanded, "then why not her? Have someone else in mind, do you?"

"If you must know," Ian blurted out, "I thought to marry someone from Dorset."

"Dorset?" Timothea made a face. "Who? Why?"

"Because," he gritted out, "of *our mother.*"

Timothea's frown deepened. Their mother was an enigma to Ian, she lived in Scotland and they were barely acquainted, but her relationship with Timothea was more complicated.

"Her resentment?" Ian reminded. "Her unhappiness. She stewed in misery at Avenelle, and we all suffered. She never recovered from being plucked from Scotland and transplanted to Dorset. She was homesick and displaced, a disastrous combination in a wife and a mother. If I marry the daughter of local gentry, at least her life will be familiar. She'll be close to her people."

"Who?" demanded Lady Tribble. "Which daughter of local gentry?"

Ian waved a dismissive hand. "Sir Nevil Flemming has six or seven daughters. Blondes of various shapes and sizes. Fond of terriers."

"*Which* Flemming daughter?"

Ian shrugged and turned away. "What does it matter? I cannot tell one from the other."

Timothea made a shrill sound of frustration and dropped

her stack of books to the floor. "The interchangeable blond daughters of Sir Nevil? Look, Ian, I've made countless mistakes in life—this I admit, readily. I am distractable, I follow my own passions, I am true to myself to the exclusion of all others. But hear me now: I was a happy wife to Tribble. Exceedingly happy, happier than ever I've been. Marriage, in my view, is precious. A gift. A *relief*.

"And it has very little to do with . . . *geography*," she went on. "Mama was unhappy because she was married to a miserable man who made no effort to know her and even less to provide the most basic comfort.

"I've seen the other side of the coin, and it's magical," she said softly. "For however long it lasts. I mourn Tribble every day. His passing left me so very lost, it was so painful to be alone, I . . . I subjected myself and our dear girls to that wretched . . . wretched—" and now her voice broke.

"Timmie," Ian said, taking a step to her. Miss Trelayne was closer, and she hesitated only a moment before she wrapped an arm around Timothea's waist.

"Have a care, my lady," Miss Trelayne whispered. "You're overtired. Our predicament is not worth upsetting you. We've kept you from your bed."

*It* is *worth upsetting her*, Ian wanted to shout. How long had he waited for some . . . honesty from his sister?

He edged closer, wanting to touch her, but touch was not naturally achieved in their family. Neither were discussions of honest emotion.

"No one can fully understand," Timothea sniffled. "I know I was wrong to be swept up by the Temple. But I was so very heartbroken. And alone. And . . ." She let out a sob.

"Timmie," whispered Ian, his reservations forgotten. He put his hands on her shoulders and tipped his forehead to rest against her hair. He was defeated and exhausted. He'd tried so very hard to restore his relationship with his sister and nieces, but he felt like he'd gone ten rounds in the boxing ring and lost.

"*No*," Timothea said suddenly. She jerked away. She

spun toward the wall, gulping in air, her shoulders rising and falling.

"I'll not speak of it," she vowed. "It's not . . . my way. I *detest* speaking of it. And you've no wish to hear it."

"That is untrue," Ian said. "I've had no other goal these last three months than to learn what happened and how I can help. I want to know all of it. I failed you by not knowing more until tonight. I was unavailable when you needed me, and I take full responsibility for that failing. I regret it daily. I was too consumed by my own scandal."

"If you want to do right by me," said Timothea, speaking between breaths, "leave it. I didn't return to Avenelle to be hounded."

She turned back, wiping the tears from her eyes in brisk, angry swipes. "My books, if you please."

Ian stared at her. She wanted to go. She didn't care about the scene in the gallery, and he couldn't ignore Miss Trelayne any longer.

He stooped to recover his sister's books.

"So . . . *marry*," Ian repeated quietly, testing Timothea's suggestion. "Marry Miss Trelayne. A woman I've only just met. *Not* a girl from a neighboring family I've known my whole life."

"You are impossible, Ian," Timothea snapped, taking the books. "In my experience, you *marry* the girl you toppled upon the gallery bench, your hand up her skirt, *not* a neighbor you can hardly identify. *If* she'll have you. And that is no small 'if.'"

And then, as Ian's face burned, his sister spun on her heal and marched out.

He stared at the empty doorway, listening to her retreating footsteps.

He turned back to Miss Trelayne. She, too, stared at the vacant door, her cheeks crimson.

"There is a small chance she cannot find her way back to her chamber," said Miss Trelayne.

Ian laughed. "You're very clever," he said. "On top of everything else."

"Your sister is scandalized, I fear."

"Another joke," he said. "Of all the many injustices suffered by my sister, scandal doesn't seem to be one of them. To her, I believe our predicament has had almost no impact."

"Lucky us," she muttered.

"Are we?" he said, making his way to his desk.

"No. I don't suppose we are."

Ian didn't reply. She was correct, of course, but it unsettled him to hear her agree so readily.

"Right," he said. "Now what? We've heard my sister's opinion. I'm sorry for the . . . the unchecked nature of that conversation. You've gotten an earful tonight. On top of everything else."

"I'm sorry to have distressed Lady Tribble."

"*Lady Tribble's* rank and money protect her from many hardships in life, but not all of them—as we've heard. You, however, have no such protection, I assume."

"No," she said.

He allowed himself to look at her, to really looked at her for the first time since he'd kissed her. Her hair was a riot of tangled red curls piled on top of her head. Her skirts were wrinkled. The cream of her skin was interrupted here and there with little pink abrasions where he'd dragged his beard.

*I did that.* The thought rose, unbidden in his mind. It was followed, unhelpfully, by, *And I want to do it again.*

Well, at least now he knew why he looked at her like a man leery of gazing into the sun. Looking at her made him burn. He turned his back and made for his desk.

"So is that the extent of your solution, to ask the servants not to gossip?"

"I . . . I should go away."

"Go? Go where?"

She stared at him.

"Sorry," he said, "I'm not trying to be obtuse; but the thought of you leaving had not crossed my mind."

Of course she couldn't *go*, he thought. He'd only just gotten her. Who would manage the twins? Who would—?

"Well, I have a cousin in France," she said. "There is also America. Canada."

"Banishment? What you're describing is banishment. Fleeing the bloody country."

"I cannot stay, Your Grace. It would ruin the girls for me to stay."

"But you've a business to launch. You have plans. The finishing school. You've enlisted a royal princess to drum up clients. You cannot move to Canada."

"No family in England will hire a stylist who disgraced herself with her employer, I assure you. I'm writing a reference book, for God's sake. A little manual called *Drewsmina Trelayne's Rules and Comportment*. I cannot proffer *rules* if I'm also known to break them."

"Disgraced herself with her employer?" he repeated, testing the phrase. It hadn't felt like disgrace. It had felt like . . . walking out into the sunlight after tromping about in a dank cave.

"This is madness," he said, his voice a growl.

He shoved up from the desk.

He stared at her.

He looked at the ceiling.

The words he wanted to say echoed in his head once, twice, and then . . . out they came.

"Timothea is correct, for once," he said. "We shall marry. Marriage will calm the immediate crisis. As to the long-term complications? I cannot say."

"Your Grace—"

"Bollocks proposal, I know."

"Lachlan," she said. "*Your Grace*. You cannot mean this."

"On the contrary, I mean it far more than I've meant the

previous calamities into which I've hurled myself. No one will perish, hopefully, because of this marriage. Rioters will not come at soldiers with pitchforks and torches. My sister will get her way for once rather than simply . . . drifting along. My nieces may continue their refinement under your incredibly generous tutelage. Certainly I'll find no one better suited to deal with the two of them, not if I searched a hundred years. I can hardly relegate you to Canada if for no other reason than Imogene and Ivy."

"But are you suggesting real marriage?" she asked, her voice a rasp. "As in, I should be a duchess—*your* duchess?"

"Yes, God help us," he said. "There will be far-reaching ramifications, so pause a moment and consider."

"Your Grace."

He continued, suddenly terrified she would actually *pause* or earnestly *consider.* "I have every intention of returning to Avenelle after I've made some effort to abolish this export tax and the girls have had their Season. Your home is in London, obviously. It's exactly the sort of scenario I'd hoped to avoid, so naturally it's precisely what we face. We'll sort out some . . . some . . . 'arrangement.' I've no wish to make you miserable in Dorset."

"Well," she began, "perhaps the 'arrangement' should mean we *appear* to be, er, betrothed, and when the gossip is forgotten and the girls have had their Season, I . . . I— Then we could dissolve the betrothal."

He studied her face, trying to discern her intent. His chest felt suddenly hollow; a brisk wind would whistle through him.

"Is that what you prefer?" he asked.

She hesitated. He tried to exhale but he couldn't seem to breathe out.

Slowly, she shook her head.

"Then we are agreed," he said, turning away. He let out a long breath.

"We are?"

"In the first place, gossip is never forgotten; you may

depend on it. Second, let us not deal in half-truths. The marriage can be managed any way we see fit. Separate households, separate lives—whatever you want. But let us simply *do* the thing. Sign the documents, go to a church, get it over with. Timothea is correct."

He hazarded another glance. She was no longer wincing but she hardly looked relaxed. Who could blame her? This was not a relaxing conversation.

He felt compelled to add, "Unless you'd rather not. Unless Canada is preferable to being married to me."

"It's not." A whisper.

He couldn't look at her. "You'll note I did not compare myself to France."

"I should be grateful to marry you, Your Grace. If you are certain."

And that was that. Ian dropped into an adjacent chair, waiting to be consumed by anxiety or outrage or regret. Instead, he felt a strange sort of exhilaration. The breathless feeling of arcing through the air on a rope swing. A weightlessness.

He looked up cautiously and their gazes locked. He was at a loss for what came next. The room fell silent. It occurred to him that he wanted to kiss her again—a compulsion so strong, he gripped the arm of the chair.

The memory of the gallery bench flashed in his brain.

Would it presume too much to try for a kiss in this moment? He narrowed his eyes, trying to judge her receptiveness. She stared back with a tight expression, cautious and uncertain. She looked at him like he was a newly discovered trap door. He presented an escape route, yes; but did he lead to freedom or a twenty-foot drop?

Perhaps no kiss at the moment, but he wondered if he might touch her. Not to snatch her up, per se—although he would do it if he could—but to simply reach out and touch her. A knee. Her hand.

The great irony of this betrothal was that it felt more reliable and secure than most hasty, forced things. It felt . . . *known*. He'd called it a surprise, and true—the notion of marrying her had come on rather suddenly—but the feeling of wanting her, of needing her, of *enjoying her* had not been sudden.

Thinking about Drewsmina Trelayne had become as familiar as thinking of Avenelle. Between the two of them, he thought of little else. That's why kissing her had been so very easy. He'd dreamed of how she would taste for days.

"Well," he ventured. "Congratulations. You've gone from a member of staff to the Duchess of Lachlan, all in a matter of days. Welcome to the family. God help you."

He rolled from the chair and rounded the desk. He began dashing off a note to his solicitor. There would be paperwork, and lawyers, and clergymen. His days of hiding from London were over.

"I find myself at a loss for what to say next," ventured Miss Trelayne. "Forgive me."

"The situation could not be more bizarre," he said, scribbling. "Do not apologize. But can you spell your given name?"

"It's *D-r-e-w-s-m-i-n-a*. But I'm called Drew by friends."

He looked up. "'Drew.' It suits you. I am Ian. You'll have heard Timothea wail it ten or twelve times."

She answered, "Your Grace."

*Or "Your Grace,"* thought Ian. Disappointment felt like a window slammed shut.

He reminded himself that a consent to marry was not an ode to summer grass or sandy beaches. This was not a romantic endeavor.

There was no guarantee that they would want the same things. He was no expert, but intimacy in marriages seemed to span the spectrum from cordial partnership, to brotherly affection, to sworn enemies and everything in between. He shouldn't expect too much. He shouldn't expect anything. They'd only been at this for an hour.

"How should we tell the girls? How should we tell anyone?" he asked, a far safer topic.

"Well," she began, "perhaps we could tell the girls in

the morning? After they've taken breakfast. You and I together, I think. If that suits you."

He shrugged. "As good a plan as any."

"Will we tell them we've experienced this . . . this . . . ?" The phrase that sprang to mind was, "surge of burning lust," but he knew that would never do.

"I think we should tell them the truth but not elaborate," she said. "That we were discovered in a compromising position and now we are forced to marry to save their reputations and mine. Just as I explained in the carriage."

It pained him to think of marriage in terms of *explaining,* or *forced,* or *compromise.* But of course, it was true, all of it.

"Right," he said. "After breakfast. Together. Tell them the truth."

"In the garden," she added. "In my experience, difficult news is easier to deliver outside. After that, we can address the staff belowstairs. The sooner they know we are betrothed and will marry—and perhaps here we could embellish a bit and say we've been planning this for some time—the sooner their gossip will have a romantic bent, rather than a scandalous one."

Ian nodded, adding *difficult news* to the list of terms that no man would wish associated with marriage.

"I'm . . . sorry, Miss Trelayne," he said. "Likely this is not how you envisioned a proposal of marriage."

"In fact I had no vision of marriage, Your Grace, and less so a proposal."

"That makes two of us," he said, returning to his paperwork. "Regardless of my sister's hounding, I had no intention of adding a wife to my rather complicated heap of problems. This was wholly unplanned."

She blinked now, saying nothing. She looked like a very stoic soldier absorbing a very unpleasant order.

"Forgive me," he corrected, "I . . . I overstate my indifference."

He thought for a moment. Bollocks, he was making a muck of this.

He started again. "*Indifference* is the wrong word entirely. We need only remember what transpired in the gallery to acknowledge my . . . enthusiasm for your—"

He stopped before he said the word *body*.

He cleared his throat. "To understand my enthusiasm. The rest of it . . . we'll sort out as we go along. You are a reasonable woman, and I am a reasonable man. Unless I deceive myself, which is highly possible."

"You are very reasonable, Your Grace," she said. "Please do not feel you need explain yourself to me."

He looked to her again. *Really*, he thought. *No explanation? Nothing more to say?*

She stared back, looking steady and settled and calm. Well, fine. That made one of them. What he did not see was an invitation—not to explain, or make some further plans, or to (God help him) share another kiss.

So be it.

So what if his attraction licked and burned, impossible to extinguish, even now?

In hindsight, it was a miracle he had resisted her for as long as he had.

As to the future, only one question remained: How would he resist her when he was her husband and she was his wife?

# Chapter Sixteen

*Dear Cynde,*

*Change of plans regarding the Duke of Lachlan and his nieces.*

*I cannot think of another way to say this, so I'll simply write the words: The Duke and I are to be married. This week. A special license is being secured and the ceremony is planned for Saturday. I will explain all of it when I see you next.*

*The wedding will be very small, with a private ceremony at St. Mark's and breakfast for the duke's immediate family in Pollen Street. The duke's sister and nieces are not yet comfortable hosting outside guests, and the duke and I wish to maintain some semblance of privacy for a time.*

*Pray do not worry. I am well. I'll come to you as soon as I am able. More soon.*

*Yours,*
*Drew*

*Dear Ana and Lord Madewood,*

I've received an offer of marriage from my current employer, the Duke of Lachlan, and I have accepted. I apologize for the shocking nature of this news, it has been a whirlwind for us all.

What this means for you, is that my time as your Spinster Boarder has, at last, come to an end. Thank you for allowing me to live as a guest in your household these great many months.

If you are amenable, I hope to send servants and a carriage to remove my belongings and set the room to rights. Do let me know what day might be most convenient for this task?

If a social call would suit you or your schedule, I would be pleased to host you for tea in Pollen Street or call on you in Golden Square at your earliest convenience. The wedding will be a private ceremony followed by breakfast with the duke's immediate family—over and done by next week.

All my best,
Drewsmina

*Mother,*

Hello.

I'm writing to inform you that a solicitor may be in touch this week in regard to the annuity I receive from Father's estate. Please cooperate. I have accepted an offer of marriage from Ian Clayblack, the Duke of Lachlan, and will marry in a private ceremony next week.

Drewsmina

~~~

THE LETTERS HAD been written in the middle of the night. When dawn broke, Drew sent a boy from the stables to deliver them.

When she wasn't passing midnight hours writing and rewriting letters, Drew had paced. When she didn't pace, she'd lain in bed, sleepless, grappling with a terrible, nagging sense of disbelief.

Was she engaged to be married?

Yes.

Well, yes—for the moment. Possibly. So it seemed. Against all odds.

Should she be mortified and ashamed about the nature of the betrothal?

Also possibly. In actuality, she felt no such thing. But perhaps this was one bit of her former life that hadn't been properly made over. Did pleasant, thoughtful women stew in horror because a handsome duke had kissed them?

God only knew.

What bothered her far more was not knowing if the duke's incredibly generous attitude would persist.

Would sunrise bring the same casual pleasantness? What about next week? What about any day for the rest of their lives, which, the last she checked, was the length of a marriage?

It was impossible to know if (or when) bitterness or outrage or resentment might raise its terrible head.

When that happened, *then* what would she do?

The questions and lack of answers were maddening, and Drew felt almost rigid with uncertainty, like a wet kerchief left to harden in the hot, bright sun. Formerly functional, now too stiff to do any good, easily mistaken for a dead bird.

When finally the household began to stir, Drew's disbelief gave way to strumming anxiety. She hid in her room until after breakfast. The loose plan had been to meet

Lachlan at an appointed time and hope to intercept the girls as they left the morning meal. Ultimately, she reached the door too early and was hovering outside the breakfast room when Lachlan clipped down the stairwell. At the sight of him, a small flock of birds launched inside her chest.

"Hello," he said, coming to a stop before her. He crossed his arms over his chest. His eyes were bright and blue and keenly observant. He had not been tossing and turning all night.

"Hello," she said.

There was too much to say and also no words whatsoever. She held her breath, waiting for him to tell her he'd changed his mind.

"Can you hear them?" he finally asked. "Through the doors?"

Relief coursed through her, granting malleability. She found she was limber enough to nod. "Still breaking their fast, I believe."

"Making the distressed sounds of traumatized innocents, are they? Their eyes forever seared by the sight of—" He cleared his throat. "Of us?"

Drew bit her lip. A joke. He appeared to have no second thoughts *and* he'd made a joke.

"Unless I am mistaken, they are feeding bacon to the cat?" she said.

"Of course they are. Ah, but here they come."

The united presence of Drew and Lachlan outside the breakfast room stunned the girls into a sort of titillated silence, and they followed them to the garden without objection.

Drew had planned this bit, one of the few things she could anticipate and control. The Pollen Street house was blessed with a lovely walled garden with a gurgling fountain, and Drew led the girls to sit on the edge. The noise of falling water would mask the conversation from eavesdropping staff. If the conversation became unbearable, the autumn foliage offered plenty of other places to look.

Lachlan leaned against the garden wall, his arms crossed, and Drew stood before them.

"Girls," she began, "I should like to apologize to you both for my behavior last night."

A pause.

This, she'd also rehearsed, going so far as to write "pause here" in her speech. The transcript had given her something else to do besides pace a trench in the rug.

"It was reckless," she continued, "indecorous, and inappropriate—both as an advisor to the two of you and as a gentlewoman. I am exceedingly embarrassed by my . . . lack of comportment."

Another pause.

She turned to Lachlan. They'd not discussed what he would say, yet another detail over which she'd agonized in the wee hours. She thought Bold Repentance would be unlikely coming from him, but she also prayed that Deep Regret would have no place in his excuses instead.

*I don't regret it*, she thought, but she said nothing. She glanced at him.

He stared back, clearly waiting for her to say more.

Drew shook her head slightly and nodded to him. *And now you . . .*

Lachlan narrowed his eyes and nodded back. *And now I . . . what?*

Drew cleared her throat. "Is there something you might say to the girls, Your Grace?" she prompted.

Lachlan looked at the twins. He exhaled. "Right. I'd like to say, what the bloody hell were you doing . . . in the gallery . . . with your mother, and *your cat*, and every member of my staff . . . when I was so very obviously engaged, so very obviously *not* seeking company, and had no wish to be disturbed?"

Drew gaped at him.

The girls laughed. "We were ever so worried, Uncle," said Imogene with faux innocence.

Ivy added, "Imogene said she heard noises. We couldn't guess what you were doing in the gallery."

He shook his head, exasperated. He turned to Drew. "How did you term what I was doing, Miss Trelayne?"

Drew blinked at him.

Imogene interjected, "Were you engaging in, 'reckless, indecorous, and inappropriate lack of comportment'?" She looked more delighted than Drew had ever seen her.

"Yes, that's it," said Lachlan and the girls laughed.

Drew looked from the giggling girls to the duke.

He raised an eyebrow. It was an expression so provocative and so thrilling and so careless, that Drew almost let out a little gasp. Heat rushed to her face.

She spun back to the girls. "You'll remember what I said in the carriage when we left the dressmaker's? I'd not planned to demonstrate the truth of this warning—not in quite so literal a fashion, but here we are. The rules I discussed apply to Lachlan and myself, just as strictly as they apply to you or any young lady. As such, your uncle and I are . . . are . . ."

She'd struggled to say the words. The notion of marriage remained impossibly . . . unbelievably . . . like something that *did not, would not* happen to her.

"Uncle and you are . . . ?" prompted Imogene. She stopped laughing but a smile remained. She eyed them as if she and Lachlan were performing magic tricks. She was waiting to catch the sleight of hand.

"We are getting married," Lachlan said blandly.

"*Stop*," Imogene said.

"Congratulations," Ivy said sweetly.

"What do you mean, 'stop'? Imogene?" Lachlan demanded. "You've heard Miss Trelayne. Her reputation will be ruined if we don't. She couldn't find work. Friends would refuse her. I was left with no choice but to marry her. Or *deport* her."

"*Stop*," Imogene repeated, louder this time.

Lachlan nodded. "It's true. Not to mention, the reputations of the two of you would suffer. No debutante can take advice about manners and comportment from a woman who—Well, from Miss Trelayne. Not after last night."

Drew's blush turned fire hot. She closed her eyes. The sky above was not high enough to contain her discomfort.

"Married when?" Imogene asked.

"Saturday," Drew rasped. She cleared her throat. She must take control of this conversation.

"But have the two of you been kissing in darkened rooms and cushioned benches all along?" asked Imogene. "From the first day?"

"*No*," Lachlan answered calmly, "we have not done. I'd never met Miss Trelayne before the day she arrived."

"And now you will simply . . . marry her?"

"Yes. Now I *will simply marry her.* But can you see our point, Imogene? In all its life-altering finality? This behavior ends only in marriage. Or ruin. Regrettably."

"But you cannot mean to lecture *us*," Imogene retorted, making a face. "We weren't found cavorting in the smoky gallery with Miss Trelayne after dinner."

Imogene shoved up. She stared from Drew's face to Lachlan's, no trace of artifice. "But do you *love* her, Uncle?" she asked.

Drew, to this point, had been mostly speechless; her memorized speech forgotten, along with her pride. But now she found her tongue. This was one question she could not hear the duke answer. She would burst into song to prevent hearing that he did not love her—

"The important thing is—" Drew said—but then she stopped.

Voices and footsteps interrupted her, there was some commotion from the garden door.

"Hello?" called a familiar high, airy voice.

*Cynde.*

Tears shot to Drew's eyes when she recognized her stepsister's voice. *She'd come.* She'd received Drew's note and sought her out. Within hours.

"You're joking," Lachlan muttered. "Not the prince, too, I hope."

"Pray forgive my rudeness," sang Cynde, bustling up the path in a dress so yellow the four of them squinted. Maids and footmen from Lachlan's household trailed the princess at a respectful distance, their expressions awed. Greenly, the butler, endeavored to lead the way, but the princess slid past him.

Drew remembered that she'd not yet gone over royal address with the girls. She darted to the fountain and hustled the twins up.

"Girls," she began, "may I present Her Royal Highness, Princess Cynde, wife of the king's seventh son, Prince Adolphus, known also as the Royal Duke of Cambridge. Pray excuse us, Your Highness, as I quickly review a proper curtsy with the duke's nieces.

"Now," Drew whispered to the girls, "for a member of the royal family we would—"

"But do you mean to instruct us?" marveled Imogene with skepticism. "Now? Even after—?"

"*Yes, Imogene,*" cut in Lachlan, "she will instruct you. The only difference is, now she will be your *aunt.*"

"But will you pay her? Now that she is to be *our aunt*?" asked Imogene.

"Curtsy to the princess," snapped Lachlan. He corrected his own posture and dipped his head in a respectful bow. "Your Highness. It is an honor to welcome you to my home."

"Like this," Drew was whispering, dropping into a curtsy.

The girls hovered for a moment, staring at the princess, and then wobbled into uneasy curtsies.

Drew stole a look at her stepsister. Cynde watched it all with barely concealed delight. She clasped her hands together as if someone had just presented her with a kitten.

"The pleasure is mine," said Cynde. "I do beg your pardon for this unscheduled call, but I'd hoped to have a private word with Miss Trelayne? As soon as you can spare her."

Drew glanced at Lachlan. He shrugged. The twins stared expectantly at the adults, as if trying to predict who would deliver the next bit of shocking news.

"Girls?" called Drew. "Can we give you the job of relaying all we've discussed here to your mother?"

"But mother does not know?" asked Ivy.

"She does not know," said Lachlan, "and you've just been given the esteemed job of telling her. Congratulations. However, do not discuss it with anyone else, if you please. Miss Trelayne and I will tell the staff. Beyond that, I would ask you, as your uncle and your guardian, *not* to gossip about it. As tempting as it is. Can you give me your word?"

"Yes," said Ivy in the same moment that Imogene said, "*Depends*."

"Go," Lachlan sighed, and the girls darted up the path, nearly trampling the princess.

"Curtsy again! Ask to be excus—" Drew called, but they had already gone.

"Highness," said Lachlan, bowing again. "You've come alone?"

"I have," said Cynde, eyeing him up and down. "Adolphus would see you, Your Grace, as soon as you are able. He expects you to attend him at Kew, I believe."

"Of this I have no doubt," drawled Lachlan. "Can I impose upon you to beg patience on my behalf? We are a bit overwhelmed at the moment."

"So I gather," said Cynde. "I'll tell him. In the meantime, I would speak to my sister."

"Indeed," said Lachlan, bowing again. He began to back away. "She could use a dash of sisterly encouragement, after that lot." He nodded in the direction the twins.

"If you'll excuse me," said Lachlan, and he was gone.

Drew collapsed onto the edge of the fountain. "Oh, Cynde. Oh, Cynde. *Oh, Cynde.*" She dropped her face in her hands.

"Are you hurt, Drewsmina?" asked Cynde cautiously, her voice deeply concerned.

Drew shook her head, not looking up.

"Are you afraid?"

Drew thought about this. She nodded.

"Of the duke?" guessed Cynde.

She shook her head. She felt Cynde plop down beside her. Silk billowed like the froth of a yellow wave.

"I can't believe you've come," said Drew, sliding her hands into a steeple against her mouth. She looked at her smiling sunbeam of a stepsister.

"Nonsense," said Cynde. "Of course I've come. Adolphus and I were exceedingly concerned. Can you say what's happened? We've read your note at least a dozen times. I don't understand."

It was a short sordid tale, not unlike the short sordid tale she'd spilled to Cynde after her first (and only) beau, James, was posted to India. Then and now, Drew had been confused and frightened; and then and now, Cynde had been thoughtful and gracious and encouraging.

Before Cynde had managed to marry a prince, her role in the family had been Resented Interloper, a step up from a serving girl. When she managed, miraculously, to escape them all and marry into the royal family, Cynde suffered the added regard of jealous disdain. And none of them had been more bitter, perhaps, than Drew.

But then Drew had been hobbled; run through by heart-break over James Summer. Cynde had learned of the betrayal through court gossip and sought her out. Drew had been too miserable to reject the overtures of her once-maligned stepsister, and they'd had their first authentic, loving exchange. After that—because of the grace shown by Cynde—Drew's transformation had begun.

Now here they were again, against all odds. Only this

time, the two stepsisters were already friends, and Drew wasn't heartbroken, she was . . . she was—

"I cannot account for what has happened," Drew told her. "I cannot begin to describe what led to my part in it. None of it is ideal, obviously. But . . ."

"You've no regret?" guessed Cynde.

Drew closed her eyes and shook her head. She was many things, but regretful was not one of them.

"And you are certain that the duke did not press himself upon you?" asked Cynde.

Drew looked into her giant blue eyes and again shook her head. "I wanted it, Cynde. God help me. I wanted it. I would . . . I would—"

"Do it all again?" suggested Cynde cheerfully. She clapped her hands. "Oh lovely. Because it sounds as if the duke has done the honorable thing and arranged exactly this. To do it all again—and for the rest of your lives too."

"Oh God," rasped Drew.

"And, why not? That's what I should ask anyone who challenges you. Most marriages are formed on far less."

Drew bit her lip. She had no model for how most marriages were formed. Their sister, Ana, had a strange, violent union with Madewood that she found very unsettling. Their mother had been married four times and counting, each union for the purpose of increasing money and rank.

"But you *want* to marry the duke," surmised Cynde carefully, "and you *are* marrying the duke, so . . . ?"

"What I don't want is Lachlan feeling forced to marry me against his will. Cynde? How could he want it? How could he want *me*?"

Cynde held up a tiny hand. "I simply cannot indulge this kind of talk. Remember what I've said about the prince?"

Drew combed through the myriad of bizarre things Cynde had revealed about her royal husband. "That he likes for you to sit naked on the edge of his bath and sing to him?"

"*No*," cooed Cynde. "I've said that I was the orphaned

daughter of an impoverished earl, living as a glorified servant to a stepmother who hated me, when that chance meeting brought Adolphus and me together. His attraction was impossible to miss, and I leapt at the chance to escape my old life and embrace whatever life he might give me instead. What did I do?"

"Wear borrowed clothes and sneak, uninvited, to a royal ball to make his acquaintance?"

"*Whatever it took* to make it happen," Cynde corrected. "And it worked, didn't it? Adolphus rescued me from your mother's house and we are both so very happy."

"Are you happy?" Drew asked.

"Of course I am happy. I am a princess, my future children are in line to be Sovereign, and I've learned to love Adolphus. In fact, we suit rather well. I quite like singing naked on the edge of his bath. How lucky for you—you seem to enjoy the duke outright, even now. There will be no 'learning to love' the Duke of Lachlan. And that is saying quite a lot. Dolph has suggested that he's odd and prickly and not well-liked."

"He is—" began Drew, but she stopped short of saying, *dizzying. In the best sort of way.*

Instead she said, "He is considerate and clever and he loves his family. He is a fine man, Cynde. I like him very much—too much, probably. But I am . . ." She gestured to herself.

Cynde raised her doll-like hand again, a royal proclamation. "You are regal, and striking, and interesting. People take you seriously, unlike me. Most importantly, you seem to be exactly what Lachlan enjoys—that is, if he is entwining himself with you in the gallery."

"I can barely understand what happened in the gallery."

"Events of the gallery may call for less intellectual study, and more for . . . instinct, if you will? Goodness knows I should never have managed to marry a prince if brains had been required."

"I've no instinct in this, Cynde. You know this. I rebuilt

my personality, trait by trait, after James left. I am a . . . a creation of loose parts. I *taught* myself to be pleasant. And that says nothing of how I loo—"

Cynde stood and began fluffing her copious skirts. "I'll not be a party to this again, Drewsmina. You didn't rebuild your personality, you allowed heartbreak to smooth away the frightened, desperate, jagged edges. It was either that or become even more bitter, which would have been very bitter indeed." She made a face. "Although this *can* happen; look at your mother. Instead, you left the lash-y, rage-y bits behind and emerged the authentic and thoughtful woman you truly are. The result is the actual Drewsmina Trelayne, lovely and clever, minus the influence of your dreadful mother."

Drew's eyes filled with tears. "But . . . but Cynde. What of my—"

"Do not say it," said Cynde, patting her hair.

"I'm not . . ."

"Tell me: Did I once mend your mother's dresses, and lay her fire, and take my meals in the cellar with her staff?"

"Yes."

"Was I, in fact, her *unpaid servant*? And yet, now do I dine at Kew Palace with the king and queen of England?"

Drew swallowed. It didn't feel the same. It *wasn't* the same.

"*Anything can happen*," carried on Cynde, her sugary voice singing with conviction. "I'll say it again: You are lovely. And distinctive. And striking. Unforgettable, really."

A tear slid down Drew's cheek. She didn't deserve a friend such as Cynde.

"You have a very great challenge with these girls," Cynde continued, "that much is clear. Even if I hadn't noticed the way the duke looked at you in the throne room—*which I did*—he should be happy to marry you solely for the purpose of shepherding them. Is their mother . . . unfit or unwell?"

"She is . . ." Drew began, her mind racing with a number of cutting descriptions that her old self, more desperate and less authentic (according to Cynde), would have pinned to Lady Tribble.

Instead she said, "She is . . . an ally."

Cynde cocked a perfectly arched eyebrow. "Indeed. Lovely. Well. If the mother is an ally and the twins need your wise counsel, and the duke, obviously, cannot keep his hands off you—"

"I would not say—"

"You must stop," moaned Cynde. "I must go, actually. Adolphus wishes to meet at the milliners to look at hats. I have but a quarter hour. How can I be of the most help before I go?"

"Help?" asked Drew. "You've done so much, simply by looking in on me. I—"

"You've explained the wedding to the girls, the sister is an ally, but what of the servants? I noticed a sort of wild-eyed, excitable look about them when I arrived."

"They are not accustomed to royal callers."

"It was more than that. They look as if they've found a diamond necklace in the street and cannot decide whether to turn it over to the authorities or sell it."

"They are scandalized, to be sure. We intend to speak to them next. Announce the wedding."

"Very good. I shall accompany you. They may hear it from three of us and see my very great approval."

"I couldn't ask you to—"

"I insist. Which way to the servants' stairs?"

"Oh no, Cynde. Lachlan will convene them in the front hall, you needn't—"

"Oh yes . . ." She turned to walk up the path, her heeled slippers clicking on paving stones. "I'm no stranger to be-lowstairs, Drewsmina. Speaking of Lady Blicken, I hope you've braced yourself for some intrigue or meddling."

"Mother and I rarely speak, honestly. I'd never told her

I'd taken this job. She is appalled by the idea of gainful employment for me. I sent a note about the wedding only to pave the way for Lachlan's lawyers."

"She will horn in. Depend upon it."

Drew made a miserable sound of foreboding and trailed behind Cynde.

"I cannot believe any of this will happen," Drew whispered.

"Trust me," called Cynde, signaling for a dazzled footman to open the garden door, "*anything* can happen."

*Chapter Seventeen*

The wedding was scheduled for Saturday, after the twins' riding lesson and before their standing appointment with the dancing instructor.

If Ian thought his rapport with Drew would change simply because they'd had an incinerating encounter in the gallery, he was mistaken.

If he thought their betrothal would precipitate some new intimacy, he was wrong.

If he thought he would kiss her again, he did not.

Their impending nuptials seemed almost . . . immaterial to the way they got on. Instead, the week leading up to the wedding was filled with new horses and dancing shoes and *no-elbows-on-the-table* at dinner. Her smiles were cautious, not unwarm, but detached. They were alone together almost never.

And why should he expect more? He felt wretched about what had happened. No, he felt wretched that they'd *been discovered*. Servants snickered behind her back—despite his threats of expulsion. Imogene grew even more petulant and difficult. Add to that the awkwardness of their brief meetings alone—short encounters he manufactured to review the paperwork for the special license or to go over trivial details about the ceremony—and was it any wonder? Their time together was taut with prolonged silences and paper shuffling. He was determined not to frighten or alarm her; not to force her into . . . more than he was already forcing her (which was a lifetime), but he had no idea how to manage it. Especially since he wanted her so bloody much.

Meanwhile, his nights were filled with hot dreams and sheet-thrashing sweat; he woke up hard and ravenous for her. She'd thrown herself into her work with the girls, and he invented reasons to watch her from a distance. When they were riding, he rode. When the dancing instructor called, he made himself an available partner.

She, in turn, positioned herself opposite his sister in dances and walked instead of rode, pulling Ivy's horse on a lead. Lessons, tutors, faux tea parties wherein social calamities were foreseen and navigated—all of this took center stage. If he was being honest, she seemed to regard Ian *less* after their betrothal than before.

It was fine, he told himself.

He had other work.

He'd learned from Rucker Loring, the estate manager who appeared outside the window at the dressmaker, that some of his tenants had embarked upon the high-risk and penalty-heavy endeavor of *smuggling*. If this was true, he'd have to intervene. He could not tolerate the people of Avenelle descending into criminal activity to get by. The penalty for smugglers was hanging. Not on his watch.

He understood their motives, of course. Their duke had made no progress reducing the export levy on their handcrafted lace and local mills had been allowed to thrive. They were angry and desperate and smuggling was common in coastal Dorset.

Loring had been sent to further investigate, and Ian had devoted no small amount of hours to planning how he might put a stop to the smuggling if it was true.

Considering all this, the wedding was . . . if not an "afterthought," well certainly it was just another thing they had to do.

"So she's simply carried on, instructing the girls?" asked an old army mate, Jason Beckett, the Duke of Northumberland, in the minutes before the wedding.

The two men were packed into the antechamber outside the sanctuary of St. Mark's awaiting the priest. In a rare fit of optimism, Ian had invited his old friend North to stand as witness.

Miss Trelayne would most assuredly have Princess Cynde at the wedding. There were no guarantees, but the princess had begun to turn up in Pollen Street at regular intervals. In contrast, Ian had no witness except possibly his butler, Greenly. Most of Ian's friends had fallen away after the riots; the last hangers-on had drifted on during his self-imposed exile. But Northumberland had been a foreign agent before he was a duke and more recently, North had been out of the country with his new wife, traveling Europe.

Now he was back in England for a time, and in London no less, and when Ian learned this, he'd sent North his card. North had written back immediately and assured Ian he would be honored to attend the wedding. At Ian's gentle suggestion, North had come alone. Ian's family simply wasn't yet prepared to entertain a duke and duchess. Ian had intercepted North when he'd arrived and corralled him inside the antechamber until the ceremony began.

"Yes, she's carried on with the girls," Ian explained to his old friend. "It's why she was hired. Honestly, her dedication to the job . . . a sort of steadfastness, I suppose . . . was what I admired from the very start. I admire it still. All of us in this house could benefit from more thoughtful, measured behavior."

"And was it her dedication and steadfastness that caused you to pounce upon her in the portrait gallery?" wondered North. "Or perhaps it was her thoughtfulness and measure?"

Ian let out a noise of exasperation and turned away, tightening his gloves. His old friend wouldn't be fooled.

"Did I ever mention my fondness for redheads?" Ian asked North.

"I cannot say that you did," North chuckled.

"Perhaps because I never realized I had one. But I do. She's lovely, Jason. Ginger hair, legs unlike any I've had the privilege of encountering, teal eyes. Freckles."

"*Teal* eyes, did you say?" teased North.

Ian frowned. "My point is, her loveliness is my only excuse for that night in the gallery. Why else would I . . . set upon a girl I barely know, in whose hands rests the future of my nieces? She's a bloody employee; *I should have known better.*"

"Devil if I know, mate," said North. "I fell in love with my interpreter when I was halfway to Iceland on a mission. But answer me this: Do you fancy the idea of kissing her again, should the opportunity strike?"

"*All. The. Bloody. Time,*" Ian stated slowly, speaking to the wall. He paused, trying to find church-appropriate words for how often he thought of putting his hands on Miss Trelayne. "It's a voracious sort of . . . sort of . . . mindlessness. A little like being drunk, and a little like anticipation, and a little like being plunged under water and needing to draw breath."

"Well said," chuckled North. "Poetic too. You always were too clever for your own good. Look, Lachlan, if your . . . er, regard is as strong as this, and if she reciprocates, then why shouldn't you marry her? Even if it's a forced union to a girl you barely know. I hear no regret, no bitterness. My God Lachlan, you seem almost . . . happy."

"I'm not happy," Ian declared.

"I don't believe you."

"And what do you know of my happiness?"

"I know you're not sulking in rain-drenched Dorset, stewing in the memory of the bloody riots. I know you've taken on your batty sister and her feral nieces. I know you've managed to find this woman to help you and are making her your duchess. In short, you're actually living your life."

"She's being made a duchess out of necessity."

"*As duchesses are wont to do,*" he said sardonically. "I don't buy it, mate. Sorry. Funny how necessities and *things you actually want* sometimes align so beautifully."

"Everything I do is out of necessity."

"Don't misunderstand, Lachlan. You face challenging roads ahead, but I can think of ten different ways to travel them that don't involve an expensive Season for Timothea's girls or marrying their governess."

"She is a stylist."

"She's about to be a *duchess*, and I don't care what you say about 'necessity.' I know you, and I know your regard for the dukedom. Unlike me, the title is not something you take lightly. I think you *want* this woman, and I think you want her because she makes you happy."

Ian thought about this. Was he happy? He felt . . . contentment. Engagement—which was nice, after years of solitude. He felt excitement, even. He thought of Miss Trelayne on the balcony, hearing the bird. Miss Trelayne in the dressmaker's shop, showing off her caterpillar bracelet. He thought of the portrait gallery.

*Oh God, the gallery.*

Certainly he would rather be *with her* than *without her*.

Certainly he'd spent the last week wishing he was with her more.

He couldn't speak to his happiness. He didn't know enough about it.

"All I know," Ian finally said, "is that I expect very little."

"Oh yes, your guttersnipe existence as a bloody duke."

"I'm not complaining. My father's gin-fueled stagger to the grave left me an estate in ruins. My mother's misery left me with a sister with terrible judgment, keen to carry on the tradition. My own cock-up with the riot left a man dead and my reputation in tatters. It comes as no surprise, then, that I'm marrying a *member of my staff* . . . who I embarrassed in a public setting . . . despite the fact that I barely know her. And yet, here we are, moments from being bound together for life. It's hardly a happy occasion but it's also . . . no surprise."

"I'll say it again," sighed Northumberland, crossing his arms over his chest. "I don't believe you."

Ian swore and turned away. After a long moment, he conceded, "Perhaps what I feel is . . . is *larger* than happiness or unhappiness? Perhaps what I feel is . . . ?"

"Desire?" guessed his friend. "It's as good a starting gate as any."

"*Possibility*," Ian corrected. "I was going to say I feel 'possibility.' Potential."

"I knew it," bragged North. "And I rest my case. Oh, and you're welcome, by the way. Best to face these sentiments squarely. Why deceive yourself?"

Ian ignored him, thinking of the unnamed . . . *what-if* that seemed to pulse in his gut like a light on the distant horizon.

Even more trickery was this: He wanted the light to be real. Or he thought he wanted it to be real. All he really knew was, real or imagined, marriage to Miss Trelayne felt like holding out an open hand to . . . to a long, lost—

Well, she wasn't a friend. Nor was she a lover—not really. *Not yet*, his brain provided unhelpfully.

No, Miss Trelayne was a long-lost chance at something like kinship. After a family that mostly ignored him, Miss Trelayne seemed like someone who paid attention, and applied herself to his benefit, and cared. If not *for him*, then at least *on behalf of him*.

Ian, lost cause that he was, would take it.

And he would kiss her again if she would have him. But he dared not make things worse by manhandling; not if she preferred to put everything that happened in the gallery far behind them.

He would assume nothing, and expect nothing, and bloody bleeding hell—he would cease running headlong into situations that redirected the course of everyone's lives.

He learned his lesson time and time again. Now he would bide his time and wait and see.

"Well, at least she has red hair," sighed North, clapping him on the back. "A trait for which you've admitted your great fondness. Well-known fact: hair color is a perfectly reasonable basis for any marriage."

"Sod off. I'm beginning to wonder why I invited you."

"No one else can tolerate you," reminded North. "And you enjoy my company. I make you feel good about yourself because I'm the only man more terrible at being a duke than you are."

"'Duke' in name only," scoffed Ian. "Doesn't your sister manage your estate?"

"She does, in fact, and she's doing a crack job. I thank Christ for her every day. And my wife contributes. Perhaps your new duchess will help improve your outlook on Avenelle and the lot."

"I cannot say how much time she'll spend at Avenelle," Ian admitted glumly. "She hopes to open a finishing school in London. It's been her dream these many years. I'd be a rotter to disrupt her plans because she's been forced to marry me. We may . . . live apart for much of the year."

"Live apart? Bloody hell, Ian—no," said North, sobering. "Bollocks to that. Find some middle ground. Have you discussed a compromise?"

"Have you not heard what I've said? We are literal *strangers*. She is a very lovely, very proficient . . . stranger. We've discussed almost nothing about this union except the need to fling it together in five days to curtail gossip."

They heard footsteps in the corridor; the old priest greeted them indifferently and ushered them to the alter.

"But will she allow you to touch her? Tonight?" whispered North hurriedly.

"I don't know," Ian ground out. It was painful to say out loud all the things he did not know.

"Well, here's my advice," North whispered quickly. "Instigate some . . . private discussion about the arrangement into which you've both just entered. Talk about where you will live, for how long, how you could make her new school happen alongside your commitments in Dorset. If nothing else, this will make the future feel less slapdash. Meanwhile, perhaps the ol' drunk-anticipation-can't-breathe feeling will strike. If she's amenable, kiss her again. Where's the harm? The longer the two of you regard kissing as a rare fluke instead of a custom, the stranger and scarcer it will become."

"Thank you for the advice," sighed Ian smugly, reseating his hat. "I bloody well know how to kiss a woman."

"Obviously," muttered North, turning to smile at the waiting priest.

Ten minutes later Ian married Miss Trelayne before a crowd of three family members, the Duke of Northumberland, and a royal Princess.

After communion, Timothea played her lute.

Imogene slept through all of it.

# *Chapter Eighteen*

> *Drewsmina Trelayne's Rule of Style and Comportment #33:*
> *Proper sleeping attire for respectable ladies should include:*
> *night rail; dressing gown—preferably a matched set*
> *secured with a ribbon belt—wool stockings; slippers; and a*
> *night cap. In the winter a shawl may provide added warmth.*

At the end of a truly exhausting, truly *odd* wedding day, Drew returned to her room to find that all of her possessions had been removed.

"Never you fear," said a maid who was fussing with the curtains. "I've seen all of Your Grace's things moved into the duchess's suite on the third floor."

"Oh," said Drew, looking around the cold dark space.

"I'm Chappy, by the way; it's a pleasure to make your acquaintance. I look so very forward to serving you in the role of lady's maid, Your Grace." She dipped a small curtsy.

"How do you do," Drew ventured, staring at the woman. She was exactly the sort of roundish, shortish, kind-faced servant for whom Drew would've, in her former incarnation, made life wretched. Now, for a reason Drew couldn't explain, she wanted to hug the woman.

The maid turned back to the curtains and yanked them closed, sealing out the moonlight. "I'd be happy to show you to your new rooms, if it pleases Your Grace," Chappy said, taking up a candle.

"Alright," said Drew, a little dazed. They were halfway down the stairwell before Drew found the words to ask, "Did Lady Tribble install you in this position, Chappy, or . . . ?"

Drew could not imagine Lady Tribble hiring maids or rearranging rooms, but the alternative meant . . . Lachlan had done it.

Lachlan, who'd been cordial but evasive these last five days; who'd made the wedding happen but in the most practical, no-nonsense manner. They were married with as much feeling and sentiment as might be given to a carriage purchase.

He'd thought of everything but said almost nothing.

He'd kissed her on the cheek at the end of the ceremony— a slow, gentle swipe of his lips that hovered, just a breath, beside her ear—then he'd ridden his own horse outside the carriage from the church to the breakfast.

Drew had followed his lead, throwing her energy into the girls and relying heavily on Cynde for conversation and encouragement.

But *someone* had installed her in the duchess's suite on the family floor. And hired personal staff. It could be only him. Lachlan made her a duchess in grand gestures but allowed the small, sweet, personal details of life to go . . . if not undone, at least unremarked.

It should have been enough.

It *was* enough.

*It's not enough.*

The thought, snipey and undermining, echoed in her heart.

*I want it all.*

Drew's desire to be a proper wife, to touch, and laugh and be adored by him, nestled into her brain like seed. It grew a little more every day, distracting her from the gratitude she felt for the duke's proposal and distracted from the girls. Worst of all, it interrupted the not-insignificant satisfaction of simply being his, his . . . his helper. With the twins. In the household. With Lady Tribble.

Before Drew had transformed, when she existed in her former role as . . . well, as Drewsmina Trelayne, Terrible Extraordinaire, Drew's every move had been powered by I-want-it-all selfishness. This had been the source of shouting at servants and competing with Ana and ridiculing Cynde. All of it in service to her unquenchable desire to have the best, the prettiest, the *most*. The result was to pummel everyone else in her path but also miss the richness of small things. When you wanted it all, you missed the beauty of a million quieter, seemingly lesser things. Birds, snowy evenings, raspberry glaze, the rising action in a good book.

There was an emptiness that came from wanting it all— not to mention heartbreak.

And oh, the heartbreak that would result in loving the Duke of Lachlan. Every time he hopped out of the way of a passing servant, or stood up to Imogene with compassion and pragmatism, every time he was gracious with his sister, she felt her heart fill with burgeoning love. And the larger her heart swelled, the sooner it would rupture.

Meanwhile, he'd not touched her since that night in the gallery. On the rare occasions they were alone together, he spoke only of legal documents and pin money and the number of tiers to their wedding cake. She had followed his lead—what choice did she have? She could hardly hurl herself at him.

When she thought back to those moments in the gallery, she could barely remember how they'd gotten from standing beside each other, to kissing, to sprawled on the bench. Some endeavors happened step-by-step, like the tying of a Windsor knot or the boiling of an egg. The gallery had been nothing like that; it'd been a sort of . . . *cascade of magic*. And Drew knew virtually nothing of magic. Except that she liked it and she wanted more of it.

*I want all of it.*

Drew exhaled, not certain what to do with that entirely useless, fruitless thought. She watched Chappy, now moving about her new room, straightening linens and arranging vases. She chatted pleasantly as she went, pointing out the window seat, the removable steps to the very tall bed, the vanity crowded with Drew's hairbrushes and pins. Drew nodded along, murmuring her approval, but her attention drifted, again and again, to the closed door in the far corner.

"And that would be the door to His Grace's chamber," Chappy finished. It would be impossible for the woman not to notice Drew studying it.

"His Grace has . . . has retired for the night?" Drew asked.

"I cannot say, madam. Would you like me to send a girl to seek out his valet?"

"No, no, that won't be necessary. Thank you. I'll—We'll sort it out." Her face reddened.

Also impossible to hide: the glaring lack of convention in the very *dry* rapport between the newlyweds. Cynde spoke often of the value of discretion among servants—by all accounts, she and Prince Adolphus lived as nudists inside their suite at Kew Palace—and Drew hoped that Chappy would be an ally in this way.

If nothing else, it felt like a luxury to have the woman help her with the buttons and fasteners on her dress, to unpin her hair, to assist her with her toilette. If Chappy thought it odd that Drew's only choice of post-wedding night rail was a thick opaque green cotton that reached to her toes, paired with a stiff wool dressing gown, she said nothing.

With a final word of congratulations and good-night, Chappy was gone.

Alone in the expansive room, Drew took a deep breath and slowly spun. She drifted from the stone fireplace, to plush chairs, to the large empty bed with taut linens pulled back on one side. All the while, she listened, carefully, breathlessly, for any sound from next door. Was that a rustle? Did she hear a thump, a cough?

Drew caught her reflection in the mirror above the vanity and frowned. Her long orange hair was down, brushed shiny by Chappy. Her gown was warm and snug. She saw a hopeful young woman, cocooned in green wool, holding her breath for a man.

*I know better*, she thought, trudging to the vanity. *Moreover, I expect better.* She narrowed her eyes in the mirror, arranging her expression into a determined sort of pride. Chin high, eyes haughty, like her mother. She frowned again. Whatever she did, she mustn't look like her mother.

She had just taken up a comb with a small jeweled dragonfly, when she heard footsteps in the main corridor. Her hand froze, midstroke. The doorknob squeaked and the heavy wood of her door swung open, just a crack.

Drew pressed the comb into her hair and then sat perfectly still. Her heart thrashed like a bird in a trap. She was suddenly aware of the weight and scratch of every fiber of her heavy night clothes. Slowly she pivoted to the door.

"I have something that I require."

It was Imogene. She admitted herself to the room by swinging the door wide.

"Hello, Imogene," managed Drew, the bird of her heart collapsing into death. "Have we discussed the importance of knocking on doors before we enter private rooms? If not, please take note. It is rude to simply admit yourself to someone's private bed chamber."

"I did knock," said Imogene.

"You did not knock," said Drew.

"I did. You weren't listening."

"Believe me, I was listening."

The girl ceased arguing and padded around the room, taking in the high ceiling and soft rugs, the large window, heavy with velvet drapes.

"You were listening for uncle," Imogene guessed, picking up the porcelain figurine of a duck from the mantel.

"It makes no difference who I was listening for," said Drew, "a lady would not enter a room if she was not invited inside."

"I didn't know anyone was here." Imogene pocketed the shiny duck.

"Which is why you shouldn't simply admit yourself," said Drew, pushing away from the vanity and crossing to her. She held out her hand. "The duck, if you please."

Imogene made an expression of pronounced innocence.

Drew fished in the girl's pocket for the duck. "What use could you possibly have for this porcelain duck?" She held it out.

"It would please my mother," Imogene said, turning away. She drifted to the bed. Climbing the steps to the high mattress, she fell back with arms splayed wide, a girl dropping into a pile of leaves.

"Very thoughtful," said Drew, replacing the duck. "More so if you were to save your pin money and buy a similar item for her yourself. What did you come here to ask me? Where is Ivy?"

Imogene rolled onto her side and propped a hand under her ear. "Is that what you intend to wear to bed? With Uncle?"

Drew froze, blinking at the girl.

How very hard she worked not to be unsettled by Imogene. The proverbial upper hand was easier to maintain if Drew remained unfazed. At one time, Drew herself dabbled in petty thievery. It staved off boredom. She'd also been an encyclopedia of rude comments, a reflection of the ugliness that she, herself, had been shown. But she *had* never and *would* never make assumptions about anyone's wedding-night attire.

Drew managed to ask, "What I wear is not your business, Imogene, surely."

"Not my business?" challenged the girl. "You're joking.

We endure *daily* discussions of *this* fabric or *that* fabric, or *this* flounce or *that*. Endless droning about what is flattering and appropriate and in fashion or out."

"Yes, but I don't speak of *my* clothes, I speak of wardrobe in general. Feign boredom all you like, but you looked gorgeous in the first gown Mrs. Tavertine sent over, and you know it, Ivy, too. And anyway, these are discussions of clothes one might wear *in the day*, not . . ." Drew trailed off, looking down at her night rail.

"Trust me, *Aunt*," said Imogene, mockingly emphasizing the word, "you are out of your depth. No man will want to ravish you in that murky, impenetrable shroud. It's the color of a pond in the summer heat."

Drew stopped trying not to be shocked and gaped at Imogene.

The girl slid from the bed and trudged across the room. "Have you nothing else? It is your wedding night, for God's sake."

She drew open the door to a wardrobe with one finger, deftly skimming Drew's dresses.

"Imogene," Drew tried, "that's enough—"

"Some men might relish the challenge of a pond-scum shroud," declared Imogene, "but not Uncle. Uncle will want an invitation. Something that says, '*I* am open for business.'"

"Imogene!" gasped Drew.

The girl scooped up a clutch of silk stockings, examined them, and returned them in a wad.

"Imogene that is hardly—"

"Have you nothing light, and silky, and beautiful? Nothing at all?"

"I . . . I am cold in the night. I prefer to keep warm," Drew managed. "But, Imogene—"

"Hmmm," mused the girl, unfurling a diaphanous ivory garment like a herald's scroll. "This will do."

"*That*," said Drew, "is a shift. It's worn under my clothes. And *you*—"

"Men do not distinguish, trust me. And anyway, it will be on the ground soon enough. Take off the green shroud."

"No. No I will not." Drew took a step back. "Imogene, need I be worried about the source of your . . . of your—"

"You'll remove the pond-green shroud," recited Imogene, ignoring her, "and you'll put on the shift. What is your plan for when he comes to you?"

"Comes to me?" Drew could but repeat the words. The girl left the wardrobe and was circling about the room. She tossed the shift onto the bed.

"Ah, no plan, I see," Imogene observed. "Why am I not surprised? It's a wonder the two of you ever managed to kiss in the gallery that night."

"That is quite enou—"

"Has he kissed you again?"

Drew sighed. "We are not having this conversation."

"He has not," concluded Imogene. "Poor Uncle."

"Poor *Uncle*?" demanded Drew.

"The key," continued Imogene, undeterred, "is positioning. Where you sit, the way you arrange yourself. Before he comes in—"

"He is no—" Drew cut herself off. She cleared her throat. "This is a wholly inappropriate conversation."

Imogene narrowed her eyes, studying Drew with open skepticism. Drew stared back.

"*As I was saying*," Imogene continued, "you should situate yourself somewhere that invites him to join you. The window seat or the trunk at the end of the bed. If you sit alone in a chair, he'll have to sort out how to shoehorn you out of it. The bed, of course, would be no work at all, and men appreciate a challeng—"

"Enough!" said Drew, finally finding her voice. "Out!" She pointed to the door.

Imogene made a face and pivoted, conveying the extreme obstinance of an aging matron or a spoiled cat. She went to the hearth and pretended to warm her hands by the fire. Reaching up to touch her hair, she made a swift move to reclaim the porcelain duck.

"*Leave the duck,*" Drew ordered.

Imogene slouched, sighed, and drifted toward the door. She was almost out when a knock sounded from the far corner of the room. The firm, *tap, tap, taps* rattled the wood on the door that adjoined the duke's bedchamber.

Drew's breath caught in her throat. Her eyes flew to Imogene. It would be impossible, Drew knew, to hide her shock and excitement and hope.

Imogene narrowed her eyes in determination and marched back to Drew.

"Take off the dressing gown."

"What?" asked Drew, clutching the heavy wool.

"Take it off, take it off, take it off," the girl chanted impatiently. Pouncing forward, Imogene forcibly yanked the dressing gown from Drew's shoulders and wrestled it from her arms.

Drew was too overcome to fight her. Her eyes were pinned to the adjoining door.

"Tell him, 'Just a moment!'" whispered Imogene.

"It's not him," whispered Drew. "It's a servant."

"It's him," insisted Imogene. "*Tell him,* 'Just a moment.'"

"I . . . I—" Drew stammered.

"Jus' a moment, Your Grace!" Imogene called, employing a working-class accent Drew had never heard.

"Now this monstrosity," hissed Imogene, jerking the wool night rail over Drew's head.

"Stop, Imogene, you cannot mean to strip me!"

Drew had six inches on Imogene, but the girl fought dirty, throwing elbows and stepping on feet, and there was no hope for it. The night rail covered Drew's face in one moment and flew across the room in the next. Drew stood, naked except for her drawers, as Imogene retrieved the ivory silk shift from the bed.

"Arms up. Hurry!" the girl hissed.

"I cannot wear a—" But then the cool silk was sliding down her arms and over her shoulders and settling in a smooth, fluttery drape against her skin.

Drew looked down at the shimmery fabric clinging to her breasts and hips. She looked up at Imogene. The girl was assessing her with a critical eye.

"I don't have a dressing gown," whispered Drew. "This isn't a proper night rail—"

"Whatever you do, do not tuck your hair away. Leave it down. The little comb can remain, but allow the length of it to fall over your shoulder like that. Yes. There you are." She flipped a long curly hank of hair over Drew's cheek and down her shoulder.

Drew's heart beat like a flock of sparrows. She was terrified and excited and breathless.

She was also very glad to be Imogene's *aunt*, because this exchange would surely result in an immediate sacking if she'd been merely the girl's stylist.

"Now, go to the window seat and wait," instructed Imogene. She scooped up the green night rail and began backing away. "Call to him."

"He might knock—"

Imogene closed her eyes and swore under her breath. "Meet him halfway, for God's sake. Call to him the moment I've gone."

"Imogene, I—" She stopped. She took a deep, shaky breath. "Thank you."

"I want that duck," Imogene replied, but she hurried to the door, taking the night rail with her. "Window seat. Call to him. *Now.*"

And then she was gone.

# Chapter Nineteen

Ian entered the duchess's suite to find it empty.

He hovered on the precipice, confused. "Hello?" he tried.

"I'm here, Your Grace." At the sound of her voice, he gripped the doorknob, squeezing the worn brass in anticipation.

*No guarantees, mate*, he told himself. *Keep calm. You've come to discuss logistical practicalities, nothing more.*

Also, there wasn't *time* for more.

Ian had business tonight on the docks of South London of all places. His estate manager Loring had sent a note after the wedding. Avenelle tenants *were* attempting to embark on a smuggling venture to sell their lace abroad.

Loring had tracked their scheme to a smuggling crew who were, at this moment, provisioning and making repairs in Blackwall.

Before Ian approached the tenants, he wanted to know everything about what they had planned. They trusted him so little after the riots, he could hardly come to them with gossip and conjecture. He must know who, and when, how much, and why. Only then could he offer some alternative to dissuade them.

As loathe has Ian was to venture out on this of all nights, smugglers were not known to remain in port for long, and they kept hidden in the light of day. Now was the time. Loring was set to meet him in Whitechapel in a matter of hours; they would ride to Blackwall and see for themselves.

It was highly unlikely that he'd spend "a matter of hours" with his new wife; but he could hardly go out without speaking to her at all. And so here he was, stepping around the door.

The room was dim, illuminated only by a low fire. His eyes adjusted slowly to the darkness. He craned his head, following the sound of her voice. He was just about to call out again, when he saw her.

She was perched in the window seat. *Perched.* Shoulders tight, feet drawn up, like a girl on a village wall. He blinked, struggling to make out the fine details. He took another step.

"Miss Trelayne?"

Outside the window, a cloud was tugged from the moon and white light flooded the alcove.

*Holy bleeding hell.* She was *not* a girl on a village wall, she was a goddess who'd fallen from the sky and settled in the window.

Her pale face was half obscured by her hair. *So much hair.* Ian stared, distracted like a—well, like a man who'd seen a beautiful woman.

"Hello," he repeated.

Her expression was open, innocent, and uncertain. It was the same way she'd stared at him in the gallery. It propelled him in a way he would not have imagined. His mouth watered and his body grew languid and heavy. The reaction was strange, because he'd never before dealt in innocents; his uncle had taught him better than to chase after virginal women. His past lovers had been aggressively assured of what they wanted and how they wanted it. The untried, open question on her face was an elixir from which he wanted to drink and drink and drink.

But first things first. He'd come in to discuss any of a

number of arrangements not yet defined about their future. To sort out where they'd live and when, to tell her of access to his carriages, to ask how he might assist in the plans for her finishing school. Perhaps all of that could wait.

He took another step toward her. Softly, he said, "Are you well, Miss Trela—" He stopped and chuckled. "May I call you Drew?"

Her large teal eyes had, remarkably, grown larger. She nodded her head.

Another step.

Her hair obscured the straps of her night rail, but he'd caught a flash of bare shoulder. Oh, and her throat—also bare. Every new glimpse of creamy skin set off a pulse of desire.

"Yes," she said, a whisper. "Call me Drew if you like."

She scooted back on the window seat. The movement caused her hair to slide away, the parting of a curtain. His breath caught. She wore a slip of ivory silk so transparent he could make out the outline of her breasts, the curve of her hip, the shape of her thigh.

Ian's body, already hardening, turned to stone; his vision became a tunnel that blocked all but her, cream skin and red hair and aquamarine eyes, glowing in the moonlight. His purpose in life became only her.

"Will you call me Ian?" he asked gently, taking another step. "We're married, after all."

"Yes," she said, and the huskiness of her voice was a caress.

She watched him advance like a cat watches a toy on a string, mesmerized, a little leery, voracious.

"I hope you don't mind the new maid. I should have asked you, but I thought of it too late. Or rather, Her Royal Highness, Princess Cynde, suggested it, too late—as in this morning. I dared not trouble you with it on such a busy day. If the woman doesn't please you—"

"She seems very proficient," Drew said. "Thank you."

"When I heard excitable voices through the door," he

said, "I worried she was somehow taking you to task. She's not a scold, I hope?"

The slightest blush stained her cheeks and throat. "No," she said, looking at her hands in her lap. "She's not a scold."

"Well, I cannot complain with her ministrations. You look . . . beautiful."

Her head shot up. "I'm wearing, um . . ." Her eyes held a look of mild horror, as if he'd caught her wearing stolen shoes.

"Beautiful," he repeated, stepping to the edge of the window seat.

He wanted to reach for her; it was almost his only thought. If he reached for her, it was doubtful she would resist him, but this felt, for some reason, like the wrong play.

He could *ask her* if she would welcome his touch, but this also felt off. Too logistical. They'd spent the day going through the motions of an event that should have, by all accounts, been far more sentiment than mere sequence. All of the formal and rote "do you takes" and "I vow tos . . ."

This moment, perhaps, called for a more intimate touch.

"Is there room for me on this window seat, Miss Trelayne?" he asked.

She blinked at him. "I thought you intended to call me Drew."

"And perhaps I will. Or perhaps 'Miss Trelayne' is too familiar and pleasant to let go. Perhaps I've not yet decided what I'll call you. I've not heard you call me Ian."

"No, Your Grace."

"Now you're taunting me." She hadn't invited him to sit but she hadn't told him to go away, so he lowered himself onto the velvet cushion. He leaned back against the cold glass and propped one foot on the ledge, resting his elbow on his knee. He took a deep breath. His heartbeat had kicked up. Could she hear it? It was deafening inside his head.

"Hello," he murmured, rolling his head to the side to look at her. She made a small noise, half murmur, half giggle.

She was nervous but not frightened. She had the look of someone who was next in line to jump over a hedge on a strong horse.

"Hello," she replied, a whisper.

"Did you enjoy the wedding, Lady Lachlan? And the breakfast?"

"Oh yes. Very much." She shifted in the seat. Her tense-shouldered, propped-knee perch was less stable with his considerable weight on the cushions. Carefully, she scooted to the glass behind them, taking pains to tuck her long creamy legs, dotted (he could now see) with strawberry freckles, beneath her. The thin silk was pulled taut across her thighs and gaped above her breasts. Her hair spilled around her in a waterfall of red. She reached up deftly to gather it over her shoulder and dropped it in her lap. This left the closer shoulder exposed to him. The silk was held in place by a lone ivory strap. Ian licked his lips. He was, he realized, *starved* for the taste of her. Had he known how much he wanted her? Could a man starve and not realize it until he was seated next to a feast?

"What about the wedding pleased you most?" he rasped.

"Well, I suppose that I liked . . ." she began softly, ". . . that when it was over, I was married," she said, finally looking at him shyly.

If she left off the words *to you*—*When it was over, I was married* to you—Ian elected not to dwell.

"Better than deportation to Canada, is it?" he ventured, lolling his head closer to her. The window box smelled of old velvet and chilly condensation, but the closer he inched, the more he smelled the soft vanilla scent he remembered as distinctively hers. He'd worn his boots, and suddenly he wanted them off. He'd worn his waistcoat, and he wanted that off too. He wanted everything off. But he'd come in to talk—a single, closed-mouth peck had been his greatest ambition—and not to do . . . whatever they were doing. He was in favor of it, strongly in favor, but he was dressed entirely wrong. Idly, he began to loosen his cravat.

"I was always wretched at being young," she volunteered, looking up.

He paused with the neck cloth. "I beg your pardon?"

"My existence," she explained. "As a young woman. I was a failure at it. That is, I was never very good at most girlish, whimsical, romantic maneuverings. Before I . . . transformed, when I looked a bit different and behaved a lot differently, I was *too much* of everything. And it put people off. Friends, would-be suitors, everyone, really. I was too colorful, too erratic, too aggressive, too . . . selfishly focused on myself.

"When I *transformed*, I seemed to be not colorful or impulsive or erratic enough. I am better off embodying a mature . . . sort of *aged* existence—that much is clear—even if I am not yet literally *old*. Well, not terribly old. I could never seem to make a go of the great mystery that is Young Womanhood—not as an identity, not really—but I'd grown certain that I'd make an excellent spinster."

"Sto—"

She held up a hand. "Oh no please, do not worry—I'd made peace with it. I'd anticipated my life 'on the shelf,' as they say. There is a pressure, an expectation, for young women to be alluring. What I've wanted is to be old enough for that expectation to . . . drop off."

"Are you saying marriage to me sabotaged your long-awaited future as some sort of . . . of—"

"Old maid?" she finished with a chuckle. "Oh no, not at all. Marriage is an unexpected change of course for me—yes. But it's not necessarily an unwanted one. I was traveling down the road to . . ."

"Spinsterhood?" he asked, still in disbelief.

She nodded sagely. "I was resigned to it. Now I find myself taking a different path. But the destination remains the same. As a married matron, I'll be protected from any expectation of . . . of allure or—"

"Stop talking," Ian rasped. His voice was just above a

whisper. He extended one finger and placed it gently on her bottom lip.

Her teal eyes flew to his.

"I'll not listen to you talk about yourself as if you do not incite desire." He removed his finger.

"As if I don't incite . . ."

"Do I appear *disinterested* in you, Miss Trelayne?"

"I beg your pardon?" This time, it was a question.

"Drew," he said. "Do I seem like a man who feels no desire for you?"

Slowly, she shrugged.

"No truly, I'd like to know," he pressed.

"I . . . I could not say, Your Grace," she tried.

Ian narrowed his eyes. They'd circled back to the *Your Grace* he realized. Fine. So be it. Perhaps he could use that to his advantage.

He eyed her, considering a kiss. It would take no effort to close the distance between them and claim her mouth. Few gestures would demonstrate his very significant desire more clearly. However, unless he was mistaken, the situation wanted something more.

He cleared his throat. He readjusted his sprawl in the window seat. "Will you look at me, Miss Trelayne?"

For a long second, she was motionless, she was holding her breath. Finally, she shook her head *no*.

"*No?*" he challenged, his voice teasing.

"No, Your Grace." A whisper.

*I was right*, he thought, *she feels some security in the title.*

"You are aware," he asked, "that a duchess need not invoke so many 'Your Graces' and 'His Graces' now that she is married?"

This won him a look. "But you refer to me as Miss Trelayne."

"Yes, I suppose I do—that is, I *have*. I quite like the name, actually."

She looked again at her lap. "Perhaps I like 'Your Grace.'"

"Well, you may be the only one. Between the twins, my disgruntled tenants, and fickle London society, starry-eyed supplicants are not thick on the ground." He frowned. "Not that you are starry-eyed. Or a supplicant."

"No, Your Grace," she whispered.

The very sweet, very bashful sort of whisper of it—in fact this entire conversation, which had become a rabbit hole of unmet desire—gave him an idea.

"I've bade you to look at me, Miss Trelayne." An order. Gentle, but there was no denying it.

She sat up and blinked at him, her teal eyes wide and bright.

"Do you know the signs of a man's desire for a woman?" he asked.

She endeavored to duck her head again, and he scolded gently, "*Tut-tut-tut.* Look at me."

Slowly, breathlessly, she turned back. "I *don't* know," she admitted, a whisper.

"But would you like for me to teach you?"

She opened her mouth to say something but he held up a hand. "Can you listen very carefully, Miss Trelayne? If I were to teach you? You are the primary source of instruction in this house, but now let us see if you might also play the pupil."

He could see her eyes searching his face, trying to decipher his tone. He'd meant to strike a balance between authority and playfulness, but this conversation had piqued his own arousal. However he sounded, it was a far cry from the easy, trusting rapport they'd fallen into when she'd joined the household. Before, they conspired; now, he corrupted.

"Tell me, Miss Trelayne," he asked softly, "how do my eyes look?"

"They look very blue, Your Grace," she whispered.

"Right, but their expression?"

"Oh. They are—? Are they tired?"

"No," he said, "not tired. My eyes are lazy. Languid. I am looking at you with eyes half closed, because when I see you, I think of bed. Bedsheets. Pillows. And . . . not sleeping so much as *before* sleeping."

If possible, her eyes grew wider. She put a palm over her throat, fingers splayed. She swallowed and told him, "I've—I've incited—" She breathed in and out quickly. "I've dressed inappropriately. This night rail . . ." She looked down. "This night rail is not a rail at all, it's a simple shift. I was compelled—I was told—"

"Shhh," he urged softly. "Miss Trelayne, given the choice, I would see you in nothing more than this. Every night. For the rest of our lives."

She stared at him.

"You please me in every way," he went on, "except when you suggest that you have no allure, that you are not *desirable*. Now I intend to demonstrate the extreme falsity of this notion."

"Oh." A little gasp. The hand her at throat drifted to her hair, and she twirled a fat, red curl around her index finger.

"Miss Trelayne?" he prompted. "May I demonstrate?"

"Yes, Your Grace." A whisper.

Ian cleared his throat. "Very good. Now. Do you see my chest, rising and falling?"

Miss Trelayne stared at his chest with intense focus, like someone trying to find the hidden imagery in a Renaissance painting.

He chuckled. "My breath is coming fast, is it not?"

She bit her lip and nodded slowly.

"Labored breath, some might call it?"

While she stared, he shrugged from his waistcoat and tossed it aside. He unbuttoned the top five buttons of his shirt, and it hung open to his bare chest. Now her gaze shifted from his clavicle to his pectorals. Her expression was mesmerized, hungry.

"Give me your hand," he ordered.

Slowly, gingerly, she slid her hand from her hair and extended it to him. He took it and pressed it over his heart. Her touch was cool and soft and far less shy than her expression let on. Her fingertips dug firmly into his skin.

"Can you feel my heartbeat, Miss Trelayne?"

She nodded.

"How does it feel?"

"Quick," she whispered.

"Very astute. Do you know *why* it's quick? Why my breathing is hard and my heartbeat fast?"

Miss Trelayne shook her head. Her hand remained on his chest, and the position tipped the two of them together; their faces only inches apart. Her knees touched his thigh. Her hair fell across his arm.

"My heart is racing, and I struggle to breathe," he repeated, "because I am *excited. You* excite me, Miss Trelayne, and I have no control over it. I lost control of my breathing and my heartbeat the moment I saw you perched in this window."

This scared her a little, as he knew it might, and she went to snatch her hand away. He covered it with his own, gently holding her there.

"I'm going to kiss you," he said, a statement.

She did not deny or invite, she simply stared, eyes wide, cheeks flushed, her hand on his heart. Very slowly—with a slowness he would classify, in fact, as *excruciating*—he leaned in, giving her ample time to move away, or hide behind her hair, or shove him onto the floor.

Instead, she closed her eyes and craned to meet him.

Ian, in an unbelievable show of restraint, kissed her once very slowly, his closed lips fitted against hers. She sucked in a little intake of breath against his mouth. He remembered the sound from the gallery; he *loved* that sound.

He allowed the kiss to settle and sink, nearly perishing with want. After a long moment, he pulled back just enough to check her expression. Her eyes remained closed, but now her face was turned up, her lips ever so slightly *parted*. Her loose-fitting ivory shift drooped at the neck, revealing the swell of small pert breasts. The winter white of her skin had ripened to a sun-kissed pink.

Ian swore under his breath. He'd never seen anything so enticing—virginal redheads in thin, white shifts, who knew?—and kissed her again. The second kiss was chaste; but the third was not so chaste, and then he delved into an entirely brazen kiss, swiping her lip with his tongue before plunging into her mouth. After that, one kiss melded into the next. Words like *allure* and *desirable* were weak and insufficient.

He slid his fingers into her hair, cupping her head to hold her in place. With the other hand, he encircled her wrist and pulled her palm from his heart, sliding it around his back. He kissed her until he couldn't breathe; kissed her until she was draped over him in a wonderful, sort of full-body drape that was just a little bit taut, rigid with excitement.

Then he kissed her until her head fell back, and *she* fell back, and the two of them tipped and he was on top of her in the window seat. He found the hem of her shift and slid his hand up the glorious length of her leg, bunching the silk at her waist. Their legs entangled.

His boots were a constricting nuisance and he reared up, balancing on one knee to remove first one, and then the other.

When he looked down on her, he saw her in a pool of red curls on peacock-colored velvet; she was creamy skin tinted pink from his touch; a rumpled ivory shift barely clinging to her body. She stared up at him, her own eyes half-lidded—but not at his face. She perused his body like a jockey assessing a racehorse. When her gaze fell to the rise in his trousers, she treated Ian to an expression that he would remember the rest of his life; likely it would be his last thought before death.

"Do you know how else you might determine how much I want you, Miss Trelayne?" he asked. How could he not?

She stared up. She shook her head.

"You know what happens between a man and woman—how did you explain it in the carriage? 'In the intimacy of marriage?' You know how our bodies will unite?"

"I . . . think," she whispered.

He threw the second boot, harder than he intended. Everything she said aroused him more.

"You *think*?" he repeated slowly. He remained on a knee above her. "And tell me, Miss Trelayne, does this thinking include a very crucial piece of my anatomy that grows very hard and urgent when I am . . . as we've said . . . 'excited'?"

She blinked at him.

"That is," he continued—it was killing him to keep up the casual, languid explanation, but it was the very best kind of death—"my body grows hard so that it can actually delve inside your body. And what makes this happen . . . this hardening . . . is *engaging* with a woman I find very alluring, a woman I want very much. A woman who is absolutely nothing like an *old maid*."

"Ah . . ." she stammered, staring up at him.

"That's you, Miss Trelayne," he whispered. "*You*. Because there is *engaging* with a woman and then there is 'engaging' with you. And what you and I are about to experience—or what I am very hopeful we are about to experience—is . . . total engagement. With my wife. Invoking my very hard, very urgent bits. You might as well know. Since we've covered my languid eyes, and pounding heart, and my heavy breath."

"Oh," she said, a whimper.

Ian dropped over her but held himself off, balancing on his knees and elbows. "Give me your hand, Miss Trelayne."

"Your Grace," she whispered, a plea.

"Come now, Miss Trelayne, we've veered this far off your road to spinsterhood, we cannot stop now."

"Your Grace," she repeated, breathless.

"Duchess," he said in a teasing sort of growl, nuzzling her neck. "The duke has asked for your hand."

Finally, she gave the answer they both required. "Yes, Your Grace," she breathed.

She raised a trembling hand. He took it up, pulled it to his lips, kissed the pulse point on the underside of her wrist, and then, never taking his eyes from her face, he slowly moved it down his body to settle it over the heavy rock-hardness of his erection.

Miss Trelayne sucked in a startled breath, but she did not shy away. Her long delicate fingers cupped him through his buckskins, squeezing slightly, and Ian thought he would perish. The pleasure was so intense, so obliterating, he barely managed to balance above her, to continue the seduction, to keep control.

"Now, Miss Trelayne," he managed, his voice a rasp, "do you doubt your allure or desirability? Can you feel how much I want you?"

"Yes, Your Grace," she said breathlessly and squeezed him again.

Ian snapped, dropping on her body like a tree felled in a storm, trapping her hand between them, kissing her mouth, her neck, her ear, her mouth again, devouring her with kisses and grinding into her hand.

Miss Trelayne let out one of her scintillating little gasps, and then something that sounded like a laugh, then a moan, and then she simply endeavored to keep up.

When he turned his head, gasping for air, he panted, "To the bed, Drewsmina. Now. Bed." It was the only language left to him.

He rolled from her and reached down to scoop her up. He tossed her over his shoulder, hair swinging over them in an arc. The movement ejected a sparkling object from her hair, and Ian responded on instinct snatching it from the air.

"A dragonfly?" he asked, studying the jeweled comb.

She said nothing but held out a hand. He placed the comb in it and she tossed it—she actually hurled it—in no specific direction.

Ian laughed and stalked to the bed. The room was not small, but he crossed it in five strides. He toppled her from his shoulder and pitched her to the center of the mattress.

"If you don't want this, tell me now," he growled.

Miss Trelayne scrambled into a half-sitting position in the center of the bed, scraping the hair from her face, gasping for breath.

"Drewsmina?" he demanded, shucking his trousers and drawers, ripping off his shirt. "Do you want it?"

"Yes," she breathed, staring hungrily at his nakedness. "Yes, Your Grace."

# *Chapter Twenty*

"Eager" did not begin to describe Drew's current frame of mind. Also not applicable: Resigned or gentle.

Voracious was more accurate. Maddened. She *wanted*, and she *wanted*, and she *wanted*—all the doubts about how she looked or whether she was wanted in return could barely be heard.

This had been Lachlan—his gift to her. He'd liberated her from all of her troubling hesitations and insecurities. She needn't worry about what to do or how she appeared; she need only follow along. He gave her no room to overthink any of it. It took her breath away.

"Off with the shift," he said gruffly, kneeing to her on the bed.

"Off?" She'd barely managed to absorb the sight of him, naked beside her on the bed, and now he was asking—?

Surely not.

They weren't even under the coverlet. The room was aglow with firelight. He would see—

"Off," he confirmed and then he reached out, grabbed the hem of the flimsy shift, and skimmed it over her head.

Drew gasped, exhilarated by the lack of choice or bother. She closed her eyes when the shift passed over her face; when she opened them again, the silk was gone and Lachlan was dropping on top of her, capturing her mouth in a kiss. She kissed him back, proud of how quickly she'd learned to kiss. She could let her mind go, could kiss him without really thinking about it. This allowed her senses to focus on the strange wonderfulness of having him drape across her. He was heavy but not thick; the absence of clothes revealed lean muscle. The gallery had only afforded her the very surface of his beauty.

He was nimble, not drooping over her so much as aligning his long taut body on top of her own. For how long had she resented her own height and thinness? She and Jericka Tavertine had worked for the better part of a year to develop patterns that made her appear less like a beanpole. But Lachlan made her feel as if her body complemented his; she was tall but he was taller. She was thin and he was strong and totally in control.

"Wait, wait," he mumbled, moving his mouth from her lips to her neck, kissing his way down. "Let me see you."

"N—" she tried, a reflex, but he was already on his knees above her, staring down with hot, hungry eyes.

Drew covered her face with one hand. Her other hand flew downward—an aimless, futile effort to cover herself.

He caught her by the wrist. "Please, don't. You're perfectly formed."

She peeked between her fingers, her heart molting at the sight of his expression, rapt, hungry, and adoring.

He swore under his breath, slow and reverent, and dropped

her wrist. Scooting back, he grabbed her legs on the outside of each thigh, and then slid his hands up the sides of her body. She shivered as his open palms moved up her thighs and over her hips. His fingers swooped as they rounded the dip of her waist; they bumped up and over, traveling the ridges of her rib cage. The journey left a trail of tingles that radiated outward like the sun and then settled in the most curious of places. It felt so very good, she closed her eyes. If she'd been bolder, more demanding, she might ask him to do it again and again. But she was not so bold, and also she found herself distracted. She felt an urgency, a warm burning in her center. A pool of warmth collected at the end-point of all of those tingles. She bit her lip and let out a little moan.

Lachlan chuckled, progressing his hands up her sides, stopping when he got to the ticklish place below her arms. She thought now he might take her up, or reverse his hands, or any number of—

He flicked his thumbs across the tops of her breasts . . . once . . . twice . . . and the sensation was so very extreme, Drew cried out and arched to him. Pleasure radiated with every pass of his hands. The burning between her legs intensified and she cried out again. Her eyes flew open and she grabbed him by the shoulders.

"Ian," she gasped, forgetting the title.

"Yes?" he asked, but he was preoccupied, not listening, watching his own thumbs with half-lidded eyes as they swiped across her breasts again.

"Ian!" she said again, if only to keep from screaming in pleasure, to keep from *begging him*—for what, she couldn't say. More. Everywhere. *There.*

He made a growling noise and dipped down to capture her mouth in a hard, demanding kiss. And then, in a flash of white-hot pleasure that stopped her thinking altogether, he transferred his kisses to her breasts. Drew gasped, holding his head, wrapping her legs around him. He'd kept himself aloft, balancing half on one knee, but now he collapsed on top of her. Drew cinched her legs more tightly around him, entwining the two of them in a full-body embrace. His thigh was pressed against her center, and the pressure ignited an entirely new ripple of sensations, unbelievably more pleasurable than before, and she arched against him, seeking more, crying his name.

"I cannot wait, Duchess," he hissed, rising up. He kissed her again hard. "Forgive me."

Drew replied with a moaning noise, pressing herself against him again.

"Can I take that as a yes?" he grunted, sliding downward, grabbing her hip and hitching one leg onto his haunch.

"What?" she rasped.

"May I finish this?"

"There is a . . . finish?" she asked.

He laughed, a painful, choked sort of sound. "Oh yes."

Without thinking, she thrust against him again and he swore and looked down, repositioning himself between her legs. She whimpered at the loss of the contact, but he moved his hand to the same spot, and she moaned.

"Typically the finish comes . . . after more time. But you are so bloody responsive and I'm overcome. I—"

And now he left off talking again, looked down, made some adjustment with their bodies. He moved his hand and she felt another pressure, hard and demanding—*better.*

*How could this be better?* she wondered. Nothing was better than the previous thing . . . until it was.

"Duchess?" he asked, his voice a groan.

Drew moaned and thrust up.

"Drew?" he demanded, breathless, desperate.

She couldn't answer, she could only burn.

"Will you take me?"

"Yes, Your Grace," she panted, canting up.

Lachlan swore, leaned in, and thrust.

Drew felt a tightness, a fullness, and a tearing sort of pain pierced the haze of pleasure. She sucked in a breath. He fell forward, balancing on his elbows, his face inches from hers. They were both panting.

Her body felt strung so very tautly, like the tightest string on a violin. He was also taut, she could feel the tension and pent-up . . . pent-up—something was so very pent—and his face was tight with something like agony.

She whispered, "What happens now?"

"Now," he breathed, "we wait."

"Wait for what?" A whisper.

"For you to relax."

"I am relaxed."

"No, you're not."

"Will *you* relax?" she asked. The moment of pain had chased away some of the mind-numbing pleasure, and she could think again. She found herself full of questions.

"I will not relax," he informed her. He shifted ever so slightly, and Drew felt a tiny pang of sensation, a distant cousin of the pleasure she'd felt before.

Her eyes flew to his. In a whisper, she asked, "Am I finished?"

"No." A grunt. "Sorry. Give me one more second to garner my self-control. I am not accustomed to virgins."

She narrowed her eyes, not caring for all of the non-virgins to whom he *was* accustomed.

"I'm going to kiss you, but I'm *not* going to move." It was a declaration and a vow.

He kissed her then, soft and slow at first, then faster, more pressure; finally a lovely combination of soft but also demanding. Drew's mind began to float. She felt another fissure of pleasure, a warmth. The wonderful, demanding burn began again, pooling in her center. Next, the need. Before she realized, her hips began to move.

"Thank God," Lachlan growled against her lips. He dipped lower to suck on her breast, and the pleasure became a fully formed, all-encompassing thing, like diving into a pool.

She called his name, but he answered only, "Careful," and kissed her.

*Careful?* she repeated in her head, wondering what he

meant. But then she stopped thinking, she could only feel. He'd begun to move, meeting her thrusts. Small at first, then harder, then powerful and deep, pumping with a force that both thrilled and beckoned her. The harder he drove, the more she wanted.

She was just about to call out his name when it happened . . . some unknown trigger in her body clicked to, and all of the building and burning culminated in a firestorm of ecstasy and light and bits of her consciousness launching into the air. She gasped and cried out in the same breath, she dug her fingers into her hair and pulled, she went taut, she hovered, she floated on every last sensation, not knowing when they would end. She blinked up, seeing nothing but fuzzy pleasure.

Finally, when the eruption seemed to pulse away, she slowly, pleasantly, sank into the mattress, still clutching his head.

"*That*," he said lowly, "was the finish, I believe."

"Oh," she said.

After a beat, she whispered, "So, we've finished?"

"No," he said. "Only you have done. I am—"

He stopped talking and thrust. "Is this alright?" he rasped.

"Oh yes," she assured him, beginning to comprehend. She pressed up a little, encouraging him. He met her thrust, and then the next, and then the next; and then he pumped into her with an abandon that Drew found wild and thrilling and all the proof she would ever need that he desired her. At least in that moment.

His finish was accompanied by a guttural shout, a hard kiss, his head thrown back, and a final thrust. She felt him empty inside her, felt his consciousness hover just as hers had. Then she felt him collapse. He draped on top of her and gathered her up, burying his face in her hair.

Drew paused for a moment, trying to carefully catalog and interpret everything that had just happened. But her mind was spinning; she could not catalog or interpret. She could only rest in a shallow sort of float-like state. Absently, she wrapped her arms around him and held him, a sweet, possessive, intimate gesture that she liked almost as much as every other intimate thing they'd done.

She stared at the ceiling, wanting to freeze time.

*It was very stupid of me to pine for spinsterhood.*

Her heart pounded, and every beat said the same thing, *I've fallen in love. I've fallen in love. I've fallen in love.*

Finally, he raised his head. He blinked at the headboard. He jostled.

"I'm crushing you," he said.

"No," she said, but she loosened her hold.

He tipped to the side, sliding from her, but he kept an arm draped loosely around her waist. They lay face-to-face. Her hair spilled a fan of orange across the bed.

"Well," he said. He settled his head on a pillow and looked at her.

"Well," she repeated. She felt suddenly very aware of her nakedness.

"Now you blush?" he asked.

"Oh, I feel sure I blushed . . . throughout?"

"You did, actually. You were glowing. But are you cold?"

"A little," she said. Now that her arms and legs were no longer entwined with his, the chill of the room had begun to encroach.

She felt very exposed, lying naked beside him. She scooped up a hank of her hair and dropped it over her shoulder, covering her breasts.

He rose up to tug a quilt from the foot of the bed and spread it over her. She was warmer, and covered, but his arm was gone. He was outside the covers and she was in. It felt terribly separate.

"Are you hurt?" he asked. His tone had changed. He sounded more like the Lachlan of their daily lives, the erratic employer, cordial but blunt.

"No," she said. Out of habit, she asked, "Are you?"

He laughed and rolled onto his back. "No," he said to the ceiling. "I'm the opposite of hurt. That was . . ." and here he paused. Drew held her breath, waiting for what he might say. ". . . probably something we both needed," he finished.

Drew did not exhale. She turned this statement over in her mind, searching for trick locks and hidden compartments. It was not a rude thing to say, she reasoned, not *unkind*, but it was still less than . . . less than—?

Well, it was *less*.

It was not *I needed you*; or even, *I wanted you*—although he'd already demonstrated this, she supposed.

It wasn't: *I will need that every night*. It was also not: *I will need* you *every night*.

It wasn't: *How wonderful*.

Or, if she was being completely fantastical, it wasn't: *How wonderful you are.*

She began to shiver; the blanket failed to keep out the chill.

Were these statements too much to ask?

*Yes*, she told herself. *Of course they are too much.*

*Careful, careful, Drewsmina, not to become greedy.*

Look how much she'd already gained. A husband. A title. A beautiful home. Nieces. *This* night with *this* man. There could be a baby. *A baby.*

Now her throat grew tight.

Only someone selfish and entirely deluded would presume *more* than these.

"Did you know," he said, "I only came to you to discuss our living arrangements."

"Oh," she said. She would stop, she thought, examining his statements for deeper meaning.

"We need not mete it out now," he went on. "It's hardly the sort of boring logistical talk one longs for in bed, is it? And anyway . . ." He leaned over the side and swiped his waistcoat off the floor, fishing in a pocket for his watch. ". . . *regrettably*, I have to leave you. I'm going out. I've . . . an errand. Someone I must meet."

"Out?" she asked, unable to keep the alarm from her voice.

"Unfortunately yes." He rolled from the bed. The cold had settled everywhere now. Her ears, her nose, her hands, her heart.

She hunched under the blanket and tried to school her features. For no reason, tears burned the backs of her eyes. He was naked before her, tugging on his clothes, beautiful in the firelight, but she looked away.

"I've no intention of intruding on another minute of your sleep. You must be exhausted. After the wedding and a full day with the girls."

"Yes," she said, turning to her back. She stared at the ceiling again. He was going. He'd come when she thought he would not, he'd consummated the marriage when she thought he would not.

He'd done so much more than expected.

He was not slinking away, or lying about it. He'd told her he would go, and now he'd do it—he would go. This happened in marriages, she supposed. Her sister Ana's husband, Lord Madewood, left their home well after dinner. How many rows had she suffered through, Ana accusing and begging him not to go, Madewood either lying or ignoring? This had not been Lachlan's way; his openness neither deceived nor excused. She needn't fret. No promises had been made about . . . about . . . errands in the middle of the night.

"I dread it, honestly," he said, shrugging into his waistcoat, "but I've a pressing matter that cannot go unattended."

Drew could not trust her voice. She nodded to the ceiling.

"What's on the schedule for tomorrow?" he asked.

"More of the same," she said, her voice a whisper to disguise the tears. "No outings, only lessons and tutors and practice. It is the day after tomorrow that we've been summoned to Kew Palace."

"Right. Well . . ." He came around to her side of the bed. He stood above her, looking down. "I think we've done the right thing, Miss Trelayne."

"Yes," she said, not knowing to which "right thing" he

referred. She could agree on so many fronts. It had been the right thing to marry; it had been the right thing to make love. It wasn't *wrong* for him to now leave her bed. He had an errand.

After a moment of staring at her face, his expression enigmatic, he leaned down and kissed her. It took her so very by surprise, her mouth fell open as she watched him descend. He caught her lips apart and kissed her thoroughly, deeply, possessively.

The kiss was so disparate from his speedy farewell, she almost bit him, trying to puzzle through it all.

But she did not bite him, she kissed him back, and closed her eyes, and coiled her arms around his neck.

He made a growling noise and pulled back, grinned at her—a grin that could have no other purpose but to crack open her heart—and then kissed her once more, hard and fast. After that, he turned away.

"Careful, Duchess," he called, walking to the door. "I might slip back into bed and then where would we be?"

*Yes, where?* she wanted to ask. *Where would we be if that happened? Where are we now?*

She said none of this. She turned her head on the pillow and watched him cross to the private door through which he'd come. There he hovered a moment longer. Again, she held her breath.

"Should I send the maid to attend you?" he asked.

She turned away. "No, thank you. Good night, Your Grace."

He tapped the door frame twice with his hand and was gone.

## Chapter Twenty-One

Dan was halfway to Whitechapel when he realized he was being followed.

He swore, cocking his ear to the sound of intermittent hoofbeats behind him, and turned off his planned route. Naturally it would come to this. First he'd been forced to leave the warm bed of his new wife to muck about in Blackwall, and now—a stalker.

Ian wasn't given to intrigue, not compared to someone like the Duke of Northumberland, but he *had* served in the bloody army, and he knew the cautious, *clip-clop* of a lone rider, just out of view.

Keeping his gait even, he reined his horse eastward, winding down one unexpected street, then another. In addition to putting him off schedule, the new route made no sense; but it would be impossible to follow except by the most devoted tail.

And follow they did. He *was* being stalked.

Ian swore again and kicked into a cantor, then a gallop. Finally, he rode full-out, as fast as the cobblestones would allow, burning up the road until a dark alley came into view. Reining hard, he whipped into the shadows and spun his horse. He leaned against the animal's neck, whispering into his ear, bidding him to keep calm and quiet. He held his breath.

Within moments, the scrambling hoofbeats of the lone rider clattered into earshot. Ian's horse shook his mane and whinnied, agitated by the frantic energy of the approaching animal. Ian bit off his glove to stroke his neck heavily, trying to quiet him.

The stalker tore up the street, slowing only briefly at the mouth of the alley. When he was five yards beyond, the hoofbeats slowed again; this time they came to a stop.

Keeping close to the wall, Ian slowly nudged his mount to the precipice of the alley. Carefully, he leaned in his saddle to peer around the corner.

The other horse was stopped, spinning and stomping in the center of the road. The rider, clothed in a voluminous black cloak with a deep hood, whipped his head about, looking right and left.

Ian squinted into the moonlight, trying to discern the rider's face. He was a small man, nearly as small as a child, but he handled the horse with expert—

Ian froze.

He stared harder.

A wheat-colored lock of hair fell loose from the cloak, so long it nearly touched the horse. Tiny black gloves maneuvered the animal—a mare, Ian now saw—by tugging on her mane.

*There was no bridle. And no reins.*

Ian swore, dropped back into his saddle and, forgetting concealment, kneed his mount from the alley.

"Imogene," Ian called.

The rider spun around and . . .

. . . there she was.

His sixteen-year-old niece, holding tight to the mane of the mare. An animal he'd bought only a week ago for the purpose of "beginner's lessons" and "learning to ride."

"Imogene—what in God's name?" He nudged his horse to her.

"Oh," said a voice that belonged, unmistakably, to Imogene. "How stealthy you are."

"Said the kettle to the pot," Ian remarked.

Her hood fell back and he saw her face. Her nose was red from the cold. Her hair splashed yellow against the inside of her hood. Her eyes dared him to reprimand her.

Ian dared.

"What the devil do you think you're doing? It's the middle of the bloody night. You're meant to be at home, in bed, not streaking across London on a horse that—unless I'm mistaken—is entirely devoid of a saddle. Perhaps you've not discerned this about me, but I *detest* surprises. *What are you thinking?*"

"What are *you* thinking?" Imogene shot back.

"No," Ian said with faux patience, "you may not answer *my* question with *another* question."

"Perhaps I won't answer your question at all."

"The devil you won't. You are aware, Imogene, that your time in London, and the Season, the tennis lessons, and even that horse on which you are riding—these are not *rights* to which you are *entitled*. They may all go away. Perhaps you cannot bring yourself to be pleasant to me or to Miss Trelayne—fine. Perhaps you cannot reveal to us what's happened to you these last five years—fine. But you *may not* run wild throughout the streets of London at all hours and refuse to answer for it. I am generous and I want you to be happy, but I'm not a fool."

"What *of* Miss Trelayne?" Imogene demanded, ignoring his speech.

He was so surprised by her question, he forgot his tirade. The very last card he expected her to play was *What of Miss Trelayne?*

"Miss Trelayne is at home," he shot back, "safe and sound. *As you should be.*"

"Shouldn't you refer to her as Drewsmina? She's your wife now, after all."

"It makes no difference how I refer to her. Not to you. And not here or now, for God's sake. *Now* we're sorting out *your* location and *your* purpose."

Imogene sat up straighter, her balance remarkable on the bare horse. The mare spun in a slow circle, stomping and shaking her mane.

Finally, the girl said, "I followed you, because I wanted to know why you left Miss Trelayne. I wanted to know where you were going."

"What difference is it to you where I'm going?" Ian challenged, although it sounded petty, and they both knew it.

"I could ask the difference to you," Imogene shot back, "where I've been in the last five years."

Ian stared at her. He cocked his head and readjusted his hat. "Oh I see. If I tell you my motivations, you'll tell me yours?"

"That's not what I said," sighed Imogene, tightening her glove. "You're the one with the secret. I'm here because I wish to learn it."

Ian said nothing. Fatigue washed over him, a wave he'd not seen coming.

"I cannot abide secrets," Imogene went on, her voice suddenly low and hard. "How disappointed I am to learn that you keep them too. All adults, I suppose, harbor secrets."

Ian opened his mouth to retort, but he closed it.

Her tone had shifted. Why did *he* suddenly feel like the guilty party?

She stared at the powerful shoulders of her horse. "One thing I can say about these last five years is, I learned a very important lesson. That lesson is, when an adult keeps a secret, it is rarely if ever a *good* secret. Rarely, if ever, does the secret translate into a boon for me or my sister. On the contrary. Secrets mean more bother. And risk. And heartbreak."

"Imogene," Ian began, but he stopped again. He was uncertain how to go on and it felt imprudent to simply guess.

He should know this bit by now; Imogene had repeated it so many times. She provoked him; it made him want to scold her as insubordinate and dismiss her as a nuisance. She precluded both with some telling revelation, usually something prescient and foreboding. It cut him like a whip. Every time.

"I want to trust you, Uncle," Imogene continued, speaking to the horse. "But your behavior must . . . must *be consistent*. You've just been married. You are meant to be tucked away with Miss Trelayne, not galloping *away* from her. When you ride away from Miss Trelayne, it feels as if you're riding away from all of us."

The whip cut him again.

"*Right*," he said finally. He let out a frustrated breath and swore. He looked at his timepiece. He looked again at his niece. She was gently stroking the neck of her mare, murmuring quietly in her ear.

She was correct of course. As loathe as he was to admit it. Secrets *did* lead to distrust. He *should be* at home with Drewsmina. Anyone as astute as Imogene would be watching and waiting. He couldn't say what she'd endured, but clearly, her past was marked by painful betrayal.

Was there great harm in revealing this business with the smugglers to his niece? That was debatable, but pursuit of him seemed almost like a test. Why he, the adult, was being put through the paces of *testing*, while Imogene, the child, roamed London freely at midnight, he couldn't say—but he did not want to fail. Not the test, not Imogene.

And anyway, he hadn't the time escort her back to Pollen Street, and she could hardly ride home alone. He and Loring had earmarked tonight for little more than surveillance and information gathering. Loring couldn't say for certain that *this* was the smuggling crew with whom his tenants had engaged. They meant to observe them and pin down proof.

*If* Imogene remained close to him . . . *if* she kept quiet . . . *if* she did as she was told—highly unlikely scenarios, one and all—perhaps tonight would not be a complete waste.

And perhaps he would pass the bloody test, whatever it was.

"Fine, Imogene," he said, reining his horse around. "I've

estate business in the docks of Blackwall tonight. And *that* is why I've left home, and *that* is where I'm going. Tangling with you has put me off my schedule and I'm due to meet my man, Mr. Loring, in Whitechapel, so I haven't the time to escort you home. My only choice is to take you with me. Would that be amenable to you?"

Imogene's eyes grew large. She nodded.

"No surprise, that. But can you promise to be a very good girl?" He kneed his horse forward. "Can you do exactly as I say, when I say it? Can you conceal yourself in that cloak and not reveal yourself until we are safe and sound, back in Pollen street?"

"Yes, Uncle," said Imogene, guiding her horse beside his.

"How compliant we now are," he sighed, kicking his horse into a gallop, trying to make up for lost time.

"But what is the business?" Imogene asked, keeping pace with his horse.

"We've suspicion that some Avenelle tenants are entering into an agreement with known smugglers. To move their lace out of the country illegally."

"Smugglers," said Imogene. "How exciting."

"It's illegal—a hanging offense."

"Why would they risk it?"

"Because the Crown levies a steep export tax on English products sold abroad. They are small craftsmen and cannot pay the export tax and also make a profit on their lace. Smugglers could, in theory, sell their lace for no tax at all."

She was quiet for a moment; then she asked, "All of this for lace?"

"Not the cloak-and-dagger-y contraband one might expect, is it?" He glanced at her. She was a remarkable rider—and all with no saddle. It was a marvel.

He continued, "Quick lesson about Dorset, Imogene. It's been the home of Flemish craftsmen for generations, and their particular livelihood is a very fine type of handwoven lace called Honiton lace. It's highly prized throughout the world. Unfortunately, their old-world technique, which is slow and meticulous, is being edged out by lace made in mills. Mills can make lace cheaply. Mills can make lace very quickly. And mills can also pay export levies. My tenants are struggling to compete."

"But why have you not helped the craftsmen be competitive?" Imogene asked.

"I've tried, but they have a long, painful history of animosity with the mills, and I have been a friend to the mill owners and their businesses. In the end they are good for our village, despite the competition they create. All of it has caused a great deal of strife. Lives have been lost—and with those lives, I lost the lace-makers' trust in me. I would pay their export taxes, but they will not allow it; they want no part of me or my solutions. Instead, they've turned to smuggling. Or, we believe they may be considering the option of smuggling. If it is true, I must find a way to dissuade them."

"And it's just so terrible, is it? Smuggling? What if the smugglers are very good? What if they're never caught?"

"Because," Ian intoned, leading them over a bridge, "smugglers of any skill cannot be trusted. They may take the lace, sell it, and keep all the profits. Then my tenants would have no lace and no money. Also, the risk of arrest is too great. My people have tangled with the law enough."

Imogene was quiet and Ian thought, *There. Now you know my deep dark secret.*

"I will help you," Imogene said finally, a concession.

Ian stifled a laugh. "Ah—no. You will *not* help me. You will remain with your sister and mother and Miss Trel—and *your new aunt.* You will learn French and table manners and embroidery."

This sounded ridiculous and now she was the one to laugh. He glanced at her.

She smiled back and then squinted into the lights of Whitechapel beyond the bridge. "Should I also learn to ride a horse?" she teased.

"Oh yes. That too. Ah, but there is my man, Loring. All

joking aside. Imogene, please. I implore you. For God's sake. Keep quiet and follow along. He will lead us to the smugglers. From there, he and I are meant to get the lay of the land. One of us—likely Loring—may approach them about weavers in Dorset."

"I will—" began Imogene.

"You will be silent and biddable, Imogene, or I swear to God, I'll pack up your bedchamber and install you with Timothea. Would you like that? Think on it, I am as serious as the tomb. Unless you wish to be attached to your mother's side and suffer, night and day, the very odd worldview that is uniquely hers, you will do as you're told."

Imogene made a face. "You play dirty."

"It runs in the family," he said. "Obviously."

IAN AND IMOGENE returned to Pollen Street just before three o'clock in the morning.

The night had been as much of a success as one could expect from stalking known smugglers through the London docks with an uninvited niece. To her credit, Imogene had been (mostly) the picture of biddability. She'd kept back, she'd said very little, and she'd done what Ian bade.

Because someone had to keep back with her, Ian had dispatched Loring to approach the smugglers. This was likely for the best, as Ian had already failed once in pretending to be a peasant. Meantime, Imogene had identified an errant spy while they waited. Smugglers, apparently, were wary of uninvited callers, and they sent out a man to canvass the area as soon as Loring approached them.

Imogene had spotted the spy, and Ian had managed to get off his horse and pretend to examine the hooves of her mare. They transformed themselves into two riders with a lame horse, and the spy left them undisturbed.

An hour later, they'd met Loring back in Whitechapel, and the man had confirmed—yes, these were the smugglers engaged by Avenelle weavers. They would sail for the Dorset coast when their boat was repaired, they would collect a season's worth of lace, they would set course for France, and sell it to the highest bidder.

Or so they'd claimed.

"I don't believe it for a second, Your Grace," Loring had said.

"Why not?" Imogene had asked, cutting in before Ian.

"Ahhh," Loring had said, uncertain how to address his employer's uninvited *niece*.

Ian sighed. "Why not, Mr. Loring?" he repeated, shooting Imogene a look.

The young steward had looked back and forth between Ian and Imogene, clearly unsettled. He cleared his throat. "Gut feeling," he finally said. "A very bad, very uneasy feeling. You've heard of a man who won't look you in the eye? In my opinion, the same goes for a man who stares *too* direct-like, who holds your gaze and won't let go. They pinned me to the wall, Your Grace, with their hard, greedy eyes. I know when I'm being sized up for a fleecing. They were too interested, and 'doin' business' with them was made to sound too easy. The profits sounded too ready. I know a liar when I meet one."

Ian had considered this. "So you told them you'd come from Avenelle, like we discussed? You said you wanted in on the shipment?"

Loring nodded. "They believed me too. Barely controlled zeal at the notion of adding raw wool to the shipment. They were practically chomping at the bit. But I'd not trust that lot with a sack of grain, let alone a year's worth of sweat and toil. The weavers will lose everything. Mark my words. I've suspected this from the beginning, and now I've seen it. I'd not have sought you out in London if I didn't believe this would come to a very bad end."

Ian nodded gravely and reached into his purse. He provisioned Loring for another week's stay in London, bade him to carry on with surveillance of the smugglers and keep in touch.

"Now what?" asked Imogene when they parted ways

with the steward. They rode side by side toward Pollen Street.

"Now," he sighed, "I cannot say. Now I . . . make certain about the smugglers. I'm unsettled by surprises. We'll continue to watch them. I want to know everything I can learn about their plan."

They rode the length of one street in silence, Ian regretting his honesty. Imogene had enough about which to worry without adding the weight of estate management, smugglers, and desperate tenants to her life.

Hastily, he added, "You need not wrestle with it, Imogene. I'm the duke, I'll sort it out. Ignorance is a very great enemy, and it's fought with careful study. I'll determine exactly what the tenants intend. When I understand their motives, I'll think of something else."

"Right," dismissed Imogene, sounding not worried at all, "what I meant was, what will you do when we've reached home? To Pollen Street?"

"Oh," said Ian. And now he felt steeped in ignorance. "Now I will . . . go to bed?"

"You will return to Miss Trelayne, you mean?"

"Ah . . . I'd not given it a great deal of thought," he said. Although that was a lie. In between managing smugglers and Imogene herself, he'd given his new wife a very great deal of thought. Their wedding night had been an odd mixture of unplanned and explosive, and he had very little idea how Drewsmina felt about it. He'd been forced to leave in such a hurry. He knew only that she'd been quiet and watchful afterward, responsive and glorious during.

None of *this*, of course, would be discussed with his niece; in fact, he'd prefer not to discuss any part of his marriage with Imogene. He glanced at her. He was curious, however, about why she'd asked about Drewsmina. Of all things. After all they'd seen and done.

"Are you worried I'll tell Miss Trelayne that you've snuck out of the house?" he guessed.

"Oh, but you mustn't," she scolded impatiently. Her expression said, *After all we've been through?*

"Mustn't I?" he said, laughing at how entitled she sounded.

"I beg you, Uncle. Please do not." An exasperated statement.

"Beg me, do you?" he said, considering. To his knowledge, Imogene had never *begged* for anything. Even on the night the three of them turned up on his doorstep, she'd simply said, "Don't you want to invite us in?"

Now she said nothing more, and he worried he'd somehow embarrassed her. "If Miss Trelayne knew you'd snuck out, Imogene, she would be concerned and alarmed, but I'm doubtful she would be vicious or petty about it. She's hardly a tyrant."

"I don't care about her tyranny," she said. "I . . . I am a private sort of girl, in case you haven't noticed. I should hate for anyone to make any assumptions about me. Or my motives."

"What assumptions or motives?" he asked, chuckling. "What care have you if Miss Trelayne assumes you are bold and wild and do as you please, even in the middle of the night?"

Imogene refused to answer and Ian was left to translate what she was, in her own way, telling him.

Imogene had followed him because his moonlit "errand" looked and felt like a secret—or, more accurately, like a betrayal of some kind.

His plans for his return—whether he went to Drew or didn't—concerned her because . . . ?

But was she worried about him betraying Drewsmina?

Did she protect her new aunt? And herself, of course, by asking Ian not to reveal it.

Imogene didn't want Drew to know she cared about her.

"Perhaps I don't mention your involvement tonight," Ian ventured. "Perhaps I won't elaborate on anything that's happened tonight. Perhaps *neither of us* says anything at all."

"You're not going to tell her where you've been," Imogene said, a statement.

"Well, I've told her I had an errand pertaining to the upkeep of Avenelle."

"Secrets."

"Not a secret," he countered. "I'm simply protecting her from the worry of it."

"You should include her," Imogene said, "in everything."

"Everything but your unnecessary riding lessons. And your foray into the streets of London this night. And—let's be honest—God knows what else. You're to keep secrets and I cannot? Even for a good cause?"

"What good cause?" Imogene asked.

They turned the corner onto Oxford Street, but he barely noticed. He was warming to this topic. "Not burdening my new wife with the highly complicated conflicts related to estate business. She agreed to become Duchess of Lachlan under very odd circumstances, no one knows this better than you. I should like to shield her, at least for a time, from my struggles as duke. She needn't know immediately that I've yet another mutiny afoot. Not literally on her *second day* as duchess. Can you allow that? It's less of a secret and more like something with which I've no wish to plague her. And for good reason; you and your sister are plague enough. If you're so very concerned about your new aunt, let us think of ways to entice her, not alarm her."

"Yes," Imogene said, her voice far peppier than before. She seemed cheered by his answer.

*Well, hooray*, Ian thought darkly. At least Imogene was satisfied. Meanwhile, giving voice to his fears aloud only made them seem more real. In his head, his tirade continued.

*I cannot lose Drewsmina before I've actually won her*, he thought.

*I cannot lose any of them. Not the tenants, the girls, my sister.*

*But especially not her.*

The next quarter hour was spent in relative silence. When they reached the mews behind Pollen Street, they stabled their horses and slipped inside. Ian made a point of witnessing his sleepy niece enter her bedchamber and pull the door shut. Next, he crept to Drewsmina's room. For a long moment, he hovered, his hand over the knob. He wanted her—her body, yes, but he'd also simply wanted to see her face and hear the sound of her voice.

But what of his own face? he thought. He was damp and grimy and smelled like smoke and exhaustion. His mind was a riot of smugglers and tenants and how Imogene had learned to ride.

Considering all these, Ian knew any contribution to his wife's night would be uneasy silence, a frustrated scowl, and, if they were lucky, loud, restless snoring.

He moved away and fell into his own bed instead, vowing to wake in time to speak to Drew tomorrow. He would seek her out before she began work with the twins. He would apologize for leaving her bed after their first night together.

He would make amends.

He would not lose her.

## Chapter Twenty-Two

*C*ight hours later, long after the household had awakened and embarked upon their day, Ian roused from a dead sleep. He cursed his sloth, dressed quickly, and trooped downstairs.

Breakfast, he learned, had been cleared an hour ago and Miss Trelayne was in the ballroom, converting French verbs with Ivy while Imogene took a tennis lesson.

Ian pilfered an apple and a piece of honey cake from the kitchens and, heartbeat kicking up, sought out his family.

*When*, he marveled, clipping up the stairs to the ballroom, *did I acquire a family?*

Only "family," surely, could compel him to erect a tennis court in his ballroom.

Imogene's first two lessons had convened in the garden but Miss Trelayne had quickly seen the very great limits of the uneven paving stones and balls swatted over the stone wall. When she pointed out that tennis in general, and the tennis *lessons* in particular, seemed to represent Imogene's first-ever true passion—an activity to which she'd committed fully, no complaints or criticism, no cynicism—some solution was in order.

Miss Trelayne had hired a robust instructor called Mrs. Chutterbuck, or Bucky, as was her preference, who tromped about in men's battle boots and could easily palm three ten-

nis balls in one hand. Bucky saw immediate potential—
whether in Imogene or his purse, Ian was never sure—and
suggested *daily* lessons for the girl at the tennis club in
James Street.

Miss Trelayne promised to take this into consideration—
daily lessons in Haymarket would involve various logistical
challenges, not the least of which included transport, chap-
erone, and wardrobe (Imogene had taken to wearing a skirt
that fell just below the knee and long pantaloons for her lessons). In the meantime, Miss Trelayne suggested they make
use of the expansive second-floor ballroom. Bucky saw the
genius of the notion and cordoned off an approximated court
in the center and strung up a net.

Imogene had been so very thrilled that Ian sent out inquiries about constructing a proper clay court on the grounds
of Avenelle. He'd not played in years but had been fond of
the game at Oxford, and Imogene would need someone
against whom to play.

He ambled into the ballroom now, crunching the apple.
Imogene was bouncing a ball on her racquet and frowning
at Greenly, the butler, while Miss Trelayne and Ivy leaned
over a book. Across the room, Bucky made adjustments to
her makeshift tennis net.

"Your Grace," Greenly was saying, extending a silver
tray over her head.

Miss Trelayne and Ivy did not look up.

"I believe he means you," Imogene said, still bouncing
the ball. "*Aunt. Duchess. Your Grace.*"

"Oh," said Drew, looking up, "forgive me, Greenly. I'm
not accustomed to the, er—That is, it will take some time
to answer to the title."

Greenly bowed graciously.

"But what is this?" she went on. An ivory card rested in
the center of the butler's tray. "I'm expecting no one. But
are you certain the caller is for me?"

"Quite, Your Grace," droned Greenly. "She is ever so in-
sistent."

"*She?*" asked Miss Trelayne, eyeing the card. "Well, it couldn't be Princess Cynde, she doesn't bother with cards. Ana will make me come to her."

"We could run through every female in your acquaintance," said Ian, stepping to the tray, "or we could simply *read the card.*"

At the sound of his voice, Miss Trelayne looked up. Their eyes met, and the cream of her cheeks and throat warmed to pink. Ian winked at her, enjoying the oddest surge of gratification. But perhaps she was not damaged from last night.

He took up the card and flipped it. "Mrs. Betina Covington-Leeds," he read. "Lady Blicken. Who the devil—?"

Ian, who'd paid a small fortune to acquire a rushed special marriage license, suddenly remembered the name from the stack of documents.

Drew's mother.

Betina Covington-Leeds, Lady Blicken, was his new mother-in-law.

"Oh no," Drew said. She took two steps back and stared at the card like it was a severed limb.

"Drewsmina?" Ian asked carefully. He studied the card again. "Should we tell her—"

Drew spun to the collected group. "Everyone, listen very carefully. If ever you've held me in even the *slightest* regard, if your feelings for me extend even one notch above hate, I implore you—*I beg you*—listen very carefully and do as exactly as I say."

Ian frowned at her. *What the devil?*

Ivy closed the book. Imogene snatched the ball from the air and raised an eyebrow.

"Who is Lady Blicken?" Imogene demanded. "The woman on the soap label, isn't she?"

"That's Lady *Lichen*," corrected Ivy.

"Quiet, please," said Miss Trelayne, placing a hand to her forehead, closing her eyes. "Lady *Blicken* is married to Viscount Blicken—at least at present—and she is . . ." a deep sigh, ". . . *my mother*. More importantly, she is no one with whom to be trifled."

She took another deep breath. Ian had never seen her so agitated. Even after being discovered with him in the gallery, she'd not appeared so distraught. He took a step closer. Would it be appropriate to touch her? He wanted to take her hand.

"Let us all endeavor to do everything exactly as I say," Drew went on, "and perhaps she will . . . we will—Perhaps the day will not be ruined."

"*Ruined?*" said Imogene.

"What am I saying," muttered Drew. "We would be very lucky indeed, if she restricted ruination to only one day."

"You exaggerate," said Ian.

She'd not wanted him to meet her family prior to the wedding—it had been her very strong preference—and Ian had complied. He was annoyed by most people and generally considered it a small triumph to make the acquaintance of fewer, rather than more.

Drew's dire warning continued. "If we are too inviting, she will linger; if we are too dismissive, she will scurry away and espouse our rudeness far and wide. If we are proud, she will deflate us. If we are humble, she will exploit us. If we are—"

"What if we are simply *not home*," Ian suggested, "to callers?"

"No. The least-damaging thing to do is to receive her for a short time and get it over with. Greenly, where did you put her?"

"The pink salon, Your Grace."

"The pink salon, the pink salon . . ." Drew repeated.

"It's the one with all of the pink," provided Imogene.

"Yes, that will do as good as any," Drew said, thinking out loud. "Is she alone, Greenly, or is the viscount with her?"

"Alone, Your Grace."

"Right. Very well." She turned to the girls. "Imogene,

Ivy, do yourselves this favor and stay entirely out of view. Ivy, take your French studies upstairs and finish in your bedchamber. Imogene, carry on with your lesson and do not leave the ballroom until I come for you."

"Surely you do not expect me to hide away without even a peek," complained Imogene. "Not after this preamble."

"Surely I do," Drew said absently. She was patting her hair, smoothing her skirts. She recovered gloves from her pockets and worked her hands into the soft leather.

"And miss out on meeting *Lady Lichen*?" complained Imogene. "You're basically suggesting that we've been paid a visit by a right demon. How often does *this* happen? I should like to see a demon."

"Remember all of the demons pointed out by Reverend Sagg?" Ivy reminded.

"Those were not actual demons, Ivy, those were simply women he did not like."

"Well, my mother is not a demon," said Drew, "but she is someone that I do not like. We needn't stoop to name-calling; believe me, it has no effect except to make her more beastly. And anyway, there is nothing to see, Imogene, I assure you. She looks like any other woman of a certain age. In fact, she's rather pretty. But heed my warning, young women far shrewder than yourselves have been taken in. Her innocent features are deceptive and she can reduce you to tears with a word."

"Challenge accepted," laughed Imogene, cocking the tennis ball behind her head, tossing it up, and serving it across the ballroom in the direction of Bucky.

The large woman caught the serve on an upswing and lobbed it back. Imogene darted to the net and returned the volley, laughing as she went.

"Do not leave this ballroom," Drew called to the girl. "Imogene, please, I beg you!"

"Begging will not be necessary," Ian cut in. He stepped to the edge of the faux court. "Imogene? Carry on with your lesson. Do not leave this room."

To Ivy he said, "Off you go. Bedchamber. French. If you encounter the cat, take him too."

"Yes, Uncle," said Ivy, hurrying away.

"There's a good girl." He turned to Drew. "And what is your vision for me? Am I expected to flee or be reduced to tears?"

"I . . . I cannot say," she said, turning to look at him. She looked like someone trapped in a burning house with no idea how to escape.

"Let us remember, just for a moment, that you sailed into the drawing room of a strange townhome and managed to face down this lot—" he gestured to the twins "—almost feral at the time. In addition to my sister with her modified lute, *and*—worst of all—me. After I'd been terrible at the palace. And you did not bat an eye, did you? In fact, you seemed to enjoy it. When I'd been reduced to pacing and drinking heavily and had moved across the country because I didn't know what else to do. Don't tell me you'll succumb to hysterics *now*. Because of one woman?"

"You do not know her," Drew said softly. "You shouldn't have to know her. On top of everything else."

"Oh yes, what a very great burden you are, Miss Trelayne, with your bothersome problem solving and niece wrangling. I've seen mortal combat, I remind you. I believe I can handle an estranged mother-in-law."

"She is terrible."

"Then let me send her away. Save you the bother."

"Not terrible for me. I'm accustomed. For you. For the girls."

"Let's see, I've mentioned the battalions of Frenchmen, bearing down on me with long guns and bayonets? Also, deadly riots. As to the girls, apparently they've endured some blaggard called the Reverend Sagg and survived?"

"She will raise the topic of the riots, you may depend on it," Drew said. "If she knows anything of your sister, she will raise this too."

He shrugged and held out his arm to her. She stared at it like a hill she wasn't certain she could climb.

He was just about to tell her that, given the choice, he preferred to *discuss* the riots rather than be silently judged on gossip, when Timothea, infamous lute in hand, entered the ballroom.

"Oh no," whispered Drew. She took his arm and held on. And then, "Oh *no*," she repeated.

Ian looked up. Trailing behind his sister, or rather *floating* behind in a pronounced sort of *glide*, was a small middle-aged woman in a dove-colored dress and flowered hat. The woman looked . . . well, if not harmless, then certainly not impossible to defeat in a fair fight. If it came to that.

"Oh yes, here we are," Timothea was saying, crossing to Ian and Drew. "And Greenly too. How fortuitous. I'm expecting a call from my herbalist and she must be admitted without hesitation. It cannot be a repeat of last week. We're lucky she's consented to return, after that incident with the footman."

Drew froze on his arm, digging her fingers into the wool of his jacket.

In that same moment, a tennis ball whizzed by their heads, bounced twice, and rolled in the direction of Timothea.

Behind them, Imogene hissed a highly inappropriate word.

"Now, now, none of that!" called Bucky. "You overcorrected on the upswing."

The ball stopped its progress at Timothea's feet. She stared down at it like she'd been approached by a small dog.

"Perhaps it was ambitious," Ian said under his breath, "to think she could be contained by the frailty of the pink salon." He began the short walk across the ballroom.

"I'm so sorry," Drew whispered back.

"It would be unsporting to do this any other way."

Drew sniffed, part laugh, part groan. She took a deep breath, she straightened, she squared her shoulders.

"There's a good girl."

"Mama?!" Imogene called from behind them. "Toss the ball, can you?"

"I don't like things flying at my face," Timothea said, "you know this."

"It's not flying in your face. It rolled to your shoe. Can you not kick it, Mama?" called Imogene.

"My *bad toe*," reminded her mother, staring down at the ball.

"I've got it!" called Bucky cheerfully.

While they watched, the large woman trotted across the room, scooped the ball up with her racket, and jogged to the net. "*Out of bounds*," she sang, jolly and unconcerned. "Obviously!"

Ian chuckled, coming to a stop before his sister and the woman who was, presumably, his new mother-in-law.

"How do you do?" he said to Lady Blicken.

Timothea drifted away, distracted by the tennis match behind them.

The older woman smiled at him with an expression well north of warmth but not entirely indifferent. There was a voraciousness to her smile, an assessing.

"Lachlan," Drew said smoothly, "may I present my mother, Lady Betina Covington-Leeds, Viscountess Blicken."

The woman's hungry smile grew, and Ian saw the glint of an incisor. She extended a small, gloved hand. Ian bowed over it. "It is a pleasure to make your acquaintance, my lady."

"Likewise, Your Grace," the woman said smoothly. Her voice was melodious and cultured. She was not, Ian observed, unattractive. She looked perfectly pleasant in a smallish, doe-eyed, I-might-be-the-prettiest-one-here, sort of boring way.

Her dress was subtle in color but snug in fit; her gloves

were the perfect match; she would wear them only with this dress. On the outside of the gray leather, she wore a sizeable diamond ring. Her hat was piled to a height that invited notice rather than begged it. On the whole, her appearance projected wealth and quality; but her *expression* . . .

Her face was tight around the eyes, there was a pinch at the corners of the mouth. The constrictions formed something like . . . shrewdness? She was actively slotting the world into a hierarchical cone inside her mind. She would not necessarily put her own self at the top of the cone, Ian thought, that left no room for ambition. Instead, she slotted everyone else well lower than herself.

"What a surprise, Mother," said Drew. "Obviously we were not expecting you."

"How could you be, you've extended no invitation." She gave a little laugh. "I was forced to take matters into my own hands. A mother's prerogative. Now that you are a mother, perhaps my motives will be less of a mystery."

"I am not a mother," said Drew calmly. "I've been made an *aunt* by marriage, as I'm sure you know. You've made the acquaintance of Lady Tribble, mother to the duke's nieces."

"Ah yes, the baroness," said Lady Blicken, casting an amused glance at Timothea.

"I'd hoped to receive you in a more comfortable room. Let us retire to a salon, and I'll ring for tea," Drew said.

"Oh, it's too early for tea, surely," dismissed Lady Blicken with a chuckle. "If I had my wish, I should have a tour of this beautiful home."

Ian frowned. He didn't like her. And not simply because Drew did not like her. It made him *tired* to look at her; and Ian had enough exhaustion in his life without being forced to squire around a judgmental bag that his wife did not like and to whom he owed nothing.

"A tour," Drew had repeated. She'd not expected this, clearly. And now he knew Drew was off her game, because she was generally prepared for most things. Meanwhile, Lady Blicken had the look of someone who, if given half a chance, would happily paw through the silver.

"Yes, of course, a tour," cooed her mother. "Unless you are not yet *comfortable* in the home. If you do not *know your way* or are uncertain of what *liberties* you may enjoy here. Forgive me if I presu—"

"I'm perfectly comfortable, thank you," clipped Drew. "You've simply taken us all by surprise."

"Surely you can be torn away from these athletic feats and shows of strength," Lady Blicken went on, squinting over their shoulders at Imogene and Bucky. She looked at Ian, shaking her head. "Since girlhood, I have dissuaded Drewsmina from any activity not serene or ladylike. What choice did I have? She is a giantess among men, and that says nothing of other females." Now she laughed. "It would've been unsightly to watch her bound after balls and charge about courts. Can you imagine? At her great height? How fortunate that your niece is so very . . . fetching and petite. When men see her play, she will *entice*, rather than *astound.*"

Ian blinked, uncertain of which statement to address first. Beside him, Drew dropped his arm.

"This way, Mother," Drew said flatly. "Let us return to the ground floor. You'll be bored by the family rooms and you've seen the ballroom." Without waiting for Lady Blicken, she began walking away.

Lady Blicken gave a little laugh, and eyed Ian conspiratorially. "Oh, we're in trouble now, Your Grace. Takes offense at the slightest wrong word, that one." She slid her tiny hand under his elbow and over his arm, a rodent squeezing beneath a cellar door. She tucked herself to his side.

"I've been told she aspires to set herself up as some manner of expert on style and comportment," continued Lady Blicken. "She's revealed no such thing to me, mind you, perish the thought; but I hear things. Take heed: If she endeavors to instruct your nieces, keep a close watch on what she allows them to *say*. Her own speech has become limited to the weather or the health of the King. She's ceased all intelligent conversation. You'll not want your nieces to become bores."

Ian looked down at her. But was this a *test*? Did she fish for a chuckle or a chortle? For him to say, *Oh yes, my new wife is out of her depth as a stylist, not to mention, boring?*

"I am, in no way, bored by the duchess," he said flatly.

"Oh yes, I suppose you wouldn't be," Lady Blicken mused.

And now he almost did laugh.

"This is a very fine house," Lady Blicken enthused, allowing Ian to all but carry her down the stairs as her gaze swung right and left. Twice he dodged a sharp-pronged embellishment on her hat.

"You've an estate in Dorset, do you not, Your Grace?" she asked.

"Aye," he said. "Avenelle. Near the village of Frampton."

She wasn't listening. Ian would lay odds that every morsel of Lachlan gossip had been ferreted out of friends and servants since the wedding. Questions were asked only to confirm and gauge reactions.

"Oh, Frampton is very pretty," said Lady Blicken. "You will love it, Mena," she called to Drew. "You'll need to mind the sun, of course, so very close to the sea."

To Ian, she said, "Her coloring barely tolerates the cold, dim light of London; summers at the seaside will be entirely out of the question. Your children may inherit her pallor and have the same aversion."

"Her interest in birding has likely prepared her for exposure to the elements," Ian said, joining Drew on the last step.

"Oh yes," sighed Lady Blicken. "The birds. Well, I aimed to make her ladylike and serene and she repaid me with field tromping and bush sitting. A great lot of bother that particular hobby has caused us, hasn't it, Drewsmina? But I took care of it, in the end. Never you fear. A dodged bullet, thank you very much. Despite all of the carrying on. And now look at you. Married to a duke. I'll not hold my breath, waiting for gratitude, despite what might have been. And with whom. *Thanks to all the little birdies.*"

"There is a gallery, Mother," said Drew briskly, "of art. Paintings, sculpture. Perhaps a good place to begin. I cannot say if the fires have been lit, but there are windows with nice light."

Drew glanced at them, and Ian felt marginally ridiculous standing with her mother draped on his arm. He tried to fix an I'd-prefer-she-not-cling expression on his face, but he couldn't be rude. Lady Blicken missed nothing. Drew's own enigmatic expression—hardly his favorite, considering how much he enjoyed her expressive face—was a testament to her mother's careful judgment of every detail. Drew had transformed herself into a moving statuary, serene and ladylike, just as she'd been taught. Not rude but not happy. Also, oddly inanimate.

"Oh a gallery," considered Lady Blicken. "Inside a London townhome. Perhaps this is where you convened the wedding breakfast? For your great many guests, none of whom included me, of course. Or your sister."

"Oh, the royal princess was in attendance," corrected Ian with feigned innocence.

"I meant her *actual* sister. Anastasia, Lady Madewood," said Lady Blicken. She kept her voice so very light, but the message was very pointed.

"We convened the wedding breakfast in the dining room," said Drew. "It was quite small."

"Which raises one question from which I cannot escape. Why should a duke of some means go so far as to *get married* . . . but maintain such secrecy? No celebration to speak of? If the bride cannot bear to invite her own mother and sister, so be it, Lord knows we are accustomed, but have the two of you no friends? What of *your* family, Your Grace?"

"Oh, my family were in attendance," he said.

Lady Blicken frowned. "If nothing else, I would have sent a gift."

"We require no gifts," Drew said, and Ian realized her tactic. She minced through each of her mother's accusation-laced statements and responded to the most innocuous one.

"It's almost as if you have something to *hide*," laughed Lady Blicken.

"Here is the gallery," Drew said, pushing open the doors. She disappeared inside. At his side, her mother still clung. Ian wondered how he could best be an ally to his wife. Left to his own devices, he would have said, "You're terrible, and no one likes you," and deserted her to find her own way out. But he was determined to not make the situation worse.

Lady Blicken narrowed her eyes at the open doorway, made a *tsk*ing noise, and smiled up at Ian: "No backbone; never has had. She flees at the first sign of censure. I blame myself."

"Ah," said Ian, "something on which we might all agree."

Lady Blicken's smile faltered and then transformed in a mischievous grin. "Aren't you a clever one. Whatever she's told you about me, I'd take it with a grain of salt. She exaggerates to detract from her own failings, and no one is immune. She does not value loyalty."

Ian could not remember ever making the acquaintance of someone so unrelentingly cruel and critical, all served with a breezy, chummy sort of smile. Unless he was mistaken, she was *flirting* with him. And holding up her own daughter as the object of their shared scorn.

Ian frowned and said, "After you, my lady."

"Oh, how spare," Lady Blicken said. "And . . . alpine? Arctic? *Cold*, perhaps is the correct word." She drifted into the room.

Ian almost laughed. She was not incorrect. The gallery was sterile and impersonal. He'd not gotten around to renovating the room or determining some solution for his grandfather's boring art collection. The woman had a gift.

She was hateful and quick but very precise, if you happened to share the most ungenerous view.

Now the viscountess drifted to the sculpture of two sheep and a ram grazing on the side of a cliff. She turned her head this way and that, considering the frozen trio with a critical eye.

"Now, this piece reminds me of you, Your Grace," she said.

Ian could guess, but he wanted to hear her say it. Her back was turned so he made a face at Drew. She closed her eyes briefly, a look that said, *I'm sorry*, and *I told you*, and *please let it end* all at once.

"In what *way* does it remind you of me, I wonder?" He came to stand beside her.

"Well, the sheep, naturally," she drawled, laughter in her voice.

*"The sheep,"* he repeated thoughtfully.

"Well, the *wool*." A chuckle.

*"The wool."*

"That unfortunate business with those wretched little weavers in Dorset? Their complaints and demands and all the unnecessary chain rattling. How noble of you to try to indulge their pathetic complaints. And what a pity they took it so very far. How could you have known? I asked Lord Blicken that very thing, *How could he have known?"*

"Follow the plight of the working classes, do you, my lady? And three years ago, to boot?"

"Oh, well certainly I studied the matter when I learned that my new son-in-law was none other than *The Shearling Duke*."

Ian bit back a smile. *The Shearling Duke*. He'd not heard this in a while. She was referencing a political cartoon in which Ian, in the wake of the riots, was depicted as a peasant shepherd with cartoon sheep conspiring against him. For a time, he'd been greeted with heckles of "His *Graaaace*, The Shearling Duke," everywhere he went. It was an expected jeer within the raucous confines of a boisterous pub, but hearing it from his new mother-in-law in his own home almost made him laugh.

"As duke to an estate that equals roughly a quarter of Dorset," he said, "those 'wretched little weavers,' as you call them, *have been* and *shall remain* my priority. Along with the farmers, shepherds, tanners, and mill owners who also make their home on my property. As such, I find the title rather fitting. I *am* in possession of a great many sheep, among other assets. Anyone opposed to this should embark on a month without wool to keep them warm and lamb to keep them fed. Those of us among the 'shearling aristocracy' take our work very seriously and it comes with no small amount of pride."

"Oh, no doubt, no doubt," mused Lady Blicken. "But it's one thing to raise the sheep or wear the wool—Britons have done this for generations, haven't we?—but quite another to *mismanage* the resources so."

"You have some experience with managing sheep, my lady?" Ian's patience was running thin. He worked to keep his voice calm, casual.

"Oh no," she proclaimed, laughing off the notion. "But I've long been a student of the harsh judgments that follow a political scandal. You will, no doubt, easily weather the harsh bite of public scorn; but as a mother, I worry for dear Drewsmina. Does she have the backbone to be the 'Shearling Duchess'? I cannot say. I've already alluded to her deep sensitivity. And it's not as if she allowed Blicken to properly dower her. Why, she wouldn't even permit us to properly house and clothe her these last few years; she lived with her sister like a poor relation. I raise it only because she is already so ripe for gossip and pity. And this says nothing of your dear nieces and sister. How your reputation may cloud their—"

"Enough!" called Drewsmina from across the room. "Enough. The duke has indulged your petty accusations for long enough. I warn you: Do not to begin with his nieces or sister. If he'll not take you to task, I will."

Lady Blicken, her eyes wide with feigned innocence, opened her mouth to protest, but Drew spoke over her. "You've other business, I know, Your Grace. Pray let us not detain you."

"I cannot leave you," he said. He'd no sooner leave her with a hungry lion.

"You can and you shall. Please. Ultimately, this quarrel is between myself and my mother. Will you excuse us? She will not stay long, I assure you."

"*'Between myself and my mother,'*" repeated Lady Blicken in a mousy voice. "Such dramatics. You were always so dramatic."

"I cannot leave you," Ian repeated.

"*Please,*" Drew said, looking at him plainly. It was the "please" that got to him. Perhaps she needed some reckoning. Perhaps his presence provoked the older woman, and he was making it worse. Perhaps the insults were more deeply wounding when Drew knew he heard them too. He remembered her sending him away when she took Imogene's rudeness to task. She was thoughtful in that way. And clearly, she'd dealt with this woman before.

"Alright," he said carefully, holding her gaze. "If that is what you really want."

"Look at the two of you," teased Lady Blicken, "with your long gazes and your implorations. And here I thought perhaps some money had changed hands for this very speedy, very 'private' union."

"It is what I want," Drew whispered to him sadly.

Ian nodded, holding her gaze for a moment more.

He turned to Lady Blicken. "I wish I could say it was a pleasure to meet you, my lady. Alas, that would be bollocks."

"I should expect nothing else from a disgraced duke with a batty sister and two—"

"*I'll walk you out, Mother,*" Drew cut in loudly. She took her by the arm and began to drag.

"Ouch!" hissed Lady Blicken. "You violate me with your mannish hands, you *tower* over me."

Drew looked over her shoulder at him once more, her face very sad and very tired and very grave. Ian squinted back in disbelief. Drew had not been exaggerating, not even a little.

Lady Blicken had yanked her arm from Drew's grasp but continued to walk. Drew followed behind her, her hands clamped behind her back, her head bowed, like a monk.

# Chapter Twenty-Three

"No," Drew snapped, "*not* that way. To the door, Mother. The call has come to an unregrettable end."

"I'm expected to find my way out, am I? Some expert on manners you've proven yourself to be."

"My manners are not on display at the moment, it is my restraint."

"Oh yes, your precious restraint. Well. Do keep in mind that few people can hide their true natures forever. Perhaps you've managed to deceive the duke, but he'll eventually see the truth."

*Do not ask, do not ask, do not ask*, Drew ordered herself.

"And which truth would that be?" Drew huffed. There were too many perceived "truths" to be seen.

"Oh, Drewsmina," sighed her mother. "You'll not trick me into speaking against you. It only makes you feel sorry for yourself. And I won't be blamed for that. I meant to teach you confidence, if nothing else."

"Come now," urged Drewsmina, striding toward the door. She could see it. So close. Almost in reach. The old hurt and desperation nipped at her heals, causing her to clomp instead of walk. Pain and defeat burned down her throat and into her gut like a hot coal on a soft rug, singeing a hole ringed in black. She struggled to breathe. Her voice grew louder. Her eyes narrowed, her jaw clenched. "Let us not feign niceties at this very late date."

"I've not come to *feign* anything, darling, I've come to *congratulate* you. You've done it, Drewsmina. A *duchess*? Against all odds. And seemingly without my help."

Drew would have laughed at this if her throat were not so very tight. She mustn't respond. Every response was mined for weakness and potential exploitation. She must be a blank page.

Her mother continued, "Although doubtful you've done it entirely on your own. That *imposter* in Kew Palace had something to do with it, I dare say. I shudder to think of your debt to her now."

They finally reached the front door, which was flanked by two footmen.

"Lady Blicken's things," Drew snapped to the servants, hating her rudeness, hating everything about this moment. Thank God she'd sent everyone away. Her mother caught up, and Drew wrenched open the door. Weak morning sunlight and cold air filled the space between them.

"What I wish I *knew* . . ." said her mother lightly, glancing around, "what would *assist me* as I curtail gossip about you all over town, is, *why the haste*? Why the secrecy? 'Tis a vain hope, I suppose, that you'll confide in me."

"Yes," said Drew. "Very vain."

"Not even to protect those nieces of his? I can only assume they are now under your care."

"Lachlan's nieces are none of your concern."

"They've been the concern of nobody for quite some time, haven't they? My God—that baroness? Their mother?" She made an exaggerated face that said, *Spare me.*

"Good-bye, Mother," Drew said. A footman had returned with her wrap and umbrella. Betina shouldered into her cloak, flashing a sensual smile to the young servant. Drew's stomach turned.

"I only raise it," her mother whispered, "because there will be talk—the chatter, in fact, has already begun. The duke made no effort to restore his reputation after the riots, his sister is clearly *mad*, and his nieces are rumored to be barely fit for decent company. And now he's married? To . . . *you*?" She looked Drewsmina up and down, her disgusted gaze as familiar as a stomachache. Drew fought the urge to slump.

"And all in a matter of days?" her mother continued. "Let me help you. Tell me what I can say."

"You can say that you have no idea, which is the truth, for once. Pray, *leave us alone*. If ever you cared for me. If ever you wanted me to be happy, even for a second."

"But are you happy, Drewsmina?" she challenged softly.

"In this precise moment? No, I'm not. In general, I am very happy." Drew said the words, not really knowing if they were true. It was always this way with her mother. She must portray the best possible result simply to counter her mother's doomsday predictions. It made Drew feel like a liar, whether things were, in fact, the best or the worst or anything in between. To forever project hopefulness made her suspicious of *actual* hope. It was one of the many, many soul-destroying tactics in her mother's terrible bag of tricks.

"Well, good for you, Miss Duchess," her mother mocked. "See that you don't allow all of it to crumble. It's one thing to marry, another to *remain* married."

"As only someone married four times can attest." Drew held the door wider.

"How cruel you are," her mother whispered, stepping through the door. "Ungrateful child—from the very start. And not pretty enough to hold the attention of a man like Lachlan for long. I'd not train up the nieces too quickly, if I were you. Once they're gone—"

Drew closed the door.

The sound of the oak sliding into place—more than a *click*, less than a *slam*—echoed in the empty hall.

Slowly, achingly, Drew backed against the solid wood of the massive door. She raised her hands, trembling now with anger and sadness and upset, to her cheeks. She stared at the grand staircase, seeing nothing, and tried to catch her breath, attempting to keep the tears at bay. She wondered, idly, how she might *lock* this door, just to make certain her mother would not somehow slither back in.

Somewhere in the distance, a clock chimed. Drew was reminded of the girls, their lessons, the day. There was no place for pity or outrage in her work here with the girls; her *life* here with Lachlan.

And what a very good life it was; so much better than she'd expected life could be. Even if they were never more than a friendly couple forced to marry because of an indiscretion.

She must never wallow, she reminded herself. She could indulge in hopefulness and fanciful dreams only if she also acknowledged how very unlikely these would be. She should cleave to gratefulness and satisfaction instead. Even if he never again came to her bed. Even if he came to her bed again but never loved her. It needn't "crumble" as her mother warned. She was a jester—she made fun—not a fortune-teller. Not a believer.

From nowhere, Greenly appeared, treading down the hall with a potted fern.

"I should like to go out, Greenly," she said, stepping away from the door. "Can I trouble you to summon the girls? Tell them to dress for the park and inquire after Lady Tribble. She may wish to join us."

"Very good, Your Grace," the butler said, reversing his direction.

"Tell them a quarter hour and have the carriage brought around, if you please. I'll call down to the kitchen for a picnic basket. Has the duke gone out?"

"I cannot say, Your Grace. Shall I seek him out?"

"No, no," she said. "Pray do not hound him. We'll carry on with our day, as may he."

And carry on, she must—she *would*. Her girlhood strategy of raging and railing only made her feel worse, but she needn't restrict herself to the house. Her mother's perfume would linger in the air like smoke. Her jabs would reverberate in the rafters. If only Lady Tribble and her herbalist could trod every room, thrushing out her very essence.

Meanwhile Drew would escape for an afternoon, allow the raw feelings and resentment to pull apart, to become so thin, they snapped into pieces and floated away.

Equally important: avoid the duke until she felt more like herself—her newer, more evolved self—and less like . . . less like she always felt after an encounter with her mother.

She must apologize to him, of course. At some point, she would apologize for her mother's rudeness in its great many forms. Only, not right away. She needed time.

There was a very strong chance that the duke did not care about her mother; that a four-times-married viscountess with appalling manners might have no impact on him except as an amusement. He might not have even noticed.

There was also the chance that he noticed a great deal, and now he *reconsidered* Drewsmina, both as an advisor to his nieces and as a wife. Families were a reflection of their members, and she and Betina came from the same lot.

Would he now be appalled by her?

Drew couldn't say—she did not *want* to say—but she would need more time to think on the damage her mother may have caused.

After *that*, she would see him. After.

And anyway, the girls deserved a break from their week of lessons and tutors and the rushed wedding. They could tromp about the pond while Drew took refuge in one of her favorite birding spots. She could sit quietly and observe a life beyond her own. Absorb the beauty of smooth, still water in autumn and the simplicity (or in some cases, complexity) of the creatures who dwelt there. If only for an afternoon.

"Your mother did not seem so very terrible to me," Imogene said, half an hour later in the carriage to Hampstead. Imogene sat beside her on the rear-facing carriage seat, and Lady Tribble and Ivy sat opposite, an open botany book on their laps. Drew had apologized to the baroness for any rudeness she may have suffered at the hands of her mother, but Lady Tribble had waved away the notion.

"Honestly, I thought she was the woman who had come to replace the drapes," said Lady Tribble. "I cannot be bothered to learn the names and affiliations of everyone who troops through the house. Now that the girls read lessons, we must have twenty visitors a week."

"Not quite twenty, my lady," amended Drew.

"I knew her instantly," said Imogene to Drew. "She looked at you like a baby looks at a crank toy. Like, with just one more crank, you might go *pop*."

"It would delight her to see me or any of us detonate on her watch," said Drew. "If you came away without feeling like a lit fuse, well then I've done my job, haven't I?"

Imogene fell silent. Drew busied herself tightening her gloves, but she could feel the girl staring at her profile.

"We are not accustomed to being shielded," Imogene finally said.

Drew glanced at Lady Tribble. Imogene rarely provoked her mother, but she was certainly capable of it. And nothing provoked the baroness more than discussing their time at T.O.E.

"I expect you were shielded quite a lot, in the care of the Reverend Sagg," Drew tried. Half of her wanted to neutralize the topic, the other half wanted to hear what the girl would reveal.

"The reverend did not shield us, so much as incarcerate us," said Imogene.

Across from them, Lady Tribble lifted the book from her lap and held it in front of her face.

"We were not incarcerated, were we, Genie?" asked Ivy.

"We were not *free*," Imogene said.

Drew held her breath, waiting for Lady Tribble to address this, to say something, to excuse or object or apologize—anything. Instead, she pulled the botany book closer to her face.

Beside her, Imogene laid her head back, balancing it on the seat back.

Finally she said, "There is a difference between having someone worry on your behalf and having someone restrict you for the sake of control."

"I would be very worried, indeed," said Drew, "if you'd been forced to tangle with my mother." She would turn the subject back to herself. The day was meant to be an escape for the girls and their mother. Now the baroness's hand gripped the reference book so tightly, it shook. And Imogene's voice had taken on a hard, bitter quality.

"I enjoy tangling with awful people," the girl said.

"Perhaps you do," said Drew, "but I mean for your life to be filled with positive, useful experiences. Not quarreling. Now that you raise it, I do rather like the idea of pitting *my* mother against Reverend Sagg in a sort of . . . battle. Seeing who might come out the champion?" She glanced at Lady Tribble, hoping she'd not offended or overstepped.

Ivy giggled, and after a moment, Imogene did too. "I should pay money to see that," she said.

"Me, too," laughed Ivy.

Slowly, Lady Tribble let the book sink. Her lips were quirked up in a small smile.

Drew said, "Oh, that reminds me. I've a coin for the two of you. Here. One of the grooms will watch over you while you enjoy the Heath—"

"John?" asked Imogene hopefully, naming the handsome groom who blushed every time Imogene came into view.

"*Buellis*," corrected Drew. "Buellis will watch over you as you take your picnic. When you've finished with your meal, you may buy yourselves and your mother a sweet from the pastry cart."

"But where will you go?" asked Ivy.

"If you can spare me, I'd like to walk to the far side of the pond. There is a stand of trees there, very good for bird-watching. I visit it whenever I need to . . . clear my head. I tend to want a head-clearing after any encounter with Lady Blicken. It won't take long. Can you survive without my relentless harping for a half hour of so?"

The girls nodded, studying the coins in their hands.

"My lady?" asked Drew softly. "Do you mind if I step away? Could you enjoy Hampstead with the girls?"

"Off you go," said Lady Tribble. "I wouldn't have come if I didn't intend to spend the day with my girls."

Ivy beamed at this, snuggling into her mother. Imogene toyed with her coin, considering her mother with narrowed, speculative eyes.

"And you'll be respectful of Buellis; give him no trouble?" reminded Drew. "Oh look, here 'tis."

She pointed out the window at the sprawling parkland, high above London. Cottages and shops formed a small village, but Drew came to Hampstead for the pond. Formerly a marsh, it had been drained some forty years ago to combat malaria. Enough of the field and water, trees and hedgerow were intact, and the area remained the bird sanctuary it had been for centuries.

The girls must have felt sorry for her, she thought, because they promised to mind the groom, to be considerate of their mother, and to stay together. Drew watched them only until they ran toward the water, the hems of their new dresses held high. Buellis struggled after them, bearing the picnic basket. Lady Tribble drifted slowly behind him.

Free at last, Drew turned away, trudging into the brush, following a faint trail known only to woodland creatures and bird watchers.

The sparrows came first, as they often did. Their compact, perfectly round bird bodies lighting on a dead limb, calling out a test chirp, hopping three times, launching to the sky. Back again—a pair of them—with an insect over which they fought and ultimately ripped in two.

Next, a brilliant wheatear, scurrying along the twig-and-leaf-strewn floor of the leafy bower.

After that, a clutch of whinchats—so many ground dwellers today—hunting for food, fattening up for the impending journey to their winter home, a continent away.

Drew had just reached for her birding journal when she heard the snap of a twig behind her. She went still, not wanting to frighten it away—whatever "it" might be. She held her breath. Another twig snapped, then the rustle of leaves. Drew listened carefully for a bird song or, if it was an animal, the snuffle and gnawing of foraging.

Instead a familiar voice called, "Hello?"

Drew almost dropped the journal. It was Lachlan's voice; hushed but unmistakable.

Lachlan. *Here.* Winding through this copse of trees in Hampstead, miles from Pollen Street.

She pivoted on the stump, and yes—there he was. He stood four yards away, boot up on a fallen log, batting away the frond of a path-blocking shrub.

She blinked at him, trying to make sure. A penguin would not have surprised her more.

"Hello," she answered, cautiously, struggling to stand on uneven sod.

He looked beautiful in the dappled sunlight soaking through the autumn leaves, tall and broad-shouldered. His overcoat hung long, billowing slightly in the breeze.

But why had he come? Was he angry she'd fled the house with the girls? Did he require something.

*Oh God, has my mother returned?*

Or, perhaps her mother had made such an impression, he sought her out to discuss it.

"I'm sorry to disturb you," he began.

"No disruption," she said.

"Will I ruin your observation, if I come closer?"

She chuckled a little at this. Any self-preserving bird had long-since fled. She shook her head.

He stepped over the log and walked the distance to her, stooping to duck low-hanging branches, stepping over divots in the moss.

If she said it didn't thrill her to see this beautiful man, clever, and strong, and decent, making his way through the brambles and briars of Hampstead to her—*only* to her, there was no other reason for him to be here—she would be lying.

If she was afraid, truly afraid, that he'd come here to chastise her, to dismiss her, it was a fear as dreaded and as horrible as any she'd known.

But he did not look dismissive or angry. He looked . . . concerned. And curious. And a little unsettled by the wildness of her surroundings. He frowned at the stump on which she'd sat and the carpet of slick moss, shockingly, almost acidic green. Beyond that, autumn foliage had begun to decay on the ground. In the distance, the black pond was obscured by mist. Overhead, a kestrel flew just above the canopy, calling out its squeaky, high-pitched *kee-kee-kee*.

"Hello," he said again, coming to her.

"Hello," she said. It felt so very good to actually look *up* when she spoke to him.

"You left without a word," he said.

"Oh yes. Well. I didn't want to bother you. I thought the girls could stand for an outing. And I find the outdoors—this place specifically—very settling after . . ." A deep breath. "Well, after I've dealt with my mother."

"I'm glad. But I wish I'd known. Unless . . . you prefer to be alone?"

"I have no preference. I would've included the girls, but I'd hoped to spot the last of the migratory birds before they're off to Africa, and bird-watching can be . . . restricting. I didn't want to impose the silence and stillness on them. Also,

I felt they could use some time alone with Lady Tribble. She consented to come, surprising us all. Imogene most of all, I think. I've left Buellis looking after them. I hope they aren't—"

"They're fine," he said, stalking around the stump. "Feeding the contents of the picnic to geese. And to Buellis. At this point, I believe the old man is undecided whether he's been given the best job or the worst job of the day."

She laughed.

"They showed me the path you'd taken," he said, "and begged me to prevent you from returning. Something about missing the arithmetic tutor, I believe."

"Oh yes. He is not a favorite."

A pause.

She waited, wondering if he would state some purpose.

She tried, "You must not have been long behind us. I'm . . . I'm sorry we left with no word. It never occurred to me you would wish to . . . to . . ."

"I wanted to see you. After the viscountess had gone."

The conversation idled again.

She wanted to ask him *why* he wanted to see her, but surely this was his conversation to lead.

"So this is bird-watching?" he finally said. "Have you room on that stump for me?"

# Chapter Twenty-Four

There was very little room on the stump, but Drew edged
sideways as far as she could, collecting her skirts. He
dropped beside her in a smooth, athletic movement, and
leaned back on his palms. This position left them hip
against hip, thigh to thigh.

He'd worked up a sweat, she realized, riding to find her.
She could feel the heat from his body. He smelled like
wind, and saddle leather, and that musky scent that was
distinctively *him*.

He'd extended his legs; his boots, ruined now from mud,
stretched long in front of them. He crossed them at the ankles, and removed his hat, tossing it to the side.

"And now we'll be motionless and quiet and wait for the
beasts to descend?" he asked.

She chuckled. "If we're lucky."

He nodded, breathing deeply. He exhaled.

He did not, for all that, seem to harbor a burning indictment about her mother's visit. Nor did he seem primed to pepper her with questions. He seemed . . . sleepy. Content. Behind her on the stump, he slid his gloved hand ever so closer to her bottom, his arm now half behind her. If she leaned back, his arm would cross her back. If she leaned sideways, she would fit against his ribs.

She did neither, sitting perfectly upright on the stump. *Her* stump. The stump on which she'd perched alone a hundred times; except now she was not alone.

"You began bird-watching as a child, did you?" he asked.

She shook her head. "Oh no. Only these last five years. Before, when I was—" She cleared her throat.

"*Before*," she amended, "I would never have considered an activity so sedentary and devoid of . . . well of any contribution from me. In bird-watching, you say nothing and give nothing. You simply wait and allow it to unfold before you. I have, in my early years, struggled to both wait and to . . . allow for things to unfold."

"So difficult to envision," he mused. "You have this natural sort of . . . calmness. An evenness. The girls would try anyone's patience, yet you manage them with such placid . . . acceptance."

She smiled. "Whether it comes naturally, I cannot say; it's more like . . . what I longed for as a child. I think of how I was treated and endeavor to do the opposite. It does cheer me to learn it *comes off naturally*, as you say. That's the worry, isn't it? That I appear forced, that I am 'putting on.'"

She dipped her head and continued, "My mother's favorite new jab is to say that I live a life of posed artifice. Honestly, I cannot account for my personality. I am nothing like my mother—my primary effort. I did not know my father; he died when I was very young. I am not the girl I used to be, so . . . who am I? The princess—Cynde—has been a great example to me, but I know I'm nothing like her."

"Perish the thought," he said, inching his hand closer

to her hip. "She's perfectly lovely, but a bit like *toy doll*, don't you think? Exactly what Adolphus requires, obviously, but—" He made a disgusted noise that was part exhale, part snort. Drew smothered a laugh.

How good it felt to sit here, she thought, in one of her favorite places, with him, talking of people they knew. How many couples had she observed from this very vantage point, hidden from view? She came for the birds but saw plenty of humans on the path on the other side of the pond. Families, friends, and couples—so many couples. Old couples, young couples, illicit couples, strangers, even, who'd met on a path and exchanged some look, some friendly word, some touch—and always she'd thought, *Oh, well. Good for you.*

Without rancor, she'd thought, *There is love in the world and we are all better for it. Not for me, of course, but at least I am without hate.*

If *now . . . today . . .* Drew wanted more than an exchanged look and a friendly word and some touch—if she wanted more than to sit and laugh with this man—well, she was only human.

But she could also be happy here, now, with *this*.

From nowhere, Lachlan offered, "I'm nothing like my father. This was a rather painful reality to me very early on."

"You wanted to be like him?"

"Oh, God no. I wanted *him* to be like someone else. He drank too much, which elicited an enthusiastic meanness; he gambled too much, which depleted the coffers of Avenelle; and he brought women who were not my mother into our home, which is a particular brand of cruelty for confused, lonely children. Luckily, he paid almost no mind to me or my sister; and I had an uncle nearby—the proverbial *second son*—and he stepped in when I was very young, acted as a surrogate father. He demonstrated integrity and loyalty and hard work where my father did not. He was loyal to his wife. I was fortunate for their care and example. He loved Avenelle, even though it would never come to him. Anything good in me comes from Uncle Stephen."

"Did your sister benefit from the influence of the aunt and uncle?"

"Sadly, no. Stephen had not yet married when Timothea was very young. He was still in the army. Her formative years were spent with our miserable, homesick mother and a succession of nursemaids."

"So very sad," said Drew. "I can see Lady Tribble trying to be a good mother to Imogene and Ivy, but she struggles with her own demons, I fear. I am happy to collaborate with her on bringing up the girls. And with whatever part you will take in it."

"I value that collaboration so very much, I married you to protect it," he said. "We are fortunate that you came to us."

It was meant as a compliment—it *was* a compliment—but Drew's chest felt hollowed out by the statement. Of course he'd married her for the twins. She knew this.

And yet.

"My guess is," he said, "your late father was a decent man, a hard worker, deeply intuitive, generous, and compassionate. I see these qualities plainly in you, and he is the most likely source."

"That is quite a list," she laughed. "I would like to think my father embodied some admirable qualities; that they were incubating inside me all of this time, a secret heritage that needed only to be unlocked. But my mother will not speak of him, and he has no surviving family. We do not know much about him, Ana and me. But he did give me the gift of birds, for all that. And I cherish it more than any bauble or property he could have passed down."

"How's that?" Now he tucked the tips of his gloved fingers beneath her bottom, like a doorstop beneath a door. Drew hopped, just a little, at the nudge.

But what did he mean, touching her? Perhaps he didn't realize his fingertips had collided with her hip? Maybe he wanted her to scoot over?

"Drewsmina?" he asked, and she turned at the sound of her given name. She was unaccustomed to hearing him say it.

He prompted, "How did he give the birds?"

"Oh yes, well, my mother will not discuss him, but she *did* frequently complain about a standing donation left in his will to a birding society in Richmond. It was a constant gripe, every year. 'Why would he leave even a farthing to strangers and wild creatures?' She hounded her lawyers for how she could undo the wasteful donation to the Birding Appreciation Society of Richmond Park. At that time in my life, my only defense against her was to vex her, so naturally I looked into it. She hated this donation, so I loved them, whoever they were. I had the wicked idea of traveling to Richmond, approaching the group, and suggesting that they ask her for a larger donation."

"And instead you found your father's passion," he guessed.

"Well, I began to explore the notion of bird-watching as a hobby. Eventually, quietly, without telling anyone—a very rare stance for me—I slipped away into the brush and sat down under a tree and . . . endeavored to see what it was all about."

"Much like I'm doing," he remarked, cocking an eyebrow. Ever so slightly, he wiggled his fingers under her rump.

Drew blew out a breath. "Nothing like you are doing."

He smiled and her stomach gave a flip. "Carry on."

"I was far too impatient in the beginning to actually observe any bird, but I would return to it, again and again. I found myself seeking out the forest or the park whenever I quarreled with my mother or Ana. At first, I did it simply because Mother hated it; but gradually I realized it . . . settled me in a way?"

"I can see it. I walk the grounds of Avenelle whenever I'm troubled; it is a balm like no other."

"After a time," she continued, "after I'd managed to be motionless long enough for the bolder birds to put on a show, I sought it out for no other reason than to see them."

"Brilliant," he said softly. "Have you any books or notes from your late father that might enrich your experience?"

"I do, in fact. They are among my most prized possessions."

"And what is your favorite bird, Miss Trelayne?"

Drew opened her mouth and then closed it.

But what of "Drewsmina?" Had he just referred to her as "Miss Trelayne?"

Yes. Yes, he had.

But was it a purposeful slip? Flashes of last night suddenly flickered in her mind's eye. The window seat. His arms. The bed. He'd called her Miss Trelayne again and again.

She cleared her throat. "There are several species that thrill me, but honestly, the bit I enjoy most is to simply observe the *behavior* of the birds—all of them. Any bird will put on quite a show given enough time. They forage for food and materials, they build nests, they sit on eggs, they fight, they migrate in formation. Nothing will make your own problems seem inconsequential like watching a baby bird flop from his nest, thrash about on the forest floor, and work out the very significant challenge of *learning to fly*."

"I'd never thought about it," he said, "but you make it sound fascinating." She could feel his gaze on her profile. She looked at her gloved hands.

"Have you ever seen a mother bird light on the edge of her nest, her beak filled with worms, ready to feed her hatchlings?" she asked.

"Yes," he said, "I suppose I have. In my tree-climbing days as a boy."

"Do you remember what happens, when she lands on the nest?"

"Well," he considered, "if I remember correctly, the babies cause a great fuss. Lots of squawking?"

She looked up. "Yes, very good. The chicks in the nest go mad, chirping and tweeting, their heads thrown back, tiny beaks open wide to the sky. It's almost deafening, the sound of chicks in a nest when the mother bird appears with dinner. But do you know the reason?"

He shook his head, looking at her with rapt attention. He was so handsome, it almost broke her heart.

"The chicks raise such a fuss," she explained, "because the mother will only feed the loudest, closest ones. This is quickly learned—actually, they *know it* innately. They're in competition with every other chick in the nest to attract the mother's attention. They'll hop and jostle on their weak little baby legs to bump closer to the edge. But the noise, in particular, is the most distinctive. Each hatchling tries to out-tweet the next in order to be fed. In every bird family, at least one baby will die because it cannot make itself heard or bump its way to the front."

"This is a terrible story," he proclaimed, frowning now.

"'Tis, I suppose, but I mention it only because this behavior seems to explain . . . my very awkward, entirely *beastly* girlhood. My mother pitted Anastasia and me against each other. In order to gain her attention—and even more elusive, her approval—we were each forced to be as loud and as demonstrative as possible. We tried to outdo each other with literal and figurative *loudness*. When Mother married Cynde's father and he promptly died—she has a talent, actually, for marrying men who are not long for this earth—we had yet another competitor in the nest, someone else to outpace and outshine and outwit."

"If I'd not just met the woman," he mused, "I would not believe you. But I can see it. How wretched."

"It was wretched, honestly. Although now it feels infantile and petty to complain about her. We were not beaten—well, Ana and I were not beaten. Cynde was a frequent target for flying shoes and hurled broadsheets. But we were not starved. We had tutors and Seasons and maids to look after us when were sick. Again, Ana and I did. It would be impossible to overstate my mother's treatment of Cynde. If anyone deserves to become a princess and live in a palace, it is Cynde." She took a deep breath.

"Please don't feel you need to justify your misery to me," he commented, staring into the pond. "Squiring her around on my arm for ten minutes was proof enough. I will say that this . . . this calmness? This serenity you claim is all new? I can only guess this frustrates her."

"That and the fact that I'm a duchess now," she added, "if I'm being honest."

"Took the wind out of her sails, did it?"

"She wanted it to be untrue," Drew said, the words out before she considered them.

"Foiled again," he sang softly. Beneath her, he widened his fingers and then brought them back together, effectively pinching her backside.

She let out a little squeak, jumped, and put her hands out to steady herself. One hand flew wide, the other landed on his thigh.

"Careful, Miss Trelayne," he warned, wrapping a hand around her waist. In one strong tug, he dragged her across the stump and tucked her against him.

She squeaked again.

"I, too, was neither starved nor beaten, but my mother was either chronically unhappy or living in another country. As I've said, my father ignored Timothea and me to the point of not knowing how old we were at any given time. Once, when I was ten, he asked me if I'd yet learned to read. When I was eleven, he asked me if I'd like to share a bottle of gin. The only reason he could tell us apart was because she was a girl, and I was a boy.

"Is there a worse existence?" he asked. "Yes. Certainly. Was it still wretched? Yes. But at least I had more than the birds to comfort and guide me. My uncle and aunt were very dear. I joined the army to honor my uncle's service. I am a good custodian to Avenelle—or at least I've tried to be—because he loved it."

*And I love you*, she thought.

It was the truth, as clear to her now as the sun streaming through the leaves, casting the stump in a golden mist.

She had fallen in love with him; and it had taken no time at all. Nothing about this surprised her. When she thought of him, she saw decency, cleverness, love for his family, the ability to admit fault, honor, generosity, and commitment to his lands. If he was also interesting and sensual, well? Why not?

Was it magical? Yes. But it also felt inevitable; like spring following winter.

Of his regard for her, she was far less certain. She couldn't explain why he'd come to this leafy bower to seek her out. Or why he'd told her the history of his parents and his uncle. Why he listened to her terrible tale of woe.

She didn't know how to ask any of this, and she was too afraid to misspeak. In all honesty, she was too afraid to *move*. Last night had been glorious in so many ways, especially because she'd been free to simply follow along. There had been little room for anxiety about being too tall or too skinny or too . . . anything. She could simply swing wide the doors to her heart, open her body, and let him in.

"So," he said after a moment.

They had *almost* kept quiet long enough to allow a bird to flutter in. Almost, but not quite.

"So," she repeated.

He laughed, not unkindly, but still a laugh.

"What?" She looked to him.

"Your expression. *I'm* meant to be the one with the perpetual scowl. Either I've rubbed off on you, or you've not recovered from your mother's visit. Or perhaps I've intruded on your time with the birds, and you resent it."

"It's not that," she said quickly.

He studied her more closely. "Perhaps it's not a scowl. Perhaps you are holding your breath."

"That is possible," she whispered. "If I'm being honest."

"Why?"

"Because I'm afraid of what . . . you think."

"Of what I think?" He frowned, confused.

"About the morning." It was not untrue. Of all the things she was afraid of, this was among them.

"My mother has ruined a great many things for me," she explained, "and it would be just like her to . . . to . . ."

"I *think*," he provided softly, "that I am *worried* about you. *I* think," he repeated, "that you may need looking after."

"Oh," she said.

She forgot to breathe. She forgot everything but the faint hope that this conversation was drifting where it might, possibly, a-million-to-one chance, be drifting.

"Do you need looking after, Miss Trelayne?" he asked, leaning back to take her in. Lazily, he perused her face, her throat, her chest, and back up to her face.

"Um," she said, swallowing. He'd used her professional name again.

"Perhaps you would sit in my lap and allow me to assess your general well-being? To consider what you may need?"

"Sit in your . . . lap?" Drew repeated in a whisper. Her heart began to drum, the beats so fast they became one constricted pulse.

She looked at him, just inches from her; she looked at the stump beneath them, a smooth round platform grown over two hundred years ago and felled, surely, for no other purpose than this. She looked around at the mirage of seclusion in a public park.

"Miss Trelayne?" he sang, invoking the name from last night.

She looked back to him, searching his face.

"Would you sit in my lap?" he whispered. "Just for a moment?"

"I . . . I don't know how," she admitted.

"*You don't know how,*" he repeated, feigning puzzlement.

She laughed nervously. "Lachlan, I'm not a small—"

She exhaled. "*I'm not small*, and my cloak is voluminous and constricting, and for all practical purposes, we're sitting in a hollowed-out log. I'm not given to clambering abo—"

He leaned in, scooped her up, and settled her, sideways, in his lap. It was a tidy movement, one boot heel braced in the sod, an arm around her shoulders, another under her knees, up and over, her cloak swinging out and then draping around them.

"Oh," she said.

"Now," he said, wrapping one hand around her bottom, leaning back on the other, bracing them on the stump, "that's better."

"Lachlan," she whispered, glancing nervously around them.

"Yes?" he said, leaning in.

She'd felt his nearness before; but *near* him and *on* him was the difference between hungry and starving. His thighs were hard, the smell of him deliciously familiar, his mouth was so close.

Drew fixed her eyes straight ahead, trying not to look at it. She tried to see through the leafy fronds of the bower. She scouted for potential passersby. Would there be innocent people who might be assailed by the sight of—

"Miss Trelayne?" he rumbled softly, dipping his lips to the sensitive curve of neck between ear and shoulder.

"Yes?" she breathed. The leaves blurred; her eyes fell closed.

"I should like to smooth away the memory of this morning," he breathed against her ear, "and *your* wretched parents; and *my* wretched parents."

She made a desperate little sound, half whimper, half gasp. Her skin had come alive, buzzing with anticipation. Pleasure radiated from the contact of his lips, raising the hairs on the back of her neck. Deep down, inside the secret place he'd initiated last night, she felt an awakening. The tips of her breasts tingled. With each nudge and nuzzle, her body came more alive, fold by fold, tip to tip.

"*This* is why you sought me out?" she breathed.

"Well, perhaps not exclusively. Actually, not even intentionally . . ." He spoke the words into the skin of her neck. "But now that I'm here . . ."

"But you cannot mean to . . . to." She huffed out a breath. "Here? Out of doors? Someone might see."

"We shall be *very, very quiet*," he said, planting kisses along the line of her jaw. "And so still. So quiet and so still, even the birds will come."

"The birds will not come," she assured him.

He was nearly to her mouth, and the torture of being kissed everywhere but her lips was too much. She turned her face to him, seeking.

"We'll see about that," he rumbled and he claimed her mouth.

She lacked the will to argue. She lacked the will to do anything but kiss him. After a lifetime of not kissing, with no guarantees of future kisses, only a fool would stop.

Her hands clenched inside her cloak. The garment was a frustration, as restricting as a sack. He sensed her distress and chuckled, sliding his fingers to the jeweled pin that held it in place in the middle of her chest.

"A spider," he observed, working the pin free. His attention to the spider was careful, delicate; he ministered to the pin far longer than necessary. She felt each brush of his fingers through the fabric.

When the pin was free, he slipped it inside the pocket of his waistcoat. He returned his hands to the cloak and pulled it apart, like peeling open a fruit. Cold air hit her throat in the same moment as his hot gaze.

His hands found her body in the next instant. He captured her waist with his large fingers, and she reached for his neck. Before she pulled him to her, she paused, settling her hands on his jaw, cradling the sides of his face.

"Thank you," she whispered against his lips, "for coming to me."

"Don't thank me yet," he warned, sliding his hands from her waist, over her hips, and down her legs.

"Oh," she said, accepting his next kiss.

Meanwhile, his hands continued southward; he moved over her knees, down her calves and, with a flick of the wrist, beneath the hem of her skirt. He clasped her ankles, squeezing the laced leather of her boots.

"Lachlan?" Drew whispered.

"Miss Trelayne," he replied. Every time he invoked that name, anticipation rose in her like a hot mist.

"Your Grace," she replied, ever so quietly.

"I beg your pardon?" he teased.

"*Your Grace,*" she repeated, louder.

He chuckled, moving again, his hands now *inside* her skirts.

Soft gloves raked wool stockings, scraped over bare thigh, and tangled with her drawers. She gasped, but he didn't linger; he moved until his hands settled over her corset at the waist. Spreading his fingers, he gripped, let out a slight grunt, and *lifted.*

Drew levitated upward in a blink. She let out a little gasp and her hands flew to his shoulders. She looked down on his upturned face.

"Up and over you go," he said.

For a moment, she panicked, not understanding what he wanted. He was turning her—*pivoting her toward him*—but she could only twist so far if her legs faced—

"There's a good girl," he rasped, raising a knee to wedge between her ankles.

One moment she was being held aloft, bracing against his shoulders, the next he was knocking her legs apart to straddle his lap.

"*Miss Trelayne,*" he hissed, resettling her on his thighs. She was *astride* him now; their bodies aligned, their faces nose-to-nose. Beneath her skirts, his hands remained tight on her waist.

"Oh," she said.

"But I wonder," he mused, "are you *moving* a bit too much? For the birds? I thought we were meant to be still. Think of their shy and abiding little bird sensibilities."

Before she could answer, he kissed her squarely, properly. His tongue probed, deepening the kiss almost instantly, and he slid his hands from her waist to cup her bottom.

"You have the perfect little bottom," he rumbled against her mouth. He squeezed, and she'd never been so aware of her own body, her legs spread, his nearness. She hopped, just a little, inching closer to him, and he used the movement to scoop his palms more solidly beneath her.

Somewhere, deep in the foggy corners of her consciousness, Drew had the errant, distant thought that she should look about them, to see if they were alone, but her eyes saw nothing more than the blur of autumn leaves, and golden light, and him.

"Did you know you had the perfect bottom?" he mumbled.

"*Shhh,*" she managed, her voice strangled.

"Oh yes, the birds," he said, nuzzling her nose with his. "They mustn't know about your bottom."

"No, the people. In the park."

"We're of no consequence to the absent people in this vacant park," he said, reclaiming her mouth. "We are bird-watching."

"We are most certainly no—"

He moaned and pressed her to him. The movement ground her burning center against his hardness. He'd aligned them perfectly to collide *just so*, and she gasped at the contact.

"Shhh, Miss Trelayne," he teased. "You're scaring the birds."

She shimmied closer, rubbing against him with a sigh.

Lachlan broke the kiss with a growl and sucked in air. He retracted a hand from beneath her skirts and brought it to his teeth, biting off his glove. The other glove came next; and now he could dig his bare fingers into her upswept hair, slanting her head to deepen the kiss.

"Careful," she whispered against his mouth. "I cannot be . . . I mustn't . . ."

"Bird-watching is naughty work," he warned.

His hands left her hair and delved inside her cloak, finding her breasts. He covered them with his palms, kneading, plucking her nipples through fine wool and silk.

"I would finish this," he breathed against her mouth.

She made a wordless sound that was half whimper, half question.

"Well said," he mumbled.

He fanned his hands over her breasts through the bodice of her gown. "Miss Trelayne?" he groaned.

"We couldn't," she said.

"Oh, we *could*," he countered. He delved one hand into the neckline of her bodice, cupping her bare breast beneath her corset.

"It's . . ." she tried. "It wouldn't be . . ."

"Do not disparage bird-watching, Miss Trelayne," he scolded. "You do love it so."

She chuckled breathily, pressing against him. She couldn't. Stop. Pressing.

"Can you look up into the trees, Miss Trelayne? Tell me about the birds."

"Whi—?"

"The birds," he whispered, "*Look up*." He nudged her jaw with his nose, guiding her head back. She let her head fall, and he attacked the sensitive skin of her neck with his lips. Meanwhile, he shifted, sliding one hand behind her back and ever so slightly reclining her.

She tried to look down, to catch herself, but he warned in a throaty whisper, "Uh-uh-uh, Miss Trelayne. The birds in the sky."

She chuckled again and did as she was told, opening her eyes, blinking up at the autumnal canopy. There were no birds—or, if there were birds, she didn't care to see them—she saw only red and gold. She was submerged in a pool of sensation, and she wanted to sink deeper, not rise to the surface.

"What do you see?" he whispered in her ear. His words were calm and curious, but his breath was labored. One of his hands held her in a reclined slant on his lap, the other was a quick but scintillating tickle of movement.

She whimpered when his fingers left her breast; but he trailed a line of pleasure from the curve of her waist, to the rise of her hip, down the expanse of her leg. When his hand reached her foot, it encircled ankle and then disappeared upward beneath her skirts. He massaged his hand up her stockinged leg with seeking fingers.

She blinked at the leafy bower above, aware now of his intent. The center of her body tingled and burned, anticipating the destination.

"Surely not," she whispered, but she widened her legs. She tried to sit upright.

"I'm waiting, Miss Trelayne, to learn of all the lovely birds we've seen," he rasped. He sucked her earlobe, kissed her jaw, her eye; he nuzzled her nose.

Beneath her skirts, she felt his hand tangle in her drawers, and for a rapturous, breathless moment, he touched her where she needed it most, sliding, testing. Drew cried out, the pleasure a piercing thrum of *good, so good.*

"Careful not to frighten them away," he warned.

"You are wicked, Your Grace," she whimpered.

"Wickedly devoted to bird-watching," he grunted, and then his hand was gone, and she felt him fumbling with his trousers. Next he rose up, ever so slightly, from the stump. His powerful thighs supported his own weight and hers. The movement unsettled her, and she grabbed his shoulders, but he was already dropping back to the stump.

"Now, let's take those beautifully long legs of yours and wrap them like . . . this . . ." His hand moved quickly beneath her skirts, hitching her right leg over his hip.

"Oh," she said.

"For the birds," he said.

Drew laughed and repeated the position with her left leg, closing her eyes against the sheer wantonness of it.

He'd tipped her upright again, nose-to-nose; but there was a newness. For one, a bareness. Her drawers had been pushed aside. Also, an unmistakable hardness. Aligned perfectly, irresistibly, with her own need.

"Do you dare, Miss Trelayne?" he whispered, sliding against her.

"Please." A gasp. She didn't stop to consider.

"I knew you were more than a hobbyist," he said, kissing her, "you're so very good at this."

Next he grunted, "Up you go."

He buried another hand beneath her skirts, hooked it beneath her bottom, and lifted her. Using one hand to guide them and the other to raise her up and slide her down, he entered her in one, deep thrust.

Drew's body was ready for him—*yearning* for him—but she was unprepared for the fullness or the depth. She cried out in surprise.

He kissed away the sound, his breath ragged, sawing. He was motionless except for his hands. He slid them from her waist to gently palm her bottom.

"Are you alright?" he rasped.

"I don't know," she whispered. She broke the kiss and tucked her face into his neck.

"Am I hurting you?"

She shook her head against his cravat.

"Have I shocked you?"

She nodded.

"Come now," he teased, his voice raspy, "making love . . . on a stump . . . in a bower . . . astride my lap? This is less shocking and more . . . more . . ."

"Illegal?" she whispered, still tucked against him.

He blew out a pained laugh, fluttering the hair at the nape of her neck. "Likely it *is* illegal. I, for one, embrace my life of crime."

He shifted, just a little, and she felt a thin sliver of that feeling of utter *goodness*. It hovered on the periphery of her senses. She inhaled, wiggled.

"I didn't mean to corrupt you," he whispered into her hair, "but I did mean to make love to you. Not when I sought you out, but from the moment I sat beside you on this stump." He kissed her behind her ear. "You have that effect on me. I suppose I am wicked, just as you said. Last night, you were a virgin, and now . . ."

He shifted again and this time she let out a happy, encouraging sort of *whimper*. The good feeling had pulsed again and she rode it. She hitched her knees higher on his hips. Her breathing became fast and labored.

Very softly, whispering into his neck, she said, "Tell me what to do, Your Grace. I . . . *I want*."

Lachlan hissed out a curse, low and guttural. His hands found her waist, tightened, and he lifted her and dropped her; lifted her and dropped her. The movements were small, discreet, but very fast, repeated again and again; the rhythm immediately found, immediately right.

She heard another of her delighted whimpers. She sounded delirious with the building pleasure, and she *was* delirious, she supposed. He nosed her face from his neck and kissed her, devouring the sound.

If she'd been in her right mind—and most certainly she was not, she was as close to mindless as ever she'd been—the rocking thrusts of their joined bodies would have shocked her. His strength would have astounded her. Their flagrant disregard for their location in a public park would have appalled her.

Later, she thought idly, she would examine this encounter for shock and astonishment, and she would be very appalled.

*I will love it*, she corrected. I love loving *him*, breathless with the excitement and careless of the rest of the world.

"I cannot hold out," Lachlan huffed, speaking against her teeth. "I'm slayed. You sla—"

He was cut off by the sound of Drew's sharp sigh; it was surprise and delight bubbling up and escaping her body. She slumped against him, her muscles and bones spent, even while her insides exploded with ricocheting pleasure. Her thoughts were reduced to a swirling *yes-yes-yes*. Breathing shut down, vision shut down, hearing—all of it dimmed to nothing but the feeling of flight.

Beneath her, Lachlan let out a guttural moan, drove into her one last time, clamped her body down on him. He gasped, ground up, and dropped his head onto her shoulder. After a beat, his hands roved from beneath her skirts. He slid them up her back and he pulled her against him in an impossibly tight embrace.

Drew burrowed into his shoulder, loving the embrace as much as she loved the coupling. She was limp, barely able to lift her head from his shoulder, and yet his endless strength seemed to fuse them. They were so close, she could feel his heartbeat knocking against hers. Beneath her skirts, they were still joined.

"Are you alright?" he asked gently. Their breath came in labored pants.

She nodded. "I . . . I had no idea."

"Quite," he agreed. "Bird-watching is exhausting. Especially that bit at the end."

She laughed and, without thinking—indeed without even realizing the words left her mouth—she said, "Oh, I do love you."

She'd not said it loudly, not a pronouncement, nor softly, not a vow. She'd simply chuckled it out. It had been a realization, like, "I do relish a brisk swim," or "I do hope there's cake with tea."

Not that tone mattered. The words had been the thing. Too significant, too revealing, too needy.

Too soon.

Lachlan's heavy breathing seemed to dissipate. He made absolutely no reply.

Drew went very still, stiller than the two-hundred-year-old stump on which they were balanced. Her eyelids dropped shut. She tried very, very hard to vanish.

*Oh, my God*, she thought.

*What in the name of all that was sensible or reasonable or sane?*

*What have I done?*

She had . . . she had . . . *regressed*.

She was her old self, her vocal, speak-first, make-amends-never self. The Drewsmina from before. From the time when she was desperate for attention and she embarrassed herself on a daily basis.

It was a repeat of her behavior in the antechamber of Kew Palace with the birds, only a million times worse.

*Oh the irony*, Drew thought, *of marrying a duke, of enjoying his warm regard—his affection, his passion—and then ruining it by professing a deep, binding emotion on the* second *day.*

*Of terrifying him*, she thought. *Frightening him away. Of introducing feelings he wouldn't return.*

She was not unlike the orphans at Kew Palace, she thought. They'd seen birds in a cage and been intrigued; but instead of admiring them respectfully, they'd plunged them into frightened chaos.

And now, the duke would break a window and set himself free.

Drew's eyes filled with tears and she squeezed them away.

Meanwhile, Lachlan's silence endured. Of course he was silent, he was a reasonable man with reasonable restraint on his mouth and his heart. He would not embarrass her, but he would also make no profession. Not to *her*, Drewsmina Trelayne. Not after a fortnight of acquaintance.

She opened one eye and glanced at him.

He stared back at her with an open question on his face. His face said, *You didn't.*

He looked at her like she'd just told a roomful of children that there was no Father Christmas.

Drew's heart flickered, went dim, and then disappeared inside her chest. Coldness spread to every extremity, except her face. Her face burned.

"Look alive," Lachlan whispered, "someone's on the path."

Her eyes shot to his. He was scanning the horizon. His arms remained around her. He held her still, but not tightly, not possessively. He simply hadn't moved from before. It was a hollow touch.

She bit her lip and looked over her shoulder, trying to follow his gaze. She saw nothing. Trees, shrubs, the pond. She looked to him again. His face gave no clues except . . . mild detachment. His eyes did not dismiss her so much as . . . forget her? Move on from her?

And now her heart did its disappearing act a second time. She shivered.

"Perhaps it was nothing," he said. "We should go back."

"Oh," she said. "Yes, of course."

"If only for the twins. Buellis can only manage for so long."

She nodded and uncurled from him, sitting up. She tugged at her bodice. She looked around them. Her words had not only killed the warmth and intimacy, the teasing and playfulness was also gone. His movements were restless and pragmatic.

Would they always come together, explode together, and then . . . discuss Buellis?

*Who am I fooling?* she wondered. *There is no guarantee that we'll come together again.*

And she'd done it with a word. Well, with *three* words.

Because she'd wanted too much. She'd always wanted

too much. He'd found pleasure with her, of this she had no doubt, and he'd been considerate of her own pleasure—but to beat back the intimacy so quickly?

It had been the same last night, with his "errand." He was passionate, and then he was . . . gone.

Perhaps it wasn't her words. Perhaps intimacy between husband and wife meant that one lover enjoyed the coupling and went on his merry way, and the other . . . the other did the same. With *no* professions of love.

She mustn't cling; this much she knew. Her sister, Ana, clung; Ana wailed and begged, and the entire household was miserable for it.

Drew's eyes filled with tears again. She was embarrassed and confused and lonely. She was sitting on her husband's lap and she felt *lonely*.

She glanced at him again. Now he was staring at her face. She gave an awkward smile and looked quickly away.

Would it be reasonable, she wondered, to ask him? To inquire as to what, exactly, he preferred in these heavy moments between rapturous embrace and daily life?

Even the most reserved, measured person was allowed to ask questions about things they did not understand. Not now, of course, not after she'd already said too much of entirely the wrong thing. But eventually.

She'd transformed herself on the principle that saying less was generally better. If ever the opportunity to ask questions presented itself, she would plan in advance what she might say—no more blurting out declarations—and she would sum it up in one or two simple questions.

This plan did nothing for her disappearing heart but it gave her brain something to do. And it motivated her to carry on with the day. She could hardly remain, mortified and heartless, on the stump. He was correct about the twins. It had been selfish and careless to leave them unattended with a groom.

He was shifting now, fidgety on the stump. She unhooked

her ankles and slid her legs from his haunches. He loosened his hold and settled his hands on her waist.

"There you are," he mumbled, catching her eyes. She cast a quick glance at his face but couldn't look at him for long.

The coronet braid in her hair was loose, she could feel it sliding to one side and see orange wisps in her periphery. She released his shoulders and felt about for loose pins.

Her gloves were in the way, her palms perspired in the leather, so she peeled them off.

He watched her smooth her hair, saying nothing. She gave a small smile, not looking at him. She cleared her throat simply to puncture the silence. She kept her gaze fixed on the horizon.

The front of her skirts was bunched at the waist, and he gingerly untucked them, pulling them to first one side, then the other.

Her cloak hung in a limp column along her spine and he reached for it, spreading it over her shoulders, shielding her.

"If I hold you steady, can you stand?" he asked, his first words in minutes.

"Probably," she said.

He took her about the waist and she glanced at him. He licked his lips and her gaze fell to his mouth. She wanted him to say more—to say *anything*—but she also wanted to kiss him again. Just a peck. Kissing him had been so very lovely. She'd wanted to kiss him the moment he'd walked into the ballroom with his apple. She would kiss him every time she encountered him, given her choice.

She wanted too much.

"Drew?" he prompted.

"Forgive me," she said, and she stepped from his lap, found balance on shaky legs, shook out her skirts.

When she was steady, he rolled from the stump and turned away, fastening the fall of his trousers, tucking his shirt, running brisk hands over his waistcoat. He stooped to the ground and recovered his gloves and hat.

Drew was reminded of her own gloves. She was too over-heated to put them on, but she would squeeze them. She needed something on which to take hold.

She glanced back to him. He was settling his hat on his head, giving his coat a shake.

"Shall we?" he said, and he held out an arm.

Another touch. He wasn't angry with what she'd said. He seemed to feel . . . *nothing*. There was no other way to put it. She'd said the most important words, and he'd said and done . . . nothing.

She went to him, forcing herself to walk smoothly. She looped her arm through, and he turned them toward the narrow trail.

"Oh look," he said.

Drew lifted her head. A medium-sized green bird, its feathers shockingly bright against the dull, worn-out tones of autumn, was perched on a low-hanging branch not three yards ahead.

"Oh," she whispered, laughing a little. "A ring-necked parakeet."

"So it is," he said speculatively, pretending to concur.

She swung her gaze to him and he gave a shrug and a wink.

*A wink.* Why? Why wink at her but not speak to her? Or speak more to her? He'd talked almost continuously during their—well, *during*.

And now?

"What should I know," he asked, "about a ring-necked parakeet?"

"Well," she turned back to the bird. "They are one of very few species of island birds to have naturalized from the tropics to Britain—brought home in captivity by sail-ors. They are rare but quite happy here. They've adapted to the cold."

"So they have," he said.

She stared at the bird a moment longer. "What a de-light," she whispered, momentarily distracted; settled and cheered, as always, by the simple visit from a bird. "I've only ever seen two or three in my life."

"I told you we were bird-watching," he said, staring up at the lime-colored bird.

"Perhaps we *were* quiet enough," she remarked. "Especially at the end."

He looked at her, studying her profile, but she kept her eyes on the bird. She would not question him, or pressure him, or endeavor to direct him. She wouldn't do anything but discover the very best way to be his wife.

If the ring-necked parakeet could adapt to the cold, by God, so could she.

# Chapter Twenty-Five

Dan had always been woefully, dreadfully *unprepared* for surprises.

It would not be inaccurate to say that he *hated* surprises.

It was chilling, really, his fear of being surprised. Or unprepared. Or being (as seen today) totally dumbfounded and speechless.

It didn't matter if the surprise amounted to something delightful or something dreadful, he hated being caught off guard.

It was why he'd stalked his tenants for months, pretending to be one of them, trying to understand their conflict with the mill owners.

It was why he stalked the smugglers now, trying to understand how and why these same tenants would engage in criminal activity rather than ask him for help.

He preferred to quietly (and, if necessary, *secretly*) observe and consider before any surprise circumstance exploded in his face.

Of course this had not worked in his favor with the riots, but not because he hadn't tried.

Drewsmina Trelayne had, thus far, been an exercise in surprises. Adolphus had forced her upon him. She'd stormed the house with practicality and compassion and her red hair and blue gowns like an avenging angel. She'd been too irresistible not to . . . well, not to wind up as his duchess.

And now this.

Ian tromped through the tall wet grass of Hampstead Heath, pulling Drewsmina behind him, wondering how he could possibly salvage any of this.

*Oh, I do love you*, she'd said—a statement that might just represent the surprise of his life.

And what had he done?

He'd made exactly the wrong response, which was no response at all, a product of all the surprises that Drewsmina seemed to have embodied since she swarmed his life.

Ian detested surprises but he did not detest her.

*Do I love her?*

He had no idea.

No one had ever said these words to him.

His aunt and uncle had loved him, but their love had been *demonstrated* more than discussed. Their influence on his life had been tenuous and fragile. They'd quietly become his surrogate parents while his actual mother and father were still very much alive. They'd been careful not to overstep, not to profess or beam or claim too much. His uncle had been terrified his older brother would take Ian away.

And so nothing had been said. Not once. Never.

As to women . . . well, Ian was no virgin. He'd been in the army, he'd become a duke when he was dashing and unattached, rather than old and long married. But he'd never before had a mistress or a sweetheart. Hell, he'd never before been with the same woman for more than one night.

Oh the irony. He'd only been with Drewsmina for a night.

Well, one night and then one afternoon in a thick copse of trees.

But still.

*Oh, I do love you.*

The words swam about in his head like fish in a bowl, beautiful but also trapped. He didn't know whether to feed them, procure a larger domicile for their comfort, or thrust them back at her.

"I do not like surprises," he mumbled to himself, crunching down the path.

Drew was behind him, scrambling to keep up. "I beg your pardon?" she asked.

"Forgive me," he said. "I'm thinking out loud."

They'd cleared the trees, walked across a field, and now rounded the corner of the pond. In the distance, his parked carriage and stallion came into view. Beyond that, the girls sat in a bright patch of sunlight.

"What was your thought?" Drew prompted.

"Hmmm?"

"You've just said you were thinking out loud," she said quietly. "It makes me wonder. Thinking of what?"

He cleared his throat. He thought about how he should answer. He'd already said the wrong thing once—that is, he'd said nothing, which had been wrong. He didn't want to do it again.

"I was simply thinking," he said, "how unsettled I can be. By surprises."

"*Surprises*," she repeated with emphasis.

She walked a few more steps and declared, "Me neither. I do not care for surprises."

Another few steps. She added, "I do believe I was surprised—by today, that is. By what happened. In the, er, trees."

The sound of distress in her voice tore a strip from his heart, and he stopped. He spun back. She was looking up to him, searching his face with large, anxious eyes.

"You didn't feel . . . coerced or . . . or forced did you, Drew?" His heartbeat suddenly pounded behind his eyes.

"Oh no," she said, shaking her head, "it was nothing like that. I wanted—That is, I want everything we may, er, do. Together. The two of us." She blushed beautifully and looked away.

"However," she continued, glancing back, "now that you

raise the topic of surprises, I realize that I may have been overcome with the unexpected, er . . . passion of it all. Which may have also led me to do . . . or to *say* . . . That is, I may have—"

Now she faltered, and it was his turn to shake his head. "You've done nothing remotely out of order, Drewsmina," he said.

She narrowed her eyes, clearly trying to gauge the truth of this.

He reached out to touch her arm, and she stared at his hand. He wrapped his fingers gently round her bicep and slid them up and down. He could no longer *casually* touch her. Every touch evolved into a caress.

"Forgive me," he said. "I've spoken out of turn."

"I don't know what I'm doing," she whispered.

"That makes two of us . . . But I can tell you that . . . what happened in the trees . . . was precipitated only by worry. My deep worry—for you. Your mother is ghastly. Please know, by the way, that I'll always be available after she's come and gone. We can pour a drink and toast her . . . undeniable ghastliness."

"Oh," said Drew. "Thank you. I felt unable to face you after you'd . . . experienced her. We . . . I—"

She closed her eyes. "I fled. I'm sorry."

"You are not a prisoner in Pollen Street," he said. "Let us all come and go as we please. Greenly told me where you'd gone. I saddled my horse and came after you. Thankfully, I found the girls easily enough. And Imogene was particularly eager to point out your little sanctuary. I was so relieved to find you. And then, when I saw you, I was—well, *excitement* is perhaps the best word for it."

"Excitement?" She opened her eyes.

He nodded. "Worry drove me here, but within moments of clapping eyes on you, it was overshadowed by desire. For you."

"Oh," she said, the anxiety dissolving from her face. She

was so very pretty. Pale skin, teal eyes, hair the color of the low embers of a fire. Remarkably, he began to feel the hot glow of need again. Even now. Less than an hour after their coupling. Desire for her had become his constant companion, licking and burning at his body and mind.

"Did you know I've never made love out of doors?" he asked softly, dipping to whisper in her ear.

She shook her head.

He kissed the whirl of her ear, lingering for a moment to nuzzle her neck.

"Lachlan," Drew whispered, "the girls."

He closed his eyes and breathed in the scent of her hair.

"Lachlan?" she prompted. "Your Grace?"

"Hmmm?" His eyes were closed. He was moments away from trailing his lips from her ear to her mouth.

"I do believe they've spotted us," Drew said. "And they are running this way. But where is your sister?"

"What?" He pulled his mouth away and looked up.

"Have they unpinned their hair?" Drew asked. "But why? Oh, there is the baroness. But . . . is she hurt? Is she lying prone on the ground?"

"It would not be the first time," he grumbled, squinting into the sun.

Imogene and Ivy were suddenly upon them, their loose hair flying and bare feet flashing beneath raised hems. "Hello, Uncle! Hello, Miss Trelayne!" Ivy shouted.

"What's become of your mother, girls? Is she unwell?" Drew asked. She became caught up in the duet of ebullient girls. She slipped free of Ian's grasp and ran ahead with the twins.

Timothea was, in fact, lying on the ground, her arms and legs spread wide like the points of a star. Ian stomped behind his wife and nieces and stared down at her.

Behind Timothea's head, her unbound hair had been fanned out like a spilled pail of black paint. Woven into her hair were a magpie's collection of natural treasures: the stiff blossom of a chrysanthemum, autumn leaves in various shapes and sizes, a twig in the shape of a T, a length of twine, a feather.

She looked not unlike a witch, albeit a good, not-unpleasant-to-look-upon witch, laid out for a ritual. Beside her in the grass, her daughters had collapsed, legs huddled beneath skirts, chins resting on knees. They held up additional hair ornamentation for Drew to peruse. Now that Ian looked closer, he saw that similar specimens from the natural world hung from their own unbound hair. The twins looked less like witches and more like proper girls who may have taken a tumble from their pony into a field.

Ivy smiled down at her mother, clearly proud of their diversion. Imogene dropped her treasures and considered Ian and Drew with shrewd, speculative eyes.

"She is not unwell," Ivy told Drew. "We are *adorning* her."

"How . . . creative," Drew said diplomatically, crinkling up her nose.

Obligingly, Timothea opened one eye.

Ivy carefully tucked a long blade of grass behind her mother's ear.

"Where were you?" asked Imogene, looking back and forth between Ian and Drew.

"We were bird-watching," Ian said. "Where were you?"

"We were here," announced Ivy, as happy as Ian could ever remember seeing her. "It's been a great many years since Mama has allowed us to adorn her. Adornment was frowned upon at T.O.E. As was sitting in the grass."

Timothea closed her eye, but she arced up her hand and found Ivy's. Enlacing their fingers, she held her daughter's hand.

"I'm glad you enjoyed Hampstead," said Drew. "If you like, we can make a point to come every week."

"What birds did you see?" challenged Imogene.

"We saw a Rhine-Nosed Parapet," said Ian.

"A ring-necked parakeet," Drew corrected.

"That's what I said."

Ivy giggled, but Imogene narrowed her eyes. "Your hair is askew, *Aunt* Miss Trelayne."

"You may simply refer to me as Drew, if you like, Imogene. And what of your hair, I wonder?"

"Let me guess," recited Imogene, "proper ladies do not weave bits of the park into their hair. Proper ladies would never even remove their hats."

"But where *are* your hats, do you know?" asked Drew, scanning the park with a hand over her eyes. "I should think a pleasant afternoon in the company of your mother, enjoying a favorite activity, takes precedence over what we may or may not do to our hair. Or our hats. Oh, I see them. And you've removed your shoes as well?"

Ian followed her gaze to a nearby bench, under which lay three pairs of shoes, a pile of stockings, and two hats.

"We wanted to feel the grass in our toes," reported Ivy, sliding bare feet from beneath the hem of her dress.

"So you did," said Drew. "Never let it be said that we did not commune with nature today."

"Agreed," said Ian, and she gave a tiny, barely perceptible start. She took a deep breath.

"If Lady Tribble is amenable," Drew continued, "let us collect our things and return to Pollen Street before the evening chill sets in. We've missed afternoon lessons for today, but there is dinner to be eaten and books to be read around the fire. Oh, and tomorrow is an important day, isn't it? Kew Palace? Properly meeting Princess Cynde and Prince Adolphus in their Throne Room. We'll need to review what's expected of an audience with a royal prince and princess."

Ian frowned. He'd actually elected to forget this. Adolphus. Princess Cynde. Go again through the motions of the crowded antechamber and throne room. He sighed, dreading the overblown, extenuated ordeal of it all.

"Will you leave me?" asked Timothea, not opening her

eyes. "I'm feeling the rotation of the earth. Right this very moment. It spins ever so slowly and I am *absorbing* it."

"No, Mama," complained Ivy, looking worried, "we must return home together. Perhaps we've enjoyed enough rotation for one day?"

"Yes," said Ian, stooping. "Home. With us. Up you go." He snatched his sister's hand from the grass and recovered the other from Ivy. With a gentle yank, he pulled his sister from the grass. She came up in a stiff line, like a trap door opening from the cellar.

"Oh, Mama," sighed Ivy, "how magical you look."

"Thank you, Vee." She patted her hair and smoothed her skirt. "What a winning idea this was, Miss Trelayne—Hampstead. I endorse a weekly sojourn."

"Likewise," Ian said, and he winked at his wife.

"Girls," said Drew, blushing and turning away, "let us collect your hats and shoes? Lady Tribble, do not trouble yourself. The girls will fetch them."

"I prefer to feel my bare feet on nature's carpet, Miss Trelayne," informed Timothea, allowing Ian to lead her to the carriage.

"Will no one call her Drewsmina?" muttered Ian. "Or Drew as she's suggested? We are married, for all that."

"We are all deciding who she is within the family, Ian," instructed Timothea. "Let her find her place for each of us, and we'll find our place for her. Only then will we know how to call her."

"Quite," Ian said, and he glanced back at his wife. She was laughing as the twins zigzagged before her, arms filled with shoes and hats, stockings streaming behind them.

He glanced at his sister. Perhaps Timmie was correct. He didn't know her place in the house or his place with her. She'd been a member of staff as late as last week. Was that the confusion?

"Timothea," he asked. "Do you remember a time, any time at all, when Mother and Father seemed to share anything like . . . like *love*?"

"What do you mean, 'share love'?" she challenged. "Did they love each other? No, no they did not."

"But you managed to get the hang of it, in spite of all that?" he asked gently. "A right marriage to Tribble? Even though you'd never been shown."

"That's one of the many wonderful things about love, isn't it?" Timothea sighed. "It's instinctual. It is waiting, latent, inside all of us, like a seed. You needn't be shown. It helps, perhaps, but love can erupt inside you, a wellspring, even if you've never heard of it before in your life."

Ian frowned. He'd never considered the notion of romantic love—not now or ever. He was too measured and considered for anything so amorphous and mythical. Only Timothea could take a rational conversation and turn it into seeds and eruptions.

"Returning to the topic of Mother and Father," he said, trying again. "So they were never 'in love,' whatever that may mean. But do you think they were ever . . . *happy*?"

"Oh for God's sake, Ian," Timothea said, reaching for the carriage door. "I never knew them to be anything but miserable; but what bearing does this have on you? None. Endeavor to be *less* intent on thinking things to death and more intent on embracing the magic right in front of you. For once."

"What?" he asked, frowning. "How does one 'embrace magic'?"

But she was turning away, climbing the steps of the carriage with bare feet, sticks and feathers swaying from her unbound hair.

# Chapter Twenty-Six

Imogene complained throughout the next day's long
carriage ride to Kew Palace.

Her dress made her look like a twelve-year-old.

The pins in her hair were giving her a headache and her
hat obscured her vision.

Ivy was sitting too close. Ivy blocked the window. Ivy's
dress made *her* look like a twelve-year-old.

She had no wish to meet Prince Adolphus and she'd already made the acquaintance of Princess Cynde.

If the royal visit intruded on her afternoon tennis lesson,
she could not be held accountable.

Drew smiled serenely, disavowing each complaint, despite
the very great honor it was, truly, for any young woman to
be invited to a royal palace to meet a prince and princess. If
Imogene came off, in the privacy of the cramped carriage,

petulant and entitled, well . . . Imogene *was* a bit petulant, and her entitlement had been a long time coming. Drew need only observe Lady Tribble's detached, uncertain style of parenting to be reminded that the girls had been through so much.

The baroness had stunned them all by gliding into breakfast in a garment that could almost be considered a proper dress and announcing she would be joining for the call to Kew. They were in the carriage now, the five of them, lively, colorful silks nestled together like sweets in a box. Drew had worn a purplish-blue gown and lavender hat; Ivy, blue; Lady Tribble, dove-gray; Imogene, apricot with ebony trim. Lachlan wore a chocolate-covered overcoat, ochre waistcoat, and blinding white cravat. It was a far cry from the muddy boots and highwayman's greatcoat he'd worn for their first encounter at Kew. Drew had taken it upon herself to have a word with Pruitt, his long-ignored and under-used valet.

Riding along, listening to Imogene's complaints, Drew had hoped Lady Tribble might gently correct the girl, but it was a vain hope. Later, Drew would tell Lachlan that the *former* Imogene, the one she'd met only a fortnight ago, *wouldn't* have complained about dresses or crowding or tennis lessons, because the *former* Imogene sat in silence, projecting an owlish sort of judgment on the world. Meanwhile, the Imogene of today had a voice, and why shouldn't she use it? Her litany of abuses were, happily, mundane. They were the average grievances of a sixteen-year-old, nothing like the highly irregular complaints she'd made about T.O.E.

*This* was progress. How much better to hear about a missed tennis lesson than that Reverend Sagg had not allowed them to *read*.

In the end, the real source of the complaining had been the girl's obvious nerves. She and her new maid had devoted more than an hour to her hair, she'd changed gowns twice, and now she fidgeted with her reticule, squinted at her faint reflection in the carriage window, jabbed her sister, and looked to the window again.

Unless Drew was mistaken, *all* of the Starry women were nervous, even the baroness. Twice Lady Tribble claimed she felt unwell or "had a terrible premonition" and asked to be expelled from the carriage on the side of the road. This suggestion had been visibly upsetting to Ivy, who clung to her mother's arm.

Lachlan had said, absolutely not. If *he* had to suffer through a royal audience, they *all* would suffer through it.

Lachlan had, Drew knew, wanted to come least of all. As far she could tell, he'd been out of the house nearly all night. All of them had retired early, hoping to look fresh for the royal visit. Less than an hour later, he'd knocked on the adjoining door to Drew's room, fully dressed, down to his gloves and hat, and informed her that he had another errand and he was going out.

Unlike the previous night, when she'd expected no knock, this night, she'd allowed herself to hope. Imogene had not come, thank goodness, and she'd managed to dress herself in a proper night rail, although the least opaque and least *woolen* of her collection, and no dressing gown.

What she had *not* been waiting for, in fact what made her throat go tight and her eyes sting, was his announcement that he'd be going out, possibly all night.

Meanwhile, he'd taken one look at her, hair down, bare ankles, and feet poking from beneath the hem of her night rail, and rolled from the doorjamb, crowded her into the room, and kissed her. As before, his kisses led to her being hoisted in his arms; his arms led to the bed; and all of it working together took them to ecstasy.

He'd made love to her more slowly this time, tenderly, whispering her name. Even so, there was no mention of his feelings for her. Thankfully this time, she also managed to say nothing.

She'd wanted to say it. The words knocked insistently on

the inside of her mouth, but she dared not introduce *I love you* into the scenario again.

Although, what did it really matter because, afterward, he'd left her. Another "errand." He'd proclaimed nothing, and allowed for no intimate sort of lingering, holding each other in bed, he'd made no explanation. He simply kissed her a final time, dressed, and was gone.

For hours into the night, she'd lain awake, waiting to hear him moving about in the next room, but his suite had remained silent.

She'd only managed to sleep after she'd slid from bed, marched to the door, and thrust it open. The cavernous suite beyond had been empty, of course, and she'd stepped inside, marveling at the high ceilings, the leather-grommeted appointments, the copper tub, twice as large as hers, the giant fireplace.

*How have I never seen this room?* she'd marveled.

The duchess's suite was perfectly lovely—truly the most luxurious bedroom in which she'd ever had the fortune of passing the night—but this? This room could easily accommodate two. The bed was massive and the fire warm and bright. There was enough room to bring in a table and chairs, to take private meals in front of the hearth. And the tub?

Clearly Lachlan's proclivity for outside-the-bed lovemaking had influenced her, because her thoughts had drifted immediately to all of the sloshy, soapy fun they might have inside that deep tub.

Drew had spun around slowly, taking it all in, struck by a very bold, very courageous idea.

What if she engineered a night—a magical night—spent in the company of her husband, in the confines of this glorious chamber? The *next* night, she'd thought, after their triumphant return from Kew Palace. She would warn him in advance so he'd not be taken by surprise. He could plan for it. It would be known and expected.

They would all be exhausted; she'd already informed

Cook to plan for an informal supper. She would leave the girls to their own devices and she and Lachlan would take the evening meal here. She would have the servants draw a bath. She would . . . she would . . . wear the shift again. Or wear nothing it all. Lovemaking would be guaranteed, of this she had no doubt, but perhaps she could remain here afterward. For the entire night. Perhaps they could talk. Perhaps she could better understand him and his regard for lovemaking—and for after lovemaking.

Only with this plan percolating in her head had Drew drifted back to her own bed and finally fallen asleep.

The next morning, the idea had endured—the first thing on her mind.

In addition to approving hair and hats and pressing everyone to eat a proper breakfast, Drew had gone over detailed instructions with Chappy and Lachlan's valet Pruitt. They would make certain the bath was drawn and that Cook prepared a private supper to be served in the duke's bedchamber, with candles, and wine.

If she'd not yet managed to include *Lachlan* in this plan—to, in essence, invite him to his own room, a destination to which he would surely already go—well, she would do it when the moment was correct.

It was the very great promise of this night that kept Drew from correcting Imogene for her complaining. Drew heard the girl, but she wasn't paying attention, not really. The royal visit was something to be endured and survived—for all of them. The invitation for Lachlan to spend a special night, the *entire* night, in her company, was the real challenge of the day. She would prioritize herself in this. For once. If ever she intended to get a full night's sleep again, if their marriage was meant to be halfway reasonable and communicative, their current pattern could not go on.

"Aunt Miss Trelayne?" asked Ivy, invoking the very odd but endearing name that the girls now called her. "But how can you know we won't accidentally encounter His Majesty King George?"

Drew smiled at her, glad to have her thoughts pulled back to the present. "Well, I don't know for certain, but honestly, there is very little chance. The prince and princess receive subjects in a far-flung Throne Room—"

"Some might even call it a *sewing* room," droned Lachlan.

"—which is not remotely near the family wing," finished Drew. "Actually, I don't believe King George and Queen Charlotte are in residence at the moment. They are at Windsor until after Boxing Day, I believe. Regardless, I've called on the princess many times and never once encountered any stray royal."

Ivy nodded, squeezing a wad of her skirts into a tight ball.

Drew tugged on the girl's gown, hoping to stave off wrinkling. "Never you fear, Ivy. You've already met Princess Cynde in your very own garden. She will be no different. And besides, she and the prince mean to check *my* progress as your stylist more than anything you may do. We'll make some small chitchat, likely about the weather; they will express condolences on the passing of your father. You will thank them, curtsy a second time, and we'll reverse from the room. They receive a steady stream of callers on Mondays, and we'll be one small party among a larger crowd—people from every corner of the country. We will be unremarkable, really, except for our fine manners and cleverness."

Ivy nodded and eyed her mother. The baroness closed her eyes, and tapped her head with a gloved hand, the gesture of someone with a headache. Why Lady Tribble had elected to join this particular foray, Drew could not say. But Drew was glad of it; the more interest she showed in the girls' lessons and outings, the better for all of them.

"Behold, the palace gates," droned Lachlan, tapping on the carriage glass. "Away we go."

Ten minutes later they were stepping from the carriage, shaking out skirts and stretching their legs. After a long walk down a series of gilded passageways and stairwells, they were admitted to the small antechamber that held callers before their audience with the prince and princess.

As before, the room held seven or eight milling subjects, dressed in everything from dull country wool to shiny, vibrant silks. In particular, Drew noticed a cadre of stylish young women, similar in age to Imogene and Ivy, preening and chattering by the doorway. Perhaps today had been set aside for the royal couple to receive several debutantes, Drew thought.

Drew shepherded her family to the only empty corner in the small room and gave Imogene and Ivy a reassuring wink. The girls huddled near their mother, their eyes wide, their hands clasped tightly about fans and reticules.

Perhaps this outing would be good for them, Drew thought. It had been precipitous of Cynde, she'd thought, to summon them so soon, but the girls had learned enough to manage it, and this relatively informal palace visit would help the girls comprehend the gravity of eventually being presented to the queen.

"They've restored the window, I see," Lachlan said, leaning down to whisper in her ear. His closeness rolled shivers down her neck and arms. She glanced at the window and smiled. He'd remembered.

She swallowed hard, bracing herself. She smiled up at him. "Lachlan?"

"Hmm?" He was looking at his timepiece.

"Later tonight, when we've returned—"

"Imogene is crying."

Ivy had made this pronouncement. She was suddenly beside Drew, pointing discreetly at her sister, who'd turned her face to the wall. Beside Imogene stood Lady Tribble, her expression panicked; she looked like someone who'd been suddenly asked to pray aloud in church.

Drew reached blindly for Lachlan, her question about their special evening forgotten. The baroness bent to whisper something to her daughter, but Imogene spun, presenting her back to her mother. And now the girl's profile was revealed to the room, and ah, yes. Ivy was correct. Imogene *was* crying. The tears were discreet, shown mostly in blotchy skin and a bit bottom lip. Drew's heart broke, just a little, to see proud Imogene losing composure—and here, of all places. Drew had never seen her so distressed.

"What's happened?" Drew whispered, coming up to them. She looked back and forth between the baroness and Imogene.

"Imogene?" Drew gently pressed. "How can I help? Should we go? This outing was meant to be exciting and fun but it's certainly not worth tears."

"We are outcasts," hissed Imogene lowly, bitterly. "Oddities. Everyone can see it." Angrily, she swiped a tear from her cheek and glanced at the circle of pretty girls near the door.

*Ah*, thought Drew. She stepped up to shield the girl from view.

"We've had no proper schooling," whispered Imogene, "we've no notion of how to behave in polite company. We have almost no clothes—"

"That's not true," said Ivy, "think of the hours we spent at the dressmaker's."

"But the dresses haven't been delivered yet, have they?" shot back Imogene.

"Mrs. Tavertine's staff has worked day and night to make the gown you're wearing, Imogene," said Drew. "And it's very pretty. I assure you, you look just as lovely, if not lovelier, than anyone in this palace. I would not have brought you here if I wasn't confident you were suited for royal company."

"I hate relying upon you to tell me what is appropriate or reasonable or how to behave. I hate being ignorant of what to do."

"London was too ambitious," Lachlan remarked, coming to stand behind them. "I knew this, and yet—"

"No," said Imogene, swiping away another tear, "I adore

London. I should never leave it, given the choice. What I *hate* is not knowing how to manage it. I hate being the . . . the bumpkin who must rely on Miss Trelayne or risk looking like a fool. And mostly—" she swiped away another tear and glared at her mother "—I *hate* that I was locked away in the bloody, bleeding Temple of Order in Eden for *five years*, only to emerge the village idiot." Her voice rose on the last "I hate," and she turned angry, narrowed eyes on her mother.

Drew inhaled slowly, hoping to demonstrate calm. She glanced at Lady Tribble. The baroness wore a look of pained shock, almost is if she'd taken a musket to the gut. Then, not unlike a gunshot victim, she squeezed her eyes closed and began to sob.

When Ivy saw this, she too bowed her head and began to whimper.

"*Alright*," sang Drew cheerfully—quietly, but cheerfully— "let us step *out* of the antechamber and find some private place to collect ourselves, shall we?" She looked to Lachlan. "Your Grace, can you lead the way?"

"Right . . ." he said, looking around. "You are all too large, I suppose, to fit out the window. We'll simply . . . go out the way we came in."

He led the way to the corridor doors, opening them just wide enough for the five of them to file out. At the far end of the landing, a footman approached with a smartly dressed young couple and a babbling baby.

Lachlan frowned, looked right and left, and opened the very next door he came to. The room was dark inside and he snatched a candle from the wall and disappeared within. Drew paused, eyeing the approaching footman. The couple stopped to admire a mural on the wall, pointing out some feature to the baby, and Drew saw their chance.

"In we go, after Lachlan," she chirped, leading them into the dim room. When everyone was inside, she quietly, discreetly shut the door.

"Calm," she called gently. "Let us all endeavor to keep calm."

"I've found the lamp," said Lachlan, his face suddenly washed in light.

The room was hardly illuminated but brighter now; it allowed Drew to see that Imogene had chosen the opposite of calmness. The girl burst into proper tears.

Lady Tribble came next, her cries only muffled as her face fell into her gloved hands.

Last was Ivy, who came from nowhere to Drew's side and fell into her arms, crying against her chest.

*This is my reward*, thought Drew, *for becoming distracted.* The romantic night with Lachlan seemed as unattainable, and indeed, as frivolous, as a proverbial golden egg.

If she felt more disappointment than was strictly appropriate, especially as three females sobbed around her, she endeavored to put the entire idea out of her head. These young women needed her, and there were worse things than being needed.

Across the room, Lachlan swore, collided with something loud and clattery, and swore again. After more profanity, he managed to light a second lamp, and then a third. Light spilled from the rear of the room and Drew looked about over the top of Ivy's hat.

Thankfully, the room appeared to be used for storage. Unused chairs and empty tables crowded the large space in no particular order. Vacant tea trolleys lined one wall, and empty vases were clustered like penguins in a corner.

Drew took a deep breath, kissed Ivy's forehead, and disentangled herself. Grabbing the first available chair, she pushed it like a baby pram across the room and parked it behind the baroness.

"Sit, if you please, Lady Tribble," she ordered. "Do take a seat."

She returned for a second chair and slid it to Imogene.

"Sit, Imogene. Breathe in three deep breaths." Imogene glared at her and dropped to the floor beside the chair.

Drew laughed in spite of herself and slid the chair to Ivy. Lachlan wove his way through the scattered furniture and stood by her side, holding the lamp.

"Now," Drew said, squaring off in front of the trio. "First I should like to say this is entirely my fault. A royal introduction was precipitous; I see that now. You are overwhelmed and afraid, and this has been my very grave error in judgment. Do not bla—"

"It is not your fault," Imogene cried. "I *want* to meet the princess. I *want* to visit palaces, and parks, and museums, and concerts, and I want to go to balls. But I don't want anyone to know about T.O.E."

"Well," ventured Drew, "we shan't tell anyone, shall we? No one needs to know. You believe that people are watching you and judging you, but in fact they are far more concerned about their own perceived inadequacies to speculate about where you've been or what you may or may not know."

"Oh yes," cried Imogene, "and what of your mother?"

"Well, my mother notwithstanding. She would be the lone, unfortunate exception to this statement, but we shall endeavor to keep as far away from her as possible. There is being confident and then there is simply self-preservation. With her, we shall avoid. Take heart, however, she is hateful even to Princess Cynde, and Cynde is daughter-in-law to the king. Also, I now outrank her and will deal with her in my own time." The words were out before she'd considered them, but perhaps they were true.

Beside her, Lachlan gave a snort.

"It is my fault." These words, muffled and bleak, came from Lady Tribble, her head still buried in her hands.

"Timmie," began Lachlan, his voice soft with compassion.

"No," she cried, snapping her head up. "I would say it."

"Yes, Mama," said Imogene, "why don't you say it?"

"It was wrong of me to allow Sagg and the Temple to swallow us up," sobbed Lady Tribble. "To swallow *me*. It is my fault that the girls have been kept from so much. Every wretched thing that we encountered at the Temple is my fault. I was . . . I couldn't . . ." She let out another sob. "I was so devastated when Tribble died. I could barely get out of bed. Meanwhile Sagg and his elders were relentless. They beckoned me. They promised peace. They promised I could learn to pray in such a way that would allow me to *commune* with Peter."

"Who is Peter?" Drew whispered.

"Baron Tribble," Lachlan whispered back.

Lady Tribble was still talking. "And there was a structure at the Temple, wasn't there? A routine. The community would look after the girls when I could not. I was desolate on the inside, lonely and—"

"Wretched," provided Imogene sourly.

"And wretched," agreed Lady Tribble. "Everything about the Temple felt consistent with what I was experiencing in my head and my heart. I couldn't . . . couldn't make out the difference between my own grief and the life we would live there. Meanwhile, our life at home, with Peter gone, had carried on. His nephew was the new baron. The servants went about their old tasks for a new lord. The world had continued, but I had not—how could I? I should have managed better, I should have. It was selfish and shortsighted and Peter would have wanted better for his girls . . ."

"Why didn't you bring us to Avenelle?" demanded Imogene. "Uncle had no idea, perhaps, about your grief or the two of us, but he would've been better than Reverend Sagg. *Anyone* would have been better than Reverend Bloody Sagg."

"High praise indeed," mumbled Ian.

Lady Tribble was shaking her head. "My memories of Avenelle are very bleak, Genie. I didn't view it as a place we would be safe or happy. Not on top of everything else. To grieve Peter and suffer Avenelle? It wasn't to be borne.

I'd not returned since Ian became duke. In my view, it was still my lonely girlhood home. And I thought—stupidly, I thought—*anywhere* but there."

"Even the Temple," marveled Imogene quietly.

"Perhaps you will never find it in your heart to forgive me, and perhaps you will, but you must know how terribly regretful I am. And that I *try*. Daily, I try. Surely you see that." She raised her hands, gesturing to the room, "I'm in a palace for God's sake. And you know how I feel about turrets."

"*I* forgive you, Mama," said Ivy, floating across the room to her mother. She came behind her chair and leaned over, draping her arms down her shoulders. Lady Tribble snatched up her hands and pressed them to her mouth, clutching her daughter like a drowning woman.

Drew glanced at Imogene. There would be no immediate forgiveness or embracing from that quarter, not for some time.

Drew rushed to fill the silence. "Part of becoming the ladies you hop—"

"A word, if I might," cut Lachlan, stepping beside her. Four pairs of eyes swung to him. *Oh thank God*, thought Drew. She had no idea what she'd intended to say.

He tabled his lantern and shoved his hands in the pockets of his coat. He cleared his throat. "Since we seem to all be confessing—"

"I confess nothing but injustice," said Imogene.

"Noted," he said. He cleared his throat again. "Since *some of us* are confessing, I should like to say a few words."

The four women blinked at him in the dim lantern light. It was as if one of the chairs had suddenly begun to speak. Drew crossed her arms over her chest, transfixed.

"Right. I feel compelled to offer up my excuse for not riding on the Temple of Order in Eden and hauling the lot of you out. It is a bollocks excuse, considering all you've endured, but an excuse just the same."

"You didn't come because I bade you not to," said Timothea. "I believed myself incapable of life at Avenelle."

"Well, I should've ignored you, shouldn't I have? If you'll indulge me, I'll endeavor to explain why I did not."

The girls leaned in. Timothea rubbed her brow with a shaky gloved hand. Drew shuffled closer to him, her heart pounding. She could kiss the snobby debutantes on the mouth. No amount of engineering could have created a healing moment such as this. It was so much more important than dresses and curling wands and watercolors.

Beside her, Ian took a deep breath. "About the time you were entering into the Temple of Order in Edam," he began.

"Eden," corrected Ivy, laughing a little.

"Right, *Eden*. About that time, I'd become closely involved with a group of tenants at Avenelle who, as their life's work, shear the wool of Avenelle sheep and then make it into cloth and lace. They have this conflict with local mill owners. I've alluded to this bit with each of you before."

"The Flemish tenants," realized Timothea.

"Right. The Flemish tenants were outraged at the competition posed by the mills. And, for whatever ill-advised reason—call it youthful naivete, call it arrogant miscalculation, call it sheer stupidity—I began to attend the angry meetings of these tenants to hear their complaints. However, I did not attend in my role as their landlord; instead I dressed as one of them, a tenant, a sympathetic lace maker from another estate. I wore a weaver's clothing and spoke in a Cornish-y accent and let on that I, too, was concerned about the future of lace making and the threat of the mills. Because of this, they took me into their confidence—which had been my goal, for them to speak plainly. I had hoped, foolishly, to convince them to *work* with the mills, to find some compromise, to appeal to the new duke for help. Well, can you guess what happened?"

"They found you out?" said Ivy, enrapt.

"No, not at first. First, they took up arms and marched on

both the mills and the home of the local magistrate to demand that the mill owners stand down. They went in with torches and pitchforks, presumably to burn all of it to the ground and fight any man who opposed them."

"All of your careful observation was for naught," realized Drew.

"Yes," said Lachlan. "For naught. Their final meeting evolved into a sort of fevered, violent rage, consumed by mob rule. There was nothing I could do to stem the tide. When I comprehended their true intent, I was given little choice but to ride ahead, to warn the mill owners, to warn the magistrate, to alert a company of army corpsmen at the nearby garrison. I feared for the safety of the village."

"Ian, oh dear," said Lady Tribble.

"Indeed," Lachlan said. "The soldiers I alerted were bored after coming home from an actual war, not to mention partial to law and order. They leapt at the chance to fight. They stormed the road, meeting the craftsmen on the outskirts of the village." Ian took off his hat, ran a hand through his hair, put it back on. He sighed. His face was tight with regret. "A terrible melee ensued," he finished.

"Oh, Ian," sighed Timothea. "But I had no idea."

"How could you?" asked Imogene, "you were on your knees at T.O.E."

Lady Tribble ignored her. "But were you drawn into the fighting?"

"I was horrified by the lot of it. My own tenants—seeing me now as an imposter and, ultimately, as a rat—fought me and launched themselves at this company of trained soldiers. The soldiers underestimated the grit and will of local men, fighting for their way of life.

"Honestly, it happened so fast and was so out of control, I could do little more than dive in and out of the chaos, dragging away injured men from both sides. Before the night was over, one man lost his life. Many were injured. Property was burned. The riot only served to intensify the ill-will between the craftsmen and the mill workers, and it burns bitterly to this day.

"And do you know what? One man, alone, embodies all the blame for that night. And that man . . . is me. I'm seen as both the inciting force behind the riot and the traitor who beat back my own tenants. I am a rabble sympathizer and in bed with the devil mills. I am the cause and the effect.

"My own tenants distrust me, even now; and most informed people in London believe I demonstrated terrible leadership and poor discretion. Other riots have followed throughout the country, days from Dorset, and my name is referenced in every report of fresh unrest.

"Who can say? Perhaps they are not wrong to call me out. But where does that leave us—how am I to go on?"

"You could move to Denmark," suggested Ivy thoughtfully.

"I could do, except that I have an obligation to Avenelle and also a love for it, despite my mishandling of the riot. I could also hide myself away, *disengage*—which is something I've tried, actually. It's the reason I did not come for you at T.O.E. Hiding is ultimately a weak plan, and it does very little good for anybody. I regret not coming for you so very deeply.

"However—and this is the point of my story—whatever you've survived in the past need not define the rest of your life.

"What does this mean?" he continued, warming to his topic, "it means that regardless of the years spent at T.O.E., Timmie; regardless how out of your depth you girls may feel because *Reverend Slogg* robbed you of formative lessons or the outside world, however significant—*regardless*. If *I* can move on from the riots—which, admittedly, is a work in progress—then you can accept whatever's happened in your past, face it, consider how you might improve in the future, and put it behind you. Move ahead, carry on. Find fulfilment and joy in your new life.

"Will you sometimes feel lost and untrained, Imogene? Yes, you will, but it is survivable, I assure you. I've survived. Avenelle is prosperous for the first time in half a century. I toil daily, even now, for some solution for the craftsman, whether they want my help or not. I've somehow managed the homecoming of you lot. We're here in London, aren't we? I've married Miss Trelayne here." He gestured to Drew, and she could do little more than blink at him, so very captivated by this speech. She did love him so very much.

"But you were forced to marry Miss Trelayne," remarked Imogene.

*Oh, Imogene*, thought Drew. *We can always count on you, can't we?*

"I *was* forced to marry her, Imogene, and who's fault was that?" said Lachlan.

Drew frowned, not caring for this answer.

"But we all rather *like* Miss Trelayne, don't we? Or Drewsmina, as I believe she should be called," he said. "A crucial part of moving on is making improvements to yourself so you may rise up, better than before. Also, allowing yourself to seek help. From others. Miss Trelayne is here to help all of us rise up."

"If I might cut in," said Drew, "I should like to add something from my own life—an experience where I was, in a way, broken and beaten and yet here I am. I lived to tell the tale."

"Oh yes, your horrid mother," enthused Ivy, ready for another story.

"Well, yes, she plays a role in it. But remember after the dressmaker's shop, when I told you I'd had a friendship with a man of whom I was very fond, but he was too poor and inconsequential for my mother to accept, and she had him sent away?"

"Oh yes, the man who would not kiss you," said Imogene.

"Yes." Drew cleared her throat. "I should like to point out that he had many other fine qualities."

"Uncle subscribes to a different brand of courtship," put in Imogene.

"Imogene, *enough*," said Lachlan.

"What I was going to say," Drew said, feeling her cheeks redden, "is that after this man was relocated to the other side of the world, I was so heartbroken, so despairing, that I entered a very dark sort of . . . mindset. For many weeks I felt an inescapable hopelessness. And it was only in this . . . midnight of my life, that my stepsister, Cynde—the very princess we came here to see—sent me a note and then sought me out. From the moment she learned of my heartbreak, she showed me great understanding and kindness, and she was an attentive friend to me until I could feel lightness again. We have been so very close ever since. And our friendship—which is among the greatest gifts of my life—would not have happened if I'd not been so very wretched from heartbreak."

"But why not, if she was your sister, after all?" asked Imogene.

"Well, because I'd been terrible to her, hadn't I? I didn't even *like* her. My mother had taught me that lovely people deserved nothing but resentment and suspicion. Honestly, before my heartbreak, there was little room for any friend in my life; I was too wrapped up in my own . . . my own self.

"Being broken, in contrast, has made me able to see others—to see myself, first and foremost, and sort out all the bits I didn't like. That heartbreak also made me able to see girls like the two of you. And I'm ever so grateful. Can you see? You may be uncomfortable and uncertain now, but eventually you'll be grateful for the times you were not on the tip-top of the world."

"I shall never be grateful for T.O.E.," said Imogene.

"No and well you shouldn't," said Lachlan. "Let us call a

spade a spade. However, I believe what Drewsmina means is that your challenging slog to normalcy will have unexpected rewards and . . . it will *fortify* you in a way. Other debutantes may seem graceful and gilded, but you are strong. And how much better strength will serve you than guild . . . or even grace."

Drew was nodding, looking at each of them, hoping they understood. They stared back, a little less enrapt by her story than the torches and riots of their uncle's.

"But do you see?" Drew asked hopefully.

"Perhaps if you'd allowed your 'friend' to kiss you," volunteered Imogene, "he might have fought harder to remain."

"Thank you, Imogene. I think, perhaps, you *have* missed my point," mused Drew.

And now everyone laughed, as she'd hoped they would.

"What I mean to say is this," she finished, "our *failure* is what allows us to grow up and improve. If everything in life floats along swimmingly, we rarely bother to make alterations, to invite new people into our lives, to make adaptations and overcome."

"But why did Princess Cynde help you?" asked Ivy. "If you had been so very dreadful to her?"

Drew shrugged. "Cynde is one of those people in whom compassion and kindness simply . . . *dwell*. She is as good and true as my mother is spiteful and disloyal. If you're very lucky, you'll have the occasion to encounter someone like that in your life. You may be that person, and you do not even know it."

"I am not that person," declared Imogene.

"Keen observation," said Lachlan.

"I can say that Cynde has had her own terrible heartbreak, and perhaps that is what made her so very kind. We should ask her. Not today of course, but the next time she is in Pollen Street."

"But have we missed our audience today?" asked Imogene.

"Well," said Drew, glancing at Lachlan and the baroness. "I cannot say. I feel certain they are receiving people well into the afternoon. But do we feel well enough to try it?"

"Oh yes, I do," said Imogene, rising from the floor. She fluffed her skirts and smoothed her hair.

"Ivy?" asked Drew.

"I don't care one way or the other, honestly," sighed Ivy. "If Genie would do it, so will I. Mama?"

"We cannot huddle in this storage room, telling fireside tales forever," said Lady Tribble. "There is an odor here. A fragrance. Hyacinth and . . . rabbit dander? Do any of you smell it?"

"*No*," Lachlan and the twins said in unison, and Drew swallowed a laugh.

"I am highly sensitive to rabbit dander," reminded Lady Tribble.

"Very well," said Drew. "Let us return to the antechamber and wait our turn. I shall try to signal a footman. He can slip a note to the princess . . . hurry the process along."

"Timothea?" said Lachlan, speaking over the sound of chair scooting and dress fluffing, "would you take the girls into the antechamber ahead of us? I should like a word alone with Miss Trelayne."

Drew paused in the act of repining the ribbon in Ivy's hair. He'd just reminded everyone to refer to her as "Drew," and now he'd invoked the name "Miss Trelayne." And it wasn't simply that he'd said it, it was *how* he said it. A little clipped. A little commanding. It elicited a fissure of desire, shot straight to her core.

She returned to the ribbon, wondering about the unexpected nature of the request. What could he possibly wish to say that couldn't wait?

"Fine, Ian," said Lady Tribble, making her way to the door. "If you can tolerate the smell. I cannot, I must keep apace of my headaches."

"I'll be right there, girls," called Drew. "Pay no mind to the other callers. Truly. The last time I called to the Throne

Room, your uncle broke a window with a fireplace poker to free someone's caged birds. In hindsight, it's best that this family keep to themselves in Kew Palace."

"There will be birds?" said Ivy, filing out of the room behind her mother and sister.

Drew chuckled, turning to face Lachlan.

"What is i—?"

*Click.* He closed the door behind them and turned the lock. He pivoted to face her, blue eyes bright and hot.

"I want you," he said, stalking to her. "So bloody much. Right now. This instant."

## Chapter Twenty-Seven

*Drewsmina Trelayne's Rule of Style and Comportment #40:
As you consider male suitors and potential husbands, seek
out mild-mannered gentlemen of a thoughtful, measured
disposition. Avoid dynamic, rousing men who may
incite breathlessness or frighten birds.*

There was no time for Drew to mull over his declaration, no mis-hearing, no stalling, *I beg your pardon?*

She'd known that purposeful look in his eye; and of course he'd stated his intentions as plainly as he'd locked the door. Now he was stripping off his gloves and tossing his hat.

Drew's heart leapt into a sprint and she bit her lip to keep from grinning. When he was nearly to her, she yelped a little and darted to the left.

"Oh, make me catch you, will you?" he said, stalking her around a table. "You think I won't give chase? Is that what you think?"

"Lachlan, we cannot," she breathed, half laugh, half gasp. Why was she running? She couldn't say, she *wanted* to be caught.

"Tell me you don't want this, and I'll stop," he suggested wryly.

"Perhaps it makes no difference what either of us wants. We're are guests of the king. Of *England*. In his palace. It's . . . rude and common and indecent, surely. The girls' confidence is tenuous at best—"

"The girls are *fine*," he said. He was nearly to her and she moved right, wading into a cluster of chairs. "They're with their mother. As they should be. She'll never step in as a proper parent if you do all the work for her."

"Lachlan?" she asked, backing deeper into the chairs.

"Hmmm?"

He came to the first chair and shoved it aside. The next two, he scooted out of the way with his leg. He was cutting a determined line to her, and she was distracted from her question. She laughed, spun on her heel, and scrambled deeper into the room.

"Lachlan, this is madness," she sang. "What's gotten into you?"

"*You*, Miss Trelayne, *you've* gotten into me. You're . . . perfect. With the girls. With my sister. I've never seen anything like it. You said and did everything exactly, perfectly right. I shudder to think what our lives would be like if you'd not come to us." He lunged for her but she darted into a sliver of space between two tables, too thin for him to fit.

"Oh yes," she sighed, "my proficiency with the twins." She was trapped on one side by the wall and on the other by *him*, hovering at the edge of the tables. She hitched up her skirts and put a knee up, climbing on top. Reaching out, she scrambled across the table on her hands and knees.

*What is happening?* she thought, elated by his attention, burning for his touch. *I'm climbing over furniture in Kew Palace like a squirrel.*

*But this is why we never speak*, she told herself, eyeing the edge of the table. *We are always either making love or minding his family.*

*Was this the rapport of a proper marriage? Was this all—*

"Now, now Miss Trelayne," said Lachlan, meeting her at the edge of the table. She tried to reverse, but he fastened his hands around her waist and snatched her up. "Did you really think you could escape?"

"Lachlan," she gasped, "we cannot. Surely."

"I hate it when you call me Lachlan," he growled, hauling her across the room.

"It's your name." She began biting off her gloves.

"*No*, it's my title. My *given name* is Ian. As I've told you."

"We're not . . . we're not well enough acquainted for me to call you Ian."

"Not well acquainted?" he mused. He set her back to the wall and fell against her. "Pray, madam, let me introduce myself."

He kissed her then, hard and deep, no preamble; the heated kiss of wild lovemaking, not the gentle urgings of a seduction.

He slid his hands over her bodice, up her neck to cradle the sides of her face. The feathers of her hat tickled the top of his head, and he flicked at it.

"No, no, no," she gasped between kisses, "you mustn't disturb my hat. I could not be more serious, Lachlan. Do what you will to me, just do it quickly and do not touch my hat or my hair or irrevocably damage my dress. Is this possible?"

"Yes," he panted, crowding her back. She flattened against the wall in a rustle of silk and he pressed against her, using the leverage to kiss her properly, nearly kissing the breath from her. Drew stopped herself just short of moaning in pleasured delight.

"Legs up," he rasped, reaching down to grab handfuls of her skirt and dragging it up. His hands palmed her bottom next, the hem of her dress bunched between his arms and her waist.

"You're joking," she said, staring at him. A feather from her hat molted downward, hanging between their faces. She blew it out of the way.

"No joke," he grunted, "up you go." He ground his hardness into her and she whimpered.

"You're not strong enough."

"Never," he growled, kissing her, "say that to me again. It's an insult to my strength." Another kiss. "And is patently untrue."

With a grunt he lifted her off the ground. "Legs," he rasped, and Drew wrapped her legs around his haunches. He leaned in, sealing her against the wall, and the weight of his body pressed his erection against her core. Drew cried out at the immediate jolt of pleasure.

"*Shhh*," he urged, laughing. "We are in an occupied palace, Miss Trelayne. You mustn't cry out."

"This was your idea," she said into his neck, anchoring her arms around his shoulders. Now her hat splayed a pouf of feathers directly in his face. He made a spitting noise.

"*Mind* the hat, please," she said, half plea, half moan.

"Hold still," he rasped, releasing her with one hand to unbutton the fall of his trousers and tug aside her drawers.

His jaw, gritted now with exertion, was just beside her mouth, and she stuck out her tongue and licked it. He growled and she moved closer, kissing her way up the side of his face. She felt bold, and she liked it. He was in charge and she liked it; but she was learning that two could play this game, and she liked that too.

"*Your Grace*," she whispered into his ear, lifting her legs higher. He growled again.

"*Lachlan*," she tried, whispering again.

"What did I say about—"

"*Ian*," she said finally and licked the whirl of his ear.

He let out a guttural moan and drove into her in one thrust. She cried out, and he turned his head, seeking her mouth. She met him, and their lips crashed hungrily together.

"That man," he ground out, driving into her, "your *friend*. He was a fool not to kiss you. He was a fool to allow someone to send him away from you."

*Man?* she wondered idly, her thoughts floating in and out on waves of pleasure. *What man?* Oh yes, her little speech. The heartbreak.

But was he *jealous*? Surely not. She could barely remember the other man's name. She knew only Ian. She loved only Ian. And in that moment, she almost said it; almost opened her mouth to free the words caged inside.

"I would never be sent away," he rasped, still thrusting. "I could never . . . I will never . . . resist you."

"He was very focused on bird-watching," she said, "when we were together."

"Bollocks," he grunted. "Never speak of him."

She chuckled. "You raised it."

"It agitates me, every time you mention him."

"He is nothing to me, Your Grace." She kissed him.

"I didn't mean to accuse."

"I don't feel accused. I feel . . . I feel . . ." She felt a little better, honestly, knowing he felt possessive, knowing he would not be so easily led by the machinations of her mother. That she was secure with him. It was . . . something.

"You feel so good," he finished for her, driving into her, using the wall as leverage. And then they stopped talking. Their communication was one long unbroken kiss and his repeated thrusts. Within moments, she fell apart against the wall.

How soon it was over, quicker than ever before; their hot passion and the high risk intensifying the flammability of their coupling.

She caught fire, and then he caught fire, and they both tried very hard to keep quiet, even while their cries went up, and his knees thudded against the wall, and she went limp in his arms, scraping the plaster with the heels of her slippers.

Her hat drooped drunkenly to one side, a flowerpot blown over in a gale.

She raised up from his shoulders and leaned her head against the wall, breathing hard.

"Are you alright?" he asked, squeezing her bottom again.

She nodded. He always asked that. It was considerate. He was the odd mixture of wildly passionate and carefully considerate. The one thing he hadn't yet been was . . . adoring.

But was it fair to say that he was not adoring, when he'd just made love to her so thoroughly, so thrillingly? Drew didn't know. She barely knew her own name in this moment, but the doubts had already begun; the anxiety about coupling with him but not . . . *mattering to him*.

Next he would hurry them along.

"We should make haste," he said and she almost laughed. He lowered her gently to the ground.

"Of course," she said.

"What's the matter?" he asked.

Her tone had given her away. She couldn't keep the disappointment from her voice.

"Nothing," she said. "Well, actually. I've something to ask you." Now was the time to ask him about tonight. There would be no better time. Even with his family waiting, even with a royal prince and princess likely waiting, there would never be a better time.

"Ask," he said, and she thought of how easy this might be, after all.

"We've never spent a full night together. Since we married."

"I know," he sighed. "Bollocks honeymoon. I'm sorry. I thought after the twins' debut—"

"I am less concerned about a honeymoon, but I should like to spend an entire night in your company. I should like to . . . talk to you. I should like to . . . encounter you without the interruption of the twins or the distraction of lovemaking."

"You want me to spend the night *with* you but not *on top of* you?"

She giggled. "No, you may—" She took a deep breath. "Of course we may be intimate, I was just hoping that you would not go. Afterward."

"Brilliant. I love it. I never intended to leave you these many nights. It's only that I've been . . ." he let out a frustrated breath, ". . . called away."

She nodded. "But what about . . . tonight?"

"Absolutely. Tonight."

"Really?"

"Of course."

"Well—lovely," she said, laughing a little. "Because I may have already made arrangements."

"Arrangements," he mused.

"Yes. For supper, shared in your chamber. To have a hot bath drawn, to—"

"Have you now?" he teased. "And here I thought—"

A loud knock sounded on the door.

Drew gasped, her gaze flying to the closed door. He'd locked it, hadn't he? She looked to him and he rolled his eyes.

Drew darted away, adjusting her drawers, smoothing her skirts. Ian stalked to the door and put a shoulder against it. "A moment, if you please."

"Your Grace?" called the irritated voice of a stranger. "Their Royal Highnesses would see you now. Your nieces and the baroness have been admitted to the Throne Room. The prince and princess are *waiting for you*."

"Very good," said Ian, shrugging deeper into his coat. "We'll be just a moment."

Drew sprinted through the room, extinguishing candles and collecting gloves. She scooped up Ian's hat and met him at the door.

"Look," he whispered, pointing to the knob. "Sneaky bastard is endeavoring to *admit himself* to this locked room."

"We *are* guests in this . . ." she looked around, ". . . storage room. Guests are generally not given liberty to engage in . . . in . . . locked-door trysts. But Ian?"

"I love it when you call me that."

"Yes. Ian, about tonight? Tonight we'll take dinner? Just you and me? In your room? Tonight I can ask questions about our marriage without you feeling . . . surprised?"

"Surprised?" he repeated, watching the doorknob begin to turn. "Oh yes—that. How delicate I must sound with my aversion to surprises. Of course, Drew, we will discuss whatever you like."

"You promise?" she asked.

"Yes, yes, whatever you like." He gestured Drew to the side.

"Crafty bugger," Ian whispered, scowling at the unseen servant on the other side of the door. And then he flipped the lock and yanked the door open in the same movement.

On the other side, a royal page was flung into the room, his hand still on the knob.

"Thank you for your patience," Ian drawled, holding out his arm for Drewsmina, guiding her out the door.

They didn't wait for the man's reply. They walked swiftly, not looking back.

"Allow me, Your Grace," called the page, scrambling after them into the antechamber, "to admit you."

"Don't trouble yourself," Ian called, pulling open the door to the thrones and escorting Drew inside.

Drew closed her eyes to the rudeness of it—this, after all her efforts to refine the twins. Now she bore down on the prince and princess with her hair unraveling, a palace page in hasty pursuit. She couldn't even say if she'd adequately adjusted her dress or squared her hat.

"His Grace, Ian Clayblack, the Duke of Lachlan," called the page, part announcement, part chase, "and Lady Drewsmina, the Duchess of Lachlan."

Ian tossed up a hand, the dismissive gesture of *thank you, but we can manage from here*, and strode to the dais. The prince, Drew saw, was seated on his throne but Cynde was up, mimicking the motion of a tennis serve as Imogene pantomimed the stroke. Or that is what they'd been doing before they'd all frozen, turned to the door, and watched Ian and Drew promenade down the long carpet. Drew was given no choice but to affect a poised expression, hold her head high, and will her cheeks to be less pink.

When they reached the foot of the dais, Ian clipped his heels together gallantly and bowed his head sharply. "Your Royal Highnesses," he said.

Drew flashed Cynde a look of apology and then dipped into a repentant curtsy. When she bowed her head, her hat listed sideways and slid almost to her ear. Imogene stepped up to slide it back in place.

"How kind of you to join us, Lachlan," commented the prince.

"Pleasure, Highness. Forgive our lateness. I had an urgent matter to attend to with my wife."

Drew closed her eyes.

"Will you show me again, Imogene?" asked Cynde, and the twins stepped away to demonstrate more tennis.

"So you say," the prince was muttering, considering Ian through narrowed eyes. "How lucky for us, we've been entertained in your absence by your dear sister and charming nieces. They will delight my mother at their presentation, that much is clear. I'm so very pleased to see it."

"Thank you, Highness," Ian said. "We are very proud. They are good girls. They honor me with their resilience."

"Quite," said the prince. "If only their uncle will muster the proper respect at their presentation next spring. Tardiness will not be tolerated at St. James's Palace, Lachlan."

"Nor should it, Highness," agreed Ian. "Pray do not worry. Perhaps I've taken advantage today, as we are old friends, you and I."

"Perhaps you have, and if my wife were not so delighted by your marriage to her sister, I should take you to task."

"I am nothing if not in favor of delighting wives," said Ian.

And now Timothea made a noise of disgust. "My God, Ian, *enough*."

"Apologies," Ian said again, but his mouth was quirking up, and the prince was struggling to contain a laugh.

"Minnow?" the prince called to Cynde. "Will you not greet your sister so we may evict her pestilence of a husband and liberate the girls to their own diversions? Lachlan is disrespectful and it sets a bad example."

Ian opened his mouth to say something, likely the rudest comment of them all, but thankfully Cynde was trotting back to her husband and climbing onto her throne.

"The girls are *jewels*, Your Grace," she said, and it took a moment for Drew to realize she was addressing her.

"Baroness," Cynde continued to Timothea, "you should be so very proud. It is a delight to see all of you. I'm so glad our families have joined."

"We are not *joined* to Lachlan's family," groused the prince. "Perish the thought." To Ian, the prince said, "You owe me a drink, Lachlan."

"A debt I shall happily honor," said Ian. "Forgive me, I've been preoccupied."

"I can see that. Have your man set something up with my scheduler. You are more interesting to me, now that you're married."

"Birds of a feather," said Ian.

"Oh, and the girls tell me you've taken the duke bird-watching!" said Cynde, clapping her small hands together. "How lovely, Drewsmina, that he may share your passion."

Drew was so startled by the phrasing of this, words failed her.

"Indeed, Highness," said Ian, bowing to her again. "I am an enthusiastic pupil of the birds. Royal visits, likewise, are rapidly gaining favor in my eyes."

"We wouldn't keep you, Highness," Drew finally managed, curtsying again.

She glanced at the girls and they dropped, immediately, into passable curtsies.

"This visit has taken up too much of your day already,"

Drew continued. "Thank you for receiving the girls and overlooking our tardiness."

"It's our pleasure, Drewsmina," cooed Cynde. "How happy I am for all of you. I'll call on you in Pollen Street very soon. Oh, but this cannot wait, I adore the new way you've done your hair."

"Thank you, Highness," Drew said and curtsied again. She gestured to the girls, setting off a second dip of curtsies.

And then, as Lady Tribble slowly shook her head, the five of them backed from the room.

# Chapter Twenty-Eight

*A*n hour after they'd returned from the palace, Ian received a note from Rucker Loring.

*Your Grace,*

*Come quickly. The usual place. As soon as you are able.*

*Unexpected but potentially disastrous development in Blackwall: Ten Avenelle tenants are en route to London with a caravan of wagons. They've brought a season's worth of lace. Spools and spools, all of their work since summer.*

*My cousin learned of their plan and rode ahead to alert us. They are to rendezvous with the smugglers in Blackwall. Not Dorset—Dorset is finished for smuggling, apparently, too many patrols at the moment. They are coming here. They were told to come within three days' time or not at all. The tenants panicked and set out.*

*They are to deliver the lace, packed in hollowed-out loaves of bread. Tonight. They're due to meet the smugglers by dawn.*

*If you intend to stop the transfer, Your Grace, come now.*

*R.L.*

Ian left his library at a run, searching for Drewsmina. He ran through the drawing room, the garden, the ballroom—nothing. His wife was nowhere to be found. Instead, he encountered Imogene at the foot of the stairs.

"What's happened?" asked his niece.

"Imogene, no," Ian said, his mind racing.

"What do you mean, 'no'?" asked Imogene. "I've not asked a yes-or-no question. I asked, What's happened?"

"I mean, 'no,' nothing has happened and 'no,' it doesn't involve you. Also, 'no' I don't have time to explain." He turned for the stairs, clipping up.

"You're going out again," she guessed, darting up the stairs on his heels. "Blackwall."

Another *no* was on the tip of his tongue, but he knew from experience he didn't have time to misrepresent the truth, not to her. He'd learned his lesson.

"Fine," he said, pausing on the landing. "I've just had a note from my estate manager. The smugglers have lured my tenants to London. Apparently, they're on their way here at this very moment, hauling carts full of lace. The exchange is meant to happen in Blackwall tonight, not in Dorset next month. If possible, I'd like to *foil* the deal before the tenants arrive. *That* is what's happened."

"Why not simply go to the tenants?" she asked. "How many roads lead in and out of Dorset? Likely, you could intercept them."

"I don't want to intercept them," he said. "Their disdain for me burns bright enough already. I want to erase their opportunity to become fledgling criminals."

"But how?"

"Imogene, I haven't the time to explain."

"Will you simply ask the smugglers to . . . go away?" she asked, undeterred.

Ian stopped. He took a deep breath. He turned back. "These are criminals, Imogene. If they're any good at it, they'll be easily spooked. They'll want less complication, not more. They'll want no hassle with an angry duke."

"You're going to pay them," she guessed.

He almost laughed at her astuteness. Her astuteness and her utter lack of confidence in his ability to intimidate smugglers.

"You are aware that I was a captain in the army?" he said. "I fought the French in a small conflict known as the Napoleonic Wars?"

Imogene crossed her arms over her chest, waiting. Now Ian did laugh.

"Fine," he said. "Here is the plan. I *do* intend to simply ask them: leave my people be. I've no interest in turning them over to the authorities, and I'm not seeking retribution. Certainly I've no desire to fight them. I'll tell them as much. I don't want anything to do with them except to compel them to *stand down*. And yes—I'll pay them if I must."

Actually, the verbalization of this very loose plan—and the mention of the army—gave Ian an idea. A potentially brilliant, almost feasible idea. First, he'd need to send out a note by private messenger. And he could not tarry, not a moment longer. There was no more time to quarrel with Imogene.

"I must *go*, Imogene," he said, turning to stride down the landing.

She called after him, "But I shall—?"

"No, no, *no*," he said spinning back. "This is not open for debate. I implore you. This, I will do entirely alone. It's as dangerous as it is delicate. The smugglers could turn tail and run or they could garrot me. The tenants could do the same. I cannot manage all of that *and* worry over your safety. And time is of the essence. I must clear out the smugglers before the tenants make London. I've no idea where they are, only that they're nearly here. *There is no time*."

Imogene narrowed her eyes, considering this. For a long moment, Ian wondered what he would do if she refused to cooperate. He didn't have time to explain it all to Drewsmina or, God help him, Timothea. Not that either of those women possessed the authority to contain the girl. She must be made to cooperate.

"Fine," Imogene finally said. "I shall keep back and look after Mama and the others."

"Perfect," said Ian, wondering why he'd not invoked her protective bent in the beginning. "*Thank you*. I should be home by dawn, and by then, hopefully this terrible mess with the smugglers will be—if not over, then far less urgent."

Imogene said nothing and Ian backed away, pinned her with what he hoped was a threatening look, and then spun again, striding to his bedchamber.

Next he bellowed for Pruitt, his valet. If ever he needed to look like a bloody duke, it was now. Also, he'd want his oilcloth tonight. The sky was low and heavy. The return carriage ride from Kew Palace had been illuminated by intermittent lightning that cracked open a darkening sky. Fair weather would, naturally, be too much to ask.

"Pruitt!" he bellowed again but didn't wait for a reply.

*Fine*, he thought, *no Pruitt. What about my wife?*

He stuck his head through the door that adjoined their rooms and called her name. Nothing. Had she gone out? Surely not so late in the evening.

He looked around his own chamber. Why the devil was it so hot? He looked at the grate. A fire blazed as if the sky were pounding snow, not rain.

Beside the fire, someone had moved his bathtub to the center of the room. And there were flowers . . . he spun in a circle . . . everywhere.

Ian frowned, wondering why Pruitt was not available to produce his riding boots, but had clearly been rearranging furniture.

It couldn't be helped, and he had no time to sort it out. He hated not to see Drewsmina before he went, but he was given little choice. He'd be forced to leave her a note.

He went to his writing desk and took up a pen and parchment. Scrawling quickly, he wrote:

*Drew,*

*I've left the house in a blind sprint and not managed to find you to explain. Forgive me? I've been forced to go out again, but pray do not worry, I should return by morning. Despite the urgency of the summons, there's no cause for alarm. It's more bother with Avenelle and tenants. I hope to reconcile the late-night nature of this business tonight.*

*Yours,*
*Ian*

He frowned at the hastily scrawled letter, and then looked up. It suddenly occurred to him that the chamber blazed with dozens of candles—scores more than he would normally use—and the brightness served only to illuminate the piss-poor vagueness of this note.

He would make it up to her, he thought. He would explain everything, whether she was ready for the burden of Avenelle or not. When he returned, he'd never bolt away in the middle of the night again.

He sealed the letter and scrawled her name.

*"Pruitt!?"* Ian called again, whipped off his coat—the room was an oven—and took up a second sheet of parchment. This letter was addressed to his old friend Jason Beckett, the Duke of Northumberland.

*North,*

*I need a favor and it is not, unfortunately, small. First, it involves riding immediately to Blackwall in the rain. Apologies to your wife for the intrusion and to your valet for the rain.*

Second, it will mean standing down a lot of smugglers. I know your Foreign Office days are behind you, but surely you can dredge up some manner of authority and menace in the name of protecting Avenelle's finest from a life of crime. I'll explain when I meet you, but trust that I would not ask this if it was not essential.

I'm setting out from Pollen Street at eight o'clock, bound for Poplar High Street. There is an abandoned mews at the corner where the High Street connects with Naval Way. Meet me there.

I anticipate no riots and no need for the local garrison, but God knows I've been wrong before. I'd not mention it except we all know that the promise of unrest is an incentive in your view.

In all seriousness, I'll owe you, Northumberland, if you'll help me sort this.

Yours,
Lachlan

His friend, he was certain, would come. North had been forced to give up his Foreign Office work when he inherited his own dukedom, and North missed the action and diplomacy of spy craft. Ian hoped their encounter would be almost entirely diplomacy with very little action, but there were no guarantees.

If Ian questioned whether it was appropriate to use the *same* salutation for both his friend and his wife—"Yours"—he didn't ponder it for long. *He had no time.* He sealed and labeled the second letter, changed clothes in haste, and wrestled into riding boots without the assistance of his errant valet.

Pruitt appeared only as Ian was bolting out the door. The valet was trudging to his bedchamber, his face shiny, his hair damp, holding a steaming bucket of hot water. Behind him, a line of housemaids held their own steaming buckets.

"My God, Pruitt, what are you about?" Ian said, barely stopping. "I've been searching for a quarter hour. Put that down. I need you to locate my wife. Give her this note. After that, find Greenly and have him send a boy to the London residence of the Duke of Northumberland with *this* note."

"But, Your Grace—" tried the steam-dampened valet, carefully setting down the sloshing bucket.

"Not now, Pruitt, please. I haven't time to debate it."

And then, without a backward glance, he strode down the landing and was gone.

FIVE HOURS LATER, Ian trudged back to Pollen Street, exhausted, jittery, soaked to the bone. He entered through the stable door, stomping mud from his boots.

The house was warm, and the heat made the cold feel more pronounced. He was racked, intermittently, with shivers, but this was not the cold. This was the stress of the night leaving his body. Good riddance. Lord, what a night.

He'd made it to Blackwall in advance of his tenants. Loring had been waiting, and he'd reported the smugglers were lurking about their boat, clearly anticipating some arrival. So far, there'd been no sign of the caravan from Dorset.

Northumberland had arrived next, God bless him, pretending to be inconvenienced. It was a shallow act. Ian could tell he'd been delighted to receive a summons to tangle with smugglers in the middle of the night.

Ian had explained the circumstances and they'd agreed on their tactic. Broach the smugglers sedately, with due coolness. Threaten with chilling authority. Finally, extract a vow of cooperation. Northumberland no longer had jurisdiction to arrest them, but he could invoke the names of customs officials who could; he could also threaten to board their small craft to examine what other contraband they might harbor.

In short, North had been the villain of the operation and Ian was to play their savior. He would interject that he wanted no trouble, that he had no desire to search their boat; he wanted only the smugglers' vow that they would keep away from his tenants, have no future designs on their lace, and if possible, be gone by the time the caravan arrived from Dorset.

If this was a vow they could give him, he and Northumberland had planned to walk away. If no such vow could be made by the smugglers, or if they didn't trust their compliance, then North would summon former colleagues and actual arrests would commence.

In the end, Ian had barely introduced himself and Northumberland before the smugglers were unmooring lines and loosening sails.

They'd easily, *happily* vowed to disappear—from Blackwall this night, but also from the lives of Avenelle lace makers forever.

If Their Graces would be so kind as to forget they'd ever encountered them, the smugglers had claimed other pressing business in Margate, and off they shoved. Good evening to you. You've seen nothing of interest here. Many happy returns of the day.

"In a storm?" North had asked the captain, annoying Ian—let them go for God's sake—but North had been so very amused by their scurried departure.

The smugglers had assured them that the clandestine nature of their work lent itself to sailing in all manner of weather; and they knew when to set out and when to remain.

Tonight, they'd preferred to set out. Urgently.

And that . . . had been that.

They'd gone, cutting a smooth line through the black water of the Thames, their boat almost immediately swallowed by the mist.

And good riddance.

Ian had breathed a sigh of relief and turned to his friend. "Thank you," he'd said. "I'm almost glad the lace makers embarked on this journey and forced my hand. I might have stewed for weeks over what to do, if my people hadn't been bearing down on London. Now it's finished. At least this bit."

"Well, you know me," North had said, "I barely take aim before I pull the trigger. Drives my wife mad. I'm happy to help. Now . . ." he'd looked around, ". . . where shall we meet these lace makers of yours?"

"Oh no," Ian had said. "That, I must do entirely alone. I'm their landlord, and it's delicate work—regaining their trust. I must do it entirely alone. Can you understand?"

"Aye," North had said, clapping him on the back. "I'd be of little help—I'm a terrible landlord, as you know. My sister, on the other hand, would be brilliant. Unfortunately she keeps strict daytime hours. She is very sensible in that way."

They'd parted ways and Ian had reconvened with Loring to wait for the caravan from Dorset. They could have ridden out, hoping to intercept them on the outskirts of town, but Ian felt it was more strategic to meet them on the docks.

An hour later, they'd come. To man and ox, they'd been tired, wet, unnerved by the size of London and complexity of the streets. Ian had endeavored to appear assured and patient, a landlord well ahead of the situation. The beleaguered tenants had assembled around him; their eyes wide with both shock and relief.

It had been Ian's goal to demonstrate quiet, graceful leadership, to shepherd them rather than condemn. For once, his long, careful study of the situation had allowed him to realize this. He knew them by name, of course, and he'd greeted each man personally. He'd ascertained their safety and well-being and examined their livestock after the long, hurried journey. He'd had Loring provide them with something to eat and drink.

Finally, he'd addressed them, standing as a group in the abandoned mews, his voice loud over the sound of the rain just outside the door. He'd hoped to strike a balance between warning about the dangers of smuggling while not condemning them for their subterfuge. He'd told them of his plan to eradicate the export levy for small craftsman but made no promises.

Finally, he'd announced that two-nights lodging in London had been arranged for their comfort and recovery. Hostlers, he'd said, had been hired to help them convey the wagons back to Dorset.

And then he'd said he'd wanted to meet with them personally—each man, if they were willing—to discuss what they might do to move forward in the wake of the riots.

Something about the night—be it the fatigue and the cold rain, their anxiety about smuggling, or the surprise meeting of their full-of-promises landlord—had lent itself to Ian's favor.

The tenants had agreed. Honestly, they'd had no choice—the smugglers had vanished and they'd not thought about what they might do next. Ian embraced it. He and Loring saw them to safe lodging and Ian promised to meet with them again in the morning. In the end, just as the storm was mounting, Ian had left the lot of them with Loring and ridden for home.

*Home.* Where he now finally, *thankfully*, could allow himself to exhale, to reflect on a job . . . if not "well done," at least a job not totally ruined.

He heard footsteps in the corridor outside the boot room, and thought of Drewsmina. His stomach clenched and, no surprise, his body hardened at the prospect. He'd been forced by necessity to put her out of his mind, and now she was all he could think about. She would help him out of his wet clothes. She would strip him, perhaps, right here in the—

"Your Grace?" It was his valet, Pruitt. Ian grimaced. Pruitt, nowhere to be seen at the onset, now would be omnipresent.

The valet ignored his expression and descended on Ian's wet clothes like a falcon on a mouse. Ian had just collapsed on the bench to have the man pull his boots when Imogene strode down the corridor, Ivy behind her, half running to keep up.

"*Thank God,*" Imogene said, sounding so very grown-up, Ian paused in the act of removing his boot.

"You're back," said the girl. "Finally."

"Hello to you, too," he said, holding out his other boot to Pruitt. "Why aren't you in bed?"

"Because I'm mad with worry about your wife."

Ian dropped his leg. He turned on the bench to stare at the girl. "Worried, *why*?" His heart, exhausted, barely beating, suddenly, remarkably, kicked back into a frenzied hammer.

"*Because,*" intoned Imogene, "I can't find her anywhere in the house, and Ivy—" and now she glared at her sister "—believes she may have gone out."

"Gone *out*?" Ian repeated, grinding out the words.

He stood up. "Surely, you are mistaken. She wouldn't go out, not in rain like this. It's pitch-black and freezing. The wind almost unseated me."

"It wasn't storming when she went out. It was only a drizzle. She's been gone two hours."

"*Two hours?*" Ian spun to his nieces, sending Pruitt scrambling against the wall. "You're serious. You believe Drew has left the house?"

"If she's not with you, then—yes." Imogene had begun to back away.

"*No,* she's not with me. She's here, with you. Safe and dry like any sensible, sane woman would be."

Imogene said nothing. She threw up her hands in a gesture of *well, there you have it*. She whirled away.

Ian followed her into the corridor, his heart suddenly too fast for his chest.

Ian called over his shoulder to his valet. "Do you know of this, Pruitt? Has the duchess gone out?"

"I was not aware, Your Grace," the valet called.

Ivy was following cautiously behind them holding the cat to her face. "But what have you seen, Ivy?" Ian asked. "Did Drewsmina go out?"

"I'm sorry, Uncle," Ivy began cautiously. "She said . . .

She told me that she was going to find you. She was ever so upset. I couldn't stop her, and I went for Imogene, but by the time I'd found her, Aunt Miss Trelayne was riding away."

"No, Ivy," Ian said, stopping and turning back to the girl. "You cannot mean that Drew has really, actually left this house? In the storm? Tonight? *On horseback?*"

Ivy nodded her head into the cat's fur.

Ian spun back to his valet. "Pruitt, go to the duchess's maid. Rouse the entire house. I want every room searched. Send Greenly to me."

Not waiting for an answer, he turned and ran.

"Imogene would have gone after her sooner," Ivy reported, sprinting beside him, "but she said we would wait to see if she returned with you."

"With me?" asked Ian, his brain a torrent of whys and hows and where, where, *where* could she have gone. London had been soaked in a deluge of cold, icy rain for the last hour.

"But where did she say she was going?" Ian demanded. He reached the grand hallway and looked right and left, forcing himself to prioritize, to think.

"Imogene!" he bellowed, the girl had disappeared. Behind him, Pruitt appeared, fluttering with a towel.

Ian waved him off. "Dry boots, a dry coat, a fresh hat. Hurry, man!" he snapped.

He spun back to Ivy. "Tell me once again. You saw her leave with your own eyes. She's not fallen asleep behind a closed door? She did not, perhaps, go out, think better of it, and come back in? *You are certain?*"

Ivy shrank back, cowed by his demanding questions, hiding her face in the cat.

"She's gone, Uncle," said Imogene, reappearing at the top of the stairs. "I checked her bedchamber one last time. It's empty. I prayed you'd return with her, but—no."

"How can I return with her?" Ian asked, panicked. "I didn't know she was gone."

"Did you leave without telling her where you were going?" challenged Imogene.

"I left her a note," he said.

"I've seen that note," said Imogene, coming down the stairs, "and it's bollocks. It's no wonder she went. This is your fault, Uncle, even after I warned you. What did I say? About secrets?"

"It wasn't a secret," insisted Ian, barely able to comprehend the situation. "I didn't have time to explain. She could have asked you."

"I didn't see her. She left without a word to anyone, save *Ivy*." Imogene glared at her sister.

"She couldn't be stopped!" Ivy cried. The cat let out a squeal and leapt from her arms. "She was so determined. And she had your letters. She said she was going to find you."

"Letters? Which letter?"

Ivy rustled in a pocket and thrust out two pieces of parchment. Ian knew them on sight. One was his note to her, the other had been the original summons from Rucker Loring.

"She's gone to Blackwall," said Imogene, "in a hurricane. *Looking* for *you*."

Ian reread the note, reminding himself of Loring's original note. "Insanity," he mumbled. "She wouldn't."

"She *would*," countered Imogene.

"Your Grace?" called Pruitt from the top of the stairs. He held up two pairs of boots.

"No, no," yelled Ian, "Neither of those! I mean to ride, man, not go to the bloody opera. Do not worry, girls. I'll find her. I'll take all the grooms. I'll send a stable boy to Bow Street."

Imogene made a noise of disgust and stomped down the stairs.

"Where are you going, Imogene? Please do not think that you're leaving this house."

"I'm going to tell my mother," she countered, not looking back.

Ian lacked the presence of mind to process this. He turned and sprinted up the stairs taking them two at a time. The cat streaked before him with a yowl, and Ivy struggled to keep pace behind him.

His mind was a riot of emotions—disbelief, strategy, terror—but he forced himself to keep calm, to prioritize. There would half a dozen ways to reach Blackwall, which would she take? As the storm intensified, where might she have reined in, seeking shelter? The possibilities were endless, and potential for danger stalked each one.

Reaching the door to his room, he flung it open, calling again for Pruitt.

"I'll need—"

Ian stopped so fast, Ivy collided with his legs.

"Oh, Uncle," she said, peeking around him. "How pretty. It's like a fairy room."

His bedchamber, he realized, blinking at the soft glow, had been transformed. The fire, now low embers. The bath, filled with water long gone cold. All the candles, guttering now from hours aflame. A small dinner table, laid for two, had been situated in front of the fire, candle wax from a tall candelabra dripped into glasses of wine.

Pruitt appeared from around the corner, two more pairs of boots in his hands.

"What the devil is this?" Ian asked.

"The design of the duchess, Your Grace," answered Pruitt, looking around. "She'd been working on it since your return from Kew Palace. Left a long list of supplies this morning and began arranging it when you returned from the royal visit."

"But . . . but," he turned around. *"Why?"*

"I would not deign to gues—"

A clap of thunder shook the house, and Ian leapt into action, replacing wet stockings and pulling on fresh boots.

Drew's maid appeared in the doorway, flushed and tearful. "I cannot find her anywhere, Your Grace," she said. "I . . . I didn't know she'd gone out. She didn't ring for me. She'd asked to be left alone. In here. She'd been so diligent about laying the supper."

"Does anyone know if she was dressed for rain?" Ian asked. He couldn't think about the room. "What shoes has she worn, Chappy?"

"The pink cloak is gone, Your Grace; but her boots remain," cried Chappy, near hysterical now. "She's gone out in satin slippers."

Ian cursed, shrugging into a dry overcoat, jamming a fresh hat on his head.

"Was she angry, Ivy?" Ian asked his niece, trying to work through her motives. "Did she seem angry?"

"She seemed . . . determined," Ivy said.

"Determined to leave?" he clarified. From nowhere, an image of his mother flashed in his head.

Before Ivy could answer, Imogene strode into the room, Timothea trailing behind her.

"*Oh look*," enthused Timothea, peering into the candle-bright room. "How beautiful."

In that moment, Ian very nearly imploded. He wanted to hurl himself out the window. He wanted to hurl Pruitt who, God help the man, was coming at him with a neck cloth. He wanted to tie Imogene and Ivy to a chair, and pick up Timothea, flip her, and shake her upside down until all the nonsense left her body. Mostly he wanted his bloody wife out of the raging storm and back in his house.

"Everybody out!" he shouted, hoping to clear the room for ten seconds, to gather his wits.

"*Except* Timothea," he amended. "Pruitt, Chappy, locate Greenly and send him to the stables. The grooms are to saddle four fresh mounts and should be prepared to ride within five minutes.

"Imogene," he continued, "go with the servants and see that it's properly done. After that, can I rely on you to keep watch here, inside this house, and receive her if she comes back before I do? Take your sister. Go."

"But—"

"*Go!*" he shouted, and the servants jumped and hurried out the door. Imogene glared at him, her eyes burning, but followed after them.

Ian took a deep breath and turned to Timothea. "You must rise to the occasion, Timmie, and watch over the girls. Imogene will want to follow me, I see that look in her eye, but she cannot leave the house after dark in a storm. *No one else may leave here.* I forbid it."

"Imogene is an accomplished rider," his sister remarked, looking unconcerned. "The instructor Drewsmina hired confirmed this."

"I don't care if she's next in line to command the royal calvary, she may not ride into a storm. Please, I beg of you, allow me to catch up to my runaway wife without having to worry about Imogene as well."

"How odd that you speak of Drewsmina as if she's *run away.* You always make matters worse than they are."

"A keen observation," he said, stalking out of the room, "considering things are very grave indeed."

"I'm merely saying," said Timothea, following him, "she's gone out to *look* for you, not *run* from you. The rain is a challenge, yes, but tamp down your hysteria about her fleeing into the night. She'll be glad you've come for her."

"I'm not hysterical," he shouted, striding down the landing. Although hysteria was as good a name as any for what he now felt. Sheer terror also applied.

*Let me find her, let me find her, let me find her.* It was the simple little prayer he'd begun to chant in his head, his only ordered thought.

"But just look at the room she's prepared for you," enthused Timothea. "The excessive heat is hardly good for digestion, but the sentiment is sweet, really."

"I don't care about the room. I don't want candles and wine and bathtubs. I want her to *remain! Here. With us.*"

"Yes, but have you considered what *she* wants? She's been perfectly lovely to all of us, especially the cat, but *you*, brother, are her very strong preference."

"She has me," he countered. "I married her. I am *in her possession*."

"Yes, you married her in the sparest of ceremonies, followed by a tasteless breakfast. And then what did you do? You set her right to work, training up your nieces."

"Need I remind you that these are *your* daughters, Timothea," he said. "And we're all better for her efforts. She loves the girls and enjoys her work with them."

"She enjoys *you*. She loves *you*."

He made a growling noise and began clipping down the stairs. "'Love' again. I need more time to reckon with . . . with *that*. And why must it be meted out *now*? Tonight? Does *love* create such an urgency, it warrants running into a storm?"

"Firstly—yes. Secondly, the love is perhaps not the urgency. It's the waiting."

Timothea began to descend the stairs, shaking her head. "Men have no imagination, I'm sorry to say. They look at a girl like Imogene and think immediately, 'How pretty. She'll do nicely. *That's* the girl for me—with the blonde hair and blue eyes and the high spirit.' And good for Imogene—truly. When it comes to her, my only concern is for the sanity of her future husband, may God preserve him. But Drewsmina, in contrast, calls for more discernment, doesn't she? She is more unique, less obvious. She's been compelled to wait for someone to sort this out. She may have been waiting *years*."

"If you're suggesting I haven't noticed that my wife is beautiful, you're wrong."

"Oh I've no doubt you can identify her many fine qualities, but does she know that you cherish her?"

Ian missed a step.

"Do you know," quizzed Timothea, "what Tribble said to me the night we met? He said, '*There* you are. I've been searching for you my whole life, and now you've finally come. *Thank God*.' It was the most gratifying thing, to be seen and to be wanted. It calmed me in a hundred different ways. I felt calmness, in fact, for perhaps the very first time in my life."

Ian turned back to her. His sister managed to be the most shocking in those rare moments when she also made the most sense.

"Women grow weary of waiting for men to take some notice, Ian," she lectured, catching up to him. "Waiting for them to warm to the notion of love. It's exhausting. I salute Drewsmina's wild ride, honestly. Clearly the flowers and candles failed to capture your attention. If you'd prefer her safe inside, out of the rain, I suggest you demonstrate that she is *seen* and that you find her *precious*."

*I do see her,* Ian thought, making his way to the bottom step.

*I saw her the very first day.*

"I did see her," he said out loud. "I was made a little breathless by the impression she made, if I'm being honest. But it took me by surprise, and I don't like surprises."

"*Life* is a surprise, Ian," Timothea said. "It's one long series of unrelenting surprises. My advice to you is to accept this between now and when you locate her. And then consider how love may be acknowledged and demonstrated on a daily basis. Beginning now. In abundance. It should be a love that is independent of the girls and me, separate from the 'duke and duchess' bit. And rise above your fear of being unprepared. For God's sake. Love is having someone at your side when you are taken by surprise. Between the two of you, you'll work together and sort it out."

Ian narrowed his eyes, squinting up at her, and then turned on his heel and ran.

# Chapter Twenty-Nine

rew had lost her way. She was despondent, unsettled, angry, confused, *and* lost, but she was barreling ahead.

*And that is merely my emotional state,* she thought, reining her horse down another unknown street, *it says nothing about the fact that I'm lost in an unknown quarter of London in a bloody maelstrom.*

Tonight represented the closest she'd flung herself to the *old way,* the volatile and selfish manner in which she formerly conducted her life. Before she'd transformed; before she'd stopped flinging.

It felt wretched. She'd wondered in these last years what a regression might mean for her. Would it feel like freedom? Like a tightly laced corset come undone? Would it spoil all the progress she'd made?

No, it would not and it did not. The way it felt (beyond wretched) was foolish and irresponsible.

And surely it had not spoiled . . . well, anything.

Ian had said Pollen Street was not a prison. She was permitted to ride out if she experienced a fit of . . . of anger. At him. For leaving. Again. For leaving ten minutes after they made love. *Every time.* For experiencing frustration at his inability to croak out the words *I love you.* In actual words. No assumptions? At the very least, she was allowed to experience frustration over her having said the words and Ian not acknowledging them.

It was reasonable, she thought, to want these things. Perhaps it was too soon for him and perhaps it wasn't, but no amount of editing herself was making these desires go away. They needed to discuss it. She was angry that they hadn't, and she'd jumped on a horse to find him and tell him so.

*You deserve to be heard*, whispered a voice in her head and it made her smile. Despite the rain. Despite the cold. Despite the fact that she had no idea where she was going or how she might find her way home. She smiled.

When she found her way back to him, he would hear all of this. She would not beg, she would not threaten; she would not even wheedle him with a pretty table and a hot bath and the timid request for an evening alone.

Her refusal to be a clingy, petulant harpy needn't translate to never telling him how she truly felt or what she wanted and needed. She had been given a voice at birth, she had abused it for a time, then she hadn't, and now she must fine some balance. She could do it. It could be done.

But first she had to find her way home.

*Thoom!* Another clap of thunder rattled the windows on the unfamiliar houses around her.

The mare Drew had chosen, Ivy's favorite, did not appear to be spooked by the rain so much as invigorated by it. She galloped along, splashing through puddles and bounding over washed-out places in the road, moving into the unknown at a faster clip than Drew would have preferred.

Half of the harrowing journey to Blackwall had been devoted to remembering the route and the other half had been simply holding on.

Had she borne eastward in Aldgate, or did she ride north? Drew couldn't say for sure.

When she'd set out, before the light drizzle had birthed this torrent, Drew had thought if she could only make it to Charing Cross, she could pick up the river and follow it east, riding parallel from the safe distance of two or three blocks. But then she'd run up against the Tower of London. The rain had increased, and she couldn't find a clear way around the tower wall. She turned northward, which she knew should put her in the correct general direction, but she also knew she must eventually correct her route back toward the water, all the while keeping clear of Bluegate Fields and Cable Street, with their storied dens of gambling and crime.

With every new block, her vow to find Lachlan—to say it all and be done with it—had grown a little less pressing. The rain was unrelenting. She was soaked through and steam rose from her laboring mare.

She'd set out in a tumult of frustration, so very fed up with his avoidance, that she'd not even thought to put on more sensible shoes.

The streets were empty—only a fool would be out on a night like this—with no one to ask which way to the river. Was Aldgate behind her or below her? She came to the end of the street and realized she had absolutely no idea which way to turn.

She could knock on someone's door, ask to be taken in, but she'd wandered into a particularly bleak, rickety row of houses, no windows, only the faintest candlelight seeping beneath doors. Would she be safer lost in the rain or pulled inside one of these dark, crouched dwellings? She didn't know. If she could only find the river.

She turned the corner onto an unnamed street, only because she'd seen the distant glow of a faint light at the far end. It could be a public house, it could be an inn.

*It could be a prison on fire*, she thought glumly, squinting into the rain.

The light, Drew discovered, came from two lanterns, their flames pushing away the night, despite the wind and rain. They were posted outside of what appeared to be a little antiquities shop.

"But could they be open for business in this storm? So late at night?" Drew marveled, approaching cautiously from the far side of the street. Through the falling rain and gloom, she read the sign posted above the window. "Godfrey's Treasure Trove. Fripperies, Oddities, Baubles, and Relics."

Drew blinked, wiping the rain from her eyes, and read it again. A gift shop? Here? In East London (or what she assumed was East London)?

Drew studied the outside of the shop, weighing prudence against necessity. The shop had a cheerful striped awning over a crooked stoop, the canvas now coursing rainwater onto a pair of statues guarding the door. The statues appeared to be a matched set of stone mice, rearing up on their hind legs, holding chestnuts.

To the left of one statue was an old bath chair, a potted rosebush in the seat. Beside the other statue, leaning on its side, was the brightly painted wheel of a wagon. The length of the storefront was littered with similarly mismatched detritus from daily life, most of it at least fifty years old. Drew saw well-loved baby dolls, their dresses translucent in the rain; earthenware bowls, overflowing with water; a pickax; another rosebush; a miniature Tudor mansion, with a thatched roof and a chimney, which could only be used to house a dog.

Drew looked right and left, making sure she was alone. Was the storefront a guise for something more sinister? She looked again. It did not appear sinister, and Drew was nothing if not an expert on shopping. Given better circumstances, she should like to take the twins here.

The inside of the shop glowed through the window from bright lantern light. Merchandise crowded the large front window. Deeper inside, Drew could just make out a man behind a counter, scribbling notations in a book.

She was just about to knee the mare closer to the window, when a boom of thunder sounded, startling the horse. Drew took it as a sign. She'd hesitated long enough. She needed help, and here was a reasonable-looking person in a . . . if not *reasonable*-looking shop, at least a shop with no clear threat. There would be no safer place to appeal this night, and she knew it.

Dismounting without a groom or a block wanted considerable effort. The cold and wet had fused her to the saddle and the horse danced nervously as Drew disentangled herself from the leather straps, pulling heavily to the mare's right flank. Ultimately, her hand slipped, her glove was a useless mush of sodden kid, and she toppled from the horse into the mud. One shoe hung in the stirrup, and she had the foresight to kick her foot from her slipper rather than snap her ankle as her body made it's ungraceful decent to the ground.

"Ouch," she moaned, forcing herself to get up and calm the skittery animal. Her slipper, she was disappointed to see, had ripped in two when she'd kicked it off, split open by a sharp point on the hobble strap.

What did it matter now? she thought. The satin shoes had been useless in the rain. Her feet would be blue, she could barely feel them in the cold. She left the useless slipper hanging from the saddle and limped across the street to the shop.

"Hello?" she called cautiously, sticking her head in the door. It was warm inside, and it smelled of freshly baked bread.

"Hallo!" called a friendly voice from behind a wide counter. It was the man she'd seen through the window, now obscured by a giant cactus growing from a basket on the floor.

"But are you open, sir?" Drew hovered in the doorway. Her cloak alone weighed two stone, it was so very wet. She would leave a puddle deep enough for fishing.

"Yes, I am!" came the voice. "A quarter hour, I'd say, before I close up for the night. You've caught me just in time. How can I be of service?"

"Ah, I hesitate to come inside, because I'm so very wet. I may spoil your floors."

"Never you fear, madam. The first thing I do upon closing is clean the showroom, top to bottom. What you see now is the dirt and grime of a busy workday. If you intend to make a mess, you've come at absolutely the best time."

Drew considered this. It would be impossible to overstate how very wet she was. She could not have been wetter if she was swimming at the bottom of the sea. But also, why had she just thrown herself from her horse if not to get in out of the storm and seek help?

"Thank you so much," she said, stepping in. The showroom, as he'd called it, was a hodgepodge of books, old furnishings, taxidermized animals, stacks of textiles, paintings of farm animals, model ships, and bowls of fruit all stacked and leaned and piled at odd angles. She stepped carefully, trying not to topple a tower of mismatched china plates or drip rainwater on the skirts of a hanging emerald ball gown.

"I'm afraid I haven't any money to make a purchase, sir. I . . . I find myself in the unfortunate position of being lost in an unfamiliar part of town. The storm, as you can see, is growing worse, seemingly by the minute, and my horse is spooked and nearly spent. I fear we're riding in circles. Can you . . . can you . . ."

And Drew realized she had no idea what she meant to ask this man to *do*.

If she had visions of him leaping forth, whipping off his jacket, offering shelter, offering tea, dispatching a servant to notify her family—she was sorely mistaken. He stood, smiling behind his counter, waiting patiently for her to . . . to . . .

What did he expect her to do? Surely not browse the merchandise and buy some antiquity? Here? Now?

She cleared her throat. "But would you be so kind as to tell me where I am?"

"Oh certainly, madam," he boomed. "This is my shop, world-renowned as such, 'Godfrey's Treasure Trove.' Mr. Godfrey, at your service."

"Right," she said. "How do you do? Forgive me, but I meant, in *what* location have I found myself?"

"Of course," said Mr. Godfrey. "But you are in *London*, madam, one of the finest cities in the world."

"Yes, I am aware that I am in London—" she lifted a sodden lock of orange hair from her face "—but can you tell me *which part*?"

"Which part . . ." he repeated speculatively, looking to the ceiling. "I'd say we are in the vicinity of Shadwell-Whitehall-Whapping-Poplar? Or thereabouts? If you want to put a very fine point on it."

Drew blinked at him. She'd become very familiar with London these last few years because of her passion for birding. She'd taken hackney cabs to the many diverse habitats all over the city and surrounding countryside. The man had just named four regions that could easily amount to five square miles.

"Right," she said. "But do you happen to know where I might seek out some assistance? A church, perhaps? Or a parish hall?"

"For that . . ." he said, speculating again, ". . . I have no good answer. I do apologize. I have the great fortune of owning various shops *throughout* the city, and this happens to be one of my newer, more far-flung locations. Regrettably, I've not had the opportunity to learn the neighborhood. Or meet the neighbors."

*What?* thought Drew, barely able to comprehend.

*Was there* no help *that he could offer her?*

She stared at him. He stared back, a faint smile on his

face. It wasn't a menacing smile, or even a petty smile, but this man had begun to unnerve her, just the same.

She cleared her throat. "Would you be able to, reliably, point me in the direction of the River Thames, perhaps? Just the general direction? I should be able to find my way to safety if I only knew the location of the river. To orient me."

Slowly, he began shaking his head, the gesture of a man who had searched his heart and mind and, yet again, come up with nothing.

Drew began to shiver.

"The river . . ." he breathed. "I do believe is . . . that way?" He waved a limp finger and pointed, remarkably, in *no* direction. "Or is it that?" He pivoted and failed to point again. "Honestly, I cannot say. I do not travel to work by boat. I come by carriage. Bad knee," he said, making a *tsk*ing noise.

"Fine," said Drew, visibly shaking now. "Do you have anything like a map of the city? I've said I have no money, sadly, but if you would allow me to merely look at a London map, and if you could but name the street on which this shop is located, I should be able to sort out the direction to the river."

"Oh, madam," he said, "but you do not require *money* to make a purchase in Godfrey's Treasure Trove. In fact, I do not accept money as payment—not ever—it has been my long-standing policy these great many years. I only accept items *in trade*."

"I beg your pardon?" said Drew. "*What* items?" Now the unsettled feeling flipped into a more chilling and tangible sense of wariness, the second cousin of fear.

What would he require of her in exchange for the map? Some . . . service? A lock of hair? She glanced around at the incongruous smattering of items crowding the shop. Was this man about to cut off a finger in exchange for a city map?

"Oh, anything you may have on your person that you find you can live without," he said. "Some items I've recently acquired in trade include a pen, a hand mirror, the shell of an ostrich egg, an illustrated book of indigenous peoples in the Americas, and a crystal rock."

"Yes," said Drew, even while she meant, *No, no, no—this has not happened to me.*

"I'm afraid I'm not in possession of anything . . . of that nature," she said. "I'm alone with only my horse and my sodden clothes." She made a sound of distress, half laugh, half sob, and she realized she was about to cry. "I don't even have two shoes at the moment."

"Oh!" said Mr. Godfrey. "But I am in search of a mismatched shoe."

"I beg your pardon?"

"The one shoe? If you can part with it, I would happily take it in trade. I've a gap in my inventory for single shoes."

"You're joking."

"No indeed. Would you be so kind as to allow me to appraise the item, madam? I can tell you immediately if it suits my needs and what I may offer in return."

"Is that so?" said Drew, irritated now. She paddled under the heavy ruined hem of her dress and removed her shoe. Unceremoniously, she dropped it on the counter in a runny wad of pink satin. It hit the glass with a wet, squishy *slap*. It seeped rainwater.

"Yes," mused Mr. Godfrey, removing a pencil from behind his ear and picking the slipper up with the lead. He held it between them like a scientific specimen. "Lovely. When it dries, I should be proud to have it. We are in business, Mrs. . . ." he faltered.

"The Duchess of Lachlan," provided Drew, a little surprised to hear the name come from her own mouth.

Although a fat lot of good it did her in this instance.

"Your Grace," said Mr. Godfrey, bowing his head. "Very good. Now, what will you select in exchange?"

"We had discussed a map of the city," Drew said, her

voice less generous every time she spoke. This exchange defied belief. If ever she made it back to Pollen Street, if ever she found a way to *hold Ian down* after they'd made love, she would tell him every unbelievable detail.

"Sorry," said Mr. Godfrey, sounding truly regretful. He was taking her shoe, still hanging limply from his pencil, through a door that led to the back. "But we are fresh out of London maps at the moment."

Drew would've screamed, if her chattering teeth didn't prevent her from fully opening her mouth. "Wh—"

"But!" said Mr. Godfrey cheerfully, reappearing, holding a small pendant on a chain. "I do have a compass!"

*Chapter Thirty*

On the stable, with four footmen gathered round, Ian had unfurled a map of the city and identified five possible routes Drewsmina might have taken from Piccadilly to Blackwall. There were no guarantees, of course, but they had to start somewhere. It was a distance of some seven miles, although not necessarily a complicated journey if she'd found her way to the river and borne east.

East London represented a whole different level of challenge; it was the most treacherous quarter of the city and the river only invited more danger. Even if she found her way, she would be vulnerable to the desperate and the vile. The grooms, some old, some young, all of them accustomed to life in Dorset and not London, would be vulnerable. All of it was risky, and that said nothing of the storm. The wind had calmed but the rain was unrelenting, a steady, punishing torrent.

Ian set off, believing the rain to be the very least of what he deserved. He took the most obvious route and, by some miracle, found her within an hour.

One hour, but those sixty minutes took years off his life.

He came upon her walking down a small, out-of-the-way street halfway between Piccadilly and Blackwall. He'd only chosen that route because he'd come upon three boys squished together on the back of the mare—*his* mare, with her distinct coloring and very fine tack—that Drew had ridden from Pollen Street.

He'd corralled the boys and horse against a wall, demanding to know where they'd gotten the mount and what had become of the rider. The boys, sopping wet guttersnipes, tough enough to be prowling the streets in the rain, shrugged off his threats. He came back at them like a lunatic, with shouts and profanity; he was so very desperate to find her.

Still, the boys were not afraid, but they were keenly interested in locating a missing duchess. They grew increasingly cooperative and admitted that they they'd simply *found* the horse walking the street alone, her reins dragging in the mud.

"Where?" Ian had demanded, spinning on his stallion, whipping around. "Where did you find her?!"

The boys had told him, describing a small side street, just blocks from Cable Road. Ian paid them, warning them that if he learned they'd *stolen* the horse from the duchess—if they'd bullied or harmed her in any way—he would hunt them down and inflict a regret they had never known.

He'd further bade them to ride the mare to his stable in Pollen Street. He hadn't the time to do more than that, and he was worried for the animal. She was Ivy's favorite.

Whether the boys were to blame or someone else, the possible reasons for a riderless horse were too terrible for Ian to consider. His elegant wife could have been a victim of theft, murder, kidnapping, a fall into the river, strike by lightning—

He'd reined his stallion around and forced himself to look on it strategically, to put the doom thinking out of his head, to find her first and fall apart second.

In the end, she was two blocks from the street where the boys had claimed to find the horse. He saw her from a distance—it could be only her, so tall and thin, moving slowly, one slim hand to the brick wall.

Ian came apart at the sight of her, there was suddenly so much rain in his eyes.

He galloped to her, calling her name. She turned round, shrinking back against the wall at the ruckus. He was off his horse before the animal clattered to a stop, swinging down, overcoat whirling, ripping off his hat.

"Drewsmina!" he gasped, running the rest of the way.

"Lachlan?" she called.

It *was* her. Thank God! He didn't even care that she'd referred to him by his bloody title.

"Drew!" he yelled. "Stop. Don't walk another step. I have you! I'm here!"

"Ian," she cried, and she fell against the wall and dropped her face into her hands.

"Drew," he repeated, a whisper now. He was upon her. He took her by the shoulders, looking into her face. Her lips were blueish and her nose was crimson but she appeared otherwise unmarred.

"What's happened?" he asked. "Are you hurt? Can you walk? What's been done to you? There were pickpockets riding your horse through Aldgate."

"Nothing, nothing's happened," she said, breathless. "I . . . I'd come out in search of you. It was an impulse, perhaps, not entirely thought through. I wanted . . . I wanted . . ."

He pulled her against him and she went, tucking her face into his chest. He opened the sides of his overcoat and wrapped the two of them together inside it. The feel of her body curled against him, the rain pouring down, the sheer, breathtaking relief of finding her, felt like—nay, it *was*— the pinnacle moment of his life, when the earth spun and the sky raged, and billions of people went on about their lives, but his heart cracked open and love poured out.

"I love you," he said, speaking into her hair.

"What?" she whispered, looking up.

"I've fallen in love you," he repeated, louder. "I love you so bloody much, Drewsmina Trelayne Clayblack, Duchess of Lachlan. My duchess. My wife."

She was shaking her head, and he almost laughed. Did she really think she could deny this?

She clutched the lapels of his coat. "You've been given a fright," she said.

He leaned back and stared into her face. Was she trying to explain it away?

"I've bolted into a storm without considering who might be worried or put out," she admitted solemnly. "It was, as I've said, impulsive and a bit rash. I am ever so glad that you've come for me, but you needn't—"

"You cannot tell me not to love you, Drew." He laughed at her expression. She looked as if someone had handed her something wild and mythical and wholly unexpected. A mermaid, a star.

"If it sounds improbable," he went on, "that's only because I'm shite at demonstrating it. And saying it. And understanding it. Although that ends now."

She stared at him, eyes huge on his face. He leaned down and kissed her hard. She took it, kissing him back, but only so much. She pulled away to look at him again. It occurred to him that she didn't believe him.

"It snuck up on me, *Miss Trelayne*," he said. "I didn't see it coming, partly because it had the look and feel of a surprise, and, as you may know, I am not fond of surprises, but—"

A clap of thunder blasted above them, and they both laughed. Down the wall, an empty gatehouse stood open, and he pulled her under the cover of the tiny overhang, out of the rain.

"But also," he continued, sobering, "because I didn't know how to identify it. I was never shown. And I wasn't paying attention. It came on so very quickly, didn't it?"

"Like a drizzle that seems manageable at first, but then turns into a deluge?" she offered softly.

"Yes," he said. "Like that. I cannot claim credit for sorting it out on my own. My sister helped."

"She did?"

He nodded. "She supports your wild flight, by the way. Likely, she wishes you'd fled sooner. But not I. I've been . . . scared beyond all reason. I cannot lose you. I've had this thought from the beginning, all on my own. I cannot lose you."

"You will not," she vowed. "And I'm sorry you had to come after me." She looked at the sky. "I thought I could manage. It wasn't raining when I set out. And then it was. And then I was lost. And then I went into a shop and when I came out, the horse had gone."

"The horse led me to you."

"I'm so glad you've found her. She's Ivy's favorite. I would have never forgiven myself."

"All of this," he said, "is my fault. Do not blame yourself—not for the horse, not for any of it. You identified love right away, you *knew*. And I . . . I couldn't see it. I could feel it in a way, I *wanted* it, even, but I didn't know what it was. I had no name for it. It scared me, this *not knowing*. I wanted desperately to slow down, to study it, to lie in wait and see what it would do—to see what *you* would do."

"Clearly what I would do is . . . jump on a horse and chase you into a storm."

"The night you'd planned for us. The meal. The candles and fire. The bathtub—I pray I've not ruined future chances to explore *the bathtub*. I have been so thoughtless."

She laughed, a tearful, joyful sound. He squeezed her and continued, "My complete lack of attention and my preoccupation with the estate is appalling. I compelled you to marry me. Marriage. Forever. And then I took advantage of the devotion you showed me—and the love. I used the girls as an excuse. I'm not surprised you rode out into a storm. Although I thought . . . I thought you were running away, not trying to recover me."

"But why would I run away?"

"I don't know," he whispered. "No, that's not true, I can think of fifty reasons, beginning with the fact that the women in my life are known runners, and ending with the fact that my sister and nieces—and myself—can be difficult. At times. Or all the time." Now he laughed.

"I've wanted you," she said. "From the beginning. I did fall in love at an alarming pace, but when you've waited as long as I've waited, and you've spent as much time on . . . on introspection, you know your own heart."

"Your courage astounds me," he said. "You knew, and you weren't afraid—or you *were* afraid but it didn't deter you—and you went after me, you went after 'us.' I'm so grateful. Because, afraid or not, I'm so bloody in love with you. It's tearing up my heart, Drew—"

She giggled at his sloppy poeticism, and he laughed too. "Oh yes, laugh, it's comical. And wonderful. And I hope to die laughing with you. Certainly, I cannot do without you."

"*Ian*," she said, and he kissed her, wanting to taste his given name on her lips.

"I want to live and breathe you," he said, between kisses. "And not as an aunt to my nieces, although I love that bit of you." Another kiss. "And not as a lover, although I *really* love that bit of you." Another kiss. "I love you as my wife, the rightful occupant of my heart. A once-missing piece, now fitted into place."

"Oh, Ian," she breathed, tears filling her eyes. "I . . . I should have run into a raging storm sooner, perhaps."

"So you are . . . amenable to this?" he asked, ducking down to look her in the eye. "Just to be certain. Because this was not what we discussed that night in the library. When we decided to marry."

"Yes, yes, yes," she said, jumping a little. "How careless of me, I've failed to make my own declarations. Of course I love you and of course I want all of it." She laughed. "I think I've loved you since you freed the birds from Kew Palace. I have loved you and wanted you and been afraid to say it because . . . because . . ." She was shaking her head.

"No fear," he proclaimed. He bit off his glove and placed his cold hand over her colder lips. "No fear. I hate that it took almost losing you for me to see it, but I am stunted and stubborn and blinded by my very healthy lust for you. Please do not allow these very real failings of mine to cause you to doubt me. Ever.

"You have," he said, picking her up under the bottom, holding her above him, "bolstered me. You have heartened me. You brought me to heel *and* you have healed me. You introduced love into my life and make me courageous enough to be the uncle and the duke I hope to be. And, perhaps . . . the father?"

"Yes, the father," she breathed, smiling through her tears.

"We will have to determine some . . . schedule that allows you to run your finishing school in London and also be in Dorset. I . . . I cannot be away from Avenelle for months at a time, it's simply too demanding to be properly managed from afar. I cannot imagine how we'll sort it, but I can divide some of my time—"

"I shall have my school *in* Dorset," she said instantly. No hesitation.

"What?"

"Why not? There is no magic to a London address. Most of the debutantes in London travel here from Dorset or Devon or Surrey or Sussex. There are unfinished young women to train up everywhere. I am not particular."

"Truly?"

"Truly. We will sort it out together."

"Thank you," he breathed. "I don't want to live apart. I didn't even want to leave you for Blackwall these many nights, but I had no choice. I—"

"But can you not tell me your business in Blackwall? The note was cryptic, but enough to set me on this path, obviously. At the time, I was . . . less concerned about your business and rather singled-mindedly determined to have some answers."

"Oh yes, Blackwall. It's a long story . . ."

He told her then, all of it, despite their wet clothes and the cold night, despite the risk that she was unready to shoulder the challenging work of being the Duchess of Lachlan in earnest.

"Oh, Ian," she said, and he thrilled at the sound of his given name. "You should have told me. I will always want to know. Your struggles are *my* struggles." She paused, studying his face, and then she repeated, "I will always want to know."

He nodded. "No more secrets—even for the sake of your protection and worry. Imogene warned me of this."

"Oh yes, Imogene is no fan of secrets—unless they benefit herself."

She laughed when she said this, and the sound filled up his heart. "Should we go home?" he asked. "I can't believe we've hashed this out in a rainstorm. But I couldn't wait to say the words." He pulled her to him. "When I realized how very much I love you, I simply couldn't wait."

"I couldn't wait to hear them," she whispered, almost to herself. She looked up at him and grinned. "Can you take me home?"

He led her to his horse and mounted up, reaching down to hoist her into his lap. When she settled in, he noticed wet stockinged feet sticking out from the hem of her gown.

"Drew?" he asked. "Where are your *shoes*?"

"Funny thing about the shoes," she said, burrowing into his chest. "Would you believe there was this little man . . ."

# *Epilogue*

*Six months later*
*May 1819*

The ballroom was lit by the glow of five hundred candles. Light spilled onto the stones of the terrace like the sun had been hung inside the house. Drewsmina stood in a dark corner with Ivy, hidden from view. The colorful crush of revelers swirled inside like stained glass come to life.

"No regret, Ivy, that you don't *share* this debut?" Drew asked her niece.

Ivy quickly shook her head, as if Drew had asked if she regretted jumping off a cliff.

"No regret," repeated Ivy, watching the dancers inside. "But will the tennis courts be restored to the ballroom after the party?"

"I'm certain that can be arranged," said Drew, rubbing a small circle on her niece's back. Ivy had not changed from her blue day dress, one of several ways she made certain she wouldn't be drawn into her sister's debut. "Has Bucky finally tempted you to give tennis a go?"

Another head shake. "Oh no, not for me—for Imogene. She does so love it, doesn't she? Whatever her feelings about balls after tonight, she will always love tennis."

Ivy paused, considering the truth of this statement. Drew and Ivy both knew that Imogene would adore balls after tonight.

"That is," amended Ivy, "I'm sure Imogene will have a

perfectly tolerable time at her debut, but if she does not, we know that her affection for tennis will endure, don't we?"

"We do know this," agreed Drew, giving the girl a reassuring smile. "But soon we'll return to Avenelle for summer, and Imogene may enjoy the new outdoor courts Ian has installed."

"It feels as if we'll never return to Dorset," Ivy sighed, frowning now as a couple strolled, arm in arm, from the ballroom onto the dark terrace.

"We will go, never you fear," said Drew. "But was there no part of London that you enjoyed, Vee?"

"Oh, London is fine, I suppose," mused Ivy. "I do like the parks and bookshops. I like my horse, but Uncle Ian has said that Socks will return to Avenelle with us."

Drew smiled at her. She'd learned not to rush Ivy when she wished to make a point.

"I should hate for any of us to be left behind in London," Ivy added. "We should—all of us—go back to Avenelle. Even the cat."

"Especially the cat," agreed Drew.

Another couple drifted to the terrace and Drew edged the girl deeper into the shadows.

After a moment, Ivy drew a shaky breath and ventured, "I worry sometimes that Imogene will refuse to return to Dorset. She loves everything about London. She will like this ball, she will *love* it. If we believe otherwise, we are only deceiving ourselves." She sounded like a fortune-teller reciting a bad omen.

Drew suppressed a laugh. "Well, I certainly hope she likes it, we've gone to a lot of effort to make it special. And look how hard she's worked, to be ready for the presentation at court. She managed that brilliantly, didn't she? She should have her special night. Both of you have been so very attentive. You've truly given the best of yourselves to all the lessons and tutors and practices. What cordial, thoughtful, interesting young women you are."

"Thank you," said Ivy after a brief, internal struggle.

Drew almost laughed. Drew had taught her this. *If you've been given a compliment about something that you, yourself, find distasteful, it is better to say "thank you" than to dismiss the compliment.*

"Ah, there you are," said a voice from the garden below.

Drew and Ivy turned to see Ian clip up the shadowy steps. He slipped an arm around Drew and pulled her close. It was impossible to hide her delight in seeing him, in having him reach for her, in standing arm in arm. The sight of him sent feathers swirling in her chest, even now. She struggled in public settings not to touch some part of him. Ian did not share this same struggle, and he touched her whenever he liked.

"Bloody hell," Ian said, frowning through the doors, "they've all come, haven't they?"

"They did all come," said Drew. "Everyone loves a party. *And* a pretty debutante who's gained the favor of the queen."

Ian snorted. "Perhaps Imogene should have met with the prince instead of me."

As promised, Imogene and Ivy were granted invitations to meet Queen Charlotte at the end of the Season. Ivy had chosen not to debut this year and respectfully declined to meet the queen, but Imogene threw herself into preparations, devoting months to almost-cheerful study of Drew's every instruction. On the queen's birthday, she'd boldly joined the long line of debutantes who were to be presented as part of the celebration.

Her appearance had, according to the gossip rags, been an overwhelming success. They described her gown and styling as "distinctive," and "ethereal," and (in one particularly vivid account), "breathtaking." Onlookers reported that she'd glided assuredly down the long hall to the throne and sunk into a graceful curtsey. Her biggest triumph, however, was the brief exchange she shared with the queen—topics covered included horseback riding, tennis, and cats—and she'd not been excused until she'd made the monarch laugh.

Ian's time with the prince regent was also a success, even without his clever niece. He'd spent the spring quietly rallying parliament, one member at a time, paving the way in case the regent could not be convinced to help. He'd worked diligently; refusing to react when various MPs alluded to his reputation as a failed rioter, and Drew had been so very proud. Finally, thanks to Imogene, he'd met the future king.

He'd been brilliant, of course—Drew devoured every detail of the meeting and refused to view it in any other light—and even Ian himself seemed satisfied with the progress. The prince had been flanked by two ministers who scribbled copious notes. Adolphus had also come. In the end, Prince George urged Ian to keep him abreast of the matter, and the ministers had asked for the dossier Ian had prepared on the export taxes and its impact on small, regional craftsmen.

When they returned to Dorset, Ian hoped his tenants would see the meeting as another peace offering. A move in the right direction. He hoped they would see it as he did, as a ray of hope.

But first, the debut of Imogene Starry. After tonight, Imogene would be officially "out" in society, free to attend parties and fetes and balls and to welcome the attention of suitors.

The prospect of this clearly terrified Ivy, and she wasn't the only one. Ian and Drew had decided that, given Imogene's relative youth and newness to London, she would have greater success in her Season if she passed another summer and autumn in the countryside. Timothea had no opinion on the matter; so the Duke and Duchess of Lachlan made the decision to debut their niece late in the current Season—the alignment with her presentation at court was a perfect excuse—and then to pack all of them up and go to Dorset until the following year.

*Next* year, when Imogene was older and hopefully a bit more measured, they would return and she could enjoy a full London Season from beginning to end. Perhaps by then, Ivy would be prepared to debut. Or not. Whatever the girl wished.

"But why have you and Imogene not come up together?" Drew asked Ian, looking around for their niece. "There's no problem, I hope?"

"God only knows," said Ian. "She looked perfectly ready to me. It was Timothea who sent me away. She wanted a few words alone with Imogene."

"Really?" Drew's mouth literally fell open. She couldn't help it. She was stunned.

"Really," Ian confirmed, tugging at his cravat. "Miracles never cease."

"But will Timothea lead her to us when they've finished?" asked Drew. "They cannot wind themselves through the ballroom unescorted. Imogene must be announced; the baroness must be announced. It was Imogene herself who chose to enter through the terrace doors." Drew slipped from Ian's arm to peer over the banister, hoping to see Imogene and Lady Tribble on the garden path.

"Pray, don't worry, Aunt," said Ivy, stifling a yawn. "Imogene will find her way."

"Of this, I have no doubt, but I should hate for her to become distracted or forget the plan. Debutante balls may be frivolous and diverting, but there is an order of events. If we mean to do it, I should like to see it done properly."

She glanced back to Ian, who was examining the inside of his hat. Ivy had plucked a leaf from a nearby potted bush and was rolling it between two fingers.

"Should I go back for her?" Drew asked, her anxiety growing. "Ian, what did your sister say?"

Ian shrugged. "Nothing really. Simply, 'Where can I go to have a word with my daughter?' And I said, 'Are you mad, half of London is filling this house. You are alone here. I'll leave; do your worst.' And then I sought out the two of you."

Drew made a noise of frustration. On the one hand, she was thrilled that the baroness was sharing a special moment with her daughter; on the other, they'd worked so very hard, and to this point, Imogene's manners and comportment in public had been flawless. Talk had already begun to circulate; Imogene was rumored to be one of the most popular and sought-after debutantes in many Seasons. Drew should hate for her to distract from that with a break in protocol on the night that everyone was properly introduced to her.

"Did you know," said Ivy casually, "that we never would have escaped T.O.E. without Imogene?"

Drew blinked at her. "I beg your pardon?"

Ian slowly lowered his hat.

The girls had passed the winter and spring settling into life as a family, their studies, and the typical diversions of average girls. For better or worse, the alarming references to their life at T.O.E. had sort of . . . fallen away. Drew felt it was important to eventually revisit the topic, but she hadn't wanted to rush them.

"What do you mean, Ivy?" Ian said carefully. "About escaping T.O.E.?"

Ivy shrugged, speaking to the leaf. "I mean, the night we escaped T.O.E., it only happened because Imogene had made this elaborate a plan—she spent weeks on it, months. So I would not worry about her finding her way to this terrace."

"No," Ian said slowly, carefully, "likely that should not be a worry. But Ivy? Will you tell us more about Imogene's elaborate plan? Your escape?"

"Oh, that," said Ivy. She shrugged. "The first bit was to awaken us in the middle of the night and sneak through a field and then to a dark wood. And the second bit was to convene with this boy Imogene had met in the village so he could collect us in his wagon."

"She stole you into the night and led you through a wood and convened with a boy and his wagon?" Ian repeated, his speech still slow. Now his voice had taken on a cautious, tense quality. Drew drifted back to his side.

"Yes," sighed Ivy. "Basically. We would be at the Temple still if it weren't for Imogene. Compared to our escape from T.O.E., this ball will not be a challenge. Especially since she's so very *moony* about it. Especially since she's *obsessed* with it."

"Ivy," asked Ian, "what happened after this . . . boy collected you in his wagon? The night you escaped?"

"Oh, we traveled for many nights, didn't we? Reverend Sagg sent the Temple guards and their dogs after us, so we hid in stables during the day because the horses disguised our scent. At night, when everyone at the Temple is locked in their sheds, Imogene made us walk. Very quickly. Mostly in streams. This is also on account of the dogs."

"And where was your mother when you were . . . er, escaping?" asked Ian.

"We carried her along," said Ivy, the lament of someone with too many potatoes in her pail. "She was very dazed for the first bit, because of Reverend Sagg's special elixir. But then she came into herself more and more, day by day. And Imogene's friend, Augustus—he's the boy with the wagon, Augustus—traveled with us for many miles, so she could sleep in his cart. But then he was forced to turn back, because his parents would be suspicious, and no one in Gloucestershire wants trouble with Reverend Sagg."

"The amount of 'trouble' I shall soon rain down on Reverend Sagg," said Ian, "will be larger than the square milage of Gloucestershire." He took a deep breath and looked at Drew. She kept a hand on his arm, firm but gentle. The noise of the party had faded away and the route Imogene and Timothea might take downstairs felt no longer important.

"But, Ivy," asked Drew, "how did you find your way to Avenelle?"

"That was the challenge, wasn't it?" said Ivy thoughtfully. "Imogene and I had never been to Avenelle, obviously; we had only heard of it. But we knew it was in Dorset, although that is a place we'd also never been. When we'd finally put enough miles between ourselves and the Temple, Imogene allowed us to travel in the light of day. And she began to ask in every village we came upon. 'We are looking for an estate called Avenelle,' she would say. 'Do you know it?' 'Have you heard of it?' 'It is the home of my uncle. My mother is a baroness. My uncle is a duke.' 'We are trying to get home.'

"No one believed us really—you saw how wretched we looked—but people were generally willing to give us direction to Dorset. It's hardly a secret, which roads lead to Dorset."

"But Dorset is two days' ride from Gloucestershire," said Ian.

"It took us eleven days," Ivy commented. "Because we were walking."

Ian spun in a circle. He turned back to Ivy. "You *walked* to Dorset from Gloucestershire?"

"Well, Imogene was very good at procuring rides for us in wagons."

"Timothea, too?" asked Ian.

"Oh yes, all of us," said Ivy. "Mama prefers to ride most of all. But we had so little money. Reverend Sagg forbade anyone in the Temple to have money. It was only what Imogene could . . ." and now she looked away, ". . . could, well, borrow. We needed money for food, obviously."

"Ivy," Ian breathed. "I'm so sorry. I'm sorry you were alone and desperate and walking across the country with no money or support."

"Oh, we were not alone," said Ivy. "We were together. And I never felt desperate. Imogene is very resourceful. Aunt Drewsmina has had to teach her about life in London, but she already knew a great deal about every other part of life."

Ivy reached out and plucked another leaf from the bush. "I only mention it because everyone was so worried about her meeting the queen and attending this ball. Please do not forget, she's already rather accomplished, for all that." Another shrug. "In a manner."

"It is an excellent reminder," Drew managed. "But will you say what happened next?"

"When we made it so far as Dorset, it wasn't hard to locate Avenelle. By then, Mama could show us the way."

"It's a miracle," Ian whispered. He looked to Drew. "It's a miracle they survived."

"It was only walking," said Ivy. "In summer. Given the choice between walking across England in summer and attending this ball in any season, I would choose to walk."

"Luckily, no one will force you to make that choice, Ivy," Drew said quickly. "But thank you for telling us. I'm very proud that you survived it, and that you persisted until you found your way to your uncle. I'm also very proud to have been made your aunt. You are very special girls. Both of you. And your mother too. Very dear—to me."

"Actually I've wanted to tell this story for some time," said Ivy. "But Mama doesn't care for it."

"Well, you've said it now. And I won't mention it to her if that is what you prefer. Neither will Ian." She gave him a hard look. He had the expression of a man who'd been asked to hold a large, wet fish.

"Not until you're ready," Drew continued. "We needn't say anything more about it except that you were very brave—all of you—and certainly Imogene is . . . is very cap—"

"Oh, there she is!" Ivy said brightly, looking beyond Drew to the dark terrace steps.

They all turned and watched Imogene float from the shadows of the garden to the dim terrace. She was a puff of white rising in the night. Her debutante's gown glowed silvery in the moonlight, the silk as delicate and flowy as the down of a swan. Her blond hair had been cut fashionably short and was swept back in jeweled pins.

Timothea ascended beside her, her skin a little blotchy, her eyes bright; she wore a gown-like, shroud-like garment of vermillion silk that trailed down the steps behind them.

Drew forced herself to smile, to reconcile the stunning

young woman, her hair dripping in flowers, with the savior who rescued her grieving mother and innocent sister by walking across England.

Perhaps *reconcile* was the wrong word; there was no doubt in Drew's mind that Imogene had done it—and likely more to boot. Drew meant only to fix the combined vision of the two Imogenes in her mind; to mingle her pride in Imogene's debut with the pride in her heroism. Imogene's personality was colorful enough to accommodate both.

"How gorgeous you look," said Drew, opening her arms.

Imogene, true to form, allowed only a brief hug, and then she stepped back and whirled, sending the delicate white gown spinning into a round disc as flowers dropped from her hair.

"Timothea," enthused Drew, "look what you've done to her coiffeur. I love the flowers."

"Oh, Mama," said Ivy, "you've 'adorned' her. So pretty. Well done."

"A bit of nature never hurts, does it?" Timothea sniffed.

"How do you feel, Imogene?" asked Drew. "Ready? You've commanded quite a crowd. The ballroom is bursting. Apparently Queen Charlotte hasn't stopped talking about your presentation. Your reputation precedes you."

"Oh, best not to say *that*," laughed Imogene, picking at the pearl fastener on her glove.

Drew couldn't help but laugh. "It's a good thing, I assure you, to be a favorite of the queen. London is aflutter with tales of the Duke of Lachlan's niece, finally out in society after weeks of rumors about her great beauty and sparkling wit."

"Never you fear," said Imogene, "I'll set them to rights."

They laughed and Drew stepped away to signal a footman. It was time. If Drew allowed herself to acknowledge the swath she, herself, was cutting through London—the matrons she impressed with her pretty nieces and her lovely manners and her sensibility; the other young gentlewomen who admired her wardrobe and her carriages and the changes taking place in Pollen Street—she didn't dwell on the praise for long. These same women had chattered and gossiped in devastating ways when she'd been less polished, less sensible, and not married to a duke. Now she wanted only genuine friends.

And anyway, she was very busy. She'd had nieces to bring up and a debut ball to plan. She had a husband to love and a future to look forward to. She had a finishing school to launch.

When Drew stepped back to the circle of Ian and his family—*her* family—she said, "I should like to take a moment to say how very proud I am of the young woman you've become, Imogene. But I should also like to say that I'm proud of the girl you were all along. I could learn something from you on that score."

"*Pity*," sang Imogene, "I haven't the patience for instruction. You'll have to sort it out on your own." And then she winked.

"And I," said Ian, "would like to say that I'm a very lucky man. Through no effort of my own, I have two clever nieces, a sister who defies definition and is never boring, and a wife who—at least in my view—delivered us all to this happy moment. I love my family and I love my wife. And if we actually survive this party and these last weeks in London, I look ever so forward to us returning home. To Avenelle. Dorset in the summer puts on quite a show."

No one knew quite what to do after that—they were a happy family, but they were very new at it—and Drew stepped up again, opening her arms to the twins, hugging them fiercely, hugging her sister-in-law, and then falling against her husband.

"Well done, Lachlan," she said. "We've done it."

"We've managed so much more than my wildest dreams," he said, holding her close. "Thanks to you. In view of that, I'm wondering if you'll accept a very small token of my love and appreciation?"

"What?" Drew asked on a laugh. She pulled away from him, confused.

"I'm bollocks at identifying the correct moments for things," he said, reaching into his pocket, "but surely we can spare five seconds right now."

Drew blinked at him, watching as he produced a tidy leather box from his coat and held it out.

Drew's heart went still, as still as the box in his hand. She stared at the gift and up at Ian. He winked. She looked back to the box, unaccountably shy about taking it.

"Go on then," he said lowly.

Drew glanced at the girls. They were fussing over the flowers in Imogene's hair. She looked back at Ian and then snatched the box. It felt warm from his pocket. It was heavy. There was no rattle inside. With shaking fingers, she pulled the lid.

*"Oh, Ian."*

Nestled inside flaps of white silk was a ring. The setting was comprised of blinking stones in the shape of an insect. It had a sapphire body and legs made of small bright diamonds. Stones of red, orange, and green added colorful embellishments. It was radiant—unique and artful but also startlingly beautiful.

"A very late, very irregular wedding ring?" Ian ventured, coming closer, staring into the box.

"Oh, Ian," she said. "It's gorgeous. I love it. I should never find its equal, even if I searched my entire life."

"Well said," he chuckled. "That is precisely the way I feel about you."

"Thank you," Drew gushed, taking up the ring and testing it on her finger. It just fit over her gloves.

She was just about to show it to the girls when the footman returned, signaling to Ian and Imogene. Ivy spotted the ring and pounced on Drew's hand, exclaiming over what type of insect it might be. Timothea gave both Imogene and her brother a peck on the cheek.

"Off you go," Drew rasped, winking at Ian.

To Imogene, she said, "Serene smile. Chin high. That's it. Oh, just look at you."

She grabbed Ivy and Timothea by the hand and they watched Ian and Imogene approach the terrace doors, now held wide by two footmen.

The last thing Drew heard before they drifted from earshot was Ian saying, "I should like to impose on your busy schedule to ask about taking legal action against the good Reverend Sagg."

"Don't bother," Imogene replied, "I've detailed plans to deal with him. In my own time."

And away they went.

# Author's Note

The so-called Luddite Riots of late-eighteenth century and early nineteenth century Britain formed the loose inspiration for Lachlan's rioting tenants.

As described in the book, the riots were uprisings mounted by discouraged craftsmen—people like weavers, stocking makers, iron workers—whose livelihood was being erased by the impending industrial revolution.

I honed in on one riot in particular, the Pentrich Uprising of 1817; although Pentrich happened in Derbyshire, not Dorset, and the key players were stockingers and quarrymen, not lace makers. The Pentrich Uprising stood out to me because the angry rioters unwittingly harbored a spy in their midst. The British government had placed a plain-clothes informant in the planning meetings, and this man, later known as "Oliver the Spy," rode ahead to warn authorities on the night of the riot. Lachlan did not spy on his tenants on behalf of the government, of course, but the historical account gave me the idea.

For better or worse, one of the building blocks of my novels is finding a way to emotionally wound one or both of my main characters. This not only makes them sympathetic, it also provides all the lovely internal conflict that stands in the way of their happy ending. As I cast around for a way to torture dear Lachlan, I dipped my toe into the tenant-landlord relationship and endeavored to weave in this history of rioting. This storyline allowed me to explore, just a little, the challenges a young duke might face as he tries to promote progress without also putting lifelong craftsmen out of work.

Honiton Lace was an actual type of lace popular at the time and, of course, smuggling was rampant in the early nineteenth century. Most smuggling involved dodging taxes on imported contraband brought *into* England rather than smuggled *out*, but I found a few examples of exports being ferried out by smugglers to escape levies.

Almost everything else, especially the Temple of Order in Eden, is a fixture of my imagination. Although the older I get, the more I realize that anything can happen, or has happened, or will happen. The Reverend Saggs of the world are very much alive and well, even now; although, thankfully, they're being routed by the Imogenes among us every day.

Start from the beginning of Charis Michaels's
Awakened by a Kiss series with

# A Duchess a Day

*An heiress with a plan . . .*

Lady Helena Lark has spent years trying to escape
her wedding to the vain and boring Duke of Lusk. She's
evaded, refused, even run away. When her family's patience runs out, they pack her off to London to walk down
the aisle. But Helena has another idea: find a more suitable
bride to take her place, even if she must look for a replace-
ment duchess every day.

*A bodyguard with a job to do . . .*

Declan Shaw, better known as "The Huntsman," is a
mercenary who can pick and choose his clientele. After his
last job, escorting a young noblewoman to France, landed
him in jail under false accusations, he wants nothing to do
with aristocrats or women. But the law isn't done with him,
and if he agrees to babysit a duke's errant fiancée, the pay-
out could make his legal troubles go away.

*A most unexpected alliance . . .*

When their worlds collide, Declan realizes that contain-
ing his new client is only slightly harder than keeping his
hands off her. Helena senses an ally in her handsome new
bodyguard and solicits his help. Together they must escape
the forces that oppose them and fight for the fairy-tale love
they desire.

On Sale Now
From Avon Books

And don't miss the second unforgettable romance in the
Awakened by a Kiss series,

# When You Wish Upon a Duke

*All it takes . . .*

After a childhood spent cavorting around Europe with
a dangerous crowd, Miss Isobel Tinker has parlayed her
experience and language skills into a safe, reliable life.
Working as a clerk in Mayfair's Everland Travel Shop, she
dreams of someday owning her own travel agency and has
vowed never to leave the familiar shores of England ever
again. When a handsome duke arrives at her doorstep, she
realizes her staid existence is about to take flight.

*. . . is faith and hope*

Jason "North" Beckett, the Duke of Northumberland,
desperately needs a travel guide. He's inherited a dukedom
but has a final mission for the Foreign Office—rescuing his
wayward cousin from Nordic pirates. Isobel Tinker is the
ideal translator, discreet and unknown, but she's also unco-
operative, stubborn, and disarmingly beautiful.

*And a little bit of trust*

In exchange for her help, North promises Miss Tinker her
own travel agency upon return and strict professionalism at
sea. Isobel cautiously agrees but soon realizes "strict" and
"professional" are not how she would describe her feelings
for the irresistible duke. As their adventure sweeps them to
the shores of Iceland and beyond, can temptation and growing trust give way to the magic of wild, passionate love?

On Sale Now
From Avon Books

# JULIA QUINN SELECTS

Looking for your next favorite romance? The #1 *New York Times* bestselling author of *Bridgerton* recommends these new books coming from Joanna Shupe, Julie Anne Long, Charis Michaels, and Beverly Jenkins.

## THE BRIDE GOES ROGUE

"Joanna Shupe is the queen of historical bad boys!"
— Julia Quinn

**MAY 2022**

In Joanna Shupe's latest Gilded Age romance, find out what happens when the wrong bride turns out to be the right woman for a hard-hearted tycoon.

## YOU WERE MADE TO BE MINE

"I am in awe of her talent."
—Julia Quinn

**JUNE 2022**

A rakish spy finds more than he bargained for in his pursuit of an earl's enchanting runaway fiancée in this charming romance by Julie Anne Long.

## DUCHESS BY MIDNIGHT

Charis Michaels will make you believe in fairy tales."
— Julia Quinn

**JULY 2022**

Charis Michaels enchants us with a romance between Cinderella's stepsister and the man who can't help falling in love with her.

## TO CATCH A RAVEN

"A living legend."
— Julia Quinn

**AUGUST 2022**

A fearless grifter goes undercover to reclaim the stolen Declaration of Independence in this compelling new romance by Beverly Jenkins.

**Discover great authors, exclusive offers, and more at hc.com**